I0565468

Promise of the Flame

Sylvia Engdahl

* *Ad* *
Stellae

Eugene, Oregon

Copyright © 2009 by Sylvia Louise Engdahl

All rights reserved. For information, write to
sle@sylviaengdahl.com or visit
www.sylviaengdahl.com/adstellae.

Author website: www.sylviaengdahl.com

Book design and layout by Sylvia Engdahl

Cover art © by Musser Remy / 123RF
and Mechanik / Dreamstime.com

ISBN-10: 0-615-31488-0

ISBN-13: 978-0-615-31488-4

FROM THE REVIEWS OF
Promise of the Flame

"Outsoars its predecessor. . . . As with all of Engdahl's work, science-fiction fans will recognize the tropes she uses, but it is not just 'for' them. . . . Engdahl has produced high-quality work over a forty-year period, but this is one of her finest achievements."

—Literary critic Nicholas Birns

"It is not necessary to read the first [book] in order to be enthralled by the second. . . . Engdahl's gift is to make her characters seem comfortable and familiar to the reader, even though their circumstances are not. . . . The ideas and futuristic possibilities are disturbingly real and will remain with the reader long after they've - finished the book."   —*Indie Reader* staff reviewer

"Right now all I can feel right now is 'wow!' What a great story with thought-provoking themes and heroic char-acters. The suspense is so much fun, I couldn't put the book down through the last couple of hundred pages. What a pleasure it is to read science fiction that doesn't deal with dark and depressing subjects."

—Amazon.com Vine Voice reviewer

"This is one of the few situations where I reach the end of a book or a series and feel like I'm saying goodbye to friends, and to me, that means it's a pretty darn good book."   —*Library Thing* reader review

BOOKS BY SYLVIA ENGDAHL

NOVELS FOR TEENS
Enchantress from the Stars
The Far Side of Evil
Journey Between Worlds

CHILDREN OF THE STAR TRILOGY
(FOR TEENS AND ADULTS)
This Star Shall Abide
(UK title *Heritage of the Star*)
Beyond the Tomorrow Mountains
The Doors of the Universe

THE FOUNDERS OF MACLAIRN DUOLOGY
(FOR ADULTS)
Stewards of the Flame
Promise of the Flame

THE CAPTAIN OF ESTEL TRILOGY
(FOR ADULTS)
Defender of the Flame
Herald of the Flame
Envoy of the Flame

NONFICTION
*The Planet-Girded Suns: The Long History
of Belief in Exoplanets*

COLLECTED ESSAYS
*Reflections on Enchantress from the Stars
and Other Essays*
From This Green Earth: Essays on Looking Outward
The Future of Being Human and Other Essays

Contents

Preface

This is the second of five novels—a duology and a trilogy—that are tied together by the concept of a flame as the symbol of the evolving "paranormal" powers of the mind and by their setting in an imaginary future in which those powers are developed first by a small group of people, and later by their successors' influence on human civilization. It is complete in itself and can be read independently, but reading it first will reduce the suspense of the earlier novel if you plan to read both. However, the two are very different, and are connected mainly by being about the same characters. This book, unlike its predecessor *Stewards of the Flame,* does not deal with the controversial dystopian view of healthcare on which that book is focused. It is a story about the difficulty of establishing a colony on a raw new planet, and for that reason many science fiction readers find it more to their taste. There is no need to start with *Stewards* if its theme doesn't appeal to you.

In the back of this book you will find descriptions of the other novels: *Stewards of the Flame* plus a trilogy set two centuries later. Each book can stand alone. When I wrote them, one at a time, I had no intention of writing another; the idea for the succeeding story didn't come to me until months, or years, later. They can be read in any order, except that each includes enough backstory to affect the suspense of the preceding one. Please note that unlike my earlier books these are adult novels and contain some material inappropriate for readers below high school age.

Sylvia Engdahl, June 2021

Increased levels of psychoactivity are most likely latent, evolutionary, and emergent in our species. But if our belief system will not accommodate these natural abilities and they are suppressed early, they will not naturally emerge in the individual; there is just too much dogma in the way.

—Edgar Mitchell
The Way of the Explorer, 1996

We with our lives are like islands in the sea, or like trees in the forest. The maple and the pine may whisper to each other with their leaves, and Conanicut and Newport hear each other's foghorns. But the trees also commingle their roots in the darkness underground, and the islands also hang together through the ocean's bottom, just so there is a continuum of cosmic consciousness, against which our individuality builds but accidental fences, and into which our several minds plunge as into a mother-sea or reservoir.

—William James
"The Final Impressions of a
Psychical Researcher," 1909

Prologue

My dear friend,

By the time you receive this I will be dead. That I say so probably won't surprise you, considering that I am a hundred and thirty years old and have been confined to my bed for some weeks. But the hour of my death is absolutely certain now. It's best that I warn you before you learn of it from the media, in case any news from so remote a colony as Undine happens to reach Earth—I am to be executed for murder. I'm sure you needn't be told that I am not guilty. The reason for my false confession I'll leave to my adopted heir Peter to explain. He will be contacting you soon for another purpose, and it's of that purpose I must speak in this, the last message you will ever get from me.

As you know, nobody officially dies on Undine. The stasis vaults hold everyone who has ever passed away on this planet, except a few that the Group I founded buried illegally in the sea. As a diagnosed murderer considered incurable, I will be put into stasis while still living, and the public will be under the impression that as long as my heart beats I remain alive. But of course you and I know better. My brain will be dead from lack of oxygen within moments; stasis as practiced here is a mere illusion of life, a parody. I grieve for the effect their failure to save me from it will have on Peter and the Group, for over the years I have fostered their fear of such a death in order to unite them against the tyranny of our Med-controlled government. But by accepting it, I will be freeing them from that tyranny forever.

By a miraculous turn of fate, the Group is about to escape from Undine. I have too little time now to give you the details of how this became possible, except to mention that it was first revealed in one of my precognitive dreams. Peter will fill you in. I ask you to trust him as you have trusted me throughout the years we have corresponded. He shares the vision we've had of a world in which the powers of the human mind are fully acknowledged.

You may already have heard from our mutual friend on Earth that he has enabled Peter to charter a starship. The Group's combined funds will be sufficient with some hacking on his part; we own the offworld bank accounts of our allegedly-living ancestors, which have been earning compound interest for generations, and all that's necessary is to evade the government restrictions on the amount that can be withdrawn. He perhaps thought it strange that all members were willing to impoverish themselves to the extent of arriving penniless on the destination world. In reality it will make no difference, for they are not going to the planet to which Fleet plans to take them. Where they are going, League credits would be worthless in any case.

I dare to say this, knowing that the authorities could not break our private code even if they suspected that I'm storing a coded message in the personal datakeeper they have not yet taken from me. And they don't suspect it, as I have given them no cause to think I'm involved in conspiracy—much less that I have led a conspiracy for more than half a century. Even when the illegal emigration of over three hundred people comes to light, they won't connect it with me, and of course long before then—within the next few hours, in fact—Peter will have transmitted the message by ansible and destroyed all trace of its existence. You must do the same. But the other information Peter sends you must be preserved, not only during your lifetime but much longer, and I write now to emphasize how important it is that you and your descendants protect the secret until the time is ripe for some future generation to act on it.

If you ever inquire about the chartered starship, Fleet will tell you that it has been lost in a miscalculated jump. Whether they will also tell you that it was hijacked, I don't know; that may or may not be made public. In any case, the Group intends to hijack it. Only Peter and Jesse Sanders, the former Fleet captain he recruited, will know the charted location of the unopened planet on which they intend to land. Undoubtedly they will face great hardship there. Nothing is known about such planets except that they are potentially habitable. So it's a gamble—but one worth taking, for those of us who envision a future in which humans have become all they can be, where psi powers are fostered and developed to an extent impossible on Earth or any of the League worlds.

You will say, perhaps, that if such a future can be achieved it should be for everyone, not just residents of an isolated, illegal colony. And so it should. That is the long-term goal. But it cannot be reached directly. For centuries individuals and small groups have tried to influence the consciousness of humankind. Some have been aware, as you and I are, that through psi this is possible, that it has occurred naturally throughout history, for good and for ill, and that in principle it could be done intentionally for the betterment of civilization. But a minority of scattered believers cannot sway the majority. The collective unconscious of a world's inhabitants overpowers any effort to alter it, except insofar as new input is gradually absorbed. In particular, the resistance against the so-called paranormal is too strong to be overcome, and it always will be unless the compatibility of psi with life as we know it can be demonstrated. Speculation is not enough. The example of enlightened individuals is not enough. There must be a psi-based culture that can be admired and emulated before the barriers raised by skepticism and prejudice can be broken down.

Many who consider themselves enlightened would deny this. They are under the illusion that if only enough

people could be converted, the merging of minds would lead
to universal peace and harmony. But a large enough percentage of people could never be converted from among
those born into an unsupportive psychic milieu. In the
Group, I have taught that we influence the future simply by
being what we are, by fulfilling our own psychic potential;
and that's true as far as it goes. More is needed, however, if
there is to be any significant effect on civilization before
civilization collapses entirely. It is already collapsing on
Earth, as I'm sure you know only too well. In my opinion
there's no hope of ever transforming it there. Yet in the
colonies lies the promise of a breakthrough in human evolution.

That, I believe, is one of the reasons why interstellar
colonization is essential not only to the evolution, but to the
very survival, of humankind. The mass collective unconscious of Earth does not extend from world to world. Individual minds that telepathically access it have sometimes
been compared to islands, connected by the ocean's floor;
and that is an apt metaphor since an ocean floor is the bed-
rock of a single planet. Thus colonies on different planets
can experiment with different outlooks—some that turn out
poorly, such as the denial of death that took hold here on
Undine, and others that represent true advance. On a new
world telepathy will produce a new collective unconscious,
provided that it is allowed to develop in isolation until strong
enough to endure.

And so the Group has undertaken to attempt this. Being obliged to come up with a name on the application for
the starship charter, Peter listed us as the Stewards of the
Flame; it comes from the recognition password we've used
for our undercover work here, derived from the reference to
stewardship of mind powers in our Ritual of commitment.
You'll be amused to hear that Fleet thinks we are some sort
of religious cult. After the hijacking we will no doubt be
branded as dangerous fanatics. But that won't matter, since
considering the vast number of unopened planets to which

we might be headed, the odds are small that we will ever be found by the League.

Yet in time—far in the future—our world *must* be found and revealed as the shining example of psi's potential that I trust it will have become. Who knows what capabilities will be developed by successive generations of children born into a culture where psi is accepted and encouraged? There is, of course, danger; the Group's members were carefully chosen but their descendants are bound to include individuals prone to misuse their powers, just as any society does. That will be as true of psi as of technology, and in neither case can the good be discarded for fear of the evil. I believe that in both areas, the gains far outweigh the legitimate grounds for such fear.

There is only one thing that truly worries me, and that is the possibility that the colony my people establish will go undiscovered too long—that it may never be discovered, and that their sacrifices and struggles will thus prove meaningless as far as any effect on evolution is concerned. So I'm counting on you, my friend, to make sure that doesn't happen. You must hide the knowledge of our destination entrusted to you by Peter, yet pass it on to those who come after you with a solemn charge to seek out the new world two hundred years from now and reveal its accomplishments to the rest of humankind.

I leave the means of fulfilling this request to your judgment, aware that you're in a position of some consequence on Earth. I must die without knowing the outcome—as indeed must the founders of that world themselves, for it will take many generations to reach our goal. I am confident that you will not fail us.

With my deepest respect and gratitude,

Ian Maclairn

Part One

1

SLOWLY, OUT OF immeasurable depths, he rose to consciousness, knowing that he must fight the impulse to drop back into sleep. Sleep? It had been longer than natural sleep—days . . . weeks. . . . What had happened to him? Gradually, he regained awareness of who and where he was.

He was Jesse Sanders, Captain of . . . of *Mayflower XI*, the starship they had hijacked. An obsolete ship, so old that it still had the stasis facilities standard in the era before it had been retrofitted with the hyperdrive. They'd been pursued; he'd been forced to jump without enough time for calculation, so that they'd come out into normal space too far from their destination world. Their life support could not have lasted if they had not gone into stasis. But they had not been sure the ancient stasis units would work. All too probably, at least some of the three hundred people aboard would die.

And if he himself died, Jesse knew, they would all die even if they survived stasis. They would have no way to land. For he was the only qualified shuttle pilot among them, and in fact the only person on the starship who had ever been in space before.

So he had set the AI controls to wake him before the others—to ensure that if he did not wake, neither would they. There would be no point in their dying while awake after all, not after the ordeal they had undergone in the hope of staying alive. Stasis, used for preservation of the dead on the Group's birthworld, was the ultimate fear of its members, the symbol onto which they projected all the other fears they'd renounced. Most couldn't have agreed to it if allowed to contemplate; they would have chosen sure death, had he not persuaded Peter to hold the Ritual that put them into altered consciousness.

Peter! Jesse sat up, flexing his arms and legs, waiting for the AI to signal that he was fit to climb out of the stasis unit. He must wake Peter even before he checked to be sure the ship was orbiting their new home. Though Jesse was Captain while in space, Peter was the leader of the Group. He alone had what it would take to bring his people through the founding of an unauthorized colony on a raw wilderness world . . . which was now going to be much harder to accomplish than he yet knew.

But it was not into Peter's unit that Jesse first looked when he was able to stand. There being nobody to see his nakedness, he did not even take time to retrieve his clothes from the storage compartment in his own unit's base. He could not endure one moment's delay before assuring himself that no harm had come to Carla.

He dared not look at her until he had checked her AI telltales for malfunction. Though during his former life as a Fleet freighter captain he had never seen operational stasis units, he had become all too familiar with them during his brief stint as a Vault attendant in the Hospital on Undine. Everyone who had ever died in that colony was still in stasis, except the few for whom the Group had managed illegal sea burial. Hearts were kept beating indefinitely, even after brain death, in the belief that human life lingered in mindless flesh. It epitomized all they despised about Undine's Med-controlled government: compulsory medical treatment, whether or not any treatment was truly warranted, throughout every stage of life and beyond.

Carla had been horrified by the prospect of stasis. She'd

had good reason. Her first husband had been sent prematurely to the Vaults—in effect, had been executed—for a crime of which he had been innocent. As had Ian, the Group's founder, who had sacrificed himself to let them escape to a new world . . . to save Jesse, their sole hope for reaching such a world, from destruction of his mind and permanent imprisonment in the Hospital's psych ward. The memory of that sacrifice, enhanced by the Ritual, had induced them to enter stasis voluntarily, but for Carla it had been harder than for the rest. Only her love for Jesse had enabled her to do it. They had been together in the moments before they lost consciousness . . . together telepathically, their bond, as always between committed couples, closer than any psi connection with others. His last memory was of Carla's mind-touch, seemingly mere hours ago. But now he felt nothing. Would he sense it if the stasis had failed, if she were gone forever?

He did not believe he could get through the hard days ahead of them without her. Yet Ian's sacrifice had obligated him; he was in any case bound by his Ritual pledge to support fellow-members of the Group—and above all, he was Captain. The lives of all who had lived through stasis were in his hands.

Steadying his heart rate as he had been taught to do, Jesse forced himself to examine the telltales. The status indicators appeared to be in order. He drew a deep breath and hit the switch to slide her unit out from the bank of those above—it was on the lowest level, next to the one from which he had emerged. As Captain he had been the last to go in; she had been next-to-last, wanting to share what might well be their final seconds of awareness before a protracted death. Now her sleep was peaceful, as far as he could tell from a glimpse of her face through the unit's translucent lid. She was deathly pale, her skin almost literally white in stark contrast to the dark frame of her tousled hair . . . but that was normal, surely. He longed to wake her, see a glow of life surge into her, take her in his arms with assurance that they'd reached the new world and all was well. . . .

But it was too soon. All might not be well. Even if the ship was in position, getting three hundred people to the surface fast enough with only one shuttle pilot was going to be iffy. The shorter the time Carla had to worry about it, the better.

On the other side of Carla's stasis unit was Peter's. Again Jesse maintained rigid control while verifying the status of the occupant; then, still apprehensive, he set the controls to "wake." He was not sure how long it would take the AI to rouse Peter. Was the waking process itself uncertain, he wondered? Did people ever survive stasis only to prove unresponsive to the automated ministrations designed to bring them back? Since those in the Vaults on Undine were brain-dead, he had no knowledge of that aspect of it. The routine use of stasis in the founding of early colonies by slow ships was a detail of history he had never studied. But he recalled now that there had been reports not merely of deaths, but of occasional insanity among passengers who were revived.

Had Peter known that? As a highly skilled psychiatrist, Peter knew a great deal that he did not talk about. He'd argued against going into stasis at first, but only on grounds that some would refuse to participate and would use up so much life support that the attempt to conserve it would prove futile. Perhaps he'd also had unspoken worries. The survival of so small a group on an unopened planet would be at best precarious. All members realized this, although, Jesse felt, their upbringing on the secluded, rich colony world of Undine blinded them to the enormity of the hardships they'd agreed to accept. Their greatest asset was their mind training—not merely their psi abilities, but their near-paranormal degree of control over the functioning of their own bodies and emotions. Without that control, which any mind impairment due to stasis would surely destroy, they might indeed have been better off dying in space.

Jesse dressed hurriedly, glancing from time to time at

the still-unconscious Peter. He was torn between the wish to draw strength from him—as during the weeks of his own mind training, he had—and the responsibility he now bore to aid him. It involved more than command of the starship. He, Jesse, was needed for his experience with the universe beyond Undine. Moreover, he'd been warned that Peter would need the friendship and support of someone less visionary than himself, vital as the vision was to their venture's success.

Peter looked almost boyish as he slept. His bright tawny hair and unlined face showed no hint of his true age. When Jesse had first met him, before being recruited into the Group, he had thought him barely thirty, or even younger. In reality Peter was three years older than Jesse himself, in his mid-forties by Earth reckoning; delayed aging—and eventual prolonged life—was one of the benefits of gaining conscious control over physiological reactions to stress. He was in most respects even wiser than his years, having been mentored since youth by the preternaturally wise Ian. Yet his isolation on Undine had made him incongruously naive when it came to practical knowledge of life elsewhere. More than once Jesse's advice had proved valuable, and in an environment totally new to them, it would be even more crucial.

Now, waiting in the eerie silence of the empty ship for Peter to wake, Jesse was struck anew by awe at the strange fate that had placed him in such a position.

He'd been burned out as a Fleet officer. Twenty years, culminating in no more fulfilling work than the routine ferrying of freighters from one well-established colony to another, a Captain by rank but little more than a console operator for all the challenge the job offered. No hope of any chance to explore the new worlds he'd envisioned when he was young. No family. Nothing to do during shore leaves but lose himself in the small solace offered by drinking—though he had never abused liquor while on duty, he'd come close to letting it rule his free days.

And so, in a bar on Undine, he'd been arrested for drunkenness. Undine had no police apart from the ambulance crews. All crime was viewed as illness there, and illness left untreated was considered crime. He had been taken to the Hospital, subjected to forced treatment as a presumed alcoholic. Carla had rescued him. Not until later had he been told that Peter, for whom she worked as a psych technician, had been the doctor in charge and had manipulated them both in order to recruit him into the Group. Eventually, he'd learned that Peter had done so because of a precognitive dream in which Ian had recognized him as the one who would take them to a new world.

Peter had withheld this secret until long after Jesse had freely committed himself to the Group and its ideals. The prospect of commanding a colonizer had not been offered as inducement, for it was, after all, to be a one-way trip. After the hijacking, none of them could go back even if it were physically possible—and for Jesse, a retired Fleet officer, to be caught would mean execution for mutiny. They had not harmed the crew they'd sent away aboard a shuttle, but they had threatened them and stolen the starship chartered for what was ostensibly mere emigration to a settled planet. The decision to found their own colony was irrevocable. They would live the remainder of their lives in that colony, out of touch with the rest of civilization. It would have been unfair, Peter said, to let Jesse make such a choice out of mere enthusiasm for the adventure.

Thus at the time he was recruited, he had guessed nothing of what was in store for him. Only his desire for Carla had gotten him through the harsh but necessary testing of his aptitude for mind training; only the consummation of their love had given him full use of the latent psi powers he had gradually—and reluctantly—discovered within himself. For a time he'd known joy on Undine, despite its tyrannical government and the danger of arrest under which all Group members lived. He'd found a lifestyle he expected would be permanent. Yet all along, unaware, he had been destined by fate to lead them to freedom. There wasn't any other way to look at it. He was the only starship captain they had ever encountered, marooned on Undine through what appeared to be mere chance . . . yet how could it have been chance, occurring so shortly before the events that compelled them to escape? Discovery of their conspiracy against Undine's laws had been imminent. Many would have been charged with murder for their hospice care of the dying, as he himself had been until Ian's self-sacrifice saved him. If he'd never gotten drunk in that bar . . .

Jesse didn't believe in fate. He was no longer sure just what he did believe. But however it had come about, he was responsible for the Group's safety now . . . and he had nearly killed them all.

With a rush, the recollection he'd been suppressing flooded into him, searing his heart. It was only through his miscalculation that the jump through hyperspace had come up short. Peter had told him not to blame himself. There hadn't been time to recheck the figures; they'd have been boarded, taken to a penal colony, if he had not acted fast. Nevertheless, it was because of his failure that they were facing a much more dangerous situation than any of them had anticipated. *Oh God, Peter,* he thought, *how am I going to get us through this? It's worse than I let you guess. . . .*

Jess? Peter's color had returned; he couldn't yet move or speak, but his mind was clearing and he evidently could communicate. Peter was a gifted telepath and their bond had been strengthened by the ordeals they had recently shared.

I'm all right, Jesse assured him, *and you will be too, in a few minutes. We've arrived.*

The others?

Carla looks okay. I haven't checked anyone else yet. I need to know the ship's status before we start reviving people.

Why didn't they wake automatically?

They wouldn't have wanted to wake, if I hadn't, Jesse pointed out. There was no need to spell it out further, but he sensed Peter's surprise at not having been informed beforehand of how the controls would be set.

What else didn't you tell me? Peter asked, perceiving at once that there was more.

A good deal, Jesse admitted. *It was hard enough to get you to agree to stasis without burdening you with details of the situation we'd be in when we came out of it.*

We're not yet out of trouble, then.

No. But if Ian's dream was valid . . . He knew that Peter had faith in the dream, and that this faith had carried him through many weeks of stress that would have overwhelmed a lesser man. Jesse, too, had gained faith—in a dream of his own, Ian, knowing himself soon to die, had come to him telepathically and had given him courage that had sustained him through several crises. It was impossible to think that after all that, they would be defeated by the mere logistics of landing on the world they had reached.

Level with me! Peter commanded.

Not until we can talk—I've got to go to the bridge first. Aloud, he said, "Do you mind if I leave you here alone for awhile?"

"Of course not. I'm starting to feel my limbs. If you climbed out of your box by yourself, I can."

"Wait for the AI's signal before you try it. Then start checking key people—but don't wake them until I get back."

Still dazed and shaky from the long sleep, Jesse climbed the companionway from the stasis deck and made his way to the bridge. The door opened to his voice, just as Carla had programmed it to do after cracking the ship's computer system in the tense hours following the hijacking. They had been locked out at first; that was why there had been so little time to evade pursuit. He was Captain of this ship, yet he had been in actual control of it for only a few minutes.

The console was, to be sure, identical to those familiar to him from freighter command. It took him no time to bring up a readout showing their position. He had no real doubt about where they would be; travel in normal space was predetermined by strict and invariable laws, and nothing short of collision with space debris could have altered his expectation. Even the establishment of a parking orbit was well within the capability of the starship's AI. Still, he found himself holding his breath as he verified the figures. There was no discrepancy. They had reached the world they'd been aiming for.

Jesse switched on the huge vidscreen and for the first time looked out at the golden, sapphire-studded sphere of the planet Maclairn.

It was not so named on any chart, of course; its star had only a catalog number. Peter had named it after Ian. It was the world seen in Ian's dream—Jesse knew this because Ian had shown it to him telepathically before either of them had any idea that it was a real place. Later, when he and Peter had come to choose a destination, he had recognized it. It fit their specifications as well as any other—habitable, but not rich in elements with trade value that would make it desirable to Fleet for eventual opening. Little detail was known about such worlds, although their discoverers had certified the suitability of their gravity, atmosphere, climate, and soil. There were hundreds of them in the astronomical database. Any one they might pick would be a gamble. They'd had no reason not to choose the one Ian had perceived.

Now, for better or for worse, they were stuck with it. Forever. They had taken a big risk in making even one interstellar jump in an aging ship without a trained crew; it would be foolhardy to attempt another, even if it were not that the power receiver and emergency cargo pods, once dropped, could not be relaunched into space. So whatever they might find or fail to find on Maclairn, they would never leave its surface.

Assuming, of course, that they could get to its surface before the starship ran out of air.

2

GRIMLY, JESSE TURNED from the breathtaking view and began examining data on the current state of the ship's life support. That was less predictable than its position; there was no guessing how much oxygen had been used up during the hours between his last check and the time they had gone into stasis. Those had been hectic hours. Everyone had been excited by the journey and the few who'd known of their impending doom must have been even more agitated, despite their ability to control physiological reactions to stress. And the Ritual had involved not only strong emotion, but the essential burning of more than three hundred candles. Conservation of air had been out of the question. His calculations had assured him that with maximum generation of oxygen from the recycling of water, it would outlast the weeks of stasis—but for how long?

Not as long as he had hoped. Jesse turned cold as he stared at the readouts on his board. The ancient *Mayflower XI*, having been originally designed to carry passengers in stasis, did not have a self-sustaining life support system. That was one of the ways in which it was obsolete. Moreover, it had not been fully stocked with consumables for its last charter trip before decommissioning. Fleet had economized, providing only a reasonable safety margin over what would be required to reach its official destination. Well, Jesse thought with chagrin, the hijacking had depended on the crew not anticipating a takeover by emigrants. He could hardly complain because Fleet hadn't allowed for a longer time in normal space than the scheduled run could possibly require. And if his own calculation of the jump had been more precise, the reserves would have been adequate. . . .

Returning to the stasis deck, he found Peter on his feet checking the status of the others. "Everyone seems okay so far," he said, "though I'm not nearly finished yet. Shall I wake them as I come to them from here on?"

"No," said Jesse. "We haven't enough air and water to wake anyone we don't need—not until just before they board the shuttle. We can't even repressurize the passenger deck; they'll have to use crew quarters."

Peter came forward and embraced him in the brotherly way customary among Group members, projecting warmth and support. Only after that did he let worry show. "It's that bad? I realize that we can't follow the original plan, but if by 'need' you mean just the advance exploration team—"

The plan had been to live aboard the starship for weeks before landing—not only during the slow approach in normal space, but later while a small party went to the surface to choose a site for the colony. It would take time to prepare people for the new life on which they were about to embark. The decision to emigrate had been made quickly. On Undine before departure, Jesse had been able to meet with only a few, secretly. He had been microchipped, his location constantly tracked by the Med authorities; his connection with Peter outside the Hospital, or even with Peter's known friends, could not safely be revealed. So what little the rest knew about settling new worlds they had gained second-hand, primarily via the local Net. Many of them possessed technical skills that would be useful. Committees had been formed and preliminary work assignments made. But there was a great deal left for them to learn from before they were ready to be plunged with minimal equipment into the wilderness of a planet not even terraformed.

Jesse shook his head. "There's not going to be any advance exploration," he said. "Where we first land is where we stay, because that's where we'll have to drop the cargo pods and build the landing pad for the passenger shuttle. We've got to get people off this ship as fast as possible."

The starship carried enough equipment and emergency supplies to found a bare-bones colony; this was standard Fleet policy, without which stealing a ship could never have been considered. Nearly everything apart from the receiver for beamed power was contained in pods that had been sealed long before this particular trip, back when *Mayflower XI* was first refitted as a charter vessel. Supposedly, the pods would ensure survival in case hyperdrive failure sent it to a solar system not on established trade routes. Starships could not call for help; interstellar comm facilities were installed only on officially recognized colony worlds. Authorized colonies received regular freight shipments. The Group was aware that they'd be thought insane for deliberately aiming to do without such shipments . . . but of course their psi powers, if revealed, would be considered symptoms of insanity in any case. So would their rejection of the all-inclusive medical care mandatory on Undine. Being used to discounting conventional dogma, they had perhaps been a bit rash in assuming they could survive.

And, Jesse reflected, they were counting on more than survival. The goal was not merely to gain freedom, but to found a society in which psi and their other mind powers were used consciously, rather than just at the unconscious level on which Peter claimed they'd been operative since the dawn of history. A society that if allowed to develop in isolation from the prejudice and skepticism of Earth-based civilization, would someday become a harbinger of what Ian had viewed as the next phase of human evolution. Was there a real chance of doing that? Had it been wrong to suppress his doubts about a few hundred inexperienced people overcoming the odds against such a venture?

Peter, as always, sensed his thoughts. *I know you feared you weren't warning us fully enough*, he acknowledged. *But Jess, I haven't been wholly open about the risks either—there are things you were never told about the psi aspect of it. All we can do is proceed one step at a time.* Aloud he added, "I take it the first step is to abandon ship before the oxygen supply gives out. Will we ever be able to come back?"

"Oh, yes, some of us will. We've got equipment for liquefying air and bringing it up from the surface. It will be a slow process, but eventually, after I've trained more shuttle pilots, we can finish what we need to do here and salvage all the stuff that's useful. In any case we won't lose access to the ship's computer before we've set up remote access to the knowledgebase." *Not unless something else goes wrong, not unless we have problems with the shuttles . . . or end up without even one pilot. . . .*

We always knew that our lives depend on your presence, Peter reminded him. *You're not going to have an accident, Jess. We've survived stasis! After that, fate won't turn its back on us.*

Best not to argue the point, Jesse thought. Quickly he said, "I've seen Maclairn, Peter! It's beautiful. I'm sorry you couldn't share the first sight of it." It seemed unfair when it had been Peter's vision that had brought them here. Peter couldn't be among the first to set foot on it, either. He must take charge aboard the starship while Jesse piloted the shuttle, and in any case could not be risked early in the landing process. They'd known this, too, from the beginning.

"The AI sensors are gathering data from the surface," he went on. "That's all we'll have for input in deciding where to land."

"Not quite," Peter said. "I think we need remote viewing more than ever, now."

Startled, Jesse nodded. Some members of the Group, he recalled, were experienced in remote viewing via psi. Trainees were normally taught that skill, but he himself hadn't been; Peter had wanted him, as Captain, to maintain scientific objectivity in selecting the colony's site. Remote viewing could yield false information as well as true visions. And yet with exploration impossible, it might be better than nothing. His own recent experience with long-range telepathy had shown him that psi was not only a valid source of knowledge, but at times an absolutely vital one.

"Okay," he said. "Let's wake the best remote viewers as well as the people assigned to the first landing team. Plus the rest of the Council."

"And Carla."

"We'd better not," Jesse said reluctantly. "She won't want to stay on the surface while I make repeated shuttle trips."

"Jess, she'll be needed here. I'm relying on her computer expertise for help on the bridge, and in any case she's got to set up this end of the ship-to-ground datalink."

"Oh yes, of course." He'd blocked that from his mind, Jesse realized, thinking only of protecting her. But she was crew now—and besides, Carla needed no protection. She was as capable as any of them of dealing with worry, and they were all very capable indeed. Membership in the Group involved a formal pledge to go past fear and become free of it. He, as the newest full member, tended to forget that they'd all had longer practice in that than he had. *It's like touching flame,* Carla had said when he'd protested that people seemed oblivious to the perils of emigrating. *We just do it—and to be able to do it, we have to know we could be burned, and be willing. . . .*

In the Ritual they literally touched flame, and were not burned. More than once he himself had taken Peter's hand in fire. It was the culmination of all he had learned in the mind training, a joyous experience that set participants forever apart from the life of outsiders. Without that, they would never have gone into stasis, in fact would never have dared to set forth to a new world in the first place. It would sustain them through whatever might meet. They would not hide from awareness of danger, or even of death, if it came to that, as in the prelude to stasis it had; the Group's way was to face hard facts squarely. But neither would they let it spoil their joy in claiming a world of their own.

Nor would he, Jesse decided. He went to wake Carla, his spirits rising in anticipation of holding her close. And for a few minutes after he helped her up, he was unaware of anything else in the present or yet to come.

"It was like dreaming," Carla told him in wonder, "not horrible at all. How could I have been so scared beforehand?"

"Stasis symbolized more than just death," Jesse reminded her. "We know now that Ian encouraged fear he himself didn't feel simply to provide a focus for the Group's resistance on Undine."

"Yes, but even after we figured that out, I was terrified. While I was going under, though, I knew you were with me—I think I knew inside, all the time I was unconscious. And now it's as if it never happened, as if it were only last night that we went to sleep."

Peter had roused the other three who, with Jesse and himself, constituted the Council; they were in nearby units on the lowest level. One by one as they revived they greeted each other warmly: Hari, the mystic, slight and brown-skinned, seemingly ageless; Reiko, whose shining black hair and girlish figure belied her many years as a scholar of soci-ology and history; Kira, physician and healer—over a hun-dred years old yet looking no more than sixty. "I knew you'd bring us through, Jesse," Kira said as she hugged him. "We were so foolish to be afraid—" But she broke off, sensing from his mind that there were worse things to fear than stasis.

Kira had been his teacher for the mind training; he was closer to her than to anyone else except Carla and Peter. He would not deceive her even if it were possible. "We're not on the surface yet," he said, "and until we are, I can't claim to have brought us to safety."

"You'll manage," Kira declared confidently. "Ian trusted you. We all do."

Rousing the other people chosen took longer than he'd anticipated, as there was no fast way of locating them among the stacked tiers. They had gone into stasis quickly after the Ritual, most still in the altered consciousness that damp-ened awareness of what they were doing. The units had been filled arbitrarily and had not been labeled with name tags. It was therefore necessary to slide out and lower every one of them, identify its occupant by sight, and then re-rack it if it didn't contain someone who was needed. If it did, no unit above could be accessed until that person had been thoroughly enough wakened to be disconnected from AI support. There was no time to wait for them to gain strength; Peter and Hari lifted them out of the units and carried them to the anteroom, where Kira and Reiko helped them revive and dress.

Because examination of the units was so slow, it was some time before Peter discovered the first death.

3

THEY'D KNOWN IT was unlikely that all passengers would emerge alive from stasis—yet because it seemed a miracle that any of them had, those awake had thrust that knowledge from their minds like a fading nightmare. It was therefore a shock to lower a unit and see its telltales glowing red, its occupant's body . . . indescribable. Jesse had been aware, even while tending the Vaults on Undine, that death in stasis would not be clean. When stasis failed, bodies decayed. That was simple biological fact. The dead had decayed on Earth during the centuries when the horrific custom of sealing them into watertight grave vaults had prevailed, but they had done so beneath the ground, mercifully hidden from human sight—and it had happened slowly because of the preservatives used. It was a faster process when a live body had been sealed into a coffinlike box with ancient, untested AI connections. The corpses were barely recognizable.

Still, Peter and Kira did recognize them. All seven of them, once the check of the passengers was complete. Jesse had been with the Group a shorter time and had not known most of the lost members personally. But Xiang Li . . . though he had met Xiang Li only once, he'd talked to him by phone and had borrowed money from him in order to leave his legally-accessible offworld retirement fund intact for application to the starship charter. Xiang Li had owned several of the safe houses used on Undine as hospices. He hadn't possessed much psi talent, nor had he any skills that would be valuable in building the colony; his contribution to the

Group over the past forty years had been his wealth and his expertise as a financier. He had nevertheless been thrilled at the thought of settling a new world. Peter was shattered by his death, and Jesse too, along with everyone else awake, wept for him. They went on to find six more to weep for.

Jess. . . . Peter, unable to express himself in words without choking up, turned to a less explicit mode of questioning. *What do we do about . . . ?* Jesse realized that Peter, having never been in space before, had no idea how to dispose of the bodies. It was up to him, as Captain, to get them into the recycler. *I'll see to it,* he told him without elaboration. *In principle it's like the sea burials we risked so much to accomplish.*

He knew that Peter felt personally responsible for these deaths. It had been he who'd proposed the hijacking plan, he who, through telepathic persuasion, had inspired everyone to come along. No matter that Xiang Li had broken enough of Undine's financial laws over the years to have been executed if caught there, or that most of the other victims would have been subjected to harsh psychiatric treatment for other alleged crimes. They were dead, and death before old age was rare on Undine. Peter had had more experience with it than his contemporaries, for his wife had died tragically in a sailing accident. But premature death was not something he could view matter-of-factly.

"Peter," Jesse said, "we ought to start manning the bridge. Will you take the watch?" Once Peter had gone, he sent everyone to crew quarters except two of the men wakened for the landing team that he assigned to help him. The stasis chamber would have to be purged of air so as not to waste any by contaminating it with odor when the sealed units were opened. That meant they'd have to work in spacesuits. As the others had never before seen a spacesuit, it would be rough going—still, they were experienced scuba divers. Scuba diving, though banned on Undine as a health risk, had been a favorite sport on the Group's private island; he himself had mastered it quickly because of his ex-

perience with a helmet and air tank. Hopefully cross training would work the other way around. He took them to the
suit locker on the deck above where they also obtained air-
tight body bags, then returned to the stasis deck and did
what had to be done.

By the time they were finished and he'd repressurized
the chamber, Jesse was feeling faint. How, he thought, could
the distastefulness of the job have had this much effect on
him, a hardened Fleet officer? He'd dealt with the recycling
of bodies before, less decomposed, to be sure. . . . Suddenly
it struck him—this was not just an emotional reaction. It
was a sign of low blood sugar. He had been out of stasis
longer than the others and the nutrients administered in-
travenously during the AI-controlled awakening process
were now depleted. His body was demanding nourishment.

Carla was sitting in the crew lounge, somewhat dazed
with grief and horror, but composed. Jesse approached her,
forcing himself to speak as if no more to her than Captain.
"Go up to the computer room and access the archived
knowledgebase," he said. "Find out how soon we're supposed
to eat after stasis, and what kind of food we can tolerate."
Their stomachs would be shrunken, he realized with dismay. They might not be able to eat the ordinary rations
they could carry easily to the surface. God, what if stasis
passengers had been fed by IV for awhile after they emerged?
He didn't know.

He told Hari to assemble the remote viewers, who were
to work in crew quarters without ever seeing the planet
through a viewport or onscreen. Then, mustering energy
through the mind skills he'd been taught for regulating
biochemistry, he went back to the bridge to join Peter. In
due course Carla reported via intercom. "Broth," she told
him. "Prepared from powder vacuum-stored on the stasis
deck. No solid food until tomorrow. And we'll require extra
sleep."

Sleep? When they'd just wakened from weeks of it?

Sleep. "Oh, my God," he said aloud. *He* could not sleep.

He had to pilot the shuttle—not once, but on many trips. If he slept, they would run out of time.

Peter sensed this thought and responded reassuringly. "You'll be awake when you need to be, Jess," he said. "The mind has that power."

"Well, sure—people can keep going long hours in a crisis. But after a certain point, aren't snatches of sleep involuntary?"

"We have control over so-called involuntary functions," Peter pointed out.

"Is there a mind-pattern for that one? I was never shown it."

"Not specifically, but the patterns you learned to match through neurofeedback were only symbols, after all. You were not shown a visual pattern for fire immunity, either."

No, but Peter had supported him telepathically when he thrust his hand into fire; the whole assembly had supported him. . . .

You'll have support—I'll see that someone qualified is on every shuttle trip, once you reach the stage where it's necessary.

Peter, Jesse ventured, ashamed to express the thought aloud, *I know we refuse all drugs, but the ship's medical stores include stimulants. . . .*

In an emergency I wouldn't stand on principle. But after stasis it might not be safe. Stimulant drugs might kill you. And then where would we be?

True enough. The Group's objection to medication was not merely philosophical; free of society's pharmaphilic bias, they knew that even medicinal drugs were apt to do more harm than good. Peter, a fully-trained member of Undine's Med hierarchy, had been forced to administer all too many drugs, to patients willing and unwilling, during his years as a Hospital psychiatrist. His judgment in such matters was to be relied on.

Carla brought them tall mugs of broth, then returned to the adjacent computer room. The stuff had an unpleasant taste and made Jesse slightly nauseous; it was hard to get down. As he finished drinking, Kira spoke urgently through the intercom. "I think you had better look at Claire, Peter," she said. "Her vital signs are okay and I sense nothing wrong internally, but I can't wake her up."

Peter froze. "How about the rest of the remote viewers?"

"Some of them seem a bit out of it, though they're walking. It's only natural that people react differently to stasis, I guess. But Claire's—not with us."

"Okay. I'll be there right away if Jesse doesn't need me."

"I don't, now," Jesse said. "It will take me a while to analyze the sensor data. But come back as soon as there's some result from remote viewing—we have to choose a landing site."

"You may have to do that without me," Peter said slowly. "If I can't come, I'll send Hari with the remote viewing report. I may be—tied up." He was blocking full projection of his feelings, which had, Jesse sensed, overwhelmed even his grief over the deaths.

"Don't hold out on me," Jesse commanded. "It's my job to know everything that affects our status."

"As I mentioned a while ago," Peter confessed hesitantly, "there are dangers about which I never warned you. Partly because we weren't free to meet during those last weeks, but also because I knew you'd have enough to worry about with the practical demands of being Captain. I hoped we'd at least get a settlement established before we ran into them. But stasis increased the chance that some of our people would . . . retreat."

"Retreat? Where? There's nowhere to go."

"Into their minds, Jess. Into altered consciousness from which they don't want to return. We don't know what happens to the mind during stasis. We all experienced some form of altered consciousness, even though it's not accessible to our memories. Those of us with strong ties to everyday reality have come back. Apparently Claire has not."

Insanity . . . his own recollection of Fleet rumors had been on target, Jesse thought in horror. "You knew this might happen when you argued against stasis?"

"I feared it. But you were right. Not to go into stasis would have meant sure death. So it wasn't a real consideration; but nevertheless it's a blow to us—if it involves more people than Claire, perhaps a serious one."

Yes. Seven people dead; at least one, perhaps more, unconscious or worse. And dangers ahead of which he knew nothing, dangers stasis had merely increased. But he could let nothing concern him now except the need to land on Maclairn.

4

CARLA SAT AT the computer, ostensibly familiarizing herself with the knowledgebase but absorbed in troubled thought. She was worried about Jesse. He was blaming himself for the astrogation error that had put them in danger—how could he not? It made no difference that he'd been forced to act on the basis of preliminary calculations, that if he'd hesitated, they'd all have ended up in a penal colony. No one in the Group would fault him for not having come up with perfect jump parameters in the too-short time given him to find Maclairn on unfamiliar charts and judge exactly how much leeway to allow so as not to risk falling into its star. But the fact remained that if his programming of the jump had been perfect, they wouldn't have run low on life support. Underneath, he couldn't forget that. She'd have known he couldn't, even if she hadn't received his emotions telepathically from the moment they embraced after her awakening.

And in fact, she'd been aware of it long before. They had made love during their first night aboard the starship. She'd insisted on that, despite strange reluctance on his part, because she could see that he was in turmoil and he refused to tell her why. He'd been closing his mind to her, which would be impossible when they were both sexually aroused. Sex strengthened the link between telepaths; they felt each other's sensations and saw through each other's eyes. He had not wanted her to see—he'd known how much she feared stasis and had hoped to spare her the anticipation of it. But of course, when they joined she'd perceived the stasis chamber he had just inspected, along with the reason he'd done so. To her shame, she had pulled away from him, screaming. It had taken her the rest of the night to get herself under control. But once calm, she'd sensed the deep guilt he felt over his failure.

That morning, after Jesse had convinced the Council that stasis was their only choice and had gone to the bridge to make preparations, she had taken Peter aside. "He'll never stop blaming himself," she'd said, "and he hasn't been taught how to cope."

"No," agreed Peter sadly. "His training had to be rushed—"

"Which I protested from the first day you told me you planned to recruit him."

"But now you know why, Carla. I was aware that we'd have to get away from Undine as soon as we could charter a starship, which meant Jesse would have to focus on being Captain. Kira and I taught him enough control of his body's reactions to give him confidence in that ability and sustain him in the Ritual. There wasn't time for more."

"There were weeks after his Ritual commitment, weeks when you let him spend his time playing with a seaplane you knew he couldn't keep—"

"You urged me to approve the purchase of that plane. I tabled my reservations because I agreed that Jesse deserved some fun. Further mind training would have been hard on him; the process of confronting old guilt-fostering memories is more traumatic for someone his age than for a younger person. I didn't want to subject him to it just before he had to lead our escape."

True. And, Carla realized, it was best not to follow the thought that if he hadn't bought the plane he wouldn't have been arrested for the alleged murder of its former owner. Too much, both terrible and wonderful, had proceeded from that ... though they'd have been spared much suffering, Jesse would not have had telepathic contact with Ian, could not have saved Peter and herself from being left behind on Undine, would never have guessed that Ian, having confessed to murder in order to clear him, had gone conscious into stasis to prove to them that such a death was no worse than any other ... in fact Ian would have died of old age in his own bed, as had been long anticipated. There was no accounting for the complex pattern of what Peter called fate.

"I assumed there'd be plenty of time later for Jesse to learn to handle guilt feelings," Peter went on. "There were issues from his past I knew must be addressed, as there have been for us all—but I had no way of anticipating he'd have real grounds for such feelings before we got to Maclairn."

"He doesn't have real grounds! We'd be in prison now if he hadn't gone ahead with the jump."

"Yes, we owe our freedom to him, to his ability to act fast without too much weighing of consequences. The average person would have frozen in a situation like that. He doesn't recognize his own strengths."

"Has he ever?" All his adult life, she knew, Jesse had suffered from unwarranted doubt of his capabilities brought on by Fleet's failure to fully utilize them. He'd been a mere boy, fresh from school, when he entered the space academy. As a young officer he'd been arbitrarily assigned to a freighter crew and had performed well, so well that he'd quickly advanced in rank and had been locked into a position from which the ponderous bureaucracy of Fleet had not seen fit to release him. Having no ties left on Earth and no chance to develop any elsewhere, he hadn't even taken the leaves to which his years of service entitled him. Once the novelty of visiting colony worlds wore off, frustration and boredom led him to solitary drinking during layovers, so it had become a vicious circle—as word of his off-duty indiscretion spread, his chance of further advancement decreased, while his efficiency aboard ship kept him tied to stultifying routine. Had it not been for his detention on Undine, he might never have escaped into a more satisfying life. It was pure bad luck that now, just as he'd been gaining confidence . . .

"He'll be at risk for only a little while, Carla," Peter promised. "When we wake from stasis I'll deal with it. There will be weeks in orbit before he's under the pressure of frequent shuttle trips."

But now there wouldn't be weeks. There would be only hours during which he would have to make one trip after another until he was past exhaustion . . . and he assumed his health was protected. He'd been led to believe that fear and worry were the only stressors people needed to overcome.

The Group's fundamental precept was that illness, when not caused by virulent microorganisms, was the result of inner stress. Trying to eliminate it by physical means was at best useless and worst could do much harm. Thus members rejected the medical care and so-called "preventative care" enforced by law on Undine and by indoctrination everywhere else. They had no chronic illnesses. Not that their lives weren't stressful, but their mind training enabled them to consciously—and with practice, unconsciously—control physiological reactions that orthodox science considered involuntary. And this led to freedom not only from illness, but from the effects of aging. Ultimately, they hoped, it would give them lengthened lives. Ian had reached a hundred and thirty, and had been on the verge of dying naturally at the time of his execution.

But, Carla thought unhappily, Jesse hadn't yet acquired such freedom. Being a courageous man, he had risen to the challenge of the Group's rigorous teaching methods and had quickly learned to control his body's reactions to fear. That was the easy part. It was harder to get into the habit of using this skill automatically when under stress, but he was well on the way to doing so. What no one had told him— what Peter had specifically warned that he must not yet be told—was that human bodies react biochemically to guilt as well as to anxiety, and that in most people suppressed guilt is more frequent and more damaging. This had been known since the time of Freud, whose theories had placed false emphasis on the sexual hang-ups of his own era and had thus drawn attention away from the main issue. The medical establishment ignored it, of course, and few recruits to the Group gave it any thought before the issue was raised. But until you learned to acknowledge all stirrings of conscience and meet them with volitional control of your brain chemistry, you were vulnerable. . . .

"Peter," she'd asked fearfully, "will he be . . . in danger? In stasis, I mean—from uncontrolled stress responses beforehand?" Human bodies were equipped to handle crises; short-term fear wouldn't kill them even if it became panic. A major stressor like stasis combined with guilt on a deep level might be another matter.

"No," Peter had assured her. "He won't succumb while unconscious; he'll know underneath that our lives depend on him, and he's not one to shrink from the responsibility. But afterward—after we wake, when he has to take charge of getting us and all our equipment to the surface of the new world, which will take time—"

"It could make him ill. Too ill for self-healing."

"Sooner or later, perhaps—but I'll intervene, of course. I'll teach him what he needs to know." Peter took her hand, gripped it. *You do realize, don't you, Carla, that a lot depends on you? You did fine in there, in the Council meeting. I know what it took for you to overcome your phobia about stasis fully enough to make him believe you trust his decision. But you've got to stay steady. The very worst thing for Jesse would be to sense terror in your mind at the moment when that stasis box closes on you. . . .*

I know. She clung to Peter's hand, trying not to let her

dismay add to his burden. He, too, was about to face over-whelming crisis; in a few hours he would have to conduct the Ritual, and if he failed to pull it off—if some refused to enter stasis despite his best effort to influence them tele-pathically—then the life support would not last. She owed courage to him as well as to Jesse. They were as close as brother and sister. She had depended on him emotionally since the death of her first husband, Ramón; and if Peter hadn't been married throughout most of that time, their affection for each other might well have developed into some-thing more. As it was, though within the Group sex between unmarried partners wasn't frowned on, she'd avoided rela-tionships completely until Jesse's arrival had shocked her out of her long, frozen years of mourning.

I won't let him know I'm still afraid, she promised. And she hadn't. She had convinced Jesse that their love over-rode all other emotion, and had discovered, in the last in-stant of consciousness, that it did. She was free now of the old nightmare, Ramón's face beneath the lid of the box into which he'd been sealed during his execution. His body was still in stasis on Undine, would be there forever, his heart kept artificially beating; but his mind was long gone. That was not only a travesty of life, as the Group had always said, but a mockery of the very real mental existence she and the others had maintained in stasis while alive. *There is life and there is death,* Jesse had said on the day she still thought of as yesterday—*there is no in between*. Her fear that stasis would be an intermediate state now seemed fool-ish and far away.

But it had been replaced by a new fear. She and Peter had been in the Group for many years, and had aged little; their mastery of the mind skills kept them physically young. Jesse had been over forty when recruited, and he had a lot left to learn, under stressful conditions, before his ongoing health was assured. Even if he got through the coming or-deal without developing any overt illness, would his poten-tial lifetime be shortened, as was normally the case with outsiders? She did not think she could bear to be old without him. God, Carla thought, Kira's over a hundred and her husband died decades ago. . . .

Though this was a real concern, she couldn't deny that at the moment it was merely masking dread on which she dared not focus. Jesse was about to make more consecutive shuttle trips than any pilot should attempt without rest breaks. She didn't know much about shuttles, but that the undertaking was dangerous seemed all too obvious. She had lost Ramón. She had almost lost Jesse to perpetual confinement in the psych ward under brain-damaging drugs. How could she now endure her life if the shuttle crashed, if he was killed?

A stupid question, she realized abruptly. She wouldn't have to endure life. If Jesse was killed in a shuttle crash, she and Peter and everyone else left aboard the starship would die of oxygen deprivation within a few days.

5

LONG-RANGE SENSORS had started collecting data about the planet several days before Jesse had been awakened from stasis, and robotic probes had been launched by the ship's AI. By now, he had access to an extensive set of figures and photos. The information from Fleet's original survey on gravity, temperature, atmosphere and soil had been confirmed, and in addition considerable detail about mineral deposits was available. This was the basis on which the settlement's site would have to be chosen. A colony that was to receive no supply shipments could not retain the level of civilization achieved by humankind unless it could establish industry during the first generation of its existence. It must therefore devote most of its energy to mining, not farming, however sentimental a picture some people might have of what pioneering had been like on ancient Earth.

Initially, there'd been some argument. A few history buffs had been reluctant to abandon the notion that settling a new world would mean living as they did during offtime on the Group's beloved island, with only the added effort of growing their own food. They imagined that a planet untouched by modern civilization might have pristine fields waiting to be planted, and would not be defaced by mines and factories until long after their own era. To be sure, lifeforms that had evolved on Earth could not eat an alien planet's vegetation; the biological difference would be too great. But wouldn't the necessary introduction of terragenic crops and livestock turn it into the equivalent of the unspoiled farmland settled by their distant ancestors?

Most members of the Group were more realistic—after all, farming on their birthworld was dependent on robotic machinery. No colony anywhere, except a few established by religious sects, wasted human time and effort on manual farm labor. However, some people envisioned a life similar to that of farmers on Undine. They didn't stop to think that the ship could carry only enough machines to serve the founding generation. As the population expanded, more would be needed, and to manufacture more, raw materials would have to be obtained. Thus mining must begin immediately. Mining, too, would be accomplished by robotic machines, but it would require considerably more human attention than the farms would.

This, Reiko had explained, was fortunate. "If we didn't have to work with high technology," she pointed out, "our kids would grow up knowing nothing about it—after a generation or two, the information in the knowledgebase would be meaningless to them. It would seem irrelevant. And so our civilization would revert to an earlier level; the accumulated knowledge of humankind would be lost to our descendants. What's more, they'd revert even in the social sense. Customs that fit their lifestyle would develop. Pretty soon women's main function would be childbearing and men, at least most men, would be unwilling to break with established ways of doing things."

"Our aim's to move forward, not backward," Peter had

agreed. "Now for the first time in human history a culture can integrate the widespread use of psi powers without any loss of the practical skills needed to ensure long-term survival. That's possible only because of the technological level we have reached. Maintaining that level must be our top priority."

Thus the site chosen for the colony must have sufficient resources for maintaining it. God, thought Jesse, how can I be sure? From mere orbital surveys of an untouched planet, how can I pick the best place for us to locate permanently? He'd failed to calculate the jump precisely. He could not afford to fail again. And yet for the second time, he was being forced to act too fast.

It was never meant to be this way. They'd assumed they could take days to explore. The plan had called for landing in several places with a team to evaluate the pros and cons of each. Jesse had not expected sole responsibility for the decision. He was not qualified for it. He'd commanded only freighters; in Fleet, he had never served on a colonizer, and not since the cadet days of his youth had he aspired to the eventual captaincy of such a ship.

Colonizer crews included geologists, mining engineers, and exobiologists, along with others trained in the skills needed to get a new settlement on its feet. While the Group lacked such experts, it did have members with related experience whose opinions would be valuable. Those people were still in stasis. He could not consult them—he must make the choice alone, possibly even without discussing it with Peter. And there would be no second chance; where he dropped the power receiver and cargo pods was where they would have to stay.

There was, to be sure, the possibility of input from remote viewing. Jesse knew nothing about that, not even what sort of information it might provide. Abruptly he recalled that Hari had said they'd need coordinates to target as soon as he was able to provide them. Well, there was no point in further delay; he had all the data before him that it was possible to get from orbit. He chose four of the most likely spots flagged on his screen and conveyed them by intercom to Hari, stating nothing more than the numbers since he had been told that remote viewers must be given no hints about what they might see. Then he turned to the retrieval of a probe that would bring back samples of atmosphere and biomaterial.

Maclairn did have native vegetation, though it was sparse in most places. The planet was predominantly arid, large areas being covered with the rocks that gave it its distinctive golden color. Its seas were small compared to Earth's oceans and widely scattered. No doubt there was life in the seas, but whether there were any land animals remained to be determined. The initial Fleet survey had established that there were no lethal bacteria, a fact that must be verified through AI analysis of the retrieved probe.

The Group had, of course, hoped to settle by the shore of a sea—Undine was a water world, so that was what they were used to. Undine's single city filled an island; mines, farms and genetically-engineered forests occupied others, generally reached by seaplane as they were too far apart for convenient boat traffic. Ian had owned the small private one on which he had built the Lodge.

The Lodge . . . for a moment Jesse was lost in the memory of it. He had fallen in love with Carla there, first lain with her by its huge fireplace, received mind training in the hidden illegal lab below ground. But the Lodge was gone. Peter had destroyed it to prevent the lab from being found after their departure. By waking time, it was only the day before yesterday that he'd rescued Peter and Carla, who'd been stranded there after the explosion, and flown them directly to the spaceport, crash-landing the floatplane on a paved pad in a desperate move to avoid capture by the Med authorities. Accustomed though he was to hyperspace jumps, it was hard to believe how far behind that now was. If even he felt disoriented, how could the others adjust so fast to the reality facing them?

They could not build the colony on the seashore. The more Jesse studied the data, the more obvious that became. The most essential mineral deposits were far from the seas. There might not even be rivers nearby; if not, they would have to depend on wells. Perhaps if there'd been more time, if the choice hadn't been limited to areas where there'd be daylight.... Though he had access to images of the whole planet, he couldn't set a shuttle down at night until boundary lights had been rigged. And landing could not wait for the progress of dawn.

No one had anticipated such harsh conditions. They'd known the freedom of the air would be forever lost to them— many had given up private seaplanes, and planes were low on the priority list for manufacture. But to lose the sea, too ... They would wake to be thrust by a rough shuttle trip into a near-barren, rocky landscape from which they could never hope to escape. And it was his fault. They would not blame him; Peter and Kira had made that clear. But he would never know how much better a life they might have had if he had not miscalculated.

The screen swam before Jesse's eyes, and abruptly he realized that the broth he'd drunk was not going to stay down. His stomach, after weeks of forced inactivity, was about to reject it. Fortunately there was a head adjacent to the bridge; he barely made it in time.

Weak and shaken, he stumbled back to the Captain's seat and called Carla on the intercom. "I started to feel sick, too," she admitted. "The knowledgebase says it's common. We have to drink some more, Jesse, and keep drinking till our bodies can tolerate it. Otherwise we won't gain enough energy to stay awake."

She brought him another mugful and he sipped it slowly, choking back nausea. He hoped he'd be over that by the time he had to fly the shuttle. Soon, however, it became apparent that it wasn't going to stop with mere vomiting. Once the liquid food had been accepted by his stomach, it proceeded to cause havoc lower down. Cramps drove him back to the head, not once, but repeatedly; and he began to feel real worry about what this boded for the coming flights.

He didn't consult Carla by voice again, but he didn't have to; unlike most Group members, they had developed an ability to converse telepathically with each other even when not in the same room. Though she was back at the computer retrieving data on the cargo pod contents, he could not have hidden his anguish from her if he'd tried. *You'll be okay*, she assured him. *But for outsiders, recovering from stasis must have been very hard.* Those who traveled in stasis in the old days, she meant—"outsiders" was how people not in the Group were usually referred to. He was no longer an outsider. . . .

Belatedly, Jesse recalled that he was expected to free himself from such sickness. For this, he did know the mind-pattern. During one hellish afternoon during his training, Kira had subjected him to violent illness in order to prove to him that his body's reactions were controlled by his unconscious mind. He'd assumed she had drugged him; when it turned out that suggestion alone had made him sick, he had finally grasped that it could also work in reverse. She had then taken him into the neurofeedback lab and taught him to enter the state of consciousness required. Though he'd healed wounds before, the management of internal distress was more difficult; he had wondered for awhile whether the game was worth the candle, considering that no microbe-borne illnesses existed on Undine. Afterward, it had dawned on him that the issue was central. It was common knowledge, after all, that strong emotions could have dramatic impact on intestinal functions—so why wasn't it obvious that they could be managed via mind skills?

He was not yet experienced enough for this to be automatic. To do it took concentration and effort. He had to remind himself that he need no more endure physical discomfort than suffer from actual pain. Group members were literally immune to pain, regardless of its severity; learning how not to suffer from it had been the foundation of his mind training. You didn't have to bear it stoically; it simply didn't bother you once you'd mastered the skill of handling it. Painkilling drugs were not merely rejected by the Group, they were superfluous.

Yet at the same time, you had to be *willing* to suffer, willing even to lose control. If you feared that, fought it, the mind skills did not work. Which was exactly what had just happened to him, Jesse realized with chagrin. He had feared that his body would betray him, interfere with the shuttle trips. If he gave in to that fear, it would. Paradoxically, unless he was willing to fly no matter what his guts did to him, he'd have no chance of avoiding the worst. What the hell, Jesse told himself. There would be no lasting damage if he was humiliated during flight. There very well might be if he delayed getting his passengers off the ship.

Letting himself relax and turn inward, he visualized the moving shapes and colors of the mind-pattern for subduing sickness, a symbolic wall-sized representation of the particular state of consciousness he wanted his brain to produce. "Remember it," Kira had said. "This isn't something we'd want to repeat for practice." He'd been used to practicing other mind-patterns, such as the one for controlling his heart rate, and no longer needed the lengthy sessions of matching his neurofeedback to hers, or to Peter's, that he'd gone through earlier in training.

Without the advanced neurofeedback technology developed by Ian, trainees could not have gained volitional control of so-called involuntary functions within mere days—a skill that yogis and shamans had once needed years of self-discipline to acquire. The feedback, combined with the telepathic aid of instructors, was what made it possible. That was the Group's secret, the reason its members were able to maintain their own long-term health. But the training wasn't easy. For the first time it occurred to Jesse to wonder how they expected to get all their future children through it.

This wasn't the moment to ponder that question; he gave it no more thought. By the time Hari arrived with the results of the remote viewing, he had gotten his mind deeply enough into the healing state to function unconsciously there, leaving him free to devote his attention to the job at hand. Which, he realized, was what Carla and the others had been doing all along. It would take more trouble than mere sickness to faze them. He hoped that on Maclairn they wouldn't encounter too much more.

6

REMOTE VIEWING, HARI explained, was far from an infallible source of information. No single person's results could be taken at face value—there would be misses as well as hits, though not as many as on Earth, where "psychic noise" from the unconscious minds of millions often intruded. The only way to judge which visions to rely on was to compare reports, taking into account knowledge of which people had been most successful in the past. Yet because there had been nothing beyond a small area on Undine except empty ocean and scattered volcanic islands devoid of life, none of the Group's members had meaningful experience with viewing at a distance. It was not known whether anyone, anywhere, had successfully remote-viewed the surface of a planet from space. Ian, to be sure, had seen their new world in a dream, but he had been extraordinarily psi-gifted.

"Anyway," Jesse recalled, "we weren't sure what he showed me wasn't merely a world he'd seen in a picture—and even if the image did originate in his dream, Peter said it could have been part of the precognition through which he saw us land. It wasn't necessarily interstellar clairvoyance."

"The distinction may not be real," Hari said. "Remote viewing sometimes shows the future, so who's to say if they are even different skills?"

"You mean some of what was viewed today may show the future of Maclairn instead of how it is now?" Jesse asked, more confused and doubtful than ever.

"Does it matter? Suppose we saw signs of a settlement—might that not mean the location was suitable for us, whatever it's like at present?"

"*Did* anyone see that?"

"Yes," Hari replied.

Astonished, Jesse could only stare at the crude drawings Hari held out to him. "It could be a miss, of course," Hari said. "It could easily have arisen from an unconscious image of what we've hoped our colony will be. We don't know, Jesse. But at the sites of the other coordinates you gave us, nothing was seen but the natural terrain. That may be accurate; there isn't much down there but rock and landlocked seas—"

"There are no seas near the coordinates I gave you."

"Then we can be sure the results weren't influenced by expectations. Everyone thought we'd settle near water."

"I know," said Jesse painfully, "but that's not where the best mineral deposits are." He frowned. "I don't understand what you do with coordinates—those are mere arbitrary numbers on a chart generated by the computer. None of your people have ever seen the chart, so how do they find the target?"

"Nobody knows," Hari told him. "That's just how it works—how it always has worked, even when remote viewing was first used on Earth in the twentieth century. You're right that it's not logical, and it's rarely possible to exclude unconscious telepathy as the underlying source of direction. It could be telepathy here, I suppose—*you* have seen the chart and know the location of the sites you picked. But you don't know how those areas look from ground level. Some of these drawings show the shapes of the mountains."

Jesse examined them more closely. They were mere rough pencil sketches, of course; remote viewers, while in altered consciousness, could record their impressions more clearly in visual form than in words. But the shapes of prominent peaks and rocks were distinctive, and in several of the sketches, they matched. Most significantly, the drawing that showed outlines of buildings included a mountain that also appeared in another one.

"It might be possible," he said, "for the computer to analyze these and compare them with the mountains as photographed from space by adjusting the perspective. I'll have Carla try it." He called her; she came and took the drawings away for scanning. What if the comparison showed them to be accurate? he thought. It still wouldn't tell him much about the suitability of the sites for landing.

"Hari," he asked slowly, "just what did you and Peter hope to learn this way? What good did you think it would do to see the terrain as it may look from the ground? It would be a great help if you were looking for something lost, or trying to find out what was going on at some location, the way I've been told remote viewing was once used on Earth for spying. But there can't be anything on Maclairn but wilderness. If there were, the ship's sensors would have picked it up."

Hari didn't answer. Troubled, Jesse went on, "You *expected* someone might see the future, didn't you? You said it sometimes happens. That was the whole point of the exercise in the first place."

"Peter didn't want *you* to expect it," Hari said. "He wanted you to remain objective, or even to serve as devil's advocate." Hesitantly he added, "It wasn't just signs of settlement we were checking for. There might have been negative premonitions—a landslide, perhaps, or—"

"Or a crash." If remote viewing had revealed anything like a crashed shuttle, he would have avoided that site without questioning the viewer's reliability. As it was, he needed more information. "Who did that drawing?" he asked.

"It's best if no one knows except Peter, don't you think? If we act on it and it later proves invalid, it would be hard on a viewer to be thought responsible, even though none of us would fault her. But I'll tell you that she's one of our most talented, and has had true viewings before."

"The shapes in the sketch that suggest buildings aren't like anything on Undine," Jesse observed.

"So I noticed. That bothered me; they could be fantasy."

"They're like the prefab shelters in our emergency pods," Jesse said reluctantly, "yet no one aboard was told any details about what we're carrying." Shelters of that design did not exist in established colonies and were unknown outside Fleet. Not even Peter had seen pictures of them. If the viewer had picked up the shapes from someone's unconscious mind, it would have to have been his own, which seemed highly unlikely.

Troubled, Jesse returned to his study of the mineral deposit data. Before long his screen signaled the arrival of output from Carla's computer comparison. The shape of the mountain shown in the settlement drawing, and in the other that showed the same one, was similar to the ground-level projection of the area's photograph. One drawing of a different area also had features compatible with photos. The rest of the drawings were so far off as to be obvious misses.

Two areas actually seen by psi, then—with confirming evidence that at least some of what had been seen of the future was potentially true. But, Jesse thought in misery, that did not really prove anything. In the first place, Peter had repeatedly pointed out that precognition was not predestination; the choice of where to land was a real choice, and if in defiance of the remote viewing result they landed elsewhere, that result would become as false as if it had been merely imagined. Furthermore, even if they built shelters where the sketch showed them, that didn't mean the Group would thrive there. Any number of things could happen to a settlement after it was built. It could be wiped out . . . or it could simply fail to obtain the resources on which their descendants' survival would depend.

And the prospect of good access to mineral resources was slightly better at the other site—which also had more hours left before dark.

"What do you think, Hari?" he asked. "Should we consider this a true enough vision to go with it?" He knew that Hari was among the Group's most talented psi teachers, one who trained advanced students in skills that most members never ventured to investigate. It would be wise to defer to his judgment.

"That's for you to say," Hari answered firmly. "You are Captain."

"I should consult Peter," Jesse declared. "He's our permanent leader, after all."

"But he has delegated the decision to you. He's working as a psychiatrist and psi adept at present. Claire hasn't awakened, and he's trying to reach her telepathically, which may require the combined focus of a lot of us—he's called on the remote viewers now that we've finished our job. There are also several other cases, people functioning physically who aren't in full touch with reality. So don't expect him back here soon."

Yet surely Peter must have a strong opinion about whether to trust the viewing. It was not like him not to express it, by intercom if he couldn't leave his patients. He was undoubtedly aware that Jesse, lacking personal experience with such matters, would give it considerable weight. And that was precisely why he was keeping silent, Jesse realized. Peter believed in fate. To him, a settlement viewed remotely in time as well as in space would seem an obvious extension of Ian's dream, a validation of all they had undergone on the basis of that dream—even of Ian's sacrificially-hastened death. Of course he favored trusting it! But he recognized his own ignorance of space exploration, and considered the Captain better qualified than he to evaluate their options.

Jesse bowed his head. God, he didn't feel qualified! He had hoped the use of remote viewing might let him off the hook. Instead, it had made the decision harder than ever.

As a former Fleet officer, he knew that the second site had a significant edge. At either place there would be sufficient resources—still, reason dictated the choice of the one where they were most plentiful. And yet ... the precognitive viewing must *mean* something. Even on Earth, premonitions were sometimes true; those with negative content were more common than others only because of their stronger emotional impact on people without the skill of trained remote viewers. There was no justification for calling positive visions less valid.

When he'd joined the Group, he had not wanted to believe in psi. During his first weeks of training he had resisted it, as had most people throughout history. Kira had explained that this was natural, that in fact it was adaptive in the evolutionary sense for psi powers not to be widely developed until after a species had expanded to many worlds. Therefore, she'd said, psi was instinctively feared, especially by people who leaned toward the pursuit of science and technology. It was too upsetting to their worldview, their confidence in the perception of the universe on which their personal self-image depended. Though his repressed fear had been a barrier to full intimacy with Carla, he had shrunk from admitting to himself that he possessed ESP and self-healing power. Peter had finally forced the issue. After that, new doors had opened in Jesse's mind, leading to fulfillment beyond anything he had ever envisioned.

He had never been one to ponder the meaning of life. Psi had given him joy in his union with Carla. It had empowered him to touch fire in the Ritual. His growing telepathic ability had saved him from destruction in the Hospital, and had later enabled him to save Peter and Carla from missing the starship's departure. These had been immediate, concrete gains from the use of capabilities he no longer classed as supernatural. Remote viewing was less comprehensible. Where did accurate visions come from, when they didn't come from mere imagination or via telepathy from anyone alive? He didn't share Peter's trust in fate . . . yet if such visions weren't meaningful, then you really couldn't be sure there was meaning in anything. Either all aspects of the universe were significant, or they weren't. You couldn't rule out some of them just because you didn't understand their source.

Jesse thought back to the moment in the seaplane, the moment when against all reason he had abandoned his clear duty and turned toward the Island in response to Carla's and Peter's telepathic calls. The distance had been too great for conscious telepathy; he hadn't been sure the calls weren't illusory. He had known only that if he ignored them, he would be denying all he had gained in the Group, all the evidence he'd been given that the human mind was more than officially-sanctioned science assumed it to be. And if he *had* ignored them, none of them would be here now; the hijacking would never have taken place. Peter might even be dead.

The Group's goal was to create a culture in which psi was widely used. If they began by failing to follow the guidance of psi, what hope had they of building their future on it?

"We'll go with the glimpse we've been given," he told Hari. Then he turned to the task of moving the starship into position for the irrevocable step of dropping the cargo pods.

7

WHEN CARLA CAME onto the bridge later, they were in low orbit, the golden surface of Maclairn filling the viewscreen and looking only slightly more hospitable than the planet Mars as shown in ancient photos taken prior to its terraforming. She came and rested her hands on Jesse's shoulders, staring outward. "God," she said, "it's awesome . . . but the land's so *dry*."

"Of course, compared to a water world like Undine. You've never seen any other, after all." He himself had seen many, but he had to admit that this one was drier than most. There weren't many clouds visible, though he knew from the climate report that it did rain sometimes, and a few of the highest mountains were snow-covered.

"I've seen Earth in vids," Carla said. "There's a lot of land on Earth, yet from space it's mostly blue and white."

"Well, we didn't expect to find a world just like Earth. A breatheable atmosphere and tolerable climate is the most we could hope for." Tolerable, but not comfortable. Not even safe for people without survival skills about which the colonists knew nothing—it was a good thing he'd had some basic training in dealing with extreme environments during his youth at Fleet Academy. Their site would be hot year-round in the daytime; though Maclairn's sun was no brighter than Undine's, its air was thinner and its day was several hours longer. A location nearer one of the poles might have been preferable, if not too cold at night for rapid crop growth. But since the comm satellite on which the all-important datalink to the starship's knowledgebase would depend must be in geosynchronous orbit, they were limited to sites near the equator.

"I'm not complaining," Carla assured him. "And there are seas, after all, even though I can't see any right now."

Sadly, he broke the news to her. "You aren't ever going to see them unless you happen to be on the bridge when we pass over one. From our settlement they won't be visible."

"Oh, Jesse. Why not?" Memory of the sea flooded into her mind, and therefore into his: the expanse beneath their plane, the swimming cove at the Lodge, the secluded shore where they'd once made love. . . .

He reminded her of the importance of mineral deposits, but did not mention the future shown by remote viewing. He'd agreed with Hari to keep quiet about that until Peter could decide how much to tell the others. Although, he suddenly realized, it would be impossible to keep it from Carla during lovemaking, when with telepathic contact intensified by sexual arousal, their thoughts and feelings merged.

"Peter just called me," Carla said. "He said I should learn what to do on the bridge in case he can't stand watch here after the shuttle launch. How soon are you leaving?"

"As soon as I've confirmed that the power receiver and cargo pods have landed. I've released them; they're now entering the atmosphere."

It was true that Carla could take the watch as easily as Peter could; there would be nothing to do except keep in touch with him by commlink, since no one would be capable of acting on system alarms without instructions. The ship was fully AI-controlled except during the initiation of unscheduled maneuvers. There should not be any alarms. Still, you didn't leave the bridge of a starship unattended, and whatever computer tasks she needed to do could be handled as well from the bridge as from the computer room. By this time she had routed knowledgebase access to all stations in crew quarters so that landing teams could study their assigned jobs.

Jesse dreaded the coming shuttle trips. Normally, he liked nothing better than flying, and much as he had enjoyed his seaplane on Undine, he had missed the faster response of a spacecraft. But too much rode on the perfection of these flights, he must make too many of them without rest, and he was tired before he'd even begun. He found himself wishing they were over, that everyone was safe on the surface and he was free to make love with Carla as he'd just been envisioning . . . even, perhaps, with hope of her conceiving a child. . . .

Oh, God. He brought himself back with a start, remembering a detail he'd forgotten, and called Kira. "Have you removed the contraceptive implants from the landing team?" he asked. "If not, it's got to be done now—mine, too. And do it for everyone who's revived from now on; you'd better wake Susan to help." Susan, as an experienced gynecologist, would be able to work faster than any of the other physicians.

"There's no rush," Kira protested. "Eager as we all are to have kids, surely nobody wants to get pregnant before we've even built shelters! The first people who land aren't likely to have time for sex anyway, least of all you."

"You're missing the point, Kira," he said.

There was a short silence. "Okay, I was being obtuse," she admitted. "Tell me where to find the surgical equipment."

He'd had a contraceptive implant since adolescence, and

so too had all citizens of Undine. Natural conception was against the law there; all children were conceived in vitro because the Med government had strict standards as to the genetic health of babies allowed to be born. The Group had boycotted this system; even legally married couples had chosen not to start authorized, medically-assisted pregnancies. It wasn't just that they disapproved of discarding every embryo whose genetic makeup wasn't perfect. They weren't willing to accept the Meds' policies on rearing children, either, and had they attempted to circumvent them, they would have lost custody. Moreover, they feared that if psi talent proved to have a genetic component, their offspring would be in danger of being medicated to suppress it. Thus a main attraction of the new world was the freedom to have families.

But that was not why the implants had to be taken out before landing. Jesse could not ignore the risk of an accident, on a later trip if not the first—and if either he or the shuttle should be disabled, everyone on the surface would be stranded there permanently. With internal contraceptives in place they could have no progeny. They couldn't get rid of the implants themselves; only a skilled surgeon could remove them. So until Kira or another qualified doctor had gone down, it had to be done aboard the starship.

This was another of the things that would have been taken care of unhurriedly during the trip if they hadn't been forced into stasis. It was no big deal, however. Though in the Hospital scans would have been used to pinpoint the implants precisely, Kira could locate them easily with her healer's sense, a form of psi in which she was especially gifted. The surgery wouldn't take long, as Group members could control their own bleeding and heal themselves within minutes. Even the few trainees aboard could do so with Kira's aid. And of course, no anesthetic would be needed.

Getting hold of surgical supplies was another matter. There were plenty in sick bay, including the instruments required for procedures involving the reproductive system, which were standard equipment aboard colonizers. But sick bay was on the passenger deck, which could not be repressurized. Even the scalpels they had displayed as weapons during the hijacking had been left on that deck. So, too, had the personal possessions of everyone aboard, plus newly-purchased clothing that would be needed immediately; the short-sleeved shirts and mid-calf pants worn on Undine would offer little protection from the sun, and besides, hot though Maclairn was during the day, its nights were cold. There were only enough flight suits in crew quarters to outfit the first few landing parties. I'm slipping, he thought ruefully. God, how could I have overlooked that problem?

He could, of course, visit the passenger deck in a spacesuit. But he couldn't collect and carry everyone's belongings by himself, and in any case, they were running out of time. The first shuttle flight couldn't be delayed much longer.

So others would have to suit up; there was no other option. Kwame and Erik, who'd helped with the bodies, were on the initial landing team; they would have time to retrieve the surgical supplies, but not much more. Dorcas, Liz and Anne would also be on the first shuttle. What other experienced scuba divers were already awake? Jesse wondered. Peter and Kira, of course, but they were busy. He didn't know the remote viewers personally, and that meant they weren't divers because he did know the people who'd been in the habit of spending their free time at the Lodge.

That left Carla. She would have to leave the bridge for awhile, as she would be the only one available to instruct people who were awakened after he had gone. With Peter and Hari otherwise occupied, he would have to teach Reiko to stand watch—when by now, he should be checking the readiness of the shuttle. Everything that needed doing depended on something else, and he couldn't be everywhere at once....

"Carla," he said, "it looks as if you'll have to go to the

passenger deck without me. Kwame will show you how to
suit up, then later you can show others. The only tricky
thing is watching the air gauge, and that's not much different from diving." A bigger problem, he realized, might be
finding a suit to fit her; like everyone born under Undine's
genetic standards, she was tall. The women in the ship's
Fleet crew had been smaller; she might have to use a man's.

"And we're to bring back clothes as well as medical supplies?" she asked. He had not mentioned this aloud, but his
thoughts were open to Carla whenever they were together,
as long as he wasn't purposely concealing them.

"As many as you can carry," Jesse confirmed, "and you'll
have to make more trips as soon as other divers are awake."
The imported warm clothing they'd arranged for was still
in shipping containers that hadn't been unpacked. As an
afterthought he added, "Pick up our personal stuff too, if
you can. Just cram everything in each cabin into the duffel
bags—we were allowed only one apiece, after all, and they're
lightweight. Maybe you can find something to tie them to,
so you can drag a string of them into the airlock."

The airlock. No one but he knew how to cycle the emergency lock between decks, which had stood open when the
entire ship was pressurized. Well, Kwame was an engineer;
he should be able to figure it out and teach Carla. They
could consult him by commlink if they needed to.

After commanding the men to go with her and telling
Kira to wake more scuba divers plus another surgeon during the wait for their return, he ordered Reiko to the bridge.
Reiko was a scholar and administrator; she had no technical training. But all she'd have to do was maintain contact
with him and watch for alarms from the AI system.

While he was showing her the board, the signals from
the cargo drop came in. He put it onscreen at top magnifica-
tion, and they watched the parachutes blossom into bright
splotches of color against the golden surface of Maclairn. Both
the power receiver and the pods were on target. Their transmissions indicated no damage. Free now to leave the bridge,

Jesse got into his spacesuit and proceeded to the shuttle deck to make sure his bird was ready to fly.

8

THEY HAD DEPRESSURIZED the shuttle bay to force departure of the starship crew they'd sent back to Undine—and, Jesse had decided, he would not waste air by repressurizing it so soon. Kwame and Erik were already used to spacesuits; the rest of the first landing team would have to wear them only to walk the short distance to the shuttlecraft. It was the least of the difficulties they would face before the day was over.

He had no choice but to depend entirely on the shuttle's AI for its status. The Fleet crew had included maintenance engineers, although their only function would have been troubleshooting. Jesse knew no more about maintaining the engine of a shuttle than he did about the engines of the starship itself. The AI was supposed to do everything that needed doing. If it failed, a captain without a crew had no recourse. In taking command, he'd gambled on there being no failure in any system that was indispensable.

They did have backup. *Mayflower XI* was carrying three small all-terrain shuttles; originally there had been another, which had been given up in sending the Fleet crew back to Undine. In addition there was a large passenger shuttle that would need a flat landing pad. Eventually, with more pilots, they could make good use of all four ships; but for now only one at a time could be flown, and so he would alternate the small ones, letting them recharge between trips, until the pad for the large one had been built. The first had already been prepared by his remote command. Though the starship was old, the shuttlecraft aboard were newer models that were familiar to him. He climbed into the pilot's seat and began a thorough, confident check of the instrument panel. The nervousness he'd felt earlier evaporated. It had been some time since he had flown a shuttle, but the touch of the controls was something you didn't forget.

Through his headset, Kira said, "I'll be ready for you in a few minutes, Jesse. I'm almost finished with the others—Dorcas and Liz were egg donors for our cryonic bank, so their implants were removed before we left."

Damn. More time would be lost while she took out his contraceptive implant. There was such a small chance—and a horrifying one to contemplate—that doing it this soon would matter . . . yet it would seem like tempting fate to let it go. Jesse put the shuttle on standby and left the bay, wearily removing the spacesuit he would have to don again within the hour. In the crew cabin Kira had used for a makeshift surgery, he submitted to the wounding of a sensitive part of his anatomy, realizing almost with surprise that he was a bit apprehensive. Carla had cut his tracking microchip out of him their last night on Undine, but that had been a far less delicate operation than the removal of an IVD. Not that he didn't trust Kira's skill implicitly, but it had been common knowledge on Earth that fertility couldn't always be restored. . . .

Managing the pain was no problem; he'd had considerable experience, so it was second nature now. He'd had fewer past occasions to call on his power of rapid healing. But with telepathic assistance from Kira, he focused on it easily, and found that it also helped his control of the queasiness he felt afterward while swallowing another meal of broth. "You're okay," she told him. "A healer sees deeper into the body via psi than could otherwise be done so quickly. Your ducts are clear now, and there's no reason why you can't become a father."

So at last, the preparations were finished, and he had only to turn command of the starship temporarily over to Peter. For that, he must talk to him in person. He was uneasy with Peter's preoccupation during the past hours. Someone had to take charge while the shuttle was gone, and no one but Peter was qualified. Kira, though next in line for

Group leadership in matters relating to mind powers, knew nothing about the ship or the situations that might arise during the first hours on the ground.

He found Peter ready to take over. "Claire's conscious," he said, "though still not functioning well. I had to bring her around before you left because it would have been impossible to deal with anything else while I was involved in that. I had to go where she was, Jess—she was out of her body so I had to meet her on that level."

"I don't understand."

"No. Your training didn't cover out-of-body experiences and now is hardly the time to stir up a topic I know is likely to upset you. But circumstances have forced you into a situation where you'll be in direct command of people just wakened from stasis, without backup from anyone trained to handle psych problems. I owe you warning of what may happen."

"You mean that in the shuttle some of them could go crazy?" Jesse asked, frowning. "Our trained people, who know how to manage fear?"

"It's not a matter of fearing physical danger." Reluctantly Peter explained, "Jess, most psi-gifted people don't have the kind of personality best suited to pioneering a new planet. Fleet gives psych tests to applicants for its academy, as you know. There's also psychological evaluation of the first settlers sent to authorized colonies. Well, there are quite a few people in the Group who wouldn't pass those tests. They aren't crazy. They simply have mental and emotional traits the opposite of what's needed for survival in space or on new worlds."

"And you're just realizing this *now*?" demanded Jesse, outraged.

"Ian and I realized it from the beginning," Peter said soberly. "It was a calculated risk. The majority of our people will be okay. In the scenario we expected, problems wouldn't have arisen at this stage. Stasis changed that, and the need to send everyone to the surface immediately, before a ground base is even built, has changed it still more."

Jesse was silent. Yet another consequence of his astrogation error, then....

Peter continued, "Going into stasis was a major trauma for nearly everybody, even though we got them psyched up to it through the Ritual. Then there were a few moments of altered consciousness after we went in. My guess is that you spent them with Carla."

They had been joyous moments. "It was as if we were together somewhere outside the boxes we were sealed into—"

"Exactly. Your body was in the stasis unit, but in your mind you and Carla met elsewhere, and it seemed more real than your physical location in what you knew might prove to be your coffin. You got into such a state even without previous experience. And if stasis had that effect on you, it's not surprising that it acted that way on people to whom that state was familiar."

"What else had they undergone that could produce it?" Jesse asked, puzzled.

"Some of us are accustomed to traveling beyond our bodies voluntarily, Jess. It's one of the ancient mind skills to which you haven't yet been exposed."

If he were not picking this up telepathically from Peter's thoughts as well as his words, Jesse thought, he would think it mere metaphor . . . and yet he *had* felt free of his body for those brief moments.... He clenched his fingers as Peter went on, "Most people were much more afraid of stasis than you were—Carla, for one, but she had her love for you to cling to, plus your telepathic presence. Many other members were also in touch with their partners. Claire had no such anchor, and she was terrified. To escape from the box in which she was trapped, she left her body behind. But she wasn't strong enough to reorient herself following stasis; I had to go after her, and other trained people had to go along to help me. During that time, of course, we were unaware of our physical surroundings and of everything happening in the ship. We met in a different place."

Jesse swallowed. "You're thinking that there may be

others—and that it could happen to them again. If what we meet is so traumatic that it overwhelms them, they could . . . escape, instead of doing what's necessary to survive."

"That's possible," Peter admitted. "It's less likely to happen in the shuttle than among those deserted on the surface before enough people to provide ongoing psychic support are settled there. And so we must be careful who we send, and in what order."

"Someone able to deal with such cases, obviously. Yet you can't go until last, and Kira can't either, at least not until everyone's awake. Is Hari qualified? He said you'd called on him to assist, and I'd planned to take him next anyway, since he's a Council member and in line to take charge."

"He's qualified to make contact with people who are out of their bodies. But there's another problem, Jess. Hari must not go until I do, no matter what pretext I must use to keep him here. It's essential for Kwame to remain in command of the ground base."

"Why? Certainly Kwame is the most competent to set it up; that's why I picked him to head the landing team. But Hari knows more about mind powers."

Peter sighed. "He does, and unlike the people I worry about, Hari is stable; he won't fall into altered consciousness at inappropriate times. He's also loyal to the Group and to his commitment to fellow-members. But he's the last person we want down there before the majority arrives—because Hari does not really want to settle a new world at all. He and his faction of the Group could not help being a wet blanket, so to speak, through their unconscious telepathic influence."

Shocked, Jesse burst out, "They don't *want* a new world? Why did they come, then?"

"Because they knew they were needed. They realized that the majority wanted it, and felt bound by our Ritual pledge to support each other."

"But the vote was unanimous."

"The vote was taken at the gathering for Ian's funeral. Out of respect for him, even those personally opposed voted for what he had given his life to accomplish."

"Do they regret it?" asked Jesse in dismay. Initially, Hari had seemed enthusiastic about the possibility that in a colony of their own, advanced psi abilities might emerge.

"Not in the sense of wishing they'd backed out. But they may well regret that any of this ever happened. Many of them would have gotten along okay on Undine, you see. Unlike those of us who were involved in the hospices and burial of bodies, Hari and his close associates were not in danger of arrest. The front group they ran for potential trainees wasn't illegal and once recruiting stopped, its true nature could have remained concealed. And the advanced psi instruction he gave to individuals was strictly private."

"But they would have been microchipped and tracked like everyone else when the government put universal heart monitoring into effect."

"I don't think they'd have objected to it as much as the rest of us would," Peter said. "Most people with strong mystical leanings live largely in their minds. You were outraged by forced medical treatment. Hari wasn't; to him the compulsory checkups were a mere nuisance. I suspect he laughed inwardly at what the Meds said about health care, knowing most of it wasn't true and feeling superior on that account. Freedom of choice in the political sense didn't matter to him because he was already free inside."

Jesse frowned. "Peter—you let these people come, knowing their hearts weren't in it? Let them give up comfortable lives for a struggle they didn't even want?"

"There are some who'd have been unwilling to stay behind, knowing they'd have to hide their powers forever without the support and companionship of the Group," Peter said. "As for the strong ones like Hari, we'd be too few to form a viable colony without them. I would not, of course, have forced anyone, but should I not have respected their voluntary sacrifice as much as I respected Ian's?"

That was one way to look at it. On the other hand, Peter was a fanatic about fulfilling Ian's dream, and if that could be accomplished only by enlisting colonists who had little to gain, then to him this was simply part of the cost. He had not forced them, but it could not be denied that he had enticed them. On the night of Ian's funeral he had made deliberate use of telepathic persuasion to achieve a unanimous vote—Jesse had been aware even at the time that he was capitalizing on people's grief. Had any of those who died in stasis not wanted to come? Was that why Peter had been hit so hard by those deaths?

Had Claire not wanted to come?

I do feel responsible for her, Peter replied silently. *But not just because she isn't eager to be a pioneer. She's one of the members I rescued from the psych ward.*

What was she accused of? Jesse had known that he wasn't the only person for whom release from the Hospital had been contrived, but nothing specific had been said to him about most of the others. Nor had he been aware that Claire was involved in their illegal hospice work.

It wasn't a criminal case. Claire was diagnosed with schizophrenia. She would have been drugged as you were after your arrest for murder, her mind destroyed although there was nothing more wrong with it than a tendency to slip into altered consciousness. . . .

Oh, God. *How many more schizophrenics did you rescue, Peter?* There had been at least one other psychiatric patient, Valerie, whose relapse had nearly led to the Group's discovery. Mental illness might be hereditary, and with so small a gene pool . . .

Carla must have known all along, Jesse realized. At the Hospital she'd been the data technician responsible for keeping psych department records and hacking them for the Group when necessary. Yet she had never told him that real patients besides Valerie had been recruited.

"You're thinking of it as the Meds do," Peter pointed out. "They don't value any form of consciousness except the one they call 'normal.' You know better. And you know from your own experience how meaningless the label 'mental illness' is. Most schizophrenics are simply people who don't have volitional control of their brain states—and that can be overcome with the same kind of mind training we give other members. Many have emerging psi capability they don't know how to handle. The terrible thing is that I couldn't always arrange to release those under my care."

"But you could sometimes? You're saying we've set out to build a colony in which some people must be taught to overcome schizophrenia, in addition to mystics who didn't want to colonize in the first place because they live mostly in their minds—"

"And in which they, along with the rest of us, must teach the next generation to cope with psi powers that may exceed those developed by persecuted minorities on older worlds. Remember that the Meds view all psi abilities as mental illness, too. If we'd revealed our possession of them we'd have been diagnosed as delusional."

True. He himself had acquired beliefs that would have branded him crazy in the eyes of fellow-officers in Fleet. But despite his opposition to the Meds' political regime and recognition of the fallacies in their view of health, he hadn't questioned society's attitude toward psychosis. "Is there no such thing as mental illness, then?" he asked Peter.

"Oh, yes. Violent patients are truly sick. And psi can be used for evil—that's sick, too. Ian and I have been careful to keep out anyone who might harm others, but without our protection the borderline patients would have been vulnerable to being damaged, and perhaps corrupted, by psychically-warped outsiders. That's one reason why we took them into the Group, and why I wouldn't have wanted them left defenseless on Undine after we were gone." He hesitated, debating how much to reveal of a deeper worry. "We don't know why some people are born with an attraction to the dark side of what's traditionally been termed the occult. We may have to deal with such people in future generations."

"So the physical dangers of colonizing aren't all we have to worry about. Not even at first, if not all our members can be counted on to pull their weight."

"They'll pull their weight in ways not yet apparent to you. But it's true that they'll also add to our problems. We never believed it was going to be easy, Jess."

He had not pictured the difficulties in quite this way. He didn't want to; there would be more than enough concrete problems to deal with. In any case, right now time was passing when he should be in flight; he had ordered the team to the shuttle bay and they were waiting for him.

"The ship is yours, Peter," he said. "Wake landing parties in whatever order you think best, but have one equipped and ready to go whenever I get back. If we delay between trips, there'll be nothing left here for the last people aboard to breathe."

Peter gripped his hand. "Godspeed, Jesse," he said. "You'll be okay. Since your first day on Undine you've met every challenge that came your way. I know you'll keep right on doing it, as Ian believed you will."

Jesse wished he could share that certainty.

9

THE MEMBERS OF the landing party, clad in spacesuits worn over flight suits, were waiting at the shuttle bay's airlock. Jesse sensed the excitement in them; their thoughts overflowed with it. With these people, at least, there was no question about their desire to be here—he had originally picked them not only for their skills but for their enthusiasm about space.

For the same reason that he'd insisted on removal of contraceptive implants, he had chosen equal numbers of men and women. Kwame, one of his first friends in the Group, was an engineer and thus indispensable to the establishment of the colony; on Undine he had worked in the power plant, but he was capable enough to take charge of the overall setup of the base. Dan had been a foreman in Undine's diamond mines and had begun studying other mining processes as soon as the decision to colonize had been made. Having spent the past few hours going over the information in the computer's knowledgebase about equipment the pods contained, these two could handle the robots that would position the power receiver and—in a just-barely-feasible race against time—build the larger shuttle's landing pad. Tomas, an electrician, would lay the power cable, set up the charging station, and rig the boundary lights for the pad. Erik was a comm technician and would establish an uplink to the comm satellite launched by the starship's AI, while his wife Dorcas, a professional cook, would be in charge of managing provisions and later of coordinating meal preparation. Corrine, a biologist, and Liz, a chemist, would focus on analysis of the new environment; their first task would be to locate surface water. Olivia was qualified as a nurse and healer; unless called on to treat someone, she would help where needed most, as would the people who arrived on later trips.

The final member of the team, Anne, was to occupy the copilot's seat as pilot trainee. She had been a security officer in the Hospital on Undine, used to dealing with the unexpected, and was also among the most experienced of the Group's seaplane pilots. Not that control of a VTOL shuttlecraft was much like flying a seaplane, but at least she had a sense of what it meant to deal with air currents, albeit in an atmosphere thicker than Maclairn's. She'd have to go back and forth on many trips; it would be better to gain one thoroughly-experienced new pilot than to expose others to a mere taste of training.

Kwame and Erik, the two now used to working in spacesuits, helped Jesse pack the hold with a supply of the powdered broth, food rations to last for the next few days, blankets, the team's personal duffels—and most importantly, drinking water, without which they could not survive even a few hours in the midday heat. There was little water to spare aboard the starship, as the life support system was set to divert as much oxygen as possible to air. But there was no telling how close to a source the pods had landed.

In addition, they loaded apparatus for liquefying air along with as many empty tanks as could be crammed in. These would add little to the starship's air supply, but there would be no point in letting the shuttle return repeatedly without cargo. Once everything had been stowed safely and the hatch was sealed, the team strapped themselves into place, first removing the bulky spacesuits, which were left behind for use by a later load of passengers. Jesse keyed in the destination coordinates and launch sequence, signaled the outer door of the shuttle bay to open, and settled back, hands resting on the arms of his contoured seat, as the little ship moved out of the starship into space. "How are you controlling it?" protested Anne, staring at him.

"It's all automated while we're in space," he explained. "The AI knows how to calculate acceleration and direction so that we'll end up in the right place—I don't have manual control until shortly before we land."

"What happens if the AI quits working?" she asked, more from curiosity than from fear.

"We die," Jesse replied frankly. "We can't afford an AI failure in a shuttle any more than we could have aboard the starship." *Or on the ground,* he added, making no attempt to shield the thought. The robotic machines in the cargo pods were essential to survival. If there was a glitch in the AI programming of one that wasn't duplicated, people would end up just as dead as if they'd been aboard a lost shuttle, at least until there'd been time to train some AI experts via the knowledgebase. The sooner everyone grasped this fact, the better. The awesome powers of mind to which the Group was dedicated could preserve health and lengthen lifespans, but they could not take the place of technology in colonizing an alien environment.

Anne didn't comment, but he sensed her dismay. She

was used to controlling every move of her seaplane and would feel helpless while unable to actively pilot a ship hurtling at hypersonic speed through the upper atmosphere. But she would have plenty of piloting to do when it came to landing—though only a short portion of the flight, that phase required human skill and judgment. He hoped it wouldn't require more than he could muster after making many trips in fast succession.

As they picked up speed relative to that of the receding starship, Jesse spoke into his headset. "*Mayflower XI*, we've just cleared the ship. Are you tracking us?"

"Roger," Reiko replied from the bridge. "You're onscreen, Jesse. I'll stand by."

For the first time directly visible, the bright surface of Maclairn loomed huge against the backdrop of star-studded blackness, evoking gasps of awe from his passengers. The crew deck of the starship had no viewports, and though he himself had seen the planet via the bridge vidscreen, the others hadn't. "God, Jesse!" exclaimed Kwame, unable to contain his exhilaration. "Ever since I was a little kid I've wished I could get into space . . . though I knew my chance of being picked to work on power satellites was pretty slim. Now it's hard to believe this is *real*. . . ."

Space travel was forbidden to Undine's citizens by strict financial laws that prohibited transfer of money offworld. Thus Undine had a small spaceport used only by freighters; passenger ships rarely called there. And that, Jesse thought, was another example of the incredible pattern of fate that had worked in their favor. If it weren't that only one large shuttle with seats was based on Undine, *Mayflower XI* would not be carrying such a craft. It had been brought to speed up the boarding of their charter party, which Fleet had thought wise to accomplish as fast as possible, considering the illegality of their emigration. A chartered colonizer would ordinarily have been dependent on transport vehicles belonging to its departure and destination worlds. He had not anticipated gaining one for use on the new planet. Yet if it were not available, he would now have to make nearly forty back-to-back trips in ten-place shuttles like this one—a clear impossibility, even apart from the fact that the starship would run out of air before that many trips could be completed.

So the presence of the larger shuttle was a miraculous blessing . . . and also, unfortunately, a source of terrible risk.

In the first place, it would need a level landing pad. The robots in the cargo pods were versatile enough to laser-blast one in rough terrain, out of solid rock if necessary. But normally this would have been done long before the arrival of colonists. Even in the emergency situation for which the pods were intended, days of preparation would precede the landing of passengers. He was going to have to get a pad built in mere hours and use it within minutes of its completion. If it weren't that otherwise he couldn't get everyone to the surface in time, he wouldn't dream of staking people's lives on anything so chancy.

Especially since the large shuttle was less automated than the smaller ones, and by the time he had to fly it, he was going to be very, very tired.

Anne, beside him, absorbed these thoughts and responded. "I'll help all I can," she said steadily, her mind's turmoil belying her words.

"You can't learn to land a heavy ship like that just from copiloting," Jesse said. "I don't know if anyone but me can ever fly it, because we can't risk it on training flights. Neither can we let a student pilot try setting it down as near our settlement as we've got to put the landing pad." The proximity of the pad to their base was among his chief worries. Without ground transportation other than the one small motorized cart the dropped pods contained, it would be necessary to locate it much closer to the shelters than was really safe—another reason why he'd have to be in top condition during every one of the coming landings. . . .

Tentatively, the little craft grazed the atmosphere— another AI-controlled process, designed for approach to alien planets, in which heat sensors determined the angle of descent. The outer hull began to glow, drawing startled cries from the passengers. "It's going to get warm in here," Jesse warned. "But we won't burn up. What you're seeing is normal." Most of them did not know even the basics of orbital flight, he realized. Coming from a world that no one for generations, other than a privileged few, had been allowed to leave, they were as ignorant of conditions elsewhere as those who'd lived before space travel existed. He tried his best to project telepathic reassurance, belatedly aware that as one of the Group's leaders his responsibility went beyond that of an ordinary shuttle captain.

Their view was obscured by the hull's incandescence. When it faded, the sky beyond the ports was not black, but yellow, and the golden planet on which they looked out was no longer a world above them. It lay below, obviously the ground—rough, mountainous ground. "It's . . . barren," Olivia said, in a voice barely audible over the hum of the shuttle's powered deceleration.

"Not really. There's plant life, though no trees. But the dominant forms are pretty much the same color as most of the rocks."

He had little chance to observe the scenery, for his top priority before landing was to brief them on desert survival. "Don't be tempted to take your flight suits off," he warned. "They're designed for extreme conditions and they'll be some protection from the heat, even though you may feel like stripping. Keep your hat brims turned down front and back to avoid exposing your skin to the sun. Don't stand around in it—when you're not doing something essential, stay in the shade of the pods." At least it was not a sandy desert; they would be okay without sunglasses and need not worry about sandstorms. "Above all," he emphasized, "drink often even if you're not thirsty." Thirst was not a reliable guide to dehydration even for normal people, and Group members, who'd learned not to mind physical sensations, might easily succumb to heat exhaustion before recognizing the danger.

"There's a sea on the horizon!" exclaimed Dorcas. "Is

that where we're going?" The news hadn't been broken to them; Jesse, after reporting to the starship that they'd reached low altitude, knew he could put it off no longer.

"We can't settle near a sea," he admitted. "All you'll see of it is what you're seeing now, from the air." The landing team's disappointment didn't need to be voiced; a wave of collective telepathic dismay surged into him, magnifying the self-blame he already felt for having had to decide on the site so hurriedly. The land around the sea looked much smoother than the region he knew the ship to be heading for, as well as more attractive. It would have been an easier place to put down. But in the long run, it would not meet their needs. "We have to go where the supply pods are," he pointed out, "and I dropped them where we won't lack the mineral resources civilization depends on."

They passed over the sea with little more than a quick glimpse, and before he could say more, his board came alive with the lights and horn calling for manual takeover. Tuning out other concerns, Jesse turned his full attention to piloting.

It had been years since he'd landed a shuttle on rough terrain. As a freighter captain, he'd had no occasion to do so, though he'd kept his hand in via simulators and during occasional side excursions from ports where he'd had layovers. He had been fully trained for it during his younger days, of course—all Fleet officers were, and once, he had hoped to be assigned to an explorer, one of the small starships sent out to survey uncharted worlds. Now that dream was being fulfilled. But, he thought grimly, he wouldn't have chosen a scenario in which so many lives depended on his perfect performance.

The shuttle could, to be sure, fly safely on autopilot; it had power to spare, even after allowing plenty of reserve for takeoff. But without a landing beacon, the AI could not choose a spot to set down. Thus it could not predict at what moment to rotate the thrusters, initiating the switch from forward flight to vertical descent—after which further level flight would be impossible. Nor could it provide sufficient attitude control in turbulent air, or steer around whatever boulders or gullies might loom in their path at the last minute. Only a human mind, responding to human vision, could make these decisions. Yet they had to be made instantaneously. You could not take time to think about them; if you did, the ship would either overshoot the landing site or it would crash.

The first landing would be the hardest; once down, they would place a transmitter to home in on. "Just observe for now," he told Anne. "I won't be able to talk you through it till our next trip." He gripped the thrust control lever, keeping one eye on his instruments while watching the ground rush past beneath them. They were coming up on the coordinates. . . .

Ahead, he spotted the bright-colored blotches of the collapsed parachutes that marked the location of the supply pods. As he approached he saw with dismay that they'd come down on a plateau, near the rim of a canyon. If the wind had been a little stronger they might have fallen to the bottom—but there was no time to grasp how narrow an escape that had been. He could think only of making sure to stay away from the edge when landing. He couldn't afford to land far this side of pods; if he did, too much of the team's time and energy would be expended on walking. Yet they lay amid rocks. Praying for a unobstructed patch of ground in the vicinity, he committed the ship to vertical movement.

"God, we're stalling!" Anne cried out.

"It has to reach stall speed," Jesse said. "That's the big difference from the kind of flying you're used to. You have to let it stall and drop—otherwise you couldn't target a landing spot. The thrusters keep it from dropping too fast."

He could sense what the others were feeling. Several of them were seaplane pilots; the rest had flown frequently as passengers to and from the Island. All their instincts told them that a plane was not supposed to fall vertically. Having spent many recent hours in his own seaplane, he too was momentarily disoriented by the sensation, and by the jolt as the VTOL thrusters cut in. But thoroughly-ingrained unconscious reactions prevailed; he lowered the landing gear and focused on maneuvering toward what seemed the most promising area of the rocky, slightly sloping ground now visible in the relayed image from the belly cam. The ship hovered for a moment. Then, gently, it settled, shuddered, and was still.

"Don't anyone move yet," Jesse cautioned. If the place they'd touched down was not solid, if the landing gear lacked firm enough contact with the ground to support the shuttle's weight, they could topple. He held his breath, checking the panel in front of him for readings that assured stability. Finally satisfied, he unbuckled his seat straps, envying the others the relief that flooded from their minds.

"Okay, folks," he said. "You are now residents of the planet Maclairn."

For most of them, imminent peril was past. For him there were many more flights to come.

10

WHEN HE FIRST stepped onto the surface Jesse was stunned by a scorching blast of heat. He had known in theory that the temperature would be high, but had not anticipated how overwhelming heat could be. Well, people had lived in desert climates on Earth, he told himself. The AI had assured him that Maclairn's was no worse.

There was no time to waste surveying their new surroundings. On future flights, Jesse would not even disembark, but initially, he must appraise the condition of the dropped supply pods and decide where the landing pad should be placed. With Kwame and the other men he proceeded to the nearest pod, repeating as they walked the orders he'd given earlier about priorities.

First, the robotic machines on which all heavy work
depended must be brought out of the pods and activated.
Next, they must be used to position the power receiver a
safe distance from the base for reception of a laser beam,
which would provide power to the recharging station until
permanent wind power stations were built. This was at best
a stopgap arrangement. Transmission would of course be
intermittent, since the orbiting starship would be below the
horizon part of the time. Moreover the beam, while essential, was a potential hazard, for though the ship's AI could
be relied upon to target it precisely, it couldn't be put far
enough away to avoid the trouble of staying clear of it. Not
only would getting there take too long, but the distance to
the charging station supplying the settlement was limited
by the length of the available cable.

Once power was established, two of the prefab shelters
must be unloaded and erected, enough space for all the
starship's passengers to cram into, not only because they
wouldn't all have flight suits but because hot though the
weather was now, after dark it was going to get cold—too
cold to sleep safely in the open air. The next few loads of
passengers would help with that job. They would have to
handle most of it manually, for the machines must be devoted to getting the landing pad built at top speed.

Kwame was fully experienced in power engineering; he
needed only physical assistance in deploying the equipment.
Leaving Erik and Tomas with him, Jesse and Dan determined the pad's boundaries. It was not ideally located; he
had, in fact, picked the smoothest ground when he brought
the shuttle down, which was closer to the supply pods than
he'd hoped to land the larger ship. But ruggedness of the
land left him no choice. The beacon for his next few landings,
to be out of the way of the construction area, would have to
be put a longer walk from them, and on rougher terrain.

Meanwhile, the women had unloaded the supplies the
shuttle had brought, as well as the empty tanks for liquid
air. Anne, following the written instructions on the lique-

fier, had started it running. The rest stood gazing at the scenery, unable to do any more work until the machines nearest the pod hatches were out of the way and the inner compartments could be opened. "Liz and Corrine, start hunting for water," Jesse ordered. "Dorcas and Olivia, retrieve those parachutes and find some way to hang them between the pods for shade. Eventually we'll make good use of them when we need clothes for children." Their own clothes were made of a durable fabric that would last many years. More such cloth was included in the supplies, he knew, but there was no telling how soon their first crop of genetically-engineered plants would yield fiber for spinning into yarn.

He realized, as he and Anne reboarded the shuttle, that he'd learned scarcely anything about the place where he was to spend the rest of his life. From space the planet had looked romantically golden, like the vision Ian had shown him in the dream. From the ground, he'd seen nothing but dirt and rocks plus a little sparse vegetation. Absorbed in evaluation of landing sites, he had not even noticed the profile of the not-too-distant mountains . . . which, he now recalled, had been seen via psi by several people from orbit. By prescient psi, in one case. Was this, then, truly the destination to which fate had led them? Or had he simply stumbled upon it, through a sequence of decisions backed by no more than chance?

The return trip was uneventful. After the brief stress of takeoff, he spent it talking to Peter by commlink and showing Anne the fundamentals of the shuttle's controls. Rendezvous with the starship was swift and fully automated; after this first time, he would be able to let her handle it. But he knew he would be too tense to get much rest.

When they docked, he wearily clambered into his spacesuit again to cross the airless shuttle bay. He left Anne to supervise boarding of the waiting passengers while he returned to the bridge to turn on the laser beamer, which would initiate power transmission only upon signal from the ground-based receiver, and to initiate an automated launch of the comm satellite. Carla wasn't there; she and several others were still moving stuff from the starship's passenger deck. Peter, on watch, greeted him with warmth and outward confidence, but he seemed preoccupied, even troubled; Jesse knew him too well not to be concerned by the extent to which he was shielding his mind from telepathic probing. It meant there was some new worry that for the present, would bear no discussion.

He found it surprisingly hard to drag himself back to the shuttle bay and suit up again. It was the letdown, he supposed—after successfully achieving one risky landing, he was naturally less keyed up when anticipating another. Because he really hadn't been awake enough hours to account for the physical exhaustion he felt. The day—assuming that his arousal from stasis counted as "morning"—wasn't half over.

The new group of passengers was composed largely of remote viewers; there wasn't enough leeway in the starship's air supply to keep them aboard now that they were no longer needed there. This, Jesse realized, contributed to Peter's uneasiness; as exceptionally inner-oriented, psi-gifted people, they would not have been his first choice for the initial ground team, although the truly unstable ones—Claire and one other—had been held back. Nor were many of them well suited for the physically-demanding job of erecting shelters. But more loads of people would arrive long before dark.

The landing, while not quite as nerve-racking as the first one, was nevertheless difficult; the newly-placed electronic beacon helped, but the ground to which it led him was strewn with sizeable rocks. Anyone free of other jobs, he decided, would have to work at dragging them away before he returned again; he could not count on missing them by luck indefinitely.

He found the robots beginning the long job of leveling the landing pad, with Kwame supervising while the others unloaded more equipment from the pods. Water had been located, a narrow river much farther from the base than he'd hoped—it was in fact at the bottom of the adjacent canyon. Corrine had tested it and pronounced it drinkable without purification, which was fortunate since carrying a supply sufficient for three hundred people was going to be a hassle; the water-bearers would have to be well hydrated before undertaking the long climb. As soon as the landing pad was finished, the next task for the robots would be to dig a well.

To Jesse's relief, more flight suits and hats had been discovered in one of the pods, which was going to make working in the sun more practical than he'd feared it would be. Fleet's planners had evidently realized that a stranded party might end up on a planet where protection from the elements was needed. Olivia volunteered for the job of instructing new arrivals on the importance of avoiding heat exhaustion. Still, it was evident that conditions on the surface were taking their toll.

"Better bring us some fresh, strong workers next time," Kwame said to him after his third landing, as the tanks filled with liquefied air were put aboard. "I don't think anyone on my team is up to erecting shelters, Jesse. We're worn out, and I'm not sure why—we've been working only a few hours."

"That's natural in this heat," Jesse said worriedly. The others, born on the cool water world Undine, would need even more time to acclimatize than he would. "You've been drinking broth, haven't you—and plenty of water?"

"Yes, but it doesn't help much. We're all bushed. It's more than just the heat—could it be the air here, do you think?"

Jesse frowned. It was possible that the atmosphere, thinner than Undine's, did have something to do with it—yet the starship's air mix had been adjusted to match even before they went into stasis. It was no less oxygen-rich than in high-altitude cities on Earth. To be sure, they weren't accustomed to working in it, and hadn't had much chance to adapt. If that were the cause, however, the new arrivals should be feeling worse than those who'd been wakened earlier, whereas they obviously had much more energy. Certainly more than he himself felt. . . .

By the time he'd made three more trips, leaving the shuttle only to switch to a newly-serviced alternate each time, he was barely able to hold himself erect—nor was Anne in much better shape. He felt guilty asking her to deal with the cargo and new passengers, yet he did not feel he could drag himself through that process again, and it was, of course, of prime importance that he remain fit to fly.

Neither Peter nor Carla, nor even Reiko, was available to speak by commlink; he wondered what crisis had taken them from the bridge. Greg, now manning it, would not admit that any problem had arisen, despite Jesse's insistence that as Captain he should be fully informed. He must put it from his mind, he realized. That was evidently what Peter intended. His job now was to focus fully on the repeated landings, which were becoming harder rather than easier because fatigue was slowing his reactions.

As they entered Maclairn's atmosphere for the seventh time, he spoke to Anne and got no reply. Glancing at her, he saw in horror that she had fallen asleep.

He was about to land; he couldn't spare attention for waking her, and it was not as if he needed her assistance. She was there simply to learn. But to sleep in such a situation—and it was less than nine hours since they'd started. It was not like Anne. She woke with a start when they touched down, puzzled and chagrined by her own lapse. Reluctantly, Jesse decided that there was no point in her returning with him; without her, he could transport one more person on each trip. She would never be able to handle a landing on rough ground in any case; what training she'd absorbed would serve only to prepare her for the retrieval of equipment from the starship later, after it was re-aired and the pad was enlarged to accommodate multiple shuttles. And so, telling her to rest, he took off alone.

During the flight his worry grew. Anne had fallen asleep involuntarily, yet she had been exposed to conditions on the planet's surface no longer than he had. What if it happened to him? Peter had assured him that it wouldn't . . . but Peter had not known that people would be overcome by fatigue so soon. He still could not reach anyone via comm except Greg, who promised to have someone experienced in the use of spacesuits on hand to help unload filled air tanks and load empty ones. There were several who'd worked with Carla on the passenger deck but hadn't yet gone down. Carla . . . she must long ago have finished that job. Where was she? Perhaps the computer had malfunctioned, he thought in dismay. If it had, and she couldn't fix it, they were in deep, deep trouble. . . .

Carla? He should be able to contact her telepathically, Jesse realized as the shuttle bay opened to receive his ship. Wherever she was in the starship, the distance could be no greater than their separation during the last weeks on Undine. If she was facing a bad situation she would surely confide in him. *Carla . . . oh, God, Carla, answer me!*

There was no response. With rising panic, Jesse docked the shuttle and prepared to suit up, all the while calling to her in his mind. The airlock cycled, admitting the new batch of passengers; he knew he must hurry to the alternate shuttle and take command. Yet he couldn't leave again without knowing she was all right.

Mechanically, he went through the process of verifying the shuttle's readiness—it was, of course, one he'd flown twice before—and then, once the cargo was loaded, of getting everyone aboard. The copilot's place beside him was empty, though he'd told Greg to send nine people this time. "One more's coming," Greg said. Jesse waited, his mind still calling to Carla, as the last person hurried toward them. To his surprise, when the hatch was sealed and she raised her suit's helmet, he saw that it was Kira.

Thank God, he thought. Kira would not hide anything from him. Yet something must have happened; she hadn't been scheduled to go to the surface so soon. Jesse turned to her, urgently pleading, *What's wrong? I can't get in touch with Carla. . . .*

She's okay, Kira assured him. *She's just sleeping. I'm sorry, we forgot that you've been used to conversing with her over distance.*

My call would rouse her, Jesse insisted. *She'd respond even without waking.*

Not now, not from the deep sleep I gave her. Aloud, Kira told him, "We didn't want to burden you with anticipation, but Peter and I consulted the knowledgebase for medical data on stasis. We've learned the instruction about getting plenty of sleep afterward doesn't mean just at night—for the first day or two, people need to sleep for a few hours after every ten awake, preferably oftener. He and the others still aboard who were first out of stasis are sleeping now."

"*You're* not." At an age over a hundred, she had often seemed to Jesse to be indefatigable; but even she must be subject to limits.

"I just woke up. Peter told me to get my sleep early and then go down to make sure the people on the surface sleep soundly. They can't work normal schedules, yet they're too excited to drop off on cue without assistance."

That made sense. Kira, as well as Peter and a few other healers, could induce restorative sleep telepathically in a willing subject—Peter had done it for him on two occasions following extreme stress. "The ability to fall asleep at will is one of the controls the mind can gain over unconscious functions," she said. "We don't teach it to most trainees because in the Group there was no point in it; very few of our people have ever had insomnia. Now they'll need help, but it's easily provided."

"That's great," said Jesse, "except that what I need is the opposite. I *can't* sleep, not for a long time yet—but if it's an aftereffect of stasis I may not be able to keep from it."

So far, only fifty-seven people were on the ground. It would be another three hours before the landing pad was ready—twenty-seven more passengers, now that he could carry nine. Could he afford to skip one flight of a small shuttle, sleep for an hour or so before having to handle the large one? No, because there would then be five people left behind after four trips in the large shuttle, which could carry no more than fifty-seven besides himself . . . his mind was foggy, he could barely do the calculation, but there had been 315 starship passengers to start with, counting the seven who'd died in stasis. It had been a mistake to carry Anne back and forth six times; if he hadn't, it would have saved a trip. . . .

"Conscious control works both ways, Jesse," Kira said. "The other reason I'm here is to show you how to manage the sleep switch in your brain. It's biochemical, you know, just like everything else we've taught you about volitional control of neurotransmitters. Your body can produce its own stimulants."

"Surely not indefinitely, if stasis has affected our stamina."

"Well, no. But you can last as long as you have to, because you do have to."

Because a lot of people will die if I don't, he thought despairingly. Kira's reassurance meant little; she could hardly have said anything else. And he sensed her underlying worry. It was by no means certain that need and determination would give him special powers. The basic prerequisite of the mind skills, in fact, was true willingness to fail and take the consequences—yet he was *not* willing to have shiploads of people die as a result of his failures. If his earlier miscalculation hadn't forced them into stasis . . . it always came back to that.

Kira frowned. "Jesse . . . everybody feels to blame for *something*. Not currently, I mean, but always, because that's how life is. In the Group we're taught to deal with those feelings—and you haven't been, so far. Set them aside for now! Dwelling on them will only distract you from the skill you need to acquire."

He was silent as they left the bay and headed out toward Maclairn. As always, his passengers' first sight of it thrilled them, but he was no longer able to share their excitement. It would almost be better, he thought, if he had to pilot the whole way instead of just during the landing; as it was, inaction brought drowsiness punctuated by jolts of terror at the thought of how close he was to dropping off.

Kira reached over and gripped his hand. "When we pledge in the Ritual to live free of fear," she said softly, "it's not just for facing danger. It's for coping with exactly this sort of situation. Weren't you shown on your very first day in the Group that the deepest, most damaging fear is of your own loss of control?"

True, you had to be willing to lose control in order to gain it. "But this is different," he protested. "I'm not about to become willing to crash a ship."

"The concept of being willing to fail is rather subtle," Kira said. "It doesn't mean willingness to incur irrevocable harm. For instance, with the firewalk and ultimately the Ritual torch, you were willing to be burned—but not to be permanently crippled; you knew we wouldn't let that happen—"

"But Kira," Jesse interrupted, "the ship will be destroyed if I lose the ability to pilot it."

"Yes. Our mind skills have never depended on blind indifference to disaster. What they require is simply that we be willing to lose *conscious* control of our reactions and let our unconscious minds take over."

"And yet it's conscious control, volitional control, that we're aiming for."

"It's a paradox," Kira agreed. "That's why human beings have rarely developed these skills spontaneously. The concept has existed throughout history; it's sometimes been expressed metaphorically—for instance, as submission to the will of God, a frame of mind that has often given strength to people whose personalities weren't in the least submissive. We don't know the source of all that's in our unconscious minds, Jesse. Even Ian didn't, in spite of all the advances he made in neuroscience. But we do know, through experience, what we gain by trusting them."

He had been taught from the beginning that willpower was counterproductive in achieving mind skills, Jesse reflected. And after all, everybody knew that if you *tried* to fall asleep, you wouldn't. No doubt it was also true of staying awake. "I could give you physiological explanations," Kira went on. "The body's mechanisms for automatic functions are different from those involved in functions like movement that are normally under conscious control. If they weren't, animals and small children would have no protection against dangerous experimentation with their own capabilities. But you don't need to know those mechanisms. Your unconscious mind knows. Through volition, you decide what you want your body to do, and as long as you don't interfere by trying to direct it in the way you direct your limbs to move, your intent will be fulfilled."

"It's not as simple as that, Kira."

"Of course it's not. Which is why our training depends on telepathic input from instructors, input at the unconscious level. Otherwise our skills would take years to acquire even for the few able to master them, as in past societies was usually the case."

Well, he was used to absorbing such input, from Kira as well as from Peter—he couldn't have imagined how to control his heart rate, or blood pressure, much less how to heal an open wound, and then suddenly he *knew* how, somewhere deep inside. Would he know, then, how to stay awake? He didn't feel sleepy anymore . . . perhaps, while she'd been talking. . . .

"Jesse!" Kira burst out, aghast at the orange glow enveloping the viewports. "You'd better pay attention to the ship now. I think it's on fire."

He turned to reassuring the passengers, thinking how strange it seemed for his role and Kira's to be reversed.

11

JESSE GOT THROUGH the next two flights without difficulty; he realized that his mind had indeed absorbed something from Kira's. He was physically exhausted, but not groggy. Though there was someone qualified to help beside him both times, he didn't need to draw on external aid.

After the second of these flights, he disembarked and inspected the newly-completed landing pad. It was ready. That was fortunate, because the latest report on the starship's air supply showed little margin remaining. The four flights of the big shuttle must be made in quick succession.

He was pleased to find that Greg had been placed in charge of the first large group of passengers and would occupy the copilot's seat. Greg was an experienced mind-skill instructor with whom he'd occasionally worked in the past; Peter had begun to train him as a backup psychiatrist now that the Group was on its own. Jesse felt comfortable enough with him to stop worrying about staying awake and concentrate on handling the larger shuttle.

It was, of course, impossible to put all fifty-seven passengers into spacesuits; there weren't enough suits available. That meant the shuttle bay had to be pressurized, thus wasting air when it was opened, something that had been figured into the calculations but was nevertheless troubling. Jesse tried not to think of what would happen if, at the end, they ran just a little short.

He also tried to shut out worry that the new landing pad might prove to be not quite as firm as it looked, a possibility about which he could do nothing. In theory, it should be tested with one of the small shuttles, and there wasn't time for that. Nevertheless, the landing went smoothly. Kwame and the rest of the initial team, having slept a few hours in the shade of the shelters being erected, were on hand to cheer. The pad's boundary lights had been set. There was beginning to be some relief from the oppressive heat, for the sun was setting—the first sunset on their new world, which Jesse was not in a mood to admire. The next landing, he thought dizzily, would have to be made after dark.

Alone in the big empty ship, returning toward a docking less automated than those of the small shuttles, he lost touch with place and time. The planet, now in shadow, was behind him; ahead there was nothing but the blackness of space, the unvarying hum of the drive . . . soon into his mind flashed images, images of rocks rising to meet him, of the vivid blue sea of Undine, of Carla. . . . In horror he jolted back, aware that his eyes had closed. It was happening; he was drifting into sleep against his will. What exactly had stasis done to his body? The warnings about a biological need for sleep could hardly have been baseless. . . .

The lights and alarms on his console got him through the docking. He could not even think of moving from the cockpit, and since there was no longer an alternate ship to switch to, he didn't have to leave his seat. He remained outwardly calm as, hurriedly, the passengers boarded. I'm Captain, he thought, I should be supervising, I should at least know what's going on, who's in charge of the starship now . . . It was too much effort. He supposed that when the time came, he could go through the motions of landing; but it didn't seem real anymore.

Michelle, another of his original mind-skill instructors, settled into the seat beside him. *You're okay,* she communicated wordlessly. *All you need is contact with another mind.* Jesse roused, and during the flight was able to respond to conversation. Michelle hadn't as much experience in providing telepathic support as Kira and Greg had, but it was enough. While putting the ship down, guided only by the constellation of boundary lights, the necessary focus on what he was doing kept him alert.

As he prepared to take off, Anne came aboard. "I've slept enough," she told him, "and I've talked to Peter on the commlink. He says I'm to return with you."

It would certainly be wise not to fly alone again, Jesse realized. But Anne, though telepathic, was not a psi instructor or healer. Why her? Surely Peter didn't think she'd learned enough to take over the controls in an emergency.

"Not of this big ship, no," she agreed. She said no more, but it was clear in her mind—Peter was worried. He wanted her back on the starship so that if Jesse's next flight should fail, if it crashed, there would still be a chance for her to save a few more people in a small shuttle. She could probably manage to land it now that the pad was available. Yet she was risking her life by returning, when she'd been safe on the ground. . . .

He was Captain. He could forbid it. Making sure that he didn't crash was his responsibility. Yet it was also his responsibility to maximize the chance of survival for as many people as possible. He had no choice but to let her come.

One more round trip—and then a one-way flight. Two more landings, and then he could sleep. Everyone would be safe, he could sleep for hours, days if necessary . . . surely he could stay awake, and sane, just two more hours. . . .

Jesse! Oh, Jesse, are you okay? She was calling to him, Carla was calling. . . . He felt Anne touch his hand and knew he was not asleep; the contact with Carla was real. He was docking, and she was awake now. *Carla . . . Carla, I need you so. . . .* Their minds joined wordlessly; he was scarcely aware of the process of reloading the ship or the coming of new passengers.

Carla, can't you come on this trip? Surely you're not needed at the computer anymore. He wanted desperately for her to come, not only to help him stay conscious but because with each passing hour the peril grew. The last people to leave the starship ran the greatest danger of running short of air.

No, she told him firmly. *I wish I could come with you, but Peter said no, and I agreed.*

In principle, he could override Peter's orders. But he had delegated the responsibility of scheduling passengers to him, and after all, once they were all on the ground he would be Captain no longer. Reluctantly, he said goodbye to her and turned to the shuttle's controls, wondering who would keep him awake this time if Carla could not.

Just before he sealed the hatch, Peter slid into the empty seat beside him.

"Peter?" he asked in surprise. "I thought you were going to stay until last." Not only that, but he had counted on Peter's presence during the final, most grueling flight.

"The time's come when I'm needed more here," Peter said. "I'll return with you. I'll be with you next time, too."

"Who's in command of the starship, then?"

"Hari. He's capable of managing the air situation, and in fact he and some of his protégés can do with less oxygen than the others if it comes to that—they can control their metabolism. They will use spacesuits; Carla's shown them how to suit up."

"If it's going to be that close, I don't want Carla to stay. Since she has no more duties, why shouldn't she come with us now?" As a full load of passengers had boarded, they would have to put someone else off; but Jesse was past caring about such details.

Peter hesitated. "Carla is your insurance," he admitted finally.

"Insurance? Against what?"

"Against not having quite enough strength to make the last trip."

Shocked, Jesse bit back an angry reply. He could see the logic. While capable of rational decision, he would of course make the last trip no matter who was left to be rescued. But if his body was weakened to the point where he couldn't think straight, he would still make it, somehow, if Carla's life hung in the balance.

"This isn't ordinary fatigue," Peter informed him. "I didn't want to scare you before I had to, but now you need to know. You will not be able to stay fully awake much longer, even with help. For this flight, probably—but not the next.

Our power over physical reactions doesn't extend to situations where the body can't respond normally. And so you'll have to rely on me to guide you through it."

"Peter, how can you? I can't handle a shuttle if I'm not awake."

"It will be like sleepwalking, Jess. Sleepwalkers do all kinds of things; they've occasionally even driven cars. They're confused about what's happening and they can't process sensory inputs accurately, but their motor skills are intact. And telepathic ability is enhanced in sleep, as you know from your contact with Ian. You and I will be in touch telepathically, and I will provide input to your brain. But you must start preparing yourself to trust it, which means letting go of fear and accepting my word that it can be done."

He had trusted Peter from the first day they'd met. Even the shock of learning that the trust had been intentionally inspired through psi had not shaken it, for there was no mistaking the sincerity of feelings communicated by telepathy. Never, except during the brief portion of his aptitude testing when that support had been purposely withdrawn, had he doubted Peter's reliability or his capacity to succeed in anything he undertook. More than once, he had thrust his bare hand into a flaming torch on Peter's command; surely the paranormal rapport now demanded of them was no greater than what they'd achieved on those occasions.

But in the Ritual, his own safety alone had been at stake. Now, failure would mean the death of more than fifty people, including Peter himself—perhaps ultimately of the whole colony if they couldn't get back to the starship to retrieve essential equipment.

"Yes, there's that," Peter agreed. "We do have to face the possibility that it won't be a perfect landing, that perhaps even if we survive it, this shuttle may be damaged to the extent that it can't lift again. And so as your executive officer, I have given orders that I hope you'll see fit to let stand. Anne says she believes she has learned enough to land a small shuttle, to make it available for future use, as long as she doesn't have to do it on rough ground."

"But Peter, she can't use the pad; it's not large enough for two ships."

"I've asked Kwame to have a second pad built, a small one. It doesn't need to withstand as much weight, of course—it can be done quickly. She will launch as soon as we've taken off safely."

"She's not ready. She hasn't ever handled the controls alone. To risk lives—"

"Only one. Anne is willing to risk her own, but not to take passengers."

Reluctantly, Jesse nodded. Rash as it was, it was unquestionably better than total reliance on his ability to land a much heavier ship while literally asleep.

"Okay, the decision's made. Relax now, and focus on *this* flight—remember, I haven't seen our new home at close range yet. After all the weeks I've been looking forward to it, I'm excited." Peter's smile was genuine. As always, to an even greater degree than most Group members, he was able to set aside fear when there was nothing to be gained by worrying. For him, Jesse realized, there was no barrier to pleasure in the sight of Maclairn's luminous crescent filling the sky. Well, it was good that he could enjoy it during the short time before the shuttle descended into the dark.

12

CARLA, TRACKING THE flight from the bridge of the starship, was in turmoil despite her years of practice in disregard of worry. She found herself gasping, feeling with each indrawn breath that the air was thinner than normal, though the gauge on the console before her showed that it was not. There would be enough air to last until the shuttle returned—not any margin for safety, but enough. Hari's people might not even need the spacesuits she'd taught them to use. The stress affecting her now was not physical. It was dread of what would soon be happening to Jesse.

Peter had been frank with her. He could scarcely have been anything else; if he'd blocked his thoughts she would have known he had reason to hide them. As it was, she had perceived both fear and sorrow in him. "I wish to God I weren't asking you to wait for the last flight," he'd said. "I want you, above all others, to live, and the chances of that flight landing safely are not large. But I must do everything in my power to maximize them—and I know you'd choose to protect Jesse's life even by putting yours in danger."

To her dismay, she'd sensed that Peter was truly afraid—not on account of his own peril, or the threat to his long-held hope of establishing a viable colony, but for her. She'd become aware for the first time that he loved her deeply, less in the familiar brotherly way than as he might have loved her after his wife died, had she ended her prolonged mourning for Ramón before meeting Jesse. He had never before revealed this. He had encouraged her relationship with Jesse, at first to draw Jesse into the Group but later because he cared about their happiness. Only his knowledge that they might both be dead in a few hours had caused him to let down his guard.

She wanted desperately to put her arms around him, comfort him, but knew she must not. If she did, they could never embrace as mere friends again. That friendship had been central to her life since Ramón's death. She'd spent part of nearly every day with Peter, either as his assistant at work in the Hospital or during offshifts on the Island. She felt no trace of doubt about her commitment to Jesse; though they had not been legally married on Undine, they were bonded in all the ways that mattered. Still, she knew with shock that in some different world, one where the strength of love was not measured by exclusiveness, she would be capable of loving Peter, too.

Flushing, she realized that he'd picked up this thought;

how could he not, when they were so used to telepathic contact? Neither of them would ever speak of it. If they lived, Peter would turn to someone else, if only for the sake of the children the colony expected all members to provide. But he already knew the members of the Group and had not fallen in love with any of the unattached ones. It was not as if he could hope to meet someone new. He would never have what she and Jesse had, what he himself had had before the loss of his wife, Lesley . . . though now, abruptly, she perceived that Lesley had not been given his whole heart. He had loved her, Carla, since her first weeks in the Group—since before she'd chosen to marry Ramón, who had been his best friend.

All along he had kept this to himself . . . even while they'd spent their free days as what she'd believed was a contented foursome. Only his exceptional telepathic control had made that possible. Had Ian known? He must have; Ian had seen deeply into people and to him, Peter had been like a son. He must have realized, too, what lay ahead for Peter. There would be hardships in the colony, and as leader he would bear the brunt of them—with no true life-partner to turn to. In the years to come, she would weep for him.

But for the present, all else was overshadowed by her fear for Jesse. "If I can help him in some way by waiting, of course I will," she'd said. "But I don't see what good it can do."

Peter had told her, then, what Jesse was facing, and what he hoped to do to enable him to land the shuttle. "There's no alternative," he said, "and so I have to believe it may succeed. Jesse's had little training in psi, but we've had strong rapport before, and he has much untapped potential. His instinct as a pilot will go against trusting it. He will fight to retain full conscious control of the ship when he's no longer capable of that. If I can't get him to let his unconscious mind take over, we will crash. Though I can help him, I can't handle the controls myself."

No. Peter was a superb seaplane pilot, but he could

hardly fly a space shuttle he had never so much as seen before. It was risky even for Anne to try flying the small one. Although, Carla realized, Anne might be safer doing so than she would be as a passenger in the final shipload, if Peter's doubts were valid.

"Jesse will come through," she assured him. "Think of how we reached him when we were stranded on the Island, think of how he learned to communicate over distance while he was drugged in the Hospital, with only a hint from Ian in a dream! And how he taught *you* to do it later, Peter— something you hadn't known was possible. We can reach his mind while he's asleep, surely, in any case *I* can—"

"That's just what you mustn't do, Carla. When he feels himself losing control he will cry out to you in his mind. He needs to know you're on board, that your life's in his hands— yet beyond confirming that, you must not respond. Any exchange with you would distract him from the contact with me that his ability to fly will depend on."

"Peter, if I thought we had only a little while to live, I *couldn't* shut him out."

"I know how hard it would be. You've got to steel yourself to the idea; it's why I'm preparing you for the worst. Of course to him, I'll project confidence. I won't let him suspect my own doubts—and you mustn't, either. He must trust me wholly in order to draw on my aid."

Slowly, she nodded. "I—can't believe it's going to end for us, after all we've come through," she murmured. "You've always believed fate led us to this world—"

"The colony—the Group—won't end, even if some of us die. Fate didn't let us down. We got here, and most people are already safe on the ground."

Without either you or Jesse to lead, they wouldn't know how to keep going, Carla thought sadly.

"Yes, they would," Peter declared aloud. "Kira and Reiko are there, and Kwame, and Greg. They'd manage. All the potential leaders are safe." But underneath she sensed that he was thinking, *If I don't get there, if not even Hari is there to teach advanced psi skills to the next generation, our big experiment could go wrong . . . psi could get out of control. . . .*

She knew that he had spent many hours with Ian discussing this possibility, absorbing Ian's advice on how to deal with it. All members of the Group had been screened for integrity and trustworthiness. Though they weren't all emotionally strong, they had no hostile tendencies and could never pose a danger to others. But who knew what might happen in generations to come among people not individually selected? Peter was trained, experienced, and exceptionally psi-gifted. Ian had believed it would be possible for him to handle whatever psychic emergencies arose and to train successors who could keep the colony safe in the future. She suspected that neither of them had pictured anything happening to him so soon unless the Group as a whole was wiped out.

Peter sighed, troubled by something beyond the imminent danger. "By rights," he confessed, "the passengers kept here till last should have been chosen by lot. I didn't do that. I picked the strongest and most enthusiastic to go to the surface, shipload by shipload, leaving those I'm least sure of. I'll never feel comfortable about it—yet it served the survival of the colony."

"Hari volunteered to stay, didn't he? He and the people he's trained to control their breathing?"

"Yes, they did, and to accept their offer was justifiable— they're the most fit to deal with a shortage of air. But I know in my heart I'd have held them till last in any case, since they aren't as eager to colonize as the others. And so I don't feel right about it. Nor do I feel right about Claire and the other unstable people who're still here, or the novices— the people who aren't full Group members that I recruited at the last minute. Those people aren't as well equipped to survive as the ones who've had mind training. The colony's too small to support dependents if nearly sixty of us are lost. Logic tells me I did the right thing. My conscience tells me otherwise. After all, civilization has been founded on protection of the weak."

She did not know what to say to him. Repeatedly he had risked his Hospital position, perhaps even his life, in bringing psych patients into the Group, as well as by helping dying people in hospices. Though he'd been ruthless in subjecting strong people to the ordeals of training, his compassion for weaker ones had more than once overruled his good sense. Now that he had assumed full leadership, he could no longer yield to that compassion. The survival of the colony had to come first. But Claire and the other former patients trusted him. The novices trusted him. Several were adolescent sons or daughters of Group members, who would also be on the last flight, not suspecting that he had knowingly placed them and their children at risk. . . .

Well, if it crashed, he wouldn't be around to reproach himself. Carla tried not to think of the other possibility— the chance that something would go wrong with the *next* flight, leaving the people scheduled for the following one stranded and Peter on the ground, perhaps, picturing their slow deaths forever after . . . and Jesse, too, helpless to prevent *her* death. Even a delay would lead to that; there wasn't enough air remaining to allow for more than a quick turnaround.

Peter took her hand, squeezed it. "I've got to go now and see that everyone for this flight's ready at the airlock when Jesse docks," he said. "You can communicate with him while he's aboard the starship, of course, and with both of us by comm after that. I've turned command over to Hari, but he'll be occupied with assembling the last passengers and monitoring the air supply. You have the watch on the bridge."

"Godspeed," Carla whispered, choking back tears. "I'll stay in touch."

"Carla—don't worry about me. I—I'm pretty sure I'm not going to die today, though reason tells me there's danger of it. Ian dreamed . . . and so far, his premonitions have proved valid."

"Did he see you on the surface when he viewed us landing, then?"

"No. It was—something else. Something I perceived only as I was going into stasis. You know that back when I said farewell to Ian, when they were about to put him into the Vaults, he planted ideas deep in my mind that I wasn't aware of till later—"

"Yes, about stasis, the reason he'd led us to fear it on Undine."

"We were in touch telepathically while he was dying, and I knew he himself felt no fear. But he was afraid for me, Carla. It was as if some last-minute revelation had made him afraid I might waver. He kept telling me not to lose courage, assuring me that courage would save me, and through me, the Group. At the time I assumed he meant that I shouldn't let my horror at his execution affect our plan. That I must put aside grief and do my job as leader. During the onset of my own stasis, though, while I was in altered consciousness, a lot more came through, things he hadn't wanted to tell me outright. Things he assumed wouldn't emerge until I was facing a crisis where I drew on my memory of him for help."

"Well, we guessed he might have foreseen our danger precognitively."

"Not that, not what we underwent while still aboard. He'd sensed some terrible ordeal ahead for me personally. Whatever new dream he'd had was vague—he knew no more of what will happen to me than he'd known why he dreamed of still being needed when he wanted to die naturally at the Lodge. But he knew it will happen on the new world. I haven't been awake long enough to think about it . . . but it must mean I'm going to get there."

Oh, God, Carla thought. It might be the same thing she'd been fearing, that Peter would get there and the last shipload of people wouldn't. That he would spend the rest of his life crushed by guilt and grief for them . . . for her. She closed her mind tight against his telepathic sensitivity, hoping no such interpretation had occurred to him.

Just before he left the bridge, Peter turned. "There's one other thing you've got to know," he said with evident reluctance. "The landing pad is very close to the shelters—too close, Jesse said. It had to be, since we're not equipped for ground transport. But that means that if the shuttle is out of control when it reaches low altitude, either on this flight or the last one, it can't be allowed to approach the pad. I—I will have to make sure that it doesn't; if Jesse loses consciousness and I fail to gain rapport with him, I will have to take over."

"But you can't—you just said you can't land it!"

"No. But I can steer it away from the settlement."

She turned cold. "Crash it elsewhere deliberately, you mean."

"I'll have no other choice, Carla. It's another reason why I must be in the copilot's seat on both flights. It's only fair to warn you, because if that should happen when you are aboard, you'd know we were going down—and in those last moments, it would be all right for you to contact Jesse. Your minds could merge even if he was too deep in sleep to handle the controls. Time is . . . altered . . . in situations like that. The moments would pass slowly. I'd want you to spend them with him, as you did when you went into stasis, rather than alone and in terror."

Would we meet out of our bodies, the way we did before? she wondered.

Yes, I'm sure you would, during that brief time. And . . . perhaps after that . . . who knows?

I won't be afraid, then, Carla assured him. *Don't worry about me, Peter—or about the others. Do what you have to do, and trust fate for the outcome.*

She had tried to put on a brave front. But now, with the flight in progress, her inner dread grew, spreading into consciousness as darkness spread across the planet below, leaving only a slim crescent illumined. She prayed she would be with Jesse when dawn came.

13

JESSE FOUND IT easier to stay awake with Peter beside him than it had been during the past few flights. Peter's enthusiasm for the long-desired experience of space flight raised his spirits, and though he was vaguely aware that a deliberate effort was being made to keep him talking, he was grateful for it. Hearing Carla on the comm helped, too, though more and more he longed to give up the effort of speaking aloud and converse as they often did, mind to mind. He managed to pull out of the daze into which he was slipping when it came time to land. To his relief, they settled onto the pad with no more than a slight wobble, quickly corrected.

And then, with the passengers disembarking as rapidly as Peter could urge them to move, Jesse slumped over the controls, unable to muster the strength for another takeoff. The sound of voices was faint and far away, as if in a dream. They didn't seem to matter anymore. What mattered was that he was too tired to lift his head, and cold, too . . . it shouldn't be so cold inside the shuttle, but he wasn't up to doing anything about it. . . .

"Jess! Jess, pull out! We need to hurry." Peter was shaking him; he opened his eyes and realized that the ship was empty except for the two of them.

"Got to rest a little while," he mumbled. "Just a few minutes, Peter. I can't lift now, not yet—"

"Yes, you can. You have to. Carla's waiting for us—they haven't enough air to last much longer."

Air. Yes, the starship was low on air; he hadn't forgotten, but surely a few minutes wouldn't make that much difference.

It will, and besides, a few minutes will make a difference to you. You'll be worse off in a few minutes, not better, and Carla will die if we don't reach her in time.

Carla would die. Ian had told him that, in the dream, Jesse remembered—he'd said that if he gave in, Carla would die. How long ago had that been? Had Ian foreseen this, not just their going into stasis? It was all mixed up, and he was so tired, he would figure it out later. . . .

". . . Heat, Jesse! Your body's losing heat. Show me how to raise the cabin temperature." Peter spoke insistently, intruding on his apathy.

Slowly, Jesse's hand moved toward the thermostat. He felt Peter's grasp his, rubbing life into his cold fingers. *Now start the takeoff sequence*, Peter prompted. *I want to learn to fly this thing—we'll be making other trips in it later. But right now we just have to do it once more. One more liftoff, to go back for the people left on the starship. For Carla.*

He got the hatch sealed, but couldn't seem to remember what came next. Then suddenly there was a red light flashing, and a loud alarm horn. It shook Jesse into action; an alarm was something you didn't ignore in space. Frantically he surveyed the console, seeking its source.

"Sorry," Peter said. "I had to revive you somehow, so I pushed what I took to be the panic button."

"God, Peter. It was the emergency evacuation warning. If you push it again the hatch will blow."

"Well, I'm not planning to push it again. Turn the damn thing off and let's get going."

Jesse complied. Carla—he realized with shock that it was not a dream; Carla was in real danger, along with more than fifty other people yet to be transported. Of course he had to lift. But, once off the ground and on autopilot, he realized that he would not be capable of setting down again. Sleep had almost overcome him. The next time he succumbed, he would be unable to bring himself back.

He switched off the comm, not wanting Carla to hear what he had decided. "Peter," he declared, "when we get to the starship, while the passengers are boarding, I need you to go to the bridge and get the med kit from the captain's locker. There are stimulants in there. I know you said stimulants might kill me, but that's a chance I have to take. I can't risk not being in shape to make the last landing."

"Stimulants wouldn't help," Peter informed him. "The medical data I found on stasis warned specifically against using them during the first few days after revival. They would kill you too soon—your heart could not stand the stress."

"Oh, God. I'm about to pass out, Peter. What are we going to do?"

"I told you what we're going to do. I'm going to help you land in your sleep."

"You seriously think we can do that?"

"Yes, if you let your subconscious mind take over. As I said, sleep-driving is a known phenomenon."

"Then I'll sleep a little now, while we're under AI control—you can wake me just before we dock. Maybe a few minutes will be enough to tide me over for one more trip."

"No," Peter said unhappily. "If this were ordinary sleep deprivation, that would be true, but what you're experiencing is different—it's more like hypothermia. Your body is so overtired that it's trying to slip back into the stasis state. If I let you sleep now, I couldn't bring you far enough out of it to make contact with my mind."

It was all his own fault, Jesse thought groggily. This was happening because his miscalculation had forced them to go into stasis. The arrival on their new world was supposed to have been a happy time. Peter and most others had expected to enjoy the thrill of it, even if hardships came later. It was something that could never be experienced again, and he had spoiled it for them, had perhaps even cost some of them their lives . . . he sensed a sadness in Peter that could only mean he was not really sure he would ever set foot on the planet that was to have been the culmination of his, and Ian's, long hope.

We'll be all right, Jess! You've already saved most of us—if you hadn't held out so long we wouldn't have had a chance. What we're going to do wouldn't have worked more than once.

I don't see how it's going to work at all.

We'll cross that bridge when we come to it. Right now

you need to focus on warming up. The mind can control body temperature—on Earth, there used to be yogis who could go naked in the snow. We didn't teach that skill in the lab because it never got very cold on Undine. On the new world we'll have to. From what I hear of the surface temperatures, we'll need to adjust to both cold and heat. Imagine yourself down there in the sun again. . . .

Remembering, Jesse began to feel warmth seeping into him. It was like the first time he'd been taught to stop bleeding, when Peter and the others, functioning as healers, had shown him the way. Without neurofeedback training, he would be unable to do it alone. But he no longer feared his own power, as he had back then. Was it possible that he did have the ability to function in his sleep?

If he did not, then it had all been a game, Jesse felt. All the training, all the fine words about becoming more than he'd been in the past . . . even the Ritual had been a game if he could not use his mind powers to save himself and others—to save Carla—when nothing else could save them. What had the Group come here for, if not to prove the value of reliance on such powers? Why else take the terrible risk they had taken? Either he was willing to trust his inner mind, or he was not fit to be among them. . . .

He lost track of time. At some point, he heard Anne's voice and Peter responding to her, and realized that she had launched in the small shuttle. Then the starship loomed ahead of them and somehow he managed to dock with it, not really thinking about what he was doing, letting his hands move over the controls in the familiar sequence as the AI gauged their approach. When he sensed that they were motionless he wanted nothing more than to lean back and close his eyes, but Peter kept after him, silently insisting that he remain in touch with the ship, even after the balm of telepathic contact with Carla drove everything else from his consciousness.

Jesse! Oh, Jesse, I'm coming, we'll never be separated again. . . . Nothing now was important except that. He had made it back to her, and would never again have to leave her behind. And he would not let her die. . . .

He barely noticed the last load of passengers boarding until Peter rose to check on them and Carla was beside him, touching his flesh as well as his mind. She held out a mug of broth; as always before a flight, it revived him slightly. He found himself able to speak aloud again. "Sit right behind me during the flight," he said. "Just knowing you're close will help."

"No," Carla said gently. "I'm supposed to sit in back and close my mind to you. Peter said we mustn't communicate— it would distract you from getting input from him. You've got to stay in touch with him, not me."

She was right, Jesse admitted. Already their minds were on the verge of blending as they did in bed; he felt his body begin to respond as if in a dream. *That* was quite possible during sleep. It was possible even when they were in separate rooms and fully conscious; it had happened while he was drugged in the Hospital. But it must not happen while he was attempting to land a ship. Nor must they meet outside their bodies as they had while entering stasis, and he sensed that this, too, might now be possible if in sleep he reached out to her.

Reluctantly he let go of her hand. Peter settled back into the copilot's seat and threw the switch to seal the hatch. Keying in the launch sequence, Jesse became uncomfortably aware that he was leaving the starship unmanned without so much as a cursory check on the status of the bridge. He was still Captain, yet he had given no instructions about how to set it on standby, and it would be too late to do anything about that now even if he were not too dazed to think it through. There wasn't enough air left for anyone to go back. Well, if they didn't crash, he would be back himself in a few days—and if they did, it wouldn't matter.

Once more he took the ship out into space, into total blackness now, since the planet's dark side was turned toward them. These passengers wouldn't get even a glimpse of it. "Most of them won't care," Peter said. "They're so relieved at having escaped suffocation that they want nothing more than to be on the ground. But for Carla, I'm sorry."

Jesse, too, wanted nothing more than to be on the ground, to sleep at last, free of responsibility for others' lives. But there was one more hurdle to overcome before that, assuming Peter did know some magic way to help him manage it. He'd reached the end of his own endurance. As the ship entered the atmosphere, its red-hot hull glowing more brightly than ever without any backdrop of worldlight, he was blinded; his tired eyes burned and he could not force them open.

"Talk to me!" Peter urged. "You've got to keep talking a little while longer." When Jesse didn't answer, he went on, "Jess, have you ever seen that old classic vid, *Star Wars*?"

Groggily Jesse called up memories. "Sure, what kid hasn't?" It had excited him in boyhood even though the quaint-looking spacecraft in it weren't anything like real ones. It had been one of the things that had led him to declare, at the age of ten, that he was going to be a spacer when he grew up.

"Do you remember the last part, where Luke has one last chance to destroy the Death Star and Obi-Wan Kenobi's voice tells him to trust the Force, and he turns off the targeting computer? Aims accurately by means of his unconscious mind alone?"

"Well, it was a fantasy film . . . not how anybody thought the future was going to be."

"But some of us know better now," Peter said. "Mythology that lasts usually has a lot of truth behind it. Why do you suppose that particular space film has been popular for centuries when the others in its series are long forgotten? It's because it got the mythic parts right. The rest of them didn't—in the later ones the Force became just something a few people could zap others with if they'd inherited the right genes. 'May the Force be with you' lost the meaning it had in the original story. That was a typical case, I suspect, of shying away from the reality of psi."

"Are you trying to say there *is* a Force?" Jesse mumbled, doing his best to respond despite the haze swirling in his head.

"Certainly. What have I been saying since the day I recruited you? The mind draws on power that's rarely acknowledged outside fantasy fiction. Whether you call it the Force or something else doesn't much matter. But it's real, Jess— real and usable, as we've proven to you many times."

Peter . . . I don't think I'm up to a philosophical discussion right now. The brief spurt of energy that had allowed him to speak was gone, and he was grasping Peter's thought directly rather than through words.

"This is not a philosophical discussion," Peter said. "I'm telling you how you're going to land this ship."

I . . . can't see, Peter, I can't keep my eyes open anymore—

"No, you can't. The sensory functions of your brain are shutting down." *And so you'll have to do as Luke did, and not count on your eyes—trust your unconscious mind to take over. Let me see for you. I can give you images, not just thoughts. Telepathy will work in the altered state called sleep, as it did between you and Ian . . . and what seems like just a few days ago between you and me, when I was drugged on the Island.*

Oh, God, Peter . . . you don't know how to bring us down! How can you tell me what to do?

You'll keep on handling the controls. You do it with your unconscious mind anyway, you know; if you stopped to think out every move you couldn't react fast enough. What do you think the old saying about flying by the seat of your pants means? Or flying blind?

Not literally blind, not without seeing instruments. I've got to know how close I am to the ground.

You can draw that from my mind, Jess. I'll watch the ground. And you can draw something more from me, as you did when you first took my hand in fire.

Yes . . . Peter had somehow imparted the knowledge of how to do that. The memory would be with him forever,

Jesse thought, even when he was not fully conscious, even when it was blending with the memory of how he had taken Ian's hand too in fire, in the dream in which Ian had come to him. Involuntarily his eyes closed, and he saw only the flame, and felt again the surge of realization that he *could* touch it, that it would not burn him while his mind was open to telepathic support. That was the transformation he'd undergone in the Ritual, what commitment to the Group meant beyond the pledge to support fellow members in more tangible ways. You had to trust your own unconscious mind. You had to believe in its power to function in ways past your understanding. Like Luke Skywalker, you had to trust the Force. . . .

He was drifting, spinning, into a dream, but he knew where the ground was, partly because Peter knew, but also because he sensed it, sensed even the location of the landing pad, and he was aware, with some astonishment, that this was how the remote viewers had seen the planet from far above. He had not been trained in remote viewing, but Peter was showing him now what in a less urgent situation might have taken him weeks of practice to grasp. It was instantaneous, as his immunity to fire had been acquired instantly, because psi functioning of this sort occurs outside time. It demanded altered consciousness; he could not have absorbed it if he'd been fully awake. As it was, the skill in flying spacecraft gained through long experience combined with a new and more awesome skill. His hands knew what to do with the controls as Peter's did not, and he knew, too, the contours of the land below them; but only through Peter was he in touch with the reality of the ship's position in time and space. Alone, neither of them could bring it down. Together. . . .

But it was too dangerous! Drawn by the settlement's electronic beacon, the ship had reached low altitude. In sudden panic Jesse jolted back to awareness, struggling unsuccessfully to rise out of sleep. He must take control. . . .

No, Jess, no! Don't fight it! You can't wake now, you'll

break the contact. Trust it! Trust your inner mind; it's our only chance.

Peter—we'll be too close to the shelters! I have to control—if I miss the landing pad I'll crash into them!

That's not going to happen.

How can you be sure it won't?

Because I won't let it.

You can't— Jesse stopped in mid-thought. Peter could. He knew without any exchange of words that Peter was prepared for that possibility. They might die if they failed, but they wouldn't kill the people on the ground. Committing himself fully, he sank once more into the dream state, and the ring of boundary lights, magnified as seen through Peter's eyes, merged with the memory of candlelight . . . they blurred into flames, a bright circle of fire. Always fire . . . time after time, the crises of his life had been marked by fire . . . hearthfire, candles, torches . . . the burning safe house he'd entered to save friends . . . the pyre that had been the Lodge . . . and now he was plummeting into the center of a flaming wheel that rushed up to meet him. His hands were on the controls but he wasn't aware of what they were doing; they acted of their own accord. The ship was on target. Beneath it, the landing lights illumined the pad within the encircling flame; he needed no eyes to know that, for he saw it with the same new inner sense that told him their speed was precisely right.

And then, abruptly, the lights veered to one side, and the ship was coming down too fast. It lurched with a force that threw him hard against his seat harness and the yoke jerked in his hands, so that he no longer had any form of power over it, and the brightness he perceived swung sharply around from right to left. Too fast for even an exchange of thought, Peter had taken over. *I'm dreaming,* Jesse thought, and I'll wake soon next to Carla . . . and Carla responded instantly, *Jesse! Jesse, I'm with you! With you forever—*

The thought cut off, and he did not have time to dream about the crash.

Part Two

14

IT HAD NOT been his fault, Jesse was assured. A sudden gust of wind could defeat any pilot; it could just as easily have happened on an earlier flight when he was fully conscious. He should thank his lucky stars that it hadn't—that the wind hadn't risen until the last flight so that the loss of the shuttle hadn't doomed anybody. Jesse knew this to be true, but he couldn't help feeling that if he had not been flying literally in his sleep, he might have managed to set down safely. And in any case, it *was* his fault that the aftermath of stasis had forced them to fly at night in questionable weather.

No one had been seriously hurt in the crash, although there'd been many injuries to be dealt with by Kira and the other healers. Jesse himself had awakened, after being carried unconscious into a shelter for ten hours of uninterrupted sleep, to learn that he'd suffered a fractured shoulder that had required setting. Peter, when informed that he was awake, had come to him and completed the physical healing process. Jesse was uncomfortably aware that he'd also attempted psychological healing, and that further attempts would be needed. For some reason everyone seemed to think he was a hero merely because he'd stayed awake longer than the medical records on stasis said should be possible, long enough to get everyone but the last shipload onto the ground without incident. He did not feel heroic. And he didn't think any future effort on Peter's part was going to change that.

The large shuttle, though only moderately damaged, might as well have been totaled for all the good it was going to do them. They had neither the facilities nor the skill to repair it. It lay some distance from the pad on the side away from the settlement, and in time would be cannibalized for materials needed by the colony. The hull, however—designed as it was to withstand the heat of entry into the atmosphere—could not be converted into usable material. It would remain intact, he supposed, for centuries, a monument to the havoc his miscalculation of the jump through hyperspace had caused.

Anne was the real hero. If it hadn't been for her courage in bringing a small shuttle down alone, they would be in serious trouble. Without a way to reach the starship, they would lack much that was needed for survival. As it was, they were no worse off than Fleet had expected a lost colony to be; the presence of the large shuttle had not been part of the standard emergency plan. To be sure, neither had the loss of consumables—they would be unable to re-air much of the ship using small shuttles alone. They would have to work in spacesuits when retrieving equipment. But that was a minor obstacle, compared to what they might have faced.

Once fully healed and well rested after a second sleep cycle, Jesse felt somewhere near normal. Emerging from the shelter, he found most members of the Group lounging in its shade, and was at first dismayed to think so many were still weakened by injury, heat, or just the aftermath of stasis. But he soon became aware that they were not so much debilitated as bewildered. Despite the telepathic undercurrents between them and the mutual trust that bound them together as a team, they simply had no idea of what to do next.

Only a few people were needed to supervise the robots, and the basic housekeeping chores had already been accomplished. All six prefab shelters had now been erected, so there would be less crowding than during the first night when, Carla told him, they had lain side by side in rows on the floor. Sleeping spaces had been assigned and one of the shelters had been made into a common area with cooking and eating facilities. The contents of the pods, other than supplies stored for future use, had been unloaded. Privies had been set up, and the construction of a well was underway. For now, water was being carried up from the canyon with the aid of the motorized cart; a duty roster had been posted for that and for meal preparation. But there being no other obvious work to do, most people were just sitting around, beginning to grasp the fact that this was *it*—they were here now forever, cut off not merely from the comforts they'd always enjoyed but from all the routine occupations of their former lives.

Catching sight of Jesse, a cluster of them approached him. "What should we be working on?" Liz asked.

"Well, that's up to Peter," Jesse said.

"Peter is busy with people who aren't fully recovered," Reiko told him, "and as soon as Carla's finished setting up the neurofeedback lab, he's got to begin training the recent recruits who can't cope with the heat. So it's for you to say."

"I haven't any authority on the surface except for being part of the Council," Jesse reminded her. "In other words, no more than you have."

"You are Captain. And since you're the only one with any knowledge of this place, no one will question your orders."

It struck him for the first time that this was true. What little he knew about settling new worlds, absorbed over the years from talk he'd heard in Fleet, was the only thing they had to turn to. Peter was the official leader; it was Peter who would inspire them to struggle . . . but he himself would have to lead in practical matters, at least for now. It wasn't a job he wanted. He no longer felt well qualified even for the space command he'd eagerly accepted. But fate had placed him here, where they could all die as easily as they could have died in space. Somehow, he had to see to it that they survived.

"Is the datalink from the ship operative?" he asked Erik.

"Yes, I checked it out while Carla was still aboard. And our phones work, though they won't in the canyon."

"Well, then, get the textreaders out of the stores and schedule the use of them. Everyone without other work should stay inside where it's cooler and get started on learning their new jobs." It had been decided before leaving Undine that everybody with a useful skill must train an apprentice, and everybody without one must either become an apprentice or gain, from the knowledgebase, some skill that nobody in the Group possessed. Farming was, of course, the highest priority, followed by mining and manufacturing techniques. There were also professional roles to be filled, such as dentistry, which could be learned through the computer's virtual reality facilities. Carla, in addition to troubleshooting computer problems, planned to study the most crucial field of all, maintenance of the AI on which their future survival would depend.

But until they could retrieve more textreaders from the starship, there would not be enough to go around. And people could not be allowed to stay idle, Jesse knew. That would be devastating to morale. It wasn't the same as at the Lodge on Undine where their joy in simply living, in having fun despite underlying awareness of ongoing danger, had so impressed him. Then, they'd been relaxing from the demands of their work. Free time would be less enjoyable if they had no work to relax from.

"I hadn't thought it was going to be so . . . empty," Dorcas said in a low voice, glancing around the rock-strewn plateau, from which the pods and shelters rose in stark contrast to the barrenness of the land. Not being near a sea was a blow from which they would not soon recover. In time, to be sure, there would be crops and eventually shade trees. In a year there would be children to care for. The colonists could not wait a year to be distracted from the new world's desolation, or even a few days. They must be fully occupied now, or they would lose heart.

Children . . . the sooner the better, Jesse thought, and

yet in the shelters there was no privacy. That in itself was a
big problem, for within the Group sex—involving as it did a
closer telepathic bond between partners than existed among
outsiders—was an indispensable part of living. And its telepathic aspect made the present setup worse. A couple making love in close proximity to other telepaths tended to project
emotions and even sensations; thus at the Lodge the cot-
tages had been widely spaced. Mere curtained partitions
would not suffice even if materials for them could be found.
As for secluded spots outdoors, there weren't any. Both the
plateau and the lower land near the river were flat and bare
of all but low rocks and ground-hugging vegetation. After
dark it was too cold to be out. Yet if people had to refrain
from sex for very long, it would be the last straw as far as
maintaining their psychological balance on this inhospitable
world was concerned.

Private dwellings must be built soon—and must in any
case be ready when the children came. "What's our building
committee doing?" he asked Reiko.

"They took charge of the erection of the shelters. Now
that that's done, they're at loose ends, since there don't seem
to be any local materials useful for building."

"Get Nathan," Jesse said to Liz, who was married to
him. "We need to talk about the next step." Nathan had
worked as a building contractor on Undine and thus had
been named head of the committee. But it was true enough
that no construction materials with which he was familiar
were at hand.

What could they build homes of, with no steel or alumi-
num or carbon fiber, neither plastics nor wood, no way even
to make bricks until harvesting of crops produced straw?
Stone, of course; there was nothing else available—and it
would provide good insulation against the temperature ex-
tremes. The robotic machines could handle stone easily. But
the robots were in use. After the well was finished the fields
for crops must be cleared, and then would come excavation
for mining. Still, in ancient times, Jesse had heard, people

on Earth built stone houses by hand, even without mortar, and they had stood for centuries. It could be done again. Manual labor would be the best antidote to boredom in any case.

"Organize teams to gather stones," he told Nathan when Liz returned with him, "and start picking sites for houses."

"How are we going to roof them?"

"Perhaps with the parachute fabric, for a while at least, until we can adapt something more permanent from the starship."

"Thatch or woven grass, maybe," said Liz, drawing on her interest in history. "There are plants near the river that might do. And there's sod—sod roofs were once common on Earth."

"Any material needs framing to hold it up," Nathan pointed out.

Jesse frowned. There had to be some way. It couldn't be impossible to construct homes on a planet without wood. They'd have it in time, of course, as the genetically-engineered trees developed for terraforming were fast growers—but not fast enough to provide shelter for the first generation of young children.

Reiko, sensing his thought, said, "Of course there's a way. Some ancient cultures used corbelled construction, piling unmortared stones in concentric circles to form a dome like an igloo. Beehive huts, they were called. A number of them still exist."

"They couldn't be very big," Dorcas said doubtfully.

"Big enough for a single room to shelter a family," Reiko assured her. "In the future, we can add rooms onto them."

There being no alternative, Jesse ordered the construction of beehive huts, telling Nathan to consult the knowledgebase for techniques. He wished that he were free to lose himself in the building of a hut to sleep in with Carla. But there would be many more space flights to make before he could do that . . . and he must get started on them before the reluctance the crash had implanted in him burgeoned into fear.

15

LATE THE NEXT day, after a short Council session, Peter called for an assembly of the Group, held in the Commons—with its tables folded and stacked—since only at twilight would it be cool enough for a crowd larger than the shaded area to sit outside. Jesse had already made a trip to the starship, taking just one helper, Bernie, so as to leave as much room as possible in the shuttle for bringing back equipment. Bernie was an experienced seaplane pilot and needed to begin learning the shuttle's controls. Eventually, he and Anne would be skilled enough for them to risk flying two shuttles at once, though one of the three, and one pilot, would always be kept on the ground.

While collecting blankets and towels from the starship's passenger deck, they had gathered up the stubs of candles left after the Ritual. But much as individual candles were desired during the memorial for the people who'd died in stasis, they would be needed more in Rituals yet to come— none could be made unless plants were found that would yield wax. And so, as the light from the setting sun faded beyond the shelter's windows, the traditional candlelight ceremony was held with a single candle burning. Such services had formerly taken place in boats, during the illegal sea burials of bodies the Group had contrived to keep out of Undine's stasis vaults. It felt somehow lacking when the song didn't echo over water—still it recalled the goal, the sense of purpose that had drawn them together and had ultimately led them to a new world. . . .

> *May the radiance of candles we light now amidst our tears*
> *Fuel the rising flame within us to be passed on through the years.*

The last time they'd sung it had been at Ian's funeral. That recollection went a long way toward dispelling the gloom some had begun to feel, though Jesse was uncomfortably aware that it might return with the realization that no fires would ever be possible.

Fire had been the focus of Group gatherings, in the huge Lodge fireplace or on the Island's beach where everything from casual cookouts to firewalks had been held. Here there was no fuel for a fire. After the ceremony, soft lights were turned on to illuminate Peter and other speakers; but no merely practical substitute could make up for the associations that were lacking.

To be sure, Peter radiated warmth. He carefully avoided opening his mind fully to the others' sensing, though Jesse knew, as must they, that the deaths and injuries haunted him. From the beginning he'd known there'd be hardship— but not tragedy, not so soon in the venture. He would not let it dim the hopeful spirit he must project. Yet like the rest, he was deeply shaken.

No hint of that came through as he spoke of the life ahead of them. "We didn't expect a paradise," he said. "We've got what we wanted, a world where we're challenged to develop our mind powers. Where they'll count for something beyond a mere demonstration of human potential."

"If the weather so far is typical, we're going to need them," Nathan agreed. "We couldn't lift stones in this heat day after day if we didn't know how to turn off discomfort. But won't it have an effect on our bodies eventually, Peter? Doesn't long-term physical stress shorten lifespan just as emotional stress does?"

"Yes, but we can avoid that," Peter assured them. "We can go further than not minding how we feel—we can accelerate and enhance physical acclimatization. The mind has the power to regulate internal temperature. Ian taught me, and we recorded feedback for it; Carla's doing the programming to turn that into a teaching pattern. Each of you will have to have several sessions on dual neurofeedback with me or another instructor, so since we've only got one set of lab equipment, it will take time for everyone to learn."

"Meanwhile, we'll stick to a safe schedule," Reiko announced. "Breakfast before dawn, all outdoor work early in the day, and back inside the shelters before noon. Studying the knowledgebase will keep us busy during the afternoons."

The meeting proceeded to the official vote on the colony's charter, something else that had originally been planned to take place aboard the starship prior to landing. On Undine, the Group's policies had not been formalized. On the new world they must be, though with such a small population it would be run more like a city than an entire planet. The charter had been drafted by Reiko, who was a historian and university administrator, and informally agreed to via secure Net communication among Group members before departure. Now it must be read aloud and approved.

"We've modified it," Reiko said, "since it's become apparent that we need a larger Executive Council and delegation of specific responsibilities. Of the existing members, Kira as you know is in charge of medical procedures and healing; Hari, of advanced psi experimentation; Jesse, of the retrieval and allocation of equipment. We propose to add Kwame, for power and engineering; Carla, for computer and AI maintenance; Dan, for mining; and Teresa, the only one of us who has lived on a farm, for agriculture. I will coordinate work and study assignments, oversee record keeping, and head a committee to plan the education of our future children. Peter, of course, will remain in charge of neurofeedback training in addition to his responsibilities in psychiatry and as Council head."

"And Jesse," Peter added, "will be deputy head. I'll defer to him in all matters related to the physical establishment of our settlement." Jesse became aware, somewhat to his surprise, that this had always been intended. Until now he had not grasped how much responsibility would fall to him in the years ahead. But he realized now that Peter would have his hands full training and counseling people in the use of the mind powers needed for survival.

The expanded Council was quickly approved by voice

vote and Peter went on to review the other provisions of the charter, some of which not everyone had seen. "We'll use single names," Peter said, "because surnames would be superfluous here. There are plenty of names available for generations to come and the computer can keep track of them so they won't be reused. Anyone wishing to name a child after someone else can use that person's original surname, or a derivative of it, or the equivalent of the given name in a different language."

"No family names?" Jesse protested. "We want to encourage family ties, after all." On Undine many children, Peter among them, had no birth families; they'd been born of host mothers by IVF, the genetic parents being unknown to them, and had been assigned arbitrary surnames. Here, he'd expected his kids to bear his surname combined with Carla's.

"We'll encourage families," Reiko agreed, "but we don't want to discriminate against children whose fathers are anonymous. To achieve population growth, all the first-generation women should give birth, yet since there are more women than men in the Group, not all can have permanent partners. Some of those who do are partnered with other women. And many are past menopause so will have to use IVF in any case; that's why we brought the DNA bank, why Ian stored his sperm. Discrimination would work both ways if we allowed it—kids without social fathers would feel cheated, and more might be expected of Ian's descendants than they could live up to."

"Are you saying those not born to married couples won't know who their real parents are, any more than the crèche children on Undine do? I thought one of our goals was to get away from that."

"Genetic ties aren't important except in connection with diseases that were wiped out long ago," said Peter. "To consider them socially significant would be to endorse the Meds' belief that personality, as distinguished from ability, has a physical basis."

"We'll keep confidential records of genetic parentage

because we need to learn the extent to which psi talents are inherited," Kira said. "But to our kids, family will mean by whom, and with whom, they were reared. Only with their birth mothers will they have an inherent permanent relationship."

Reiko said, "You weren't involved in this discussion before we left, Jesse, because you were being tracked and to meet face to face would have put us in danger. I know having been born on Earth will make the changes here seem more radical to you than they do to us. But even on Earth, for centuries there has been confusion about surnames, what with all the serial marriages on top of inconsistency in passing on the father's name or the mother's. And the tradition whereby genetic fathers had rights and responsibilities is a holdover from the time when there was no choice about pregnancy and both women and children were viewed as the property of men."

"Well, presumably dads will still have responsibilities, even if not based on genetics."

"Moral responsibilities, yes, once they've chosen to take part in the rearing of a child," Peter said. "Legally under our charter, though, that choice won't be binding. The birth mother—but not the genetic mother, when they are different—has a natural tie to her child because she carries it in her body for nearly a year, and as it develops, an unconscious telepathic bond forms. That's why people have always sensed that children belong with their mothers—contrary to common belief, it had nothing to do with whether women are better fitted than men to care for offspring too old to nurse. Here, since we're aware of telepathy and want to foster it in our kids, we'll respect that bond."

"The failure to recognize it was one of the worst aspects of the system on Undine," Kira pointed out. "Crèche babies were taken from their host mothers and no amount of loving attention from caregivers could wholly compensate for that. And incidentally, it's why Earth's experiments with artificial wombs never worked and never will."

Peter continued, "Dads, and for that matter grandparents and social siblings, will also bond telepathically with kids, of course—but later, and less irrevocably. If a couple splits up, the children will remain with the woman who bore them."

"But won't her legal husband have any rights? Or any obligation to contribute financially?"

"That's another thing," said Reiko. "We don't intend to make marriage a legal institution here. There is no reason for the government to have anything to do with who is sleeping with whom, or for how long. Marriage is a private matter between two people who make a commitment to each other, in some cases a religious commitment. The pretense that it has civic significance has been a farce ever since women became capable of self-support."

Absorbing this slowly, Jesse felt his initial dismay fading. He and Carla had not registered their marriage officially on Undine because to document his connection to her would have been to risk revealing some of the Group's secrets, thus endangering Peter and perhaps Carla herself. They had not felt any less married on that account.

"Think of all the senseless argument there once was on Earth about gay marriage," Kira added. "The root of the problem was not that same-sex couples were denied privileges, but that heterosexual couples had privileges that were obsolete. By the end of the twentieth century there was no longer any logical reason for making legal distinctions between married people and singles—it was grossly unfair not only to gays but to longtime friends, such as older people, who shared homes without being sexually involved. It would be pointless to continue such distinctions here."

"Worse than pointless," Reiko said, "because we do have more women than men, and most of them are heterosexual. Not everyone in our own generation would have a chance to be married unless we endorsed polygamy."

He hadn't thought of that. It meant not everyone had a chance for a committed relationship either. Yet he supposed that had been true even on Undine, for Group members, having once experienced intimacy with a telepathic partner, could no longer enjoy sex with outsiders. Brief relationships within the Group, on the other hand, were never merely casual; the telepathic component guaranteed immediate emotional involvement.

"Okay," Jesse conceded. "But I think you've overlooked one big flaw in the idea of keeping biological descent secret. How are the kids to know who's ineligible as a sex partner? In a colony as small as this, their friends might easily turn out to be brothers and sisters."

"How do you think it worked on Undine?" Kira asked.

"With the crèche children whose genes came from the DNA bank, you mean? Well—" He broke off, realizing that he had not thought.

"There was no genetic disease on Undine," Kira said, "because of the criteria used in selecting embryos created through IVF. And so there will be none here, since none of us have defective genes to pass on. In the culture we're used to, incest was not defined in the same way as on Earth. Crèchemates were off-limits, and of course immediate family members in the case of children raised by parents. Genetic relationship wasn't a consideration. Actually it was rarely as important a factor on Earth as has traditionally been thought. Incest is taboo in most cultures simply to keep girls safe within their own households and to ensure that kids don't develop sexual feelings toward the people they live with."

"None of the IVF kids will be more than half-siblings in any case," Reiko pointed out, "since we won't use DNA from the same two parents for more than one implantation, any more than they did with the crèche children on Undine."

The talk turned to the colony's monetary arrangements: credits would be earned for hours of work or study useful to the colony—one hour, one credit, regardless of the work's nature—and would be charged for meals and for goods from the common stores. Everyone was starting from scratch, of course; all their assets had gone toward charter of the starship and would have been meaningless on an isolated world anyway. In time, when people had accumulated credits and began trading them for handmade goods, a true economy would develop.

By the time the vote on the charter had been taken—again by voice, as no one objected—it was a relief to get out of the jammed-packed Commons and retreat to the relative spaciousness of the five other shelters, in which everyone slept fully clothed. There would be no mattresses until they could be brought down from the bunks on the starship. Jesse, settling beside Carla on the hard section of floor allotted to them, hoped that beehive huts could be readied soon.

16

THE WORST ASPECT of shelter living proved to be the lack of water for bathing. The building of the well was a slow process—the pods had not, of course, contained a drilling rig, so it had to be driven by the general-purpose robots. The water table proved to be low, and though the preprogrammed machines "knew" how to get to it, the people involved did not. They were constantly referring to the knowledgebase for instructions, and more than a few false starts were made before Hari pointed out that water might be located by dowsing.

"There's nothing magic about it," he said. "It's simply another form of remote viewing, one that was used on Earth long before anyone knew what it involved." Jesse hid his skepticism, thinking that at the very least such an attempt might rouse enthusiasm among the psi-focused faction of the Group, who had a tendency to isolate themselves from practical concerns. To his surprise, they found accessible water fairly quickly. But it was at a greater depth than had been hoped, and several attempts at tapping it were aborted when the drive-point hit rock. When success was finally achieved, the well had to be surged. A windmill had to be set up to power the pump. So for some days the settlement's supply was limited to what could be carried from the river in the canyon, and even drinking water had to be rationed.

A shortage of water was not something Group members, accustomed as they were to the water world Undine, had ever imagined. They took it in stride, but they were not happy about it. When it was discovered that one of the large bottles kept in the Commons kitchen had been knocked over, spilling its contents over the floor, tempers flared—not so much from the waste as because nobody took responsibility for it. It was upsetting to find that anyone among them would fail to own up to such carelessness. The Group was founded on mutual trust. Its members were pledged to support each other. If they couldn't count on full honesty within the settlement, the years ahead would be grimmer than had been foreseen.

Especially disturbing during the wait for the well's completion was the impossibility of staying clean. The dry plateau was dusty, and the nightly winds made it worse. So there were plenty of volunteers to fetch water, despite the hike in the morning heat, for the river and adjacent pond offered a chance to wash off.

On the third morning after his recovery, Jesse and Carla joined the water-bearers. "The pond's not so full as it was yesterday," Corrine observed as they approached. "And the river has shrunk, too."

To his dismay, Jesse saw that it was not very deep. He had imagined something too wide to wade across. The stony riverbed spread out on both sides of the stream that meandered down its center—was it full in some seasons, or was this evidence of a long-term climate change? No one had thought to mention it, as they had nothing to compare with. There were no rivers on the small islands that dotted Undine's seas.

"Well, I'm going to cool off," declared Edris, one of the

recent recruits. This early in the day the canyon wall provided shade, so it was safe to expose skin. Stripping down to panties, she stepped into the pond, the water coming barely up to her knees, and began sponging her body. Suddenly, with a look of astonishment, she froze for an instant—and then began to scream.

In that instant Jesse had seen what was happening to Edris and horror had surged through him. Her arms, and presumably her legs, were covered with crawling blackish creatures that looked like some obscene cross between a spider and a newly-hatched frog. It was all he could do to keep from letting out a yell, though he quickly brought his responses under control, calming his heart and stomach. The others, apparently, had done the same, but telepathically he sensed that only their mind training was keeping them from panic.

Edris had no mind training. She continued to shriek hysterically, though she'd managed to stumble out of the pond. Jesse ran to her and suppressing his revulsion, started to pull the disgusting things from her body. *Carla, can you help her?* he pleaded silently. He himself did not have enough psi skill to reach Edris's mind, but Carla had some healing experience, as did many of the others.

They gathered close around Edris, focusing reassurance, and gradually her sobs abated. Carla moved forward, reaching out to help detach the creatures, but Jesse stopped her. "No," he said. "Stay back, all of you. We don't know anything about them." *They might be poisonous*, he added, not want to say this aloud. Edris wasn't yet a trained telepath and, he hoped, might not pick up the thought.

They had seen no life on Maclairn other than tall wiry grass, rushes, and in some areas, ground-hugging shrubs. Data collected from orbit had shown no sign of animal life, but lower forms such as this would not have been detected, and they were not widespread enough to have been collected by a probe. There was no telling whether they'd be permanently harmful to humans, though red welts were appearing on Edris's skin where he'd removed them and his own fingers stung fiercely.

Corrine, Jesse questioned, thankful that she was present. *You're the biologist—what are the chances that these things are dangerous?*

It's not likely. They're biologically alien, after all, so they're not going to feed on us. They shouldn't hurt us, any more than touching the primitive sea plants on Undine did. But without lab work I can't be sure.

"Take a specimen," he ordered, "and find out what you can about them right away."

They filled the water bottles quickly from the river, sacrificing one in which to carry specimens, and loaded as many as possible onto the cart. With the rest in backpacks, they climbed the long trail to the settlement. Everyone was too shaken to say anything. These people, Jesse realized, had never seen any wild creature before, let alone a repulsive one. There was no animal life on Undine and none had been imported during its terraforming. There were no domesticated animals either, other than caged chickens, as its government disapproved of red meat and no food was available for pets. Insects, lizards, and the like were totally beyond the colonists' experience.

"I don't know why I got so upset," Carla confessed as they reached the settlement. "It's not that I was afraid—it didn't occur to me that they might harm us until you warned me. But I cringe inside just thinking about them. It's not rational."

"No, but it's natural, after all," Jesse said. "That's how most people feel about spiders and other crawly things."

"I've heard that they do. I never understood it until now."

Peter, when the situation was discussed in a quickly-convened Council session, had an answer. "It's part of our genetic heritage," he said, "because spiders, snakes, and similar lifeforms often were poisonous on Earth. But it's not like other instinctive fears. It's not activated in a person who hasn't been exposed to someone else's reaction—

that was proven many years ago in experiments with monkeys. They showed no fear of snakes until shown pictures of other monkeys reacting to snakes, yet when shown pictures of monkeys conditioned to fear harmless things, they didn't pick it up. I might add that actual observation isn't necessary, though scientists have assumed that it is. A telepathic reaction has the same effect, probably a greater one."

"So we felt horror because we saw and sensed it in Edris?" Carla asked. "But why did *she* feel it? What started the chain?"

Jesse said unhappily, "If telepathy can do it, then *I* started it. Edris didn't scream until I had seen those creatures. I felt the way people on Earth do because I grew up there. It's part of the collective unconscious milieu you're always talking about, isn't it, Peter, the one that doesn't extend beyond a single planet?"

"Yes," Peter agreed. "That's how it must have happened."

"God, then I'm contagious—I've psychically contaminated a whole new world."

"We mustn't let that happen," said Kira. "We're going to live the rest of our lives where these creatures are around. There may be others just as abhorrent. Unless they're proven dangerous to us, we don't want our kids to fear them. We'll be happier not recoiling from them ourselves."

"You're right," declared Peter, meeting her eyes. "You know what has to be done."

Kira nodded. The other Council members, too, seemed to grasp his meaning, and resign themselves to an idea they clearly were not eager to accept. It took Jesse awhile, but he knew Peter too well—and sensed too much in Peter's mind and Carla's—to shut the thought out of his own. The Group's way was to face all fear squarely. The Ritual pledge demanded it of them, not arbitrarily but because it was the key to the stress control that preserved their health. If the crawlies were in fact harmless, they could not allow themselves to be bothered by them.

"What about Edris?" Carla asked. "She's not trained—"

"No, she's not had even the basics beyond the initial test," Peter confirmed. "I didn't dare recruit her until the last minute. Her parents are among the most powerful citizens of Undine—they own several rich mines and her mother is high in the Hospital administration. Edris is barely eighteen, too young to have developed control over her emerging psi talent without help, and if they'd sensed that she was planning to leave we'd have been exposed in short order."

"So this will be the first step in her training," Kira said. "Something comparable was arranged for each of us early on, wasn't it?"

Yes. For Jesse, it had involved a phobia of deep water, acquired during a near-drowning episode in early childhood. Peter had induced him to defy it, and afterward, learning to swim and to scuba dive had been enjoyable. There would be nothing to enjoy in what was now being asked of them.

That night he slept poorly, dreaming of creepy, crawly things—not from fear, but because the incident was still another case of his having unintentionally hurt the colony. He had polluted its psychic environment. The effect could extend to generations as yet unborn if he failed to fully overcome his distaste for handling such creatures.

In the morning, after Corrine had pronounced native lifeforms harmless, the entire Council hiked to the pond, accompanied by everyone who'd been present the day before. Edris had suffered no physical aftereffects once Kira had healed the red welts, but she was pale and withdrawn. No one had told her what was about to happen. It had been hard enough to persuade her to come along under the pretext that she needed to avoid developing reluctance to take her turn at carrying water. Still, like most young recruits she idolized Peter and would probably obey him. He would provide telepathic support; but even so, the lesson would be harsh.

They formed a circle around the pond, silently, in no mood for the light banter that normally enlivened Group gatherings. Peter smiled—sincerely, Jesse thought; Peter truly believed that the harder a thing was to do, the better it made people feel to find themselves able to do it. "Okay, folks," he said, pulling off his shoes, pants, and shirt. "Let's get it over with." Without further comment he waded into waist-deep water and stooped to stir the bottom with his hand.

Edris gasped and put her hands to her face, hiding her eyes; but Kira gently pushed them down. "No, Edris," she said. "You have to watch."

Peter rose, his arms covered with the horrific crawlies, and deliberately spread them onto his upper body. Repeatedly he did so until his skin was swarming with them. Edris dropped to her knees and vomited; no one had stopped to think that unlike themselves, she hadn't yet acquired the ability to subdue nausea. Telepathically, Kira put an end to it; self-healing was a more advanced skill than a trainee needed to be concerned with at this stage.

"Jesse," said Peter. It was a command. Jesse had expected this and resigned himself to it. For more than one reason, it was necessary that he be called first. He did not hesitate; after discarding his outer clothing he moved quickly toward the water. *Are you okay with this, Jess?* Peter asked silently.

I have to be, don't I?

Yes. But they'll share what's in your mind, you know— I picked it up unconsciously myself and was nearly bowled over by the effect on me. So a lot depends on how you handle it.

Jesse knew what was required of him. You weren't supposed to fight your feelings; the point was to be willing to experience them fully. That was the paradox fundamental to mind training: if you were willing to accept the worst— the loss of control over yourself—then the worst wouldn't happen. It didn't matter whether it was something large and significant, like handing fire in the Ritual or staying awake to fly, or a small thing like undoing the damage he'd done through his instinctive reaction to a trivial threat. The secret of the Group's resistance to illness and aging lay in refusal to be ruled by genetic mind programming.

He stepped into the pond and scooped up crawlies as Peter had done, not allowing himself to cringe as they squished beneath his bare feet. He didn't try to pretend that he wasn't repelled by them. The only course open was simply to relax and accept this as he would any other discomfort. The sting was quite intense where they clung, but his control over pain reduced that to insignificance; the worst part was the tickling sensation as they crept over his back and chest. He didn't let himself wonder how long he would have to endure it. He must remain in the pond as long as Peter did, and Peter would not move until everyone else had joined them.

One by one the others were called, until only Kira and Edris were still out of the water. Peter waded close the bank and held out his hand. "Come, Edris," he said. "I won't lie to you—it's not pleasant. But it will work like the testing at the Lodge, where I showed you that you're stronger than you thought you were."

Edris shrank back, drawing close to Kira. "I—I *can't*," she whispered. No one needed to hear her voice; the intensity of her emotion was telepathically overwhelming.

"This is how we gain mind powers in the Group," Kira told her. "One way or another, you'd have to do something hard, you see. If it wasn't this, we'd find some other way to challenge you—we'd have done it before now if we hadn't been busy setting up living quarters. You'll feel *good* afterward. You'll know you needn't ever be held back by fear."

"It's a matter of whether you trust us," Peter said. "If you don't, it was a mistake to come with us to Maclairn—but you're here now, and you can't go back. You won't be happy unless you learn to live as we do."

He was urging her telepathically more than with the words, projecting warmth and confidence. Jesse sensed that Peter trusted *her*—that he would never have recruited her if he had not been sure that she had what it would take to absorb mind training. It could not be forced on her. The effectiveness of the teaching ordeals depended on voluntary submission to them; it was the willingness, not the action itself, that empowered the learner. And it was Peter's psychic skill and charisma that made frightened novices willing.

Jesse held his breath, knowing that his mind, too, was broadcasting and that the slightest waver of his own self-control would destroy any chance of success for Edris. Slowly, she moved forward, side by side with Kira. She had not taken her clothes off, but wet clothes would be a small matter compared to what was being accomplished. As they stepped into the water, she let go of Kira's hand and reached for Peter's. He squeezed it, then drew her close to him in an embrace. Crawlies crept from his body to hers, but she did not pull away. Then together they waded out of the pond, and the others followed.

It took some time for everyone to pull the clingers off and toss them back into the pond. By the time they were finished and had healed first Edris's welts and then their own, the charged psychic atmosphere had been dispelled. "It's hard to believe how awful those creatures seemed to me," Carla said as she dressed. "We made such a big deal over nothing."

"It wasn't nothing," Peter said. "If we hadn't nipped it in the bud the aversion would have gotten permanently established here. Once it had spread to the whole population it would have been much harder to wipe out."

"If it's a genetically-based fear and can be triggered by mere pictures," Jesse remarked, "I don't see why you hadn't acquired it as kids from horror vids."

"Horror vids involving animal life aren't permitted on colony worlds," Peter told him. "Haven't you ever wondered why starship libraries don't contain any? Earth has always banned their export as a measure to protect extraterrestrial lifeforms. It's one of the few government trade regulations I think is wise."

Of course, Jesse realized. The average Earth citizen's reaction would have been to kill the crawlies—if possible, to exterminate them. That hadn't occurred to anyone yesterday. And horror vids often portrayed even intelligent aliens as repulsive; what kind of precedent would that set if similar ones were ever encountered?

Edris, dressed in Peter's dry shirt, had been embraced by each member of the party in turn and was now beginning to bloom. In fact, everyone was getting high—the normal aftermath of a telepathically-shared challenging experience. Jesse threw his arm around Carla and she pressed close to him, wishing, as they all did, that couples had someplace private to go. He recalled what Peter had told him when he was new to the Group, *In the case of potential sex partners a shared high often does lead to bed*. To his dismay he saw that Edris's worshipful focus on Peter, now greatly strengthened, was not being discouraged in the way Peter usually discouraged adoration from the trainees he instructed. What was the matter with him, that he failed to notice that she was in danger of falling in love with him?

A recruit's acquisition of full telepathic ability did demand sexual contact with an experienced Group member, if necessary prearranged and brief—but for the leader to take part personally would give him the wrong sort of status. In the past Peter, like Ian before him, had carefully avoided arousing any such expectation. Now. . . .

Jesse did a double take, suddenly aware of his own obtuseness. Peter's wife had died more than a year ago on another world, and there were fewer men than women in the Group. His genes would be needed, especially since he was among the most psi-talented of its members, and there was no reason to think they should be provided solely through artificial insemination. A relationship now would be seen not as exploiting his position, but as serving the colony's future. Edris, who must bear a child and had no men of her own age to choose from, was naturally attracted to Peter; if the attraction was mutual, what would be the harm in it? The fact that he was more than old enough to be her father really didn't matter—she might not even have been told yet that he was older than he looked. The slow aging of members had been one of the Group's closest-kept secrets on Undine.

Carla, too, was watching them. *It would be a good thing, Jesse,* she told him silently. *I don't think he'll bond with her in the way you and I are bonded. But he needs someone, even if just for a little while.*

Why not permanently? Jesse wondered. Well, Carla had known Peter far longer than he had and she was like a sister to him, so no doubt she knew.

17

THE LOWNESS OF the river worried Jesse. There had been no sign of clouds in the days since they'd landed—not in itself a concern in so short a time, but how did they know it would rain soon enough for the raising of a crop before their stores ran out? He was struck anew by the terrible chance they had taken. It was something he'd known from the beginning, of course. They had never had any grounds for believing Maclairn was a place they could survive. He had pushed it out of his mind, supporting Peter's enthusiasm for the sake of sparing the Group futile worry. After all, they'd had no real choice other than to submit to increasing regimentation on Undine, something none of them were willing to do. But the time had now come when practical problems must be faced squarely. Land must be prepared for planting, and some decision about irrigating it must be made.

It had been obvious from the beginning that the plateau on which the pods had landed was not suitable for farming. Even if they dug a lot of wells there would be no means of pumping sufficient water from them, for there were barely enough parts for wind pumps available to meet future drinking and sanitation needs, and there was no telling how soon they'd be able to manufacture more. Rain could not be relied on. So water for crops, at least part of the time, must be obtained from the river—which meant putting the fields in the valley despite the long-term inconvenience of climbing to and from them.

Jesse inspected the land with Kwame, who, having consulted the knowledgebase, assured him that a mechanical irrigation system could be constructed using a water wheel to drive a vertical bucket chain. This would dump water into a raised holding tank, thus allowing the fields to be watered by gravity. The pods had contained the necessary components of such a system. But, Jesse knew, it would depend on the river retaining enough water to turn the wheel. The flow was sufficient now, but every day it grew less.

The sooner they got a crop planted, the better. So the robots were set to work clearing fields, moving the stones from them to piles against the canyon wall from which they could eventually transport them for use in building. Plowing then followed. This, like the leveling of the shuttle pads, was automated work, requiring only two men to supervise while Kwame and several helpers built the irrigation system. Meanwhile, Teresa selected the seed. Only grain for food would be grown first, although they'd been supplied with genetically-engineered plants that could meet many other needs. More fields would be prepared later, but it would be best, Jesse decided, not to risk too much seed until they'd learned what problems they'd encounter and how to cope with them.

As the days passed and the excitement of mere presence on a new world wore off, morale within the Group flagged. Living on Maclairn was not what anyone had expected. "I don't know just what we did expect," Kira remarked over supper one night, "but certainly not this. Half the time our people are working to the point of exhaustion, but the other half they're bored to death."

The amount of work to be done apart from hut construction was surprisingly small, and it fell to the individuals with the technical skills it demanded. On Undine, most Group members had held clerical or professional jobs for which the colony had no need. Being unused to manual labor, they were willing to build stone huts but limited as to the number of hours per day they could spend at it, even apart from the rule that all outdoor work must stop before the onset of noonday heat. The heat ruled out sports or exploratory hikes during the afternoon. The neurofeedback equipment, which at the Lodge had been available for games when not otherwise needed, was in use around the clock for basic mind-training of the novices and the training of everyone else to control body temperature.

Thus there was nothing to do in free time but study or read, and as there weren't enough textreaders to go around, this often had to be done on the miniature screens of personal datakeepers. There were only a few computers with monitors. Furthermore, since it got too cold to stay outdoors after sundown and the shelters had no extra space, evenings had to be spent in sleeping quarters where there was no room to do anything but read, listen to music through earphones, or watch vids on the tiny personal screens.

The Commons being too small to hold everyone with the tables in place, people ate in shifts, which were rotated because only those served last could linger to enjoy community fellowship. Meals were unappetizing. The food, chosen by Fleet to provide maximum nutrition while requiring minimum storage space, had been stowed decades ago in the emergency pods and had to be reconstituted with water. The alien native vegetation was inedible. There was, of course, no fruit, much less wine. So even eating offered no break in the monotony.

The worst of it was that there was no immediate prospect for change. It had been decided to build the huts one at a time, with everyone working together in shifts, and schedule use of them night by night so as to give as many couples as possible a chance to be alone. Not until there were enough for everyone would they be permanently occupied. That wasn't going to happen soon, and even when it did, the windowless beehive huts would be cramped and cold. Their decor could hardly be made homelike.

Free time on Undine had been spent swimming, scuba diving, picnicking on the shore, relaxing beside fireplaces or campfires . . . it had revolved around water and fire. The new world lacked both; even in the future when trees had grown, wood would be too precious to burn. Yet to the Group's members, fire was the symbol of all they most valued. It recalled not only the exultation of the Ritual, but their commitment to mutual friendship and support. To many couples it also symbolized their love, by tradition first consummated by the Lodge fireplace on a night when all others withdrew. That they would never sit by a fire again was not a deprivation anyone had anticipated. Trivial it might be beside the true hardships of colonization—yet nothing could change the fact the opportunities for recreation on Maclairn were virtually nonexistent, and there were not enough challenging jobs to make up for the lack.

Not surprisingly, frustration built up, and the unaccustomed sexual restraint necessitated by the public sleeping quarters aggravated it. The Group's mind training had been designed to overcome fear and anxiety, not frustration. Vaguely, people knew that the same principles could be applied. They could control their physiological response to the stress well enough to avoid stress-induced illness. But their carefree enjoyment of life in defiance of danger, the hallmark of membership that had so impressed Jesse during his days on the Island, had faded.

He himself was too busy to give any thought to that. Day after day he returned to the starship, dismantling equipment and loading most of it aboard the shuttle personally with the aid of only his copilot. To bring more assistants would reduce the payload of each flight, and besides, few people had gained enough experience in working in spacesuits to be of any help. It was hard work, although he lowered the ship's gravity to lighten it. The thought of all that hinged on the flights made it even more exhausting. Always in the back of his mind was an awareness that someday the wind might gust again. He was not personally afraid of what might happen to him in another crash—but until everything essential to the colony's long-time survival had been retrieved, all three pilots and shuttles were indispensable.

And in his case, it wasn't just a matter of equipment retrieval. He alone had knowledge of what resources existed aboard *Mayflower XI* that could be made to serve some useful purpose. Only he could deal with emergencies such as interruption of the power being beamed to the surface, which would be needed until enough wind power was being generated to support the settlement. Moreover, though Anne and Bernie were now competent to handle cargo flights, they were not yet ready to carry passengers, and there was one thing for which passengers would have to be brought up. The lab facilities for producing embryos to be used in IVF could not be moved into the crude accommodations available on Maclairn. Sooner or later biologists must come to the starship for that—which like so much else, had been expected to be finished before establishment of the colony.

Every time Jesse came up against such a thought, a realization of yet another difficulty resulting from the astrogation error that had prevented well-planned settlement of the new world, he cringed inwardly. But he was too fully occupied to do so consciously. On each return from space, he'd barely emerged from the shuttle before someone came to him with a new issue to be settled. There were no more suitable stones within carrying distance of the building site; could the robots be diverted to hauling them for a couple of hours per day, perhaps? Not yet, he decided, because pressing as the need for huts now was, nothing overrode the need for maximum speed in getting a crop planted. There wouldn't be enough wire to provide power to all the huts if they were spaced widely enough for future addition

of rooms; should they be built closer together? No, because
stone huts would be permanent whereas wire could eventually be manufactured. If people not earning credits through
other important work chose not to participate in building
huts, would they be eligible for a turn at sleeping in them?
Should they be required to work in order to eat, or could
they run up a credit deficit indefinitely? It went on and on.

It was not that none of the other Group members were
capable of making such decisions, but that someone had to
take charge. The question of credit deficit was one for the
Council, Jesse ruled; but the Council could not meet daily.
He had assumed Peter would handle issues that arose between sessions. But Peter, too, was overworked, and was
rarely on hand. His main job was the healing of people who
had not fully recovered from stasis—of whom Claire was
not the only one—and the training of the recent recruits;
after that came temperature-control training for three hundred people, which required individual neurofeedback sessions. Kira, Greg, and several others assisted, as they were
experienced neurofeedback instructors as well as powerful
telepaths. But Peter had to oversee and to conduct many
sessions personally. The colony could not afford members
without adequate mind training; the avoidance of cata-
strophic illness depended on it. And, shaken by conditions
on the new world, even some of the longtime members sought
his counseling and encouragement. Jesse wondered, at first,
why Peter did not step in with his usual charisma and create an occasion to raise Group morale en masse telepathically, which he was surely capable of doing. But concentration on the weakest links evidently had priority.

"There's more to it than that, Jesse," Carla said when
he mentioned it to her. "Yes, in a crisis he could do as he did
at Ian's funeral, and again on the night we went into stasis.
But he can't encourage ongoing dependence on him. The
colony has to be able to stand on its own. If, God forbid,
something were to happen to him—"

True, Jesse realized. The point was to create a culture,

not a cult. Peter would be treading dangerous ground if he allowed the Group as a whole to rely on him emotionally.

Only a few people seemed oblivious to the frustrations of their new life—Hari and his circle of friends. From the start they had seemed able to tolerate the heat, and before long Jesse realized that Hari already knew how to control his temperature, without benefit of neurofeedback, and had taught others who were exceptionally receptive to telepathic instruction. They worked their shift of hut-building like everyone else, then—when not studying new jobs—they sat apart in the shade of a shelter, apparently content to do nothing. When in contact with others at work or at meals they showed no signs of depression or even discouragement; they simply remained untouched by what went on around them. Whether this was the retreat Peter had spoken of, Jesse wasn't sure; if so, Peter was making no attempt to interfere with it. And perhaps it was something more positive than retreat. It occurred to Jesse, noticing their silence one afternoon, that they might be meditating.

The weather continued to be dry. Dust rose from the newly-plowed fields; then, once the irrigation system was set up, water flowed through the furrows without sinking in. The tireless robots had to cultivate deeper before the soil could be fertilized with the essential nutrients supplied by the pods. Refertilization would depend on human waste—which, Reiko assured them, had been commonly used for farming in some cultures on Earth—and later on supplements of chicken manure. There were cryogenically-preserved chicken embryos aboard the starship, but chickens couldn't be raised until enough grain had been grown to feed them. Like so many other aspects of establishing the colony, the list of crucial farm tasks was circular.

Would it have been better to have chosen a different site? Jesse wondered. Could he have located a better source of water, perhaps? Crops couldn't have been irrigated with seawater, of course; Undine's island farms had been dependent on large desalination plants built by its terraforming team. But perhaps there were lakes somewhere on Maclairn, or at least wide rivers. The remote viewers might have been able to find one. His failure to ask them was yet another mistake that might prove fatal.

When he awoke one night with fierce spasmodic pain in his back, he was startled—it was an old problem, but he'd thought it had been solved. Once Kira had explained its source in unconscious fear of the strange new powers he was gaining, the pain had not recurred. Well, he was skilled in dealing with pain now. He adjusted his perception to the point where it no longer bothered him, and went back to sleep.

In the morning, he sensed that Carla knew. "There's more to mind training than what leads up to the Ritual, you know," she ventured with a troubled look.

He had long suspected this, but nothing direct had ever been said to him about it. He knew there were psi powers and forms of consciousness to which he had not been introduced. But that was the last thing he needed to be concerned with, Jesse thought grimly. He could barely keep his head above water with what he was already handling.

Several times during the next few nights the pain came again. Carla said nothing, but he knew that she couldn't have avoided awareness of what he was feeling. During the day her eyes were worried, but her mind was closed to him. There was something troubling her that she chose not to discuss.

If only they could make love, Jesse thought. He hungered not merely for Carla's body, hidden from him now for the many nights they'd slept within arm's length of other couples, but for the full merging of minds on which he'd come to rely. They had been apart much too long. There had been weeks before departure from Undine—weeks during which he dared not let her come to his apartment lest their connection become known to the authorities—and then the one miserable union aboard the starship when she'd pulled away in terror, perceiving his knowledge of the choice between stasis and death. All that should be behind them!

They'd looked forward to the new world as a joyful resumption of their life together. Yet so far, lying side by side but unable to satisfy their longing for each other, they were worse off than before.

The building of a prototype hut proceeded slowly. It took much planning, much trial and error, and much back-breaking hauling of stones. Since no flooring materials were available, the ground had to be leveled and sufficiently smoothed to serve as a floor. The technique of corbelling had to be deduced from study of the ancient huts pictured in the knowledgebase. No one was really sure how large a circle to start with to provide enough interior height. There were too many volunteers to work efficiently after the stone-gathering stage—most were merely in the way—yet it did not seem wise to start on more huts until it was certain that the first one wouldn't collapse.

Jesse held back from getting involved, aware that if he offered any advice, all the questions would soon be brought to him. There was no good reason why a starship captain should know more about building stone huts than anyone else, but he had learned that in the eyes of the inexperienced settlers—perhaps even in Peter's—the title of Captain endowed him with magical ability to resolve any problem connected with the new environment. It was ironic, he thought ruefully, considering how inadequate he'd proved to be in the one skill, astrogation, in which they'd had a right to expect him to excel.

18

LOAD AFTER LOAD was brought down from *Mayflower XI*—electronic gear, seating, mattresses, pots and pans from the galley, dishes and utensils, all the food aboard—and Jesse began to think about dismantling built-in furniture and even interior walls. He flew each day, accompanied by Viktor as pilot trainee, while Anne and Bernie, with the other two shuttles, took turns so that space transport would always be available to the settlement. The seats in the shuttles, except for the pilot's and copilot's, were designed to fold down to create cargo space, and they were left down, as no passenger flights would be made soon.

Checking over his ship after landing one evening, when the people who'd gathered to meet it had carried away its load, Jesse was struck by a long-ago memory and then by mounting excitement. What a fool he'd been! How could he have overlooked a resource that every cadet aboard a Fleet starship was well aware of?

That night as they left the Commons to scurry through the cold wind to their sleeping quarters, he drew Carla back. *Don't say anything to anyone,* he told her, *but come along with me. I've got a surprise for you.*

They crossed the dark plateau to the shuttle pad in silence. Carla asked no questions; his newly-heightened mood was enough to tell her that it would be a pleasant surprise. He helped her inside the ship and turned on the heat and lights. "The hatch is locked," he pointed out. "Not that it needs to be when nobody knows we're here. But after tonight we'll have to tell the others—there are three shuttles on the ground at night and one in the daytime. That's privacy for four couples a day. We don't need to wait for huts."

"Oh, Jesse!" Her eyes brimmed with tears, happy tears.

"I should have thought of it sooner," he said with chagrin. "On Fleet training cruises, cadets used to sneak into the shuttle bay after hours and fold down the seats. Everybody knew, even the officers, though they never admitted it—I suppose because in space there was nowhere else young people could make out."

Saying no more aloud, they shed their clothes and coupled quickly, needing no foreplay because with them, as with all telepaths, arousal was transmitted less through physical contact than through the uninhibited touch of each other's minds. He had feared that having held back so long, she might not be able to respond instantly, but it was as if there had been no lapse at all. He became one with her, seeing through her eyes, feeling her body as his own, just as she was experiencing *his* feelings. Simultaneously they climaxed, neither knowing nor caring which body produced the sensations. No communication passed between them, not even silently, for communication is a meaningless concept when no separation exists.

Not until afterward, when they were two again, did he exult in the beauty of her body, the perfection of her breasts, the contours of her beloved face. And then, for a long time, they exchanged thoughts, not as in telepathic conversation, with words, but simply knowing what each other knew, absorbing each other's memories and perceptions. They knew that the new world would be a good world, if not for them, then for their descendants. That however frustrating their lives might be now, their love and the children that would come of it would make everything worthwhile. And they knew that a child might already have been conceived.

I wanted to be first, Carla admitted. *The first to give birth on our new world. Until tonight I didn't think there was much chance, but now—*

It's likely now, I guess, Jesse replied. It had not occurred to him in bringing her here, but the thought pleased him. *Should we increase the odds, maybe? We won't get another chance soon; there'll be too many other people in line for this place. So let's make the most of tonight.*

They made love again, slowly this time, drawing it out as she had long ago taught him to do when helping him develop telepathic power. Before they'd had much sleep it was morning—time for her to go, and for him to fly.

The next evening when he landed, the building committee came to him. "We placed the capstone today," said Nathan. "The hut's ready to occupy, and so tonight we'll let couples draw lots. But we think you and Carla should have it first. Not because you're Captain—I know you wouldn't want it on that basis—but because you've earned everyone's gratitude."

Jesse was deeply touched. "Thanks," he said, "but we're not eligible now. We've had our night of privacy, didn't Carla tell anyone?"

"I did," Carla said, joining them, "but the builders weren't around at the time. We're already set to draw queue positions for the shuttles. With the hut there'll be room for one more couple per night. But I think that the first night it should be offered to Peter."

"Peter?" Nathan exclaimed in surprise. "I didn't know he had a partner."

"Well, I'm guessing," Carla said, "but I don't think he'll turn you down. It might be just the encouragement he needs. Peter's been under an awful strain since before we left Undine. He deserves a break."

"Peter's not shy about asking for what he wants," Liz said dubiously, "and he generally gets it."

"Does he?" A shadow touched Carla's face, and Jesse was suddenly aware that her openness to him last night had not been quite total. A small corner of her mind had not merged with his. Peter was as close as a brother to her; it was possible that he had secrets she had promised him to keep.

To everyone's amazement, Peter took Edris to the hut that night. The next day she was glowing, and at breakfast, for the first time since the landing he seemed to have regained some of his normal ebullience. But Jesse had become too much of a telepath to be fooled, and he knew that the others weren't fooled either. Was it only that the burden of leading a precariously-established settlement weighed heavily on Peter—or had he paired with Edris merely for her sake and that of the children they both owed the colony? No mention had been made of marriage, after all.

The brief celebration was cut off when Dorcas went to the kitchen to check on the day's supplies and came back frowning. "Another water bottle's been spilled," she told Peter. "Let's keep it quiet—people got upset last time. But I made it plain then that whoever did it could speak to me privately without confessing to everybody, and no one has come forward. I don't like it; those large bottles would be awfully hard to knock over accidentally."

"Surely nobody would do such a thing on purpose," Reiko protested. "Aside from the fact that we've always trusted each other, there'd be nothing to gain."

"How well do we know the new recruits?" asked Erik.

"Well enough," Peter said, looking thoughtful. "I've vouched for their integrity by bringing them here."

"Besides," said Carla, "none of them have been near the kitchen since I brought out our breakfast rations, just a few minutes ago, and I was last in line to serve a table. There was no spilled water then."

"If you were last, who has been in there?" Dorcas asked. One person from each table picked up the food for a meal, and since there was no knowing how long the provisions from the pods would have to last, no refills were allowed.

"No one—" began Reiko, puzzled; but she broke off at the sound of a crash. Jesse jumped up and ran to the kitchen. It was deserted. Two more bottles lay on their sides and the floor was littered with ration packs. Yet no one had come out. He'd had his eyes on the doorway the whole time.

Peter and Dorcas joined him. "Are you sure, Jesse?" Peter asked.

Jesse nodded, bewildered. "It doesn't make sense," he said.

"As a matter of fact, it does," Peter replied. "I've half-way expected something like this, but now's not the time to mention it to the Group as a whole. I'll simply announce that I'm on top of the situation and that nobody need worry about it—it will be taken care of. The person involved is not to blame."

That afternoon Peter called the Council together, inviting Dorcas, as chairman of food preparation, to come too. "It's not surprising," he said, "that a group of psi-gifted people under stress would include a poltergeist."

"A what?" Jesse asked.

"A poltergeist. Someone with the psi power to move objects without touching them—but unconsciously, usually without being aware that it's happening."

"Traditionally, poltergeist activity was thought to be caused by ghosts," Reiko said. "But by the twentieth century, the few scientists who took the phenomenon seriously realized that it's a form of psi."

"Ability to move objects with the mind—PK—isn't necessarily unconscious," Hari began.

"No," Peter agreed, "but I assume you're not experimenting with water bottles yourself, Hari. Do you know anybody who might be?"

"We couldn't do it on that large a scale if we wanted to," Hari admitted. "Not yet, anyway."

"We've got more pressing concerns right now than psi experiments," Peter said. "The logical assumption is that this is happening unconsciously, as was fairly common on Earth considering the size of its population. Statistically it would be unlikely to have occurred on Undine. Here, though, we all have psi talent—and we have several likely candidates."

"Doesn't it usually occur among disturbed adolescents?" Kira asked.

"Yes," said Peter, "but Claire is barely past adolescence, and she is certainly disturbed. I suspect she's the one responsible, yet her problems don't seem the sort that would lead to poltergeist activity. It's generally the result of repressed anger, not anxiety."

"Peter," said Carla, "you're shutting your eyes to the obvious! Haven't you noticed that Claire has every reason to be jealous of Edris? She's emotionally dependent on you as a therapist, however hard you've tried to avoid rousing any romantic feelings. And now she sees you're in a relationship with another woman."

Chagrined, Peter admitted, "I suppose that's true."

"Maybe I'd better be the one to talk to Claire," said Kira.

"No, she would interpret it as rejection if I stopped coun-

seling her, and she does need psychiatric help. This isn't
going to go away immediately."

"Do we want it to go away?" Hari demanded. "We're
here to develop as much psi power as we can! If Claire has
latent PK ability, maybe she can learn to channel it."

"We want healthy expressions of psi," Peter declared.
"The last thing we need is to encourage advanced powers in
people who aren't psychologically stable."

It was agreed that he and other Council members would
calm the speculations of the rest of the Group, saying if
pressed that the mysterious spills were caused by a poltergeist but not revealing her identity. A few more minor inci-
dents occurred, but the excitement soon died down.

About two weeks later—weeks according to the Maclairn
calendar that had been adopted, which like Undine's was
based on ten-day intervals—Carla was waiting at the pad
when Jesse brought the shuttle in to land. Not waiting to be
within speaking distance, she told him joyfully, *It's as we
hoped—I'm pregnant!*

No words were needed to express their mutual elation.
When he'd emerged from the ship and she was in his arms,
Carla asked, "Have you thought about what to name him?"

"Not yet," Jesse said, smiling. "It will be awhile before
we know whether we have a son or a daughter, after all."

"We know. Kira says it's a son. She can tell through
psi—through her healer's sense. I can too, actually, though
I got her to confirm it."

"But the baby's body isn't even formed this soon," he
pointed out, puzzled.

"Chromosomes are what determine gender, Jesse."

"You can see the *chromosomes*? Something invisible to
the naked eye?"

"We *know*. Psychic knowing isn't some kind of X-ray vision! Even remote viewing isn't—viewers get visual images
only because that's how the brain interprets the knowledge."

"Well, if it's a son, I'm glad," Jesse said. "As for a name,
do you have any ideas?"

"I think we should name him after Peter," Carla declared. "Kelstrom—Peter's former surname—and Kel for short."

It was fitting. Peter was the nearest thing to a relative she had now, as well as his own closest friend—and for the first child born on Maclairn to be named for the man whose vision had brought them here was surely appropriate. "That's a good name," he agreed. "We'll call him Kel."

19

CARLA WAS SUPREMELY happy at the prospect of bearing a child. On Undine, she'd resigned herself to childlessness, something that had weighed more heavily on her after her union with Jesse than it had before. Natural conception being banned on Undine, the idea of offspring as the fruition of love had died out there; but from Jesse's perspective she had absorbed it, and had felt a sense of incompleteness that only now was being dispelled.

The news of her pregnancy, quickly passed around, bolstered everyone in the colony. Soon a few other women announced that they were expecting, and the postmenopausal women pointed out that unlike those who could conceive naturally, they did not have to wait for an opportunity to have sex. Kira strongly endorsed this view and declared that it was time to begin IVF. Susan, the Group's gynecologist, started giving hormone treatments, while Corrine and another biologist were sent up to the starship to prepare embryos. Not wanting to leave them stranded at night without emergency transportation during the three days the embryos must be monitored prior to freezing, Jesse too stayed over, which gave him a chance to scour the ship for any possibly-useful materials that had been overlooked.

IVF was routine on Undine and involved none of the difficulties it had entailed during its early development on Earth. Embryos could be safely implanted in the small infirmary that had been established at one end of the Commons; the starship's facilities were needed only to produce them. A cryogenic storage unit with a portable power supply was available; it had been used to transport the Group's small DNA bank, consisting of Ian's stored sperm, that of several other men, and the eggs donated shortly before departure by young women members. The only problem was the matter of which women would carry babies fathered by Ian.

Everyone wanted that privilege, both because of Ian's status as Founder and because his very exceptional talents might well appear in the kids. Some younger women who weren't in committed relationships, plus all the lesbians, declared that they should be eligible. This issue proved contentious enough to be taken to the full Council, which decreed that IVF would be reserved for women who could not produce their own eggs. Furthermore, as it had already been decided that the genetic parentage of children conceived in vitro would not be made public, it would not be revealed to the birth mothers themselves. It hadn't been to the host mothers of crèche children on Undine, so this was not a departure from custom, but it was nevertheless a disappointment to many. And there remained the question of how to determine who the fortunate candidates would be.

Carla was too absorbed in her own pregnancy and in her work to pay much attention to this, though her computer access could have told her who was chosen and as a Council member she was entitled to know. Moreover, she was deeply worried about Jesse's health. During the merging of their minds during lovemaking, she had perceived that he was still blaming himself for the colony site's deficiencies and the problems caused by their precipitous landing. His agony over it was largely submerged now; he was too busy to think about it. But that made it all the more dangerous as far as the biochemical effects were concerned. Already he was having backaches, and he was tuning out pain that should be viewed as a warning.

That, of course, was the danger inherent in the Group's ability to experience pain without suffering. It was great to have that ability, and she knew she would be thankful for it during childbirth. But the pain of childbirth was normal and temporary, as was pain from injuries. There was no harm in suppressing it. Pain not caused by physical trauma was another matter. Such pain was a reaction to stress, and stress, if not dealt with, inevitably had health consequences. Peter had never intended to let someone who'd been taught to suppress pain go so long without full mind training. He'd promised to complete Jesse's—but there had been the temperature-control instruction for everyone, plus many cases of people less strong than Jesse whose need of his attention was more obvious.

Obvious, thought Carla, but not as crucial to the colony—if Jesse got sick, its success would be seriously threatened. Peter surely knew that! But Peter's judgment, she felt, was impaired by overwork and emotional involvement. It wouldn't affect his body; Peter had superb control of his physiological functioning and was virtually assured of remaining in perfect health for the rest of his life. But he was as subject to psychological stress as anyone, and his compassion toward the more troubled members, combined with the responsibility he bore for having led them into peril, was wearing on him. Then too, there was the hopelessness of his love for her. . . .

Had she done the right thing by pushing him into a relationship with Edris? she wondered. She'd known he felt mere attraction to Edris, not love. He might never have acted on it if she hadn't seen to it that he was offered an opportunity that would have been awkward to turn down. But she couldn't bear to think of his loneliness. And, to be honest, she'd thought taking a partner might help him forget what he could not have, and thus make her feel less sorrow over the situation she'd unwittingly created.

How long would she be able to keep the truth from Jesse? It had been hard enough during their night together, when it had been all she could do to isolate that one corner of her mind. Once they were able to merge every night, it might not be possible—and yet it *must* be! Jesse wouldn't doubt her faithfulness to him. He'd feel no resentment against Peter, either. But he would grieve, as she did, for Peter was a friend about whose happiness he cared. Knowing that he stood in the way of it would be one more burden than he should have to shoulder.

Peter, of course, had expressed joy about their coming child and had been touched when told that they'd named the boy after him. If he had guessed that this was her acknowledgement of a wish to be two people at once, he hadn't let on. But she hoped he would take it as a sign that she felt more for him than she could ever admit openly.

Because she knew Peter was too fully occupied to take on Jesse's further mind training, Carla decided to consult Kira. Kira wouldn't be able to use techniques that demanded a psychiatrist's skill, but at least she could determine whether any physical damage had already occurred. And she could warn him not to turn off pain without acknowledging its cause.

There were currently no injuries among the settlers that required healing. Kira was now often asked to confirm pregnancies, and would handle some of the prenatal care once there were too many expectant mothers for Susan to examine. She was also helping Peter in the neurofeedback work with the trainees. But her caseload was not large at present and, Carla thought, that was a good thing, because Kira hadn't been looking well lately. She was, after all, over a hundred years old, and though like Peter she was too skilled in controlling her own biochemistry to get sick, it was natural enough that her energy might wane. Surely it was no more serious than that.

Carla sought her in the infirmary, where she usually spent mornings in case someone needed medical advice. To her dismay, Kira was hunched over on the cot, a sick basin in her lap. *Oh my God, Kira,* she cried silently. There was no illness on Maclairn, not that kind of illness. No one had experienced nausea since they'd adjusted to the broth they'd had to drink on awakening from stasis—at least no one but herself and a few other women who'd had bouts of morning sickness. If as powerful a healer as Kira was vomiting, the colony must be facing must be some dreadful new disease.

Kira sat up. "I'm fine," she said. "Sorry you saw this— I'm not suffering, just letting my body adjust."

"Kira," Carla protested, "there's nothing here that should make us sick, not unless you've been holding out on us. As a member of the Council, I have the right to be told what's causing it."

"You do," Kira agreed. "I can't keep it secret much longer in any case. I'm pregnant."

"Pregnant? You?" Carla burst out incredulously. "That's not possible—"

"At my age, you mean? Age has nothing to do with eligibility for IVF. What matters is the condition of the body, and as you know, mine is younger than my years."

True, by outsiders Kira would be assumed to be an exceptionally healthy woman in her sixties. She had a good figure and on Undine had enjoyed sports such as scuba diving as much as anyone. But to raise a family . . .

"Ian lived actively till he was a hundred and thirty,' Kira pointed out, "and when our child is eighteen, I'll be ten years younger than that."

"*Our* child?" Kira, you don't mean you used Ian's sperm yourself?"

"I suppose I'd be thought presumptive and selfish," Kira admitted. "Somebody had to test our makeshift setup here before IVF was offered to others, and since I'm in charge, it had to be me—still I could have used an embryo for which there was less competition. But Carla, I believe I had the right."

Yes, thought Carla, as head of medical procedures she did have the right, but if it ever came out it would be viewed as an abuse of her position. No one in the Group had ever claimed privileges on such a basis. Peter would have considered it unthinkable.

"Peter knows," Kira assured her. "He encouraged me."

"That's—not like him," Carla said weakly. "It's not as if it were your own genes, so that it could be justified on the basis of your psi talents. Who is the genetic mother, by the way?"

"Arwen. The most gifted of our remote viewers. She hasn't been informed, of course; only the Council will ever be told."

"Well, the child should surely be gifted," Carla conceded, "and since psi-bonding in the womb is something we want to encourage, I don't doubt that you're the best one to prove how much effect it can have. But the *right*? Even the Council may not see it that way."

Kira said, "Sit beside me, Carla. This is something I'd prefer to explain to each of you privately—though you can pass it on to Jesse if you wish."

Surprised, Carla sat down. She waited silently.

"I didn't mean that I have the right by virtue of my position in the Group," Kira went on. "I meant that for the past eighty years I have been longing to bear Ian's child, and he once told me that if he were willing to have a child by anyone, it would be me."

"He *told* you that?"

"We were lovers when I was young," Kira said.

"But . . . but—"

"Yes, he was older than I was, thirty years older—not much more than the age difference between Peter and Edris. He was a professor and I was a medical student."

"The relationship was—brief?" Kira had been married during many years of her life, Carla knew, though Ian had never married. Since the founding of the Group, Kira had been one of his closest friends. When he was dying in the hospice she had lived there and cared for him. No one had ever suspected anything more between them.

"It lasted nearly two years," Kira told her. "Ian was over fifty, and he had never found a woman who shared his convictions fully enough to fit into the life he planned. For awhile he thought I might be that woman. He asked me to marry him. But I was young and foolish. I wanted children and he was unwilling to have them, for the reasons the Group always refrained from having them on Undine. Besides that, I was excited about embarking on a medical career, and I didn't think it was necessary to resist Med rule on Undine to the extent that Ian did."

Carla nodded. That part, she had known. Kira had become a cardiologist and had risen high in the Hospital hierarchy before turning against it.

"I loved him," Kira went on, "yet I felt we disagreed on too many important issues. I decided not to marry him, and we broke up. A few years later I married someone else."

"Did you have children, then?"

"One daughter. And it ended just as Ian had said it would. She inherited my psi talents and was too immature to hide them. When I protested against the drugs the Meds were giving her to suppress alleged mental illness, I lost custody. I wasn't even allowed to see her again—they considered me a bad influence. They put her into a crèche when she was six years old."

"Oh, God, Kira. All these years, when we thought we knew you so well—"

"I never told anyone about my former relationship with Ian. The time came when I deeply regretted my marriage, but Ted was a good man and I couldn't bear to hurt him by walking out. I threw myself into my work, and then when Ian formed the Group I agreed to join. He, of course, never let on that there had been anything more than friendship between us. By the time Ted died, to show favoritism would have weakened Ian's mystique. But we went on loving each other till the end of his life."

Carla's head was spinning. *Like me and Peter,* she thought, *but much worse, because above all I want to be with Jesse, whereas Kira stayed with her husband only for his sake....* "Peter knows all this?" she asked.

"Yes, he does now. Though they were as close as father and son, Ian didn't reveal confidential information until the last weeks, when he was turning leadership of the Group over to him."

So Peter, too, was aware of the comparison—aware that even in long-term hopeless love, he was following in Ian's footsteps.... Abruptly Carla cut off the thought, realizing that given her telepathic sensitivity, Kira might pick it up.

Carla, dear—did you think I haven't already picked it up from Peter himself? He doesn't guard his thoughts from me, as he does from the others. He thinks of me as a grandmother.

How long have you known?

Longer than you have. Since soon after Lesley died.

I was blind to it! But if I hadn't been, I wouldn't have been free to marry Jesse ... and it's Jesse I want more than anything! What's wrong with me, that I love Peter too?

"Among us," Kira said aloud, "among telepaths, love is more than physical union. And though the sexual relationship may be exclusive, the psychic one is not, for telepathic affinity can exist with more than just one person. We're going to have to get used to that on this new world, where our aim is to build a culture based on psi. It changes the rules. The mind's capacity for loving communion is infinite. That's something to rejoice in, not mourn."

"You're saying that what I feel for Peter is—okay?" Carla whispered.

"Of course it's okay. One of the great fallacies underlying Earth's culture, in modern times anyway, has been the assumption that all love other than family love must have a sexual expression. Yes, physical attraction exists in most cases, and there's no denying that sex enhances the telepathic bond. But that doesn't mean love isn't real without it, or that love that's not sexually consummated somehow cheats one's chosen mate."

"Yet a physical connection does mean something to you. You've wanted Ian's child, used his sperm now to have his child."

"Because I want to see something of him reflected in my child, as I'm sure I will." Kira smiled. "I've named her Ivana, which is a feminine form of Ian."

As Carla absorbed this, Kira added, "It's also a way of honoring a love that can't be openly expressed. You understand that—why else did you name your son Kelstrom?"

20

FROM THE RIM of the plateau, people watched the fields sprout in the valley below, brilliant green squares against the surrounding yellow-brown rock and the native growth that blended with it. Day by day the new plants grew. They were, of course, genetically engineered to produce a crop much faster than their ancestral species once had on Earth. Growth was facilitated by the fact that there were no weeds; the fertilizer that gave life to terragenic crops was poisonous to the planet's native vegetation. Besides eliminating the work of weeding, this reduced the need for water, since there were no competing roots to soak it up. Nevertheless, the jury-rigged irrigation system provided barely enough— and still there was no rain.

Jesse, looking down on the land daily as he brought the shuttle in, became ever more aware that though surveillance from the starship showed scattered clouds elsewhere in the region, there were none anywhere near the settlement. The planted fields were green dots clustered in the alien desert, an oasis both in the literal sense and as a human refuge. And water was not the only thing on which that oasis depended, he remembered. Just as vital were the robotic machines, without which preparation of farmland would have been impossible. Most members of the Group took the robots for granted; they had never lived on a world without them. Neither had he, but his experience was wide enough to make him uncomfortably aware of how vulnerable they were to wear and damage.

He worried about this when he had time to think about it. The content of the pods had been chosen to provide for emergencies; it had never been intended to serve the ongoing needs of a permanent colony. Fleet had expected that settlers stranded on an unopened world would eventually be found and that supply ships would be sent. The Group had deliberately picked a planet on which they would not be found. They had gambled on its being a world that would support them. Ian and Peter had, of course, known that some worlds might lack the resources needed to establish industry, but they had considered the chance of not being stuck on such a world worth taking. The few other members knowledgeable about technology had gone along, as had Jesse himself. In the first weeks after landing, they had been so thankful to have gotten to the surface safely and arranged for food and shelter that they had ignored the long-term problems. But now, it was becoming clear that survival on Maclairn would be very, very dicey.

Given enough water, crops could feed an expanding population indefinitely. But food alone could not meet the colony's needs. There must also be fiber crops and trees. With wood, it would be possible to construct any number of things that had bootstrapped civilization on ancient Earth— such things as looms, molds for clay pipe manufacture, and the shoring of mines. Wood was also essential to provide charcoal for smelting. Mineral deposits nearby were adequate, that having been the basis on which Jesse had chosen the site. But could enough metal be gotten out of the ground and put to use before the robots gave out?

"Machines were made on Earth as far back as the Iron Age, centuries ago," said Carla when he expressed this concern. "Originally, didn't people mine iron with stone tools?"

"Yes, but consider the time frame," Jesse said. "On Earth, people lived off the land. Farming wasn't dependent

on machines and so it didn't matter that industry was developed slowly, over generations. We have to do it much
faster. And trees require a lot more water than grain does—
which may be why this planet doesn't have any native ones."

He did not discuss his doubts with Peter, who had other
things to worry about. Peter had delegated responsibility
for the physical welfare of the colony to him. He was determined to bear it without complaint. That was the least he
could do, considering that he was the one whose miscalcula-
tions had brought them to this pass. In any case, he would
put off mentioning the dwindling water supply until the
Group's new recruits completed their mind training, after
which Peter would be freer to consider it.

That time was almost at hand, and the Council began
making plans for the Ritual—in fact for six Rituals, spread
over several weeks, as it would be too risky to handle fire
with more than one inexperienced person at a time. Unlike
past recruits, these were partially aware of what the occasion involved, since they had of necessity been present during the Ritual held aboard the starship. But they had been
blindfolded to keep them from seeing what was really happening. No novice given time to contemplate in advance
would be capable of thrusting a hand into flame—the courage to do so depended on unquestioning trust in one's teachers and in one's own mind power, as well as on the combined telepathic support of all those present. That support
was sufficiently strong only in the moment when the whole
assembly touched the flame of candles. Which presented a
problem, because there were not enough candle stubs left
for even one Ritual, let alone six.

"We never had the whole Group together at the Lodge,"
Reiko pointed out. "Sometimes no more than about fifty
people came to an initiation. So giving candles to only fifty
each time should be okay."

"The rest will feel excluded," said Kira. "The Ritual is
for participation, unity—to turn members into mere observ-
ers will ruin it."

"It's either that or not allow anyone but the candle-bearers to attend," Peter said, "and that would be worse. The nonparticipants will be carried along. The strong telepaths will feel the flame physically even if they don't personally touch it, you know."

"There's that," Kira agreed. "A telepath who panicked could even be burned that way, just as much as with a candle."

"Which is why it's up to those of us with the torch to see that no one does panic."

And mainly, thought Jesse, it was up to Peter. The Ritual was extremely demanding for the leader, who must hold all minds in focus, at the same time giving power to the novice and protecting him or her from harm. To preside six times in close succession would drain Peter. As usual, he was asking more of himself than anyone should have to go through—especially considering that one of the novices was Edris.

"If we've no new candles," inquired Hari, "what are we going to use for a torch?"

Aboard the starship, they had used a makeshift torch, a cluster of candles bound to a rod. But tall candles, not stubs, would be required for that. "Surely we've got something that will burn," Teresa said. "Cloth of some kind, maybe."

"Yes," Kwame agreed, "but a wad of cloth won't produce an open flame unless it's soaked in oil, and we don't have any oil."

For a moment everyone was stumped. Then Jesse said, "How about alcohol?"

"We don't have that either, do we?"

"We can make it. There's bound to be some local plant we can distill. It wouldn't be safe to drink, but it would burn."

And so Corrine was asked to analyze the native succulents, while Tomas was assigned the task of searching the knowledgebase for instructions on building a still. Jesse retrieved a boiler from the starship's galley and pipes from its plumbing. Alcohol for fuel would have many future uses besides making torches, he realized.

The other problem that had to be solved was where to hold the rites. On Undine, it had been done in the Lodge, around the central fireplace, for which there could be no substitute. There was scarcely room in the Commons, and besides, a prefab shelter would offer no aura of solemnity. After some discussion, Peter decided that by now nearly everyone had enough training in temperature control to make an assembly outdoors without shade feasible, provided it began as the sun was setting and was over before the night wind rose. "We'll be challenged to maintain our body temperature while also dealing with flame," he said, "and the strongest among us will have to carry the less experienced ones along. But in the Ritual, stimulation of telepathic support ties will be a good thing."

If three hundred people gathered on flat ground, however, most would not be able to see what was going on. So it was decided to have the robots build an assembly ring between the two shuttle pads, semicircular and graded into tiers with a dais on the open side. This would serve for all general meetings of the Group, as well as in years to come when it would be needed for the Rituals of their adolescent children; and with the latter use in mind, it was made larger than necessary for the present population. Framed by the shuttles, a symbol of the migration to a new world, it turned out to provide a surprisingly impressive atmosphere.

The Rituals went smoothly, and everyone was elated by the experience, as always. Apart from Peter, with Hari and Kira alternating as his backup, only the novices' personal sponsors were full participants—the plunging of a hand into fire was not something to repeat often. Nevertheless, the rite raised Jesse's spirits. *"We are stewards of a flame that will illuminate future generations. And we now seal our commitment with the symbol of the mind's power, which is fire."* At that moment, as he touched the flame of his candle, he was linked with all of them, a part of something noble and worthwhile; and for a time afterward he did not worry about whether or not he was to blame for any of their problems.

They were all in it together, pledged to each other, and nobody thought any less of him because of what had happened. He felt, albeit briefly, that there was no need to think less of himself.

But two nights later he awoke in pain again, and though he subdued it, he was aware that it was not going to stop coming. He was tired, not from physical effort—he hadn't been doing as backbreaking work as the hut-builders—but simply from the strain of being in charge of the Group's survival. That they still trusted him despite his failures made it worse. By now everyone was concerned about the lack of rain, but they had faith that the irrigation system would keep working. What if it didn't? He had no more control over that than over the weather, yet if the crop failed, if they all starved—now or later—he would never know that the lack of time for choosing a site had not been the deciding factor.

The next afternoon when he landed, bearing scrap metal gleaned from the starship, Peter was waiting at the pad. "We've not had much chance to talk privately lately," he said. "I had to concentrate on the trainees. I neglected you and I'm sorry, Jess—but I knew you were strong enough to manage on your own. Don't think I'm not aware of the load you've been carrying."

"Are you aware that whatever I manage to accomplish may not do any good?"

"Yes. We're in the hands of fate, all of us. This may not be a place where we can survive. And yet I don't believe that it's not. Ian's dream led us here—"

"Not to this particular site. That was my doing."

"Was it?" Peter sat down in the shade of the shuttle and motioned for Jesse to join him. "We can as easily say it was Arwen's doing, for having viewed this place remotely, or that it was mine, for delegating the choice to you. But I realize that you can't see it that way. And the responsibility for not helping you deal with such feelings is definitely mine."

"Well, Peter, I'm dealing with them in the only way I

can. Nothing you could have said would have made it easier."

"No, but I could have taught you how to avoid physical effects from them." At Jesse's startled look he went on, "Yes, I know about the backaches; I'm a telepath, after all, and you are not shielding your mind from me. But it wouldn't matter if you were. Everyone suffers physical effects from guilt feelings, Jess—it's a major cause of stress-based illness. The particular symptoms stress produces depend not only on genetic predisposition but on the collective unconscious of a society, and you grew up in one where back pain was prevalent."

Jesse swallowed his impulse to deny this idea. "I wasn't entirely honest with you," Peter continued. "I led you to believe you were protected just from being able to deal with fear. Yet normally, our trainees go through a second phase of training."

Surprised, Jesse asked, "Why didn't I, then?"

"Because I needed you to be Captain, and I didn't want to upset you in a way that would interfere. Unfortunately we can't start it now, either. You are indispensable in the job you're doing, and I can't risk losing you even briefly."

"Does it—this training—take up that much time?"

"Not time, but it affects emotional stability. You would come through okay, but your ability to work might be temporarily lessened. You'd feel worse, for awhile, than you do now."

Jesse bit his lip. "You're admitting that I do have a cause to feel guilty."

"Only a more immediate cause than in the past. Everybody feels guilty, even without knowing why—it's part of being human."

"Peter," Jesse declared, "that's hogwash! You sound as if you're defending the old notion of original sin! It's contrary to everything you've always believed about human nature."

"I'm not saying everyone's guilt feelings are warranted. The point is that they exist even when unwarranted, which is how the concept of original sin arose. It's a protective mechanism. None of us escape it, but we in the Group can control our physiological response to the stress. Otherwise we'd end up with serious illnesses sooner or later, as do the majority of people on Earth and on Undine."

Skeptically Jesse argued, "Kira once told me that people get physically sick from stress because tired, stressed-out cavemen lived longer, and passed on more genes, if they didn't feel well enough to go hunting for predators. I understand that. But she was referring to natural stress resulting from fear. Fear is protective because there were a lot of real dangers in the prehistoric world that cavemen needed to avoid. What's protective about guilt, short of it being an advantage to the species for people to feel guilty over things like murder?"

"It's an unavoidable result of volition, which enabled us to evolve into human beings," Peter said. "Volition means making choices. If there were no emotionally unpleasant consequences for bad choices about minor things, humans could not learn to make decisions about major ones. Any parent who has raised a child knows this. Psychologists have therefore often blamed early upbringing for the guilt feelings of adults. But it goes much deeper than that. It is built into us, into our genes, because early humans who didn't learn to choose carefully often died young."

That made sense. "Is it like the evolutionary origin of physical pain, then? Like learning not to touch a hot stove because that hurts?"

"Not usually. Most choices don't produce direct physical harm."

Jesse frowned. "Sickness preventing an unfit caveman from fighting is one thing," he protested. "But what good would later illness do primitive humans? They wouldn't connect it with choices they'd made earlier. Neither do we, usually."

"It's more complicated," Peter agreed. "Guilt feelings in themselves merely cause emotional pain. But emotional pain is stress, and stress produces physiological reactions in your body that over time, lead to illness. Getting sick from that is a side effect, not a benefit. And it usually doesn't happen until people are long past childbearing age, which is why natural selection didn't counter it."

"So you teach us not to feel emotional pain over our mistakes."

"Of course not. Is that how we handle fear?"

Well, no. The idea had always been to experience the fear consciously instead of shrinking from it—to accept the physiological responses and alter them. That was what neurofeedback training enabled people to do. "I suppose you mean we shouldn't suppress guilt," he said. "But I *don't* suppress it, Peter, and that doesn't prevent backaches, if feeling guilty is what's causing them."

"That's because you're not yet aware of your body's biochemical reactions at the time they occur. In the case of fear, they were obvious. They're more complex with guilt feelings and harder for us to induce in a way you can recognize—and they continue, so that you have to deal with them constantly over a long period. It's hard, Jess, but it's worth it, because that is what prevents not only illness, but aging. You haven't thought you'd age more slowly just from controlling your body at moments when you were worried or afraid, have you?"

"I've never really believed that," Jesse confessed. "But the rest of you don't age—"

"Because we've all learned this additional skill. It requires facing and reexperiencing all the little things you ever felt guilty about, even during early childhood. It takes altered states of conscious to recall them. Psychiatrists who recognized that suppression can lead to illness were using hypnosis for such purposes way back in the twentieth century, but they often did more harm than good. They aimed to make their patients *not* feel guilty about the past, which is counterproductive as well as impossible—people ended up feeling guilty *about* feeling guilty, as if it were some sort of abnormality. And that just compounded their problems."

"You're saying, then, that I'm going to age at the natural rate after all." Jesse felt a rush of disappointment, despite not having been convinced that he'd stay young.

"For the time being. But there are plenty of years ahead to change that. Kira was older than you are now when she learned. So were Ian's contemporaries."

There might not be any years ahead, Jesse thought ruefully. But then, if they all died soon, his rate of aging wouldn't matter. "Peter," he said slowly, "It's all very well for you to say we can learn to not be affected by guilt that's not warranted. But after all, you've never failed in anything more important than the little things you say bother everybody. You don't really know how it feels."

"Oh, Jess. Is that what you think?" Peter turned to him sorrowfully, continuing silently, *I was responsible for seven deaths in stasis—I induced those people to come. I'll be no less responsible than you if everyone dies here. I was indirectly to blame for Valerie's suicide on Undine, and she was hardly the only patient with whom I failed. I gave many of them, including you, damaging drugs, which haunts me even though it was to prevent worse harm being done to them by other doctors. On top of that, there are things I can't ever tell anyone because it would hurt those involved. Not just results I didn't intend, but wishes I'm ashamed of. . . .*

On the verge of protest, Jesse held back. Peter did not want to be talked out of such feelings any more than he himself did. And if Peter—the most admirable man he had ever known—was harboring them, it must be true that they were universal.

21

A FEW DAYS later, Jesse was eating breakfast when Teresa burst into the Commons, obviously more upset than she was allowing herself to show. "Jesse," she said breathlessly, "there are—*creatures* on the farm! Big creatures, like the crawlies, only huge—"

Oh, God, thought Jesse. They had not seen any animal lifeforms other than the crawlies and he had begun to be confident that there were none. If these posed a danger, they might be in big trouble. "I'll come and take a look," he said. "How many are there?"

"I saw four or five near the pond."

He and Peter, along with Corrine and several others who were free, hiked down to the valley. The creatures were indeed like the crawlies, and they were indeed huge—longer than a man's arm and shaped like twelve-legged toads. Blackish, spidery toads. "It's a good thing we were desensitized," murmured Corrine. "Otherwise, from what I've heard of how people react on Earth, we'd be having screaming hysterics."

"They're certainly related to the crawlies," Jesse said, realizing that they probably *were* crawlies, full-grown. "So are they harmless?"

"They're not actually poisonous. But I don't know, Jesse—the crawlies gave us red welts. Touching any this big might produce serious skin burns."

"Well, it's not as if we couldn't heal burns," said Peter. "What worries me more is what they'll do to our crop."

"They won't eat plants alien to their biology."

"No, but their sheer weight may crush the stalks. There were a lot of crawlies, evidently newly hatched. Even a small percentage of them loose in a field—"

"It's worse than that," Jesse declared. "If they get into the grain, it may poison us. The fact that skin contact isn't poisonous doesn't mean their excretions are safe to eat."

"Oh, God. What are we going to do?" Teresa said. "If more come we can't possibly chase them all off."

"We can't take a chance with any plants they touch," said Jesse. "They'll have to be buried. As for the creatures, I hate to say it, but we've no choice but to kill them."

Everyone gasped. Killing was not part of Undine's culture; since there had been no animals there, murder was the only form of it they knew. "How can we?" Corrine protested.

"It's not going to be easy if there are very many," Jesse said, "because we'll have to post guards and the fields are too big to patrol reliably. We may lose part of the crop. But it's the only thing we can try."

"I mean, how can we go about killing them? What would we use for weapons?"

"Oh. Well—" He drew breath; it had to be said. "There are guns aboard the starship." Guns were prohibited on Undine; none had ever been imported. The mere mention of them was taboo. He had told Peter alone that he had access to those in the captain's locker. And of course, he was the only person who knew how to handle a gun. All guards could do was spot the creatures and call him, yet he could hardly be on patrol all day and all night.

That day he went up to the ship and examined the guns available. A colonizer was not heavily armed; unlike a freighter, which might have to defend its cargo against pirates, it was provided with only a few sidearms, locked away. He had checked before the hijacking to be sure *Mayflower XI*'s officers would not be carrying them. There was no point in taking more than one, he decided, as they'd be less protective than dangerous in the hands of untrained people. He chose a laser gun rather than a firearm. It needed no ammunition, could be set at low intensity if that proved sufficient, and might also prove useful as a cutting tool.

A watch had been set up, but no crawlies had been seen to enter the fields; the few that were visible remained in or near the shrinking puddle that had been the pond. "I think they must stay underground during the dry season," Corrine reported. "Perhaps it's drier than usual now and they're being driven out by thirst. But they haven't gone near the farmland. Let's hope our plants are not only inedible but repellent to them."

Taking no chances, Jesse used the laser to dispatch those in evidence, creating a ghastly mess that Dan grimly helped him bury. As dusk came on, more men came down to stand guard, checking the perimeters of the fields with flashlights throughout the night with Jesse on alert. No crawlies appeared. So it was decided that since he could not stay up all night every night, they should simply inspect the crop regularly and destroy any plants that were crushed. None were found, but he continued to carry the laser gun when he visited the valley, just in case.

The colony had settled into a routine and expansion of its resources was underway. During the interval between planting and harvesting, the robots had been put to work excavating a copper mine in the nearby foothills of the mountains. The location of the richest ore had been determined from orbit, so all that needed doing, for the present, was to dig it out. The mining of iron would have to await availability of charcoal for smelting, but copper would be more immediately useful in any case; it was easily worked and could be used for many things besides the wire badly needed to transmit power. Materials, not power itself, were the limiting factor in the colony. The settlement's ongoing need for power could be met by wind turbines, while beamed power for use in industry would be available from the starship for many years.

The building of the stone huts was going more quickly now that the method was well established, and enough were finished to enable most couples to spend two nights a week in private. In their spare time people were gathering the native grass-like plants and rushes to weave into mats, sandals, baskets, and baby cradles, as well as small tables and other furnishings for use when permanent quarters became available. The plan was for a hut to be given to each woman, with or without a partner, upon the birth of her first child.

Hari and his close friends still sat apart from the others when not working with the builders, their hands busy with mat-weaving but their minds seemingly far away—although Hari himself spent a good deal of time with a textreader. He had been a university professor on Undine, Jesse recalled. He had taught anthropology and had been considered an expert on the shamanic practices of Earth's ancient cultures. Did he regret the choice that had led him to a new world he did not really want to settle? Would he have been happier continuing in his old life? If so, he never said so. He was simply . . . aloof, as if his surroundings were not worthy of notice. In Council meetings he was generally silent; but he was adept in remote viewing, and in the Ritual his telepathic power was strong.

Peter, now that the initial training of the novices and temperature-control instruction was complete, began to take more part in the ongoing social life of the settlement. He was still concerned about Claire, who caused no more poltergeist disturbances but walked around in a dream much of the time, and several of the others who did not seem to be adjusting well; but they no longer absorbed as much of his time and attention. He seemed more relaxed during meals, and even to have regained some of the boyish sparkle so characteristic of him in the old days, the days at the Lodge when Jesse had first known him.

Edris was pregnant. Perhaps, Jesse thought, excitement about becoming a dad had distracted Peter from the burdensome side of serving as father-figure to the whole Group. He himself found it awesome. Carla's pregnancy was visible now, and day by day his awareness grew of the child developing within her. Their son . . . before long they would be a family. It would mean a tremendous change not only in their lives but in the settlement's; he could not quite picture how it was going to be when there were infants to care for. No doubt there would be problems. Nevertheless, he was looking forward to it.

The arrival of kids would bring renewed focus on the colony's purpose, Carla said. "We wanted to build a new culture," she reflected, "but now that we're here, it's just— ordinary. We've escaped from Med tyranny and we don't have to worry about arrest anymore, and of course we're freer to talk about the things that matter to us without looking over our shoulders. But we always did use telepathy between ourselves and heal our own physical problems, and now it's no different as far as psi is concerned. Teaching kids our ways, we'll be making real progress toward the future. Toward a society that will demonstrate human potential."

Yes, Jesse thought, when their descendants were discovered, as was being prearranged by Ian's friend on Earth. That wouldn't happen until the distant future, after there'd been time for a new society to develop. And it was true that as far as their own lives were concerned, something had been missing so far. The Group had given up all former comforts in favor of hard, monotonous work—manual labor in many cases—and there was not a lot to show for it. A few prefab shelters, a few stone huts, set in the middle of a desolate plateau far from the now-fertile fields necessary to life . . . mere survival was of course an accomplishment, but in itself, it could never be a fully satisfying one. Simply being with good friends was a less central source of pleasure when you were with them constantly, all day and all night, than when you could meet them only in safe houses.

One evening they tried building a fire to gather around by piling native brush in a circle of stones, but it didn't last long enough to be of much use. For a few minutes, though, sparks rose into the dark sky and Jesse remembered beach fires on the Island, sitting with his arm around Carla while they sang old ballads passed down from ancient Earth. And, touching the minds of the others, he was aware that they all remembered, and mourned the things that were lost forever, even while they rejoiced in the thought of the things that would someday come.

22

SO FAR NO one had been seriously worried by the lack of rain. Drought was outside the settlers' experience. They had come from a water world dotted by small islands, where water for farms had been piped from the desalination plants.

Rain had not been a matter of concern there and had attracted little notice. No Group member had any technical knowledge of meteorology, but surveys from the starship—plus the existence of native vegetation—showed that Maclairn was not totally dry. Jesse had seen clouds in the region from orbit. That they might fail to provide water before the crop died was inconceivable.

But as harvesttime approached, people started getting nervous. The plants in the fields grew tall and set grain—and then began to yellow, not the warm yellow of ripening, but the faded hue of drying leaves. A day arrived when it became evident that if no rain fell within the week, they would wilt.

The Council, in dismay, sat silent; nobody knew what to say. Even Peter was at a loss for words. There was no use talking about more irrigation; the river was down to a mere trickle and the water wheel that powered the pump would no longer turn. The ditches had run dry. "How long will our stores last if we lose this crop?" Kira asked, finally bringing into the open what till now they'd not dared to think about.

Jesse was familiar with the inventory of stores. "Long enough to raise one more," he said, "if we allocate food carefully. We'll need to have rationing."

Kira frowned. "That won't save a lot when so many of the women are pregnant. Our unborn children must be nourished."

Jesse . . . is there really danger to the babies—to Kel? Carla questioned.

Yes, but we'll deal with it. The men will go hungry, if necessary.

It was at this point that Hari spoke up. "There are clouds," he said. "I've seen them through remote viewing. So have some of the others—we've been searching for them."

"I've seen them too, from the shuttle," Jesse said. "That doesn't help much, since we can't control the wind."

"The shamans of ancient cultures could bring rain," Hari said. "In dry regions rainmaking was very common. And even in modern times, a few individuals on Earth had the gift for it. Communities used to hire them, and it paid off."

"But rainmakers were frauds, weren't they?" said Kwame. "When rain did fall through their apparent efforts, it was just coincidence."

"Some were frauds. Not all of them. The ancient shamans and the witches of medieval times certainly weren't. Plenty of cultures depended on rainmaking ceremonies. In some years rain would have fallen anyway, but in others they'd have starved if they'd taken no action."

"How is that possible?" protested Dan. "There's just no way—"

"How is remote viewing possible? For that matter, how is healing accomplished, or telepathy? We have staked everything on our belief in psi powers. We came here to develop new ones—new to us, anyway. It's time we started doing it."

"Are you saying that rainmaking is simply another psi power, Hari?" Teresa asked. "A power we can actually use?"

"I don't know if we can do it. I believe we should try."

"But how? They performed rain dances—I've seen that in vids," Jesse said. "You can't tell me that dancing to the beat of drums really has an effect on the weather."

"Of course it doesn't," Peter agreed. "The dance and the imagery used are simply metaphors, just like the many other traditional metaphors that we know represent underlying concepts. The drums do have an effect, but as an aid to entering altered states of consciousness—what we ourselves do with neurofeedback instead of sound."

"Then there's some altered state for making it rain?"

"Possibly. Not a state specifically for that, but altered consciousness is certainly involved," said Peter slowly. "I had not given any thought to rainmaking, but Hari is right. It was sometimes done successfully, and has long been recognized as a form of psi—of PK, psychokinesis."

"We've attempted psychokinesis in the past, and none of us have gotten anywhere with it," Reiko said.

"Yet we know that it's real, and that some individuals did develop it on Earth."

"What's psychokinesis?" asked Jesse, who had never heard the term before.

"Affecting matter by mind alone—the poltergeist activity is just one form of it. Actually fire handling, and even some forms of healing, may involve PK. But the term usually refers to moving objects."

"People did this? Not just unconsciously, like Claire?"

"Oh, yes. But the talent is much rarer than those we've been using in the Group."

"I'm not so sure that it's as rare as we've assumed," said Hari.

"I know you've always believed it's not," Peter replied. "But Ian didn't have it, and you've never succeeded in achieving it yourself."

"It demands emotional pressure, like all the other things," Hari argued. "We've never been under the right kind of pressure before. We are now."

"Ian *did* have it," said Kwame, "if you count fire handling. And that means we all do."

"That's true," Peter said thoughtfully. "The reason fire handling works is that it *has* to work—when we put our hands in fire we don't stop to question whether it will or not, and our minds don't wander. We're not distracted by stray thoughts because we know, even at the unconscious level, that we'd be burned if we let that happen. The emotional pressure is overwhelming, far greater than anything we feel when we're just experimenting with psi."

"But that comes instinctively from the unconscious mind," Carla said. "We know, logically and consciously, that our survival depends on rain—but would the instinct that maintains our minds' focus be operative during a rainmaking ceremony?"

"Probably not," said Kira. "I suspect that shamans were supported by a tradition that went back generation upon generation—concepts perceived in metaphorical form that were well established in the collective unconscious. And there must have been telepathy involved during shamanic training, just as our own mind training depends on telepathy."

"It had to start with somebody in each locality, though," Teresa pointed out.

"Yes, and occasionally individuals in industrial cultures did learn to do it," Hari declared.

"They'd often received instruction from a shaman," said Peter. "Telepathy must have been responsible for that, too. So the question is whether we can transfer our capabilities to a new use merely on the basis of our past experience with psi. Hari, have you any idea how to go about it?"

"I suggest that we start with remote viewing—see the clouds, and then reach out with our minds, draw them to us. And visualize the rain, which is a technique some shamans used apart from community rain dances. That's all most of our people can do. But it may take something more on the part of those of us with advanced training."

Hari and Peter exchanged glances. "You're thinking we'll need to go where the clouds are," Peter said, nodding.

"Good God, Peter, that could be risky," Kira protested.

"We knew when we came here we would have to take some risks with psi. This is not a large one, and only a few of the most experienced people will be involved."

"*You* will be involved. We can't afford to have you mixed up in rash experiments."

"Can we afford to lose the crop to drought if there's a way we can try to save it?"

Peter, you mustn't! Ian warned you— Carla's plea came through clearly to Jesse; she wasn't shielding it from him, though it was directed to Peter.

He didn't mean I should hide from risk, Peter responded. *He was urging me to meet it with courage.*

Why would he? When have you ever done anything else?

Jesse frowned. The others all seemed to understand what was being proposed, and he was uncomfortable with his own ignorance. He had always known there were things going on in the Group of which he hadn't been informed, esoteric things that Peter felt he wasn't ready to learn about. But he was second in command now, and for this particular risk he'd be doubly responsible. "The only way to get where the clouds are is in a shuttle," he said. "I'm not ready to take it into a storm with you aboard, Peter—we agreed you and I should never fly at the same time in any case, and Anne isn't qualified to fly through storms."

Peter turned to him. "We won't physically fly," he said. "We're talking about going in our minds, the way I once told you I went to bring back Claire."

"You mean, with your mind somehow separate from your body?" Jesse asked incredulously.

"Yes. It's an altered state of consciousness that some-times occurs spontaneously, as it did with you and Carla when you went into stasis. Throughout history, people have learned to enter it intentionally, and that's easier for us because we know the mind-pattern for it—we learn it through neurofeedback. In itself it's not at all dangerous."

"Not in itself," Kira agreed. "But in the Group we've just been traveling around places familiar to us, leaving our bodies behind to see them from a different perspective, some-times from above. Shamans made prolonged, terrifying jour-neys into unknown regions. They interacted with natural forces we don't know how to deal with, certainly not on a planet alien to us in the middle of a storm. The trauma could have physical effects."

"I don't see how just imagining something in your mind—"

"Of course you do, Jesse," Kira reminded him. "Haven't we taught you from day one that your mind does affect your body?"

"It's more than imagining," Peter said. "Out-of-body experiences are akin to remote viewing—we see real places that we could not see with our physical eyes. The difference is that we perceive ourselves as actually being there. And though we cannot touch physical objects with the body we perceive, Hari is suggesting that in that state we may be able to use PK to move them."

"Move the clouds to our valley?"

"Yes, and if necessary condense the moisture in them so that rain will fall."

It was clear that the more Peter considered this idea, the more promising it seemed to him, Jesse thought nervously. He himself was dismayed by it. The underlying fear of psi that had plagued him during his training was rushing back. It wasn't possible that people could, or should, move out of their bodies! Yet apparently they believed they'd been doing it, and as for unlikely possibilities . . . Hari and his friends had located water for the well.

"Are we agreed that we should attempt this?" Peter asked the Council. "Through remote viewing and visualization mainly, but with a few of us, not including any of the pregnant women, going further?"

Everyone assented, with Jesse, despite his reluctance, relying on his trust in Peter's judgment. Thank God that Carla wouldn't be eligible, he thought; he knew she would have followed Peter anywhere if given a chance.

At sunset that evening the Group gathered in the assembly ring, hushed and expectant. On the dais a few people sat in a semicircle: Hari, Arwen, and several others, plus Kira to monitor the physical well-being of those whose minds left their bodies. Peter alone was standing. He would use his charismatic power, Jesse knew—he would telepathically stir the assembly as he had on the night of the firewalk, at Ian's funeral, and during the Ritual aboard the starship. His voice was low even when amplified by the wireless mike he held, but few needed to hear words.

"This is a time when everything depends on the merging of our minds," Peter said. "No one of us has the power to do what must be done if we're to survive. We are not trained shamans, and it's likely that even the best shamans could not have brought rain without the active backing their people unconsciously provided. Often the rainmaking ceremony was a religious one. The people needed rain for sustenance, and they prayed for it. I ask those of you to whom that concept is meaningful to pray. But whether or not you view it as prayer, I ask you to reach out with your minds to a higher power. Let it show you the clouds. Even if you're unable to view them remotely, visualize rain falling from those clouds, water touching your skin, the dampness of the earth beneath your feet. . . ."

There should be a chant or a song of some sort, he and Hari had agreed earlier. But none of the songs known to the Group would fit. So they had settled for recorded electronic music such as was used during the Ritual and had often been played at the Lodge. As always, Jesse soared at the sound of it. He surrendered to the beat, not thinking, conscious only of the warmth of Carla beside him and the touch of her mind, of many minds, rising into the clear sky, reaching, searching for the soft clouds that lay somewhere beyond his sight, clouds dripping moisture onto the thirsty ground, wet puddles soaking into it, his arms and his face wet with the welcome rain. . . .

He lost track of time. Then all at once he was aware that Peter was no longer speaking, had not said anything aloud for some time. The music had stopped. Peter, on the dais, was scrambling to his feet beside Hari, who lay trancebound beside him, with Kira kneeling to grasp his hand. The others around them seemed somewhat dazed.

Overhead, the sky was clear. But above the mountains a few wispy white clouds were forming.

23

IT DID NOT rain that night and the clouds came no nearer. "But I was there, surrounded by them," Peter said. "And they swirled around me, not randomly but as if I had some control."

"Was it frightening?" Teresa inquired.

"No. It was joyous—I felt free, as if I were one with the wind and the sky and could float there forever, that I need never be tied to a planet's surface again—"

Kira frowned. "That's the danger," she said.

"Don't worry," Peter reassured her. "I didn't forget my responsibilities. I could have gone farther, much farther, but I knew better than to do it."

Hari had remained in trance longer than the others, and they'd found it hard to revive him. "You shouldn't have gone without a prearranged signal to bring you back," Kira told him, shaking her head over his still-evident pallor. "What's more, I think you went farther than you should have without guidance."

"There's no one here to guide us," Hari said. "We do what we must to save our people."

Peter met his eyes. "I saw clouds," he said. "But I think perhaps you saw something more."

"An old shaman, white-haired, stepping out of the thunderclouds to greet me. He was dressed as they dressed on ancient Earth, but he had Ian's face. He sent me back to help us try again."

Jesse's skin prickled. He and Peter had both seen Ian after his death, when they had need to. But Peter had said that it was not a ghost, that it had happened simply because everyone's unconscious mind contained an image that symbolized wisdom.

"The human mind tends to perceive concepts in personified form," Peter agreed. "Traditionally, shamans and other out-of-body travelers have met spirits in human or animal form, and have been given advice by them. We are less apt to because we grew up on Undine, which does not have the collective unconscious rich in metaphor that on Earth was built up over thousands of years. But you, Hari, have been steeped in those metaphors through your long study of Earth's cultures. It's natural that you'd meet them when free of your body."

"Be that as it may, we failed," said Hari. "Yet we found

that we *can* have some effect on the clouds. We must keep on, over and over if necessary—"

"I don't believe that will be enough," Peter declared. "I spent most the night reading up on the ancient customs. I think I know what went wrong, and how we can overcome it."

The Council, encouraged, waited for him to continue. "We know that rainmaking depended heavily on metaphor," he said. "A few shamans could bring rain just by visualization, but in most cultures they led traditional ceremonies that produced not only the intense focus of all participants, but full commitment to the effort based on a belief that life and death depended on it. Not just a rational belief that the crops would die if it didn't rain. An emotional conviction that failure to perform the ceremony successfully would upset the proper order of the universe they knew. That it would call down the wrath of the gods, a metaphor for disaster, often fatal disaster."

"But Peter, such ceremonies involved symbols that acquired meaning over many generations," Reiko said. "They weren't created suddenly to meet the occasion, as we must create ours."

"That's true. But there were universal elements, and one of them—at least before a ceremony became routine and outworn—was that the stakes in the event itself were high. Usually it involved sacrifice. The sacrifice of animals to appease the gods was very common, in rainmaking ceremonies as well as on other occasions. Some cultures even practiced human sacrifice; the Aztecs sacrificed victims to the rain god."

"Well, we can hardly—"

"Of course not. Blood sacrifice isn't the point. The point is that there was a cost to making rain, or at least risk of a cost. For example, in the Hopi Indian rain dance, the dancers carried poisonous snakes. Risk enhances all psi, as we have said many times. Furthermore, humans have always known underneath that changing the natural course of things isn't free. We didn't succeed because we assumed it *was* free—that we could just sit back and visualize such a change, or attempt to hasten it, without any significant risk to ourselves. Because our unconscious minds did not believe that, the psi forces they released had little power."

"If that's true," Reiko said, "there's no way we can change it. You and Hari, and the others who went out of their bodies, took the only risk there is to take—and as you said beforehand, it was not a large one. I doubt if the ancients, short of those that practiced human sacrifice, paid much either. Those that sacrificed animals usually feasted on them afterward. The sacrifice, or the risk of it, was purely symbolic, and symbols can't be manufactured out of thin air. Their meaning is absorbed over a long period of time."

"I'm afraid Reiko is right," Hari agreed. "Symbols acquire the power to arouse awe at some time when there's a real connection with risk, and the unconscious association clings to them. They are sanctified by tradition. We have no such symbol."

"But we do," said Peter. "We have the Ritual."

Startled, everyone stared at him. The Ritual was the closest thing to a sacred rite that could exist outside of a formal religion; the idea of using it for a practical purpose seemed almost blasphemous.

"As I said yesterday, the Ritual works because we know we'd be burned if it didn't," Peter went on. "Every one of us has had the experience of thrusting a hand into flame with full knowledge that to lose focus would mean serious injury. And that association does cling. It is passed on from person to person, from one year to the next—the onlookers who touch only candle flame are as committed to what they're doing as the full participants. They are thrust into altered consciousness. So far we've used that state only to overcome our own fear and to aid the novice who needs our support. We can do more with it, now that we need to."

"There'd be no harm in trying it, I suppose," Reiko conceded.

"Supposing that it might work," Carla said, "there's no way we can do it now that the candles are all gone."

"We're going to be on this planet for the rest of our lives," Kira declared. "In future years we'll need to hold the Ritual for our children. So now is as good a time as any to find a substitute for candles."

"Braid dried grass into tapers," suggested Teresa.

"They wouldn't burn long enough," Kwame said.

"They're needed for only a minute or two before we touch the flame."

"Yes, but it takes a lot of time to light them all."

"We'll have to have more torches," Jesse said, "so that many people can light their tapers at once. There's plenty of alcohol on hand to make torches."

This necessitated scouring the wrecked shuttle for material to be used for handles. Meanwhile, people went to work braiding long grass tapers. It was dusk, and getting cold, before they were ready and the Group was again gathered in the assembly ring.

To his own dismay, Jesse was apprehensive. He was to be a full participant, and though he had done it three times before, he found himself doubting his psychic strength. For one thing, Kira would not be in the inner circle, and because she had been his teacher, he had always relied on her familiar mind-touch as well as on Peter's. But no woman so far along in pregnancy must place her hand in fire, Peter had decreed, for there was no knowing what effect the extreme alteration of consciousness required would have on an unborn child. So even with Jesse, one more person was needed. The other Council members had been chosen for practical skills, not psi-giftedness, and were not good candidates. Peter chose Greg, who was a reliable, experienced neurofeedback instructor and had occasionally participated as the sponsor of a novice. Nevertheless, with Hari distracted, in danger, perhaps, of drifting off into the clouds again . . .

Carla was quiet, white-faced. "I have a bad feeling about

this thing," she confessed to Jesse. "Peter drives himself too hard! To do the Ritual with a crowd of three hundred people and only one fully qualified backup, when he's worn out from yesterday's experiment and a night with little sleep—"

"We have to do it, Carla," Jesse said, drawing her close to him. "Unless we're willing to give up on trying to save the crop, Peter has no choice."

"I know. But I'm afraid for you—and for him. What if he collapses? We couldn't get along without Peter even temporarily."

That was true. "If Peter did not do this, we'd be in worse trouble than if we simply lost the crop," he told her. "The confidence in him that keeps us going depends on his active leadership. It would be lost if he took no steps to deal with the situation—even if they're just symbolic steps. Even if they fail, it will matter that he tried, that he can be counted on to act whenever we face a crisis."

After a lingering kiss he left her and made his way to the dais, where Peter, Hari and Greg waited. Looking back, he watched as one by one the torches of the outer circle were lit, forming a bright ring of flame around them. Once again, a ring of flame . . .

Above, the cold sky was still clear. The stars were coming out. *How empty space is between the stars,* Jesse thought suddenly, *and how far we are from the nearest peopled world. We are cut off forever. We cut ourselves off on purpose. Now if we die for lack of rain, no one will know what we tried to do here. Not even our hopes will live after us. Was it wrong to take such a chance? Or does trying to move forward matter in itself?*

It matters, Jesse, Peter responded. *It has always mattered and always will, from ancient times to the remote future.* Quietly then, over the lowered background music, he began to speak of the future, inspiring the rapt assembly to have faith in it. They were spellbound. Jesse could feel their telepathically-shared emotion as a tangible force.

Reiko came forward, carrying the Ritual torch, while all

around the encircling torches were extended, ready for the people to light their tapers. It was almost time. Peter began the familiar words: "Unfaced fear is the destroyer. We will acknowledge fear and accept it, we will go past it and live free. . . ." But at the end, just before the climax, he added, "We believe we will receive what we need to survive and flourish here, as we take fire into our hands and turn the power of our minds to the clouds that will bring us rain."

There was a brief pause for the lighting of the tapers, hundreds of sparkling dots beyond the ring of brighter flames, and then the torch was before him and Peter was saying, "And we now seal our commitment with the symbol of the mind's power, which is fire." Unhesitatingly, Jesse extended his hand to Peter, scarcely noticing that Hari and Greg did the same, and it was bathed in fire yet felt cool— and at the same time he felt the coolness of water on his face and on his body—cool, not cold like the freezing air— and rivulets of water were running beneath his feet. As he looked up, the stars faded out and he saw billowing clouds. The projected sensory images were so clear that for the moment, he did not doubt their reality, nor did he question his perception that all the others saw and felt them, too. Certainly Carla did, for she cried out to him, *Jesse! It's raining! My arms are getting wet! Oh, thank God, it's raining. . . .*

And then he was jerked back to normal consciousness as Hari slumped to the ground, tranced, and Greg pulled back, staring in dismay at the reddened, blistered skin of his hand. With surprise, Jesse saw that his own was also blistered, as it had been after the Ritual on the starship, and that Peter's looked even worse. He had delayed their withdrawal to buy more time for the intensified shared consciousness of the Group to take effect. "There had to be some cost," Peter said soberly. "We can heal flesh, after all, more easily than we can move clouds."

There was, of course, no pain; their control over pain perception had long ago become automatic. Jesse let himself focus on it, slipping back into an altered state that was easier to maintain than it would have been if his hand had been undamaged. Reaching out with his mind, he became aware that some of the onlookers, too, had received burns; the grass tapers had burned down too quickly to avoid them. It did not bother them. They knew their hands would heal, without scars, within a few minutes.

Hari's condition was more worrisome. "I knew he might leave his body again," Peter said, "but he's staying away too long. He's not as attached to the real world as most of us are. As a psychiatrist, I would discourage him from psychic journeying. Yet as leader here, I know that his dedication to the Group is strong and that his gifts are very powerful. It may be that he can make a real difference."

It was another half hour before Hari roused, and then only because Peter and Kira rubbed his hands and called to him with their minds. The assembly had dispersed. Carla and the rest of the Council, along with Arwen and several others, had come to the dais, concerned that he was gone so long. "Is he someplace where there are clouds?" Carla wondered. "I *felt* the rain. I can't believe it's not real somewhere."

At that moment Hari opened his eyes. "It's raining," he said dazedly. "There were towers of clouds, layer above layer . . . bursting with rain. . . ."

The stars still shone in a cloudless sky. But when dawn came and streaks of red, unusual on Maclairn, glowed in the east, piles of billowing thunderheads hovered over the mountains at the head of the canyon.

24

THE AIR SMELLED strange that morning. There was a pungent odor that hadn't been noticed before on Maclairn. People took up their usual work, but the Council was drawn to gather again by the promise, or at least the hope, of impending rain. "We seem not to have failed completely," Peter said. "But we can't be sure those clouds will come any nearer, or release any precipitation if they do. It's too soon to call ourselves rainmakers."

Hari still maintained that it was already raining somewhere not far away. He had seen the clouds gather around and above him, had felt soaked by the water in them, had looked down on mountain highlands darkening as it fell. And he had heard thunder, which hadn't been part of the Ritual visualization. He was convinced that it must have been real.

"Then did we actually influence the weather?" Kwame asked, speaking for them all. "Or is it just coincidence?"

"It's a strange coincidence if after all these weeks, clouds are around today," said Reiko.

"Too strange," Peter agreed. "But it could be synchronicity, which is a different concept from statistical coincidence. There's no knowing whether we had any direct effect—we'll never know, unless we produce it more than once."

As he was speaking Arwen burst into the Commons, now empty of everyone but the Council. "Peter," she said breathlessly. "I need to warn you. It's raining in the mountains."

"That's what Hari says. It's good news that you both sense it." A remote viewing by Arwen was likely to be accurate; by this time the whole Council was aware that it was she whose drawing had led to the choice of the colony's site.

"It's not good news," she said. "It's raining too hard. The river is going to flood."

"It may not be raining as hard by the time the clouds are over us," Kwame argued. "Probably it won't be, if a lot of rain is falling from them now."

"There'll be a flood," Arwen insisted. "I've seen it. I *know*."

Jesse remembered, with a chill, that Arwen's drawing of the site had shown the future rather than the present. "I think we should take this seriously," he said. "Some of the farm attachments for the robots are stored near the river; it's been dry so long I hadn't stopped to think that it might rise quickly when rain did come. We'd better go down there and move them to higher ground."

"Yes," Peter agreed. "If it rains the river will rise eventually, and it's best to be prepared."

It was decided that all five men would go without calling on others to help; it would do no good to start a rumor of flooding that people might exaggerate out of proportion, especially if Arwen's foresight proved mistaken. The women Council members, who were avoiding excess physical exertion during pregnancy, stayed behind.

As they started down the trail Jesse, thinking that dampness might bring out the giant crawlies, went back for his laser gun. "I'll catch up," he shouted.

He found Arwen in tears, with Kira and Carla trying ineffectively to calm her. "It's not safe to go down to the valley!" she told him hysterically. "It's worse than I saw at first. You can't stop the flood and you'll just be swept away."

This was not like Arwen, who was generally a quiet, level-headed young woman, the most promising of Hari's students. "We couldn't be swept away when it's not even raining yet," he began, but Kira shook her head. "It's no use reasoning with her—apparently she's seeing different time frames superimposed. Precognition is like that sometimes. It doesn't stick to the rules of reality."

"I don't know," Reiko said. "Flooding can happen very suddenly. History records flash floods on Earth where trees were uprooted and hundreds of people drowned. Sometimes whole communities were destroyed within minutes. I think you should get the important equipment to as high ground as possible, Jesse. And I think you should hurry."

Jesse nodded and headed for the trail again, but Carla ran after him. "Jesse, don't go," she pleaded.

"If there's real danger, I have to," he declared. "Since our phones don't work down there, I have to warn the others. But there can't be any danger yet when the sky is still clear."

"I guess not. All the same, Arwen scares me—she seems so *sure*."

"Then Peter has to be informed, doesn't he?"

She paled. "Yes! Yes, of course he does. Go, but hurry

back, Jesse—all of you hurry back. Don't stick around waiting for it to start raining."

By the time he got down to the valley floor the others
were already far ahead of him, moving the farming attachments for the robots out of the dry riverbed near the pump
tower. The air was still, and the sun seemed not quite as
bright as usual, though no clouds were visible—the canyon
walls obscured the view of those hovering over the mountains. From somewhere upstream came a roll of distant thunder. It set Jesse's nerves on edge and he began not merely
to hurry, but to run.

He had reached the river when the first crest of water
rolled down toward him, spilling over the banks as it came
and spreading out to swirl around his feet. In amazement
he drew back, shouting out to the others, but they were out
of hearing. It had reached them first, and they were frantically trying to drag the machinery out of its way. In moments the river had been swallowed up and the whole span
of the ancient riverbed was underwater. The second crest
took down the pump tower; the waterwheel had already
been washed far downstream.

Jesse struggled to make headway toward the place where
Kwame and Dan now huddled against the canyon wall. He
soon realized that was impossible—the current was so strong
that he would indeed be swept off his feet. He clambered up
the bank nearest him just as a third crest bore down on the
valley, inundating the farmland.

The crop was gone by the time it started to rain.

It was not the soft rain they had so desperately con-
jured up in last night's vision. It was a downpour. Water
fell in sheets, washing brush and rocks down the cliff behind him to join those from upstream already being carried
by the flood. Overhead, lightning split the sky, and thunder
drowned out the roar of rushing water.

He could not see from where he clung whether all the
farm machinery had been preserved. He doubted it. He did
see Peter and Hari who, having pulled the plow to safety,

were stranded on a ledge near the niche into which they'd
shoved it. They had all better stay where they were, Jesse
decided. It had to stop sometime, and in any case the water
was still rising. It would be dangerous to try to reach the
trail.

Hari stood erect on the rock, shaking his fist at the sky.
He was throwing all his psychic force into a futile effort to
stop the rain, Jesse realized. He blamed himself. Perhaps
he'd indeed had a part in bringing on the deluge. . . .

Suddenly Hari turned. *Peter!* he cried out. Jesse heard
it in his mind, though to his ears it was inaudible over the
thunder. As if time were stopped, he watched an avalanche
of rock fall down the wall toward the outcropping where
Peter was standing. Hari rushed toward Peter, attempting
to push him out of the way. As the rock slide hit, the ledge
plunged to the valley floor and they both disappeared.

Heedless of the risk, Jesse abandoned his own perch
and scrambled toward the place where they had fallen. *Peter*, he called, *Oh, God, Peter, answer me!* This could not be
happening. Peter could not be under those rocks! Yet they
had communicated telepathically over distance before, when
the need was urgent. . . .

Breathing hard, his legs scraped by sharp stones, he
finally reached the rock slide. Peter was lying half covered
by a boulder. Hari was not in sight, and it was all too obvious that his body must have been buried.

Jess, Peter cried silently. *I . . . passed out when I was
hit. I heard you call, I think. . . .*

"Oh, God. Oh, Peter—are you hurt, or just pinned?"
Peter's legs below mid-thigh level were hidden beneath the
boulder and small jagged rocks were heaped on the lower
part of his body. Frantically Jesse began throwing them
aside, ignoring the laceration of his hands.

"One leg is crushed, I think," Peter said. "I've stopped
the bleeding. The other feels whole, but I must be bruised . . .
where the rocks were."

At least he wasn't suffering from pain, Jesse thought in

despair. Peter had too much experience in teaching others to deal with pain to be affected by it himself. He was also a skilled healer who could heal himself of ordinary wounds; but this was past anything ordinary, and besides, he was trapped. There was no way the boulder could be moved. Even several men could not do it; it would take the robots, which of course were inaccessible.

"Where are Kwame and Dan?" Peter asked weakly.

Jesse stood and surveyed the area. Kwame and Dan were higher up the canyon wall, on the other side of the slide; for them to cross might cause it to slip further. "They're okay," he told Peter, "but they can't get to us. Even if they could, they couldn't help. There's just nothing they could do."

"And Hari? He pushed me aside . . . otherwise the avalanche would have killed me. But now he doesn't answer me—"

"Hari can't answer, Peter."

"He's dead, then?"

"I think so. The boulder fell directly on him."

"Oh, God. He died blaming himself for the storm, when the fault was mostly mine."

"It wasn't anybody's fault," Jesse stated firmly. "Remember what you've been telling me all this time."

There was a long silence. Then, with resignation, Peter murmured, "I'm going to die too, Jesse."

"No, you're not," Jesse lied.

"The water is still rising, isn't it?"

Jesse looked over his shoulder. It was rising fast. They were close enough to the valley floor for Peter to be covered by it, even if some way were found to prop up his shoulders. *All we need to do is wait,* he told Peter. *The storm will end, and then help will come.* He could call Carla for help—they alone could reach each other over this distance. But he would not do it, because she'd suffer agony if she knew, and it was far too late for anyone from the plateau to get to them.

Peter said in a low voice, "I'm not afraid of death. But . . .

I'm *needed*. There are dangers ahead I never spoke about—dangers I'm the only one trained to deal with."

"I'll pull us through somehow," Jesse said. He doubted that he could do it, yet Peter must not die without hope for the colony.

"Oh, Jess—of course you will, in the physical sense. But once psi powers are unleashed in a new generation . . . some kids may misuse them. With even Hari gone—"

There was no answer to that.

The rain was still falling in torrents, and what once had been fields had become a vast, muddy lake. Most of the water had come from higher in the mountains, Jesse realized. It had moved in a massive wave through the valley, carrying whatever vegetation had grown there on its surface. Rocks, and boulders almost as large as the one pinning Peter, had been swept along. When the flood receded, they would remain, but the fertilized soil would not. The farm would be a wasteland. And when drought came back, there would be no way to irrigate; the lost pumping system could not be replaced.

Could they ever plant again? The plow, at least, had been saved; it hadn't been touched by the avalanche. But the spreader, planter, and combine might have been lost. And without Peter, could they summon the will to keep trying—or would grief sap their spirit?

In desperation Jesse threw himself against the unyielding boulder, knowing it was hopeless, knowing that there was no way he could move it, but unable to just sit and wait. His hands, raw from his furious attack on the smaller rocks, were oozing blood. He did not bother to manage the pain; it was nothing compared to the pain in his heart.

How long, do you think? Peter queried.

I can't say. He could, but he wasn't going to. It would not be much longer before Peter drowned, but he need not learn that until it became undeniable.

"You can't stay here, you know," Peter said aloud. "You have to get out before the water rises any higher."

"I won't leave you, Peter." It would be unthinkable to leave while Peter was alive. There would be time enough later to reach higher ground.

"Think of Carla. For Carla's sake, you've got to go!" Peter burst out with vehemence. *Think what it would do to her to lose you, to lose both of us, after Ramón! Don't let me die believing she may be left alone to grieve . . . I can't face that. Everything else, but not that.*

Had he always cared that deeply for Carla? Jesse wondered, surprised. She was like a sister to Peter, but he had not realized their bond was so close as to dominate his thoughts when he was dying. "Don't worry," he said reassuringly. "I'll be safe. You know how much I love Carla, you know I wouldn't put myself at risk of deserting her."

He could not think beyond the moment, could not imagine how he would endure watching while water soaked the ground beneath Peter and then gradually covered his body. To support his head would buy only a brief respite; still, they could not surrender even a few moments of the life left to him.

As Jesse stooped, clearing a space to crouch, Peter's eyes suddenly lit up, as if some miraculous door had opened before his eyes. God, thought Jesse, he's seeing visions, like what people say about near-death experiences. Was it true sight? There might be something in the old myths he himself had never believed, because Peter's powerful mind *couldn't* cease to exist . . . was survival after death any more incredible than traveling out of one's body to move distant clouds?

"Jess," Peter whispered, "is that the laser gun you're wearing? You've got the laser?"

Jesse froze. Surely Peter wasn't suggesting. . . . Yes, it would be easier to die quickly than to wait, horribly injured, for the flood to slowly drown him—but both suicide and mercy killing were against the Group's deepest convictions. No member, least of all Peter, would request it. On the other hand, Peter wanted him to escape and knew he wouldn't leave before it was over. . . .

You don't understand! Peter's thought was urgent. *I want to live, Jesse! With the laser you can get me out.*

God, Peter—I can't cut away a boulder this big with the laser gun! If I could, I'd already be doing it. He wondered if Peter's injury was so serious that he'd lost the capacity to think clearly.

The water was creeping over his own shoes. He would have to move away soon or be swept off his feet. Yet he couldn't leave Peter to die alone.

"I want to live," Peter repeated, with great effort raising his voice. "I can live without legs if I have to, and there's no time now to lose."

Legs? *Oh, my God.* In a rush of startled relief mixed with anguish, Jesse grasped what was being asked of him. *I can't do it right, I don't know how,* he protested. But he did know, of course. It would not require a surgeon's skill; the laser could easily cut through flesh and bone.

It doesn't matter how. Just do it. That's your strength, Jesse—you're a man who can act fast, without agonizing over a decision till afterward.

There was no choice. The shock might kill Peter, or at least make him too weak to keep control of his own pain and bleeding. But if it was not done, he would surely drown.

Grimly, not letting himself think about the horror of it, Jesse drew the laser and amputated Peter's legs.

Part Three

25

WITH THE STRENGTH of desperation Jesse lifted Peter and staggered higher onto the rock slide. Peter had passed out, but was losing no blood. The stumps of his thighs had been cauterized by the laser; Jesse vaguely recalled having read that in ancient times, surgeons had seared amputations with hot irons.

The footing was at best precarious. He knew that very likely the rocks would slip and they would both fall into the rising flood. There was nothing he could do to prevent it and insofar as he thought about it at all, he realized that if it weren't for Carla he would not really mind drowning, if Peter drowned. He did not see how he could endure the memory of what he had done if Peter did not live.

After seemingly-eternal minutes he found his arms level with a ledge wide enough to hold Peter. He lowered him onto it and then climbed up himself, too exhausted to wonder what he would do next. He could not have carried the full weight of a man's body this far, he realized numbly. A legless man did not weigh as much. Would Peter have to be carried everywhere from now on? On a world where bionic limbs were unobtainable, he would never again be whole. Not even prostheses could be made here....

Jesse? Jesse? Oh God, Jesse, answer me if you're there!
He was suddenly aware of Carla's telepathic cry. It dawned

on him that she must be frantic—the people on the plateau would have seen the flooding of the valley. She must have been calling him for some time. Unconsciously he had closed his mind to her while he believed that Peter would die, for he could not bear to let her know what was happening. Now she was their only hope of rescue.

Carla! he called urgently. *I'm here, I'm okay. But Peter's been hurt.*

Jesse—oh, Jesse, is it bad? He felt her surge of terror and recoiled from the thought of how she'd react when she knew the whole of it. For now, he would skip the details.

It's bad, he admitted. *But he's alive. When you see, Carla, just be glad that he's alive.*

If either of you had died, I'd have known, she responded, *yet I sensed something terribly wrong. I tried to tell myself that was just from worry, not psi. . . .* Struggling for composure, she went on, *I'll send people down with a stretcher.*

No—we can't reach the trail. The others can wait for the water to recede, they're stuck on a different ledge from ours, and they're not in danger. But we need to get Peter to a healer. You've got to guide men to where we are, so they can lower ropes. Rope, thank God, was among the limited supplies provided by the pods, as was the stretcher. He hoped there was enough. There would be nothing at the edge of the plateau to anchor a rope; many men would be needed on the upper end.

The thunder had ceased. Belatedly, he shouted to Kwame and Dan, who were not in a position to see him and had assumed that Peter died with Hari. He told them no more than that he was alive, then tersely acknowledged their reply. After that, alone, he gave way to silent tears.

The wait for Carla to set up the rescue seemed interminable. *Lower the stretcher and some blankets,* Jesse had ordered. *Peter can't climb. He'll have to be pulled.* The slope above the rock slide was not steep; the stretcher would not be hanging, but could be dragged. Nevertheless it wouldn't be an easy process, and he tried not to think of the shock people would feel once they saw what could not be hidden.

Jesse . . . are you still here? Peter was regaining consciousness. Immediately Jesse was engulfed by pain, the physical pain that Peter was now in no shape to manage. It knocked the breath out of him. He had felt pain telepathically before, on Undine, when Zeb was dying. But that had been nothing to the pain that now seared his legs, paralyzing him. Peter's pain was like his own . . . it nearly swamped him until he remembered that he must deal with it as if it *were* his own. That was how healers did it, how he himself had been taught. You must voluntarily suffer before shifting to the altered state in which you did not mind pain, then draw the patient or trainee along with the shift. It had been Peter who'd done this for him, in the beginning . . . the memory was suddenly vivid, revived by the shared agony. Peter, beside him in the neurofeedback lab, his voice calm, steady, despite the fierce pain he was letting himself experience . . . the dual mind-patterns blazing red on the wall in front of them . . . and then the breakthrough, the moment when all suffering ended and their patterns matched and they were high, not from the pain but because they had succeeded in altering their perception of it.

He must take the lead role now. *Peter . . . it doesn't have to hurt . . . merge your mind with mine, remember the pattern. . . .* He had lessened Zeb's suffering more than once— Kira had said his ability to do it would grow. She'd said even those not born as healers could do it for close friends. *Peter, I'm shifting now, follow me. . . .*

Abruptly, the pain ceased to matter. It didn't lessen, but was neutralized by a discrete form of perception that once learned, was never forgotten—a state in which the sensation of pain simply wasn't unpleasant. But to enter that state required volition. A semiconscious person could not do it unaided, because pain was nature's mechanism for protecting those too weak or immature to avoid injury without a warning they couldn't ignore. The infirm, animals, children . . . children! Jesse thought. We'll have to teach them, subject them to pain during training. He had not thought about this before. It was one thing to put Group recruits through it; they were volunteers. But the children . . . somehow he'd assumed they'd acquire the skill naturally, as they would telepathy. He had lived so long among people who were immune to physical suffering that he'd forgotten that the kids wouldn't be. Who could he have trusted to teach Kel, if Peter had died?

At last people appeared at the top of the cliff. The roped stretcher came down, and Jesse managed to get Peter onto it, covering him with blankets that he knew wouldn't do much to soften the impact on those anxiously waiting above. There was no escape from the need to warn them; they were entitled to an explanation. *Peter was pinned down under a boulder,* he told Carla, as he tied the last knot and signaled for the ascent to begin. *He'd have drowned if I hadn't done what had to be done to get him out. Tell everyone that, now, before they see him.*

He stood, guiding the stretcher over the rock ridge and onto the slope as the rope went taut and it began to rise. When he could no longer reach it, he dropped back onto the ledge, depleted, and sat slumped over in utter misery, wondering if he'd have the strength to climb when the rope came back to him. Looking down at the valley, he realized that the crop was gone and the irrigation tower was gone and that both were irreplaceable, but he was too numb to absorb what it would mean. Nothing beyond Peter's fate seemed important now.

In due course the rope was dropped again and Jesse stumbled up the slope, gripping it in his raw hands with the end tied around his waist for safety. He dreaded what he would meet at the top. He did not see how he could face Carla.

The whole Group was gathered there. Most of them had not yet seen Peter, but as they were within telepathic range of each other, even those not carrying phones were aware that he was injured. Kira was kneeling beside the stretcher, oblivious to everything but what her healer's sense was telling her. Carla was standing beside it, white, frozen, and her agony seared through Jesse, an even deeper pain than he'd expected. He went forward to comfort her but she drew away, shielding her mind from him. Perhaps, he thought wretchedly, she couldn't help feeling he was to blame—what other emotion would she try to hide? From the moment of their first union they had shared all sorrows.

"He was trapped, Carla," he said gently. "The water was rising and there was no other way to free him. I did what he asked, to save his life."

She didn't respond. Realization of what Peter was facing had overwhelmed her. But after the first she bore it calmly, as did the others. Their mind training took over; they were too well practiced in self-control to cry out or even to weep. Weeping would come later. For the time being they simply followed, silently, as the stretcher was carried back to the Commons and into the small infirmary. Not until Kira pulled the curtains, declaring that to heal Peter's injuries she must be undisturbed, did Jesse remember that he also had to tell them about Hari.

It was not necessary to announce in words that he was dead; through telepathy, now enhanced by the magnitude of their emotion, they knew. But Hari's heroism must be made plain. Jesse was filled with chagrin at the way he'd underestimated Hari. Quiet, solemn Hari, who had taken little part in the fellowship of the Group, who according to Peter, had not really wanted to come to Maclairn. He'd shown vitality near the end, to be sure, when he brought the rain—if indeed he had brought it. He had blamed himself when it proved to be too much. Had he believed that a sacrifice was demanded after all by the metaphorical rain god upon which he and Peter had called?

"He gave his life for Peter," Jesse said, "but I think in a sense it was for all of us. He wouldn't have been standing up on that ledge if he hadn't tried to defy the flood. It was a symbol—he knew, of course, that he couldn't hold it back. But there are worse ways to die."

"It was archetypal," Reiko agreed. "The leader—or the shaman—stands between his people and the forces of nature. When there is need, he offers himself. That was true in all preindustrial cultures, back to the beginning of time."

"Then Peter, too—" murmured Teresa.

"Yes, Peter too," Jesse agreed. "It wasn't just that we needed rain. They saved the plow instead of climbing to safety. If they hadn't, we couldn't plow new fields."

"These things aren't random," Reiko said. "All history proves that they are not, though we don't understand them. Peter calls it fate. But he was involved by choice, as Hari was, and in his heart he was willing to take upon himself whatever fate sent our way. That's the mark of a true leader, the thing we have always sensed in him."

"But it's not fair that he should be the one to suffer!" Edris burst out. "He doesn't deserve it!"

How young she was, Jesse thought. He too was outraged by the unfairness, as everyone must be—but you learned, after a few years, that it did no good to dwell on it.

Nor was this the time to dwell on the question of what was going to become of them, now that the crop was lost and the farmland laid waste. Yet people were starting to be aware of all that had happened. They would not know what to do next unless someone took charge. The Council had to meet soon—and, Jesse realized abruptly, as deputy he was now the head of it, for the time being, anyway.

Quietly, he went to Greg, telling him to get the crowd outside and to see that Dorcas had help preparing the noonday meal. Nobody would feel like eating, but it might be their last full one for a long time, perhaps for as long as they lived. Food rationing must begin tomorrow, he knew. It might make no difference in the long run, but they must try to survive as long as possible.

The Council members remained in the Commons, seating themselves at the table nearest the infirmary. By this time Kwame and Dan had arrived, worn out, as Jesse himself was, from the rough rope-assisted climb. For a long time they said nothing, sharing grief too deep for words. Kira appeared briefly to ask that more healers, Olivia and Ingrid, be sent for; then once they'd taken over, she joined the others.

"I've healed the flesh," she said, "but the stumps will take longer. And he will need surgery after a few days. One cut wasn't made high enough; there are bone splinters in the leg that was crushed that will have to be removed."

"Is Peter conscious?" asked Carla.

"Not now. He came around for a moment, but I sedated him telepathically. His body needs rest. And he mustn't think yet about the future."

"Will he live, Kira?" Jesse asked.

"Yes, of course. The internal injuries were minor, though there's some nerve damage where the rocks lay on him and I'm not sure how much functioning he'll regain."

"There may not be much life ahead for any of us," said Kwame grimly. "There's no way we can plant again, plow or no plow. When those fields dry out, they'll simply parch, and we've lost the only equipment we had for irrigating them."

"What have we done?" Carla whispered. "Oh, God—what have we done?"

26

"WE DID THE only thing we could do," declared Kira. "The crop would have wilted if we hadn't tried to bring rain. Our belief in the power of psi was what brought us here—it would have been wrong not to use it. We lacked the knowledge to use it well. But that's how it is with any human advance. If it costs us our lives, we won't be the first humans to die trying to move forward."

"That's what Peter would say," Reiko agreed.

"What he *will* say," Kira added, "when he wakes."

Carla said sadly, "I'm not thinking just about the flood. I mean . . . were we right to come here at all? To reject the medical techniques available on Undine? We were so sure we could do without them—but in the Hospital, Peter could have been given new legs."

Nodding, Kira said, "That goes to the heart of the issue. There's a price for everything, Carla. We gave up medical technology and we're paying now for that. But on Undine and elsewhere, they're paying the price of having too much. Not just the price in money as was always assumed on Earth. The price was the loss of the latent self-healing capability that's our human birthright."

"And besides that, the loss of freedom," Dan said.

"Freedom means risk," Kwame said. "We knew that, even if we didn't picture crippling among the things we were risking."

"Major accidents are rare compared to the sort of illness that nearly everyone on other worlds suffers from and eventually dies from," Kira pointed out. "So it's a small risk balanced against a much larger one."

"But can't a world have the best of both?" Teresa asked. "Medical technology where it's really needed, but not imposed where it isn't necessary?"

"In principle, yes—we hope that in time this one will," said Kira. "But for the short term, we were forced to choose."

"Technological advances always involve a stage of indiscriminate use," Reiko explained. "To fund the research required to provide for rare, extreme situations, something based on related technology has to be sold to the general public. On Earth that was true of all the stuff pushed on consumers that many people felt wasn't needed."

"It was certainly true of medication," Kira agreed. "Treatment for serious illnesses couldn't have been discovered if the pharmaceutical companies hadn't raised money by promoting unnecessary drugs for minor conditions and alleged prevention. Then, of course, people got used to relying on drugs, and a whole industry grew up surrounding that, followed by a bureaucracy that culminated in the situation on Undine."

Jesse frowned. "You're not being consistent," he objected. "A moment ago you declared that we should pay the price for progress. Now you're saying that it's better to pay the price of rejecting it."

"It depends on whether there's innovation involved," Reiko said. "Progress in medical technology was necessary in the past, first to wipe out infectious disease and then to control other sickness that people had no other way of dealing with. Evolution hadn't reached the stage for mind power to be used as we use it. What's more, we couldn't do it ourselves without neurofeedback, which depends on all that was learned about the brain by medical science."

"We're not Luddites," Kira pointed out. "Our sacrifices here are real sacrifices. But they're only temporary, a cost of developing something new. "

"Both technological and psychic advancement are essential to human evolution," Reiko added. "From the twentieth century onward, thought on Earth was dominated by two conflicting fallacies—some people believed technology alone would shape the future, while others claimed there was too much of it and only spiritual development truly mattered. In reality, they are complementary, and neither can be cast aside."

"We couldn't have had interstellar colonization without the advances that led to space travel," Kwame said. "If our species had remained confined to Earth it would have been wiped out by starvation and war. We'd be fools to deny our debt to high technology or the fact that we need it to survive here—still humankind needs mind powers, too, even if gaining them means we personally lose some of its benefits."

"We knew we'd face hardship, maybe even be killed, if we settled a new world," Carla said, "just as pioneers always have. I accepted that gladly. But when it's Peter who has to pay in a worse way than anybody imagined—"

"Peter would be the last one to choose legs at the price of giving up Ian's vision," Kira told her.

True enough, Jesse thought. And yet Ian's vision might

not come to fruition anyway. Ian had seen them landing in his dream, but he had not seen beyond that. Perhaps there had been no future for him to see.

Nevertheless, Ian had trusted him with the Group's safety. He could not hope to inspire people as Peter had. Still it was up to him to keep them going until Peter was well enough to take charge again.

Knowing he must act before anyone broke down in tears, Jesse turned the Council discussion to practical matters: food rationing and plans for the immediate future. Heavy work with stone would have to be curtailed, for the largest ration must be given to pregnant women—more than half the colony's population. Everyone else would be short on energy.

They would suffer no more from hunger than from any other physical discomfort. Nor would they have trouble confronting the likelihood of death. Any such fear they might have felt had been burned out of them by the acceptance of stasis, the symbol onto which all ordinary fears had been projected during their training on Undine. All the same, what lay ahead would be grueling. It was despair, not fear, against which they were unprotected. How could they feel anything but despair when there was no hope of raising enough food to sustain the settlement?

Almost all the women were pregnant. They were facing not only childbirth on a world ill-equipped to ease the process, but the care of infants, something they knew little of and hadn't been reared to expect. On Undine newborns had remained in the Hospital for their first year, with mere visits from their mothers. They were fed what the Med authorities deemed a more reliable form of nutrition than breast milk. Here there would be nothing to supplement human milk. And how much of that could a woman provide if she herself was near starvation? They wouldn't be able to stretch the food supply as far as might otherwise be possible, once the babies came. They would have to give top priority to providing for offspring they knew couldn't live to grow up.

"That was the main reason we came—to have kids," said Carla, her voice unsteady. "Not just to be free ourselves, but to build a better society for the generations after us. What's worth the risks we took, if we can't aim for that?"

Jesse drew breath. If even Carla felt that way, the people with less strength than hers would give up. The Group's morale would be unrecoverable. He could not let that happen.

"We *must* aim for it," he declared, "whether it's possible or not."

"But if we can't plant a crop—"

"We can plant on the plateau. The ground's damp now; it will be easy to till."

"There's not much room, when we have to stay clear of so much space around the power receiver," Kwame pointed out. They could not even cross that space when the starship was overhead; a beacon atop the receiver lit up during the unsafe hours.

"Besides," said Dan, "I thought we decided there's no way to irrigate the plateau."

"Not with enough wells to do without rain," Jesse agreed. "But hardly anybody outside the Council knows that."

Most Group members had no technical background. Kwame was the only trained engineer. Dan, Nathan and a few others had begin studying the knowledgebase before leaving Undine and had continued to do so; everybody else had simply taken their word for what could and could not be done.

"You're suggesting we should prepare land where crops can't thrive, waste our fertilizer and seed on it, and tell people there'll be a harvest?" Teresa protested, shocked.

"Tell them to hope for one, yes. The Group can't survive without hope, Teresa."

"Jesse is right," Kira said. "What's more, our unborn children's development is at stake. We know that the telepathic bond between mother and child is formed before birth. It's not verbal communication, of course. Only emotions and outlook come across. And emotions affect the brain physically—that's what our way of staying healthy is based on, after all. A child exposed only to hopelessness would be warped, mentally and physically, long before being born."

"That may well account for some of the warped minds that have plagued human society throughout history," Reiko added. "Psychologists failed to find valid causes in either heredity or environment. They didn't count emotional environment in the womb."

Carla stared at Kira in dismay. "But then *my* child, and yours—"

"That's why we have to act as if there's a future," Kira told her. "Even if it means lying, not only to the others but to ourselves."

"It's not necessarily a lie," Dan said. "For all we know, this could be the start of a rainy season."

From what the starship's weather surveillance AI had told him, Jesse didn't think so, but he refrained from comment. "Are we agreed, then?" he asked. "Can I count on you all to back me up if I call for the preparation of fields?"

Solemnly, they nodded. They still looked on him as Captain, as did the rest of the Group. They relied on him for the settlement's safety, and what he ordered, they would do. It was way too late to worry about whether he was equal to the responsibility.

That night he slept from sheer exhaustion, but awoke before dawn. Carla lay beside him, her face wet with tears. Lacking privacy, he could not comfort her in the way that he longed to do. Their minds could not merge fully without a union of their bodies. And perhaps, he thought, she did not want them to. She was holding something back, as she had been since her first sight of Peter's injury; it had touched her in some deep way beyond what she might have felt for a brother. Peter had been part of her life long before their marriage, to be sure. He had been her first husband's best friend. But, Jesse thought, Peter was his best friend, too. *Oh, Carla*, he cried silently, *don't you know how it hurt to do what I did to Peter? Do you think I wouldn't understand how you feel?*

In the morning he called the Group together and announced the rationing plan, first privately warning Nathan and the handful of others knowledgeable enough to question the promise of new fields. Few people seemed unduly worried. They did not grasp the seriousness of the situation and besides, they were still emotionally absorbed by their sorrow for Peter. Their distraction, Jesse felt, was probably a good thing.

As soon as Kira allowed it, he went to Peter's bedside. Peter was still sleeping most of the time, which she said was the best way to recover from trauma. "The body needs energy to heal," she told Jesse, "even when a healer initiates the process. He's awake briefly now to eat, since we have no means of intravenous feeding. But don't tire him."

Jesse approached with sinking heart. What could he possibly say? Peter would sense his agony, of course; they'd had too much experience with communicating telepathically when facing trouble to close their minds to each other. *You stuck by me after you were forced to harm me in the Hospital,* Jesse thought, *and now that it's the other way around, I wish I could do as much for you. But I don't know how to give support the way you did. . . .*

Peter, arousing from a doze, opened his eyes and managed a weak smile. "Jess!" he said. "Jess . . . don't grieve. This was fated to happen . . . it's what Ian must have seen."

Ian saw . . . this? Jesse was to shocked to speak. As far as he knew, Ian's prescient dreams had all been encouraging ones. Peter had never suggested otherwise.

"Not this specifically. He dreamed only that I would face some terrible test here. He didn't want me to worry beforehand—he planted the warning in my unconscious mind, the way he did the things we learned aboard the starship. But while I was going into stasis, it emerged."

"You mean you were *anticipating* something bad happening to you?"

"I wasn't losing any sleep over it. For all I knew, it might not happen until I was an old man."

"But Peter, why would he give you such a warning? If he didn't suggest any way to escape, what purpose did it serve?" Ian's precognition had always been purposeful. If he'd had random foreshadowings of trouble, he had refrained from saying so.

"He was . . . telling me not to lose courage, Jesse." *He wanted me to feel, when it did happen, that some good would come out of not giving up.* Peter fell back against the pillow, too spent to say any more aloud.

Jesse too was silent. Ian had believed courage was the answer to everything, and this had indeed proved true on a number of occasions. But those situations had been different. When Ian had come in a dream to give him courage, he had already known that he, Jesse, would be released—had known that his own sacrificial plan to bring this about would enable the Group to reach a new world. There could be no release from what Peter must endure.

But then, Ian hadn't foreseen what sort of trouble would strike Peter. Perhaps he'd merely sensed that whatever it proved to be, he wouldn't have to live with it for long.

27

WHEN THE FIRST meal shift gathered for lunch Jesse found Dorcas worrying about Claire, who had seemed even more dazed than usual since the rainmaking Ritual and this morning had not wakened. Uneasily Jesse realized that she, who'd had trouble returning to her body after stasis, had very likely been drawn out of it again during the visualization. Perhaps Peter had needed to help her return; he didn't talk about patients' problems when it wasn't necessary to inform anyone. In any case, things had begun falling off tables spontaneously again, although Claire hadn't risen from her mattress. Apparently she was causing poltergeist activity not merely unconsciously, but during prolonged sleep.

"She's been emotionally dependent on Peter," Dorcas said, "and now when he's in no shape to support her, she's scared. She's retreated, and with Hari gone nobody knows how to bring her back."

The idea of someone being "out of the body" still disturbed Jesse deeply. He was not sure he could ever get used to it. Some of the others had done it during the rainmaking, he knew, though not to the extent Peter and Hari had. He was told that to reach Claire's detached mind would require more skill and experience than any other individual possessed, and because a collective attempt to do so without leadership struck him as dangerous, he forbade it. The last thing the Group needed was to have more people lost in inner space.

By afternoon the flood had receded. Jesse looked down on the devastated valley with despair, realizing that restoration could not be attempted for years, if ever. The soil, having been loosened by tilling, had been washed away, leaving patches of bare rock. Larger rocks were strewn here and there over what once had been planted fields. The lake had reverted to a river; it still overflowed its banks, but that would not last long. Its channel had undoubtedly been deepened. It would be impossible to raise water from it even if they still had the pumping system.

He and Kwame walked along the rim of the plateau as far as the place from which they'd climbed. Far below, the rock slide with its huge boulder jutted out from the canyon wall, forming a small peninsula under which Hari lay. And also Peter's . . . he cut off the ghoulish thought and turned quickly to Kwame, asking, "Can anything besides the plow be salvaged, do you think?" They could not see even that from where they stood.

"We can go down there and investigate once the trail is clear," Kwame said. "But Dan and I didn't manage to hang onto the other implements. We're going to be planting seeds and spreading fertilizer by hand from now on, I guess."

Reiko had been reading up on flash floods. "They were common on Earth, especially in desert regions," she told them during supper. "They happen when clouds stay too long in one place and drop more rain than the land below can absorb. We should have known, I suppose. During the Ritual Hari gathered thunderheads in the mountains where he traveled in his mind, and he didn't realize that they should be kept moving."

"None of us could have known," Jesse said, "considering that Undine had no land except small islands. And except for when I was a kid, I hadn't lived on a planetary surface until I went there."

It was his and Carla's turn to sleep in one of the private huts. To Jesse's dismay, she wasn't eager to. "Would you mind terribly if we didn't go?" she asked. "I—I just don't feel like it, and it's too bad not to give someone else the chance, if—"

Never before in their marriage had she been reluctant for sex. Was it due to her pregnancy? he wondered. He had not thought she was close enough to term for it to make a difference. Anyway, they wouldn't have to do much more than undress to get aroused enough for enhanced telepathy. . . .

That was just it, he realized. He sensed that she shrank from the full mind merge arousal would bring. She was keeping something from him. It wasn't only grief for Peter, which they both felt, and which sharing should help them to bear. Somehow Peter's tragedy had triggered feelings she did not want him to know about. He couldn't believe she really blamed him for what he'd been forced to do. Carla wasn't prone to irrational anger. Yet now, when he needed her most, when they needed each other . . . Crushed, Jesse nodded and agreed, "Perhaps this isn't a good time. Maybe you can trade our turn in the hut with some other couple."

Kira was on the same meal shift that they were, but she hadn't appeared for supper. That troubled Jesse. A number of healers were sharing Peter's care, so he could see no reason why she wouldn't take meal breaks. As usual, he and

Carla retired to their sleeping place after eating, there being no place else to sit if they weren't going to the hut. She was quiet, not even communicating silently. He tried to read, but could not concentrate on it. Even the music in his earphones was more irritating than relaxing.

Finally, with his nervousness increasing, Jesse got up and went in search of Kira. Walking from one shelter to another, he scarcely noticed the cold. But he glanced up at the stars and was impressed anew with how far off they were.

He met Olivia coming out of the infirmary, and could sense at once that something wasn't right. Feeling that to express this aloud might somehow confirm it, he queried, *Is Peter doing okay?* He knew even before she replied that he was not.

He's feverish, Olivia told him. *Kira's keeping her thoughts to herself.*

Jesse pushed aside the curtain and confronted Kira. "If he's not recovering as fast as he should, I have a right to know," he declared.

"You do," Kira admitted, "though I didn't want to worry you yet. His fever is rising. It's normal to have some degree of fever after a serious injury. But I'd healed his wounds. I'd eliminated the natural inflammation. It almost seems as if there were some kind of infection."

"I thought organisms of this world couldn't infect us," Jesse said, chilled. "I thought their biology was too alien to ours."

"So did I. I'm sure it's true of bacteria, but a virus— viruses aren't even alive. They're just bits of genetic material that invade cells of a host, and they adapt and evolve very fast. Normally we in the Group throw off viral illness, like other illness, because we start out healthy and can consciously control our physiological responses. But Peter is weakened now, and hasn't been conscious most of the time. And of course none of us have any natural immunity to whatever viruses may exist here."

"Could it be contagious? Are we going to have to isolate him to protect the others?" That would be nearly impossible in a shelter without interior doors.

"No—it's not a respiratory illness. It entered through his wounds before I healed them. Any of us with minor injuries could self-heal before that happened."

Jesse looked over at Peter, who was still unconscious; he was flushed and sweating. "Is he—in danger?" he asked in a low voice.

"I don't know, Jesse. We can't predict what an alien virus would do to us. His immune system is strong, and for that very reason it may produce a violent response."

"But why can't you heal fever, as you did the wounds?"

"Healing simply speeds up and enhances the natural processes of the body," Kira explained. "Fever is a normal reaction of the immune system—a defense, a means of attacking the invading organism. If it goes high enough to damage his brain I can induce his body to lower it, but that won't cure the underlying illness. It will simply allow the virus to take over."

Puzzled, Jesse questioned, "You can't combat the virus itself?"

Kira shook her head. "I don't think so, at least we've never been sure we can do more than stimulate a patient's unconscious reactions. If we can—if healers sometimes physically alter cells—it's through PK, as Peter said when we were talking about rainmaking. But that's not usually needed and there's no evidence that we possess such an ability."

"We used PK to bring the rain clouds," Jesse said. "Hari did, anyway, whether or not the rest of us did more than channel power to him."

"That's true. But we've just discovered that we can tap such power, and I've no way of knowing how to use it against a virus."

Clearly they couldn't count on it. "There are drugs and medical supplies in sick bay aboard the starship," Jesse said vehemently, "and now isn't a time to forgo their use. Tell me what to bring down." He would not wait for dawn; he had flown at night during their landing and he could do it again. He would have to call Tomas to activate the pad lights. . . .

"Nothing from the ship would help," Kira said. "Drugs don't affect viruses unless designed to target specific ones, and lowering a fever with analgesics simply masks symptoms."

"What can you do, then?"

"Nothing beyond keeping him hydrated." She thought for a moment, then added, "There is one thing you could get. The sick bay probably has IV equipment. So far he's been able to drink, but that may not last."

"I'll go now," Jesse said, eager to do more than stand aside and worry.

"Wait till morning and take Olivia with you. She'll know what to bring."

It was just as well to wait, he admitted. There'd be couples now in all the shuttles, and it would be awkward to turn one of them out if it wasn't an emergency. He did not want the Group upset until more was known.

As he landed the next day, despair once again swept over him. The settlement no longer looked like an oasis. There was no sign of anything green, and the destruction wrought by the flood was all too apparent from the air. One tiny patch of life clinging to the vast, desolate surface of a barren planet—how had they ever thought they could thrive there? They had arrived empty-handed, with one duffel apiece plus the content of the starship and pods, expecting to found new civilization out of nothing. It had been absurd. He alone had previously traveled beyond safe, fertile Undine; why had he let them take such a risk when he'd known they weren't experienced enough to judge its magnitude?

Peter was burning with fever. Kira accepted the IV equipment thankfully and put it to immediate use, assistants having sterilized a supply of water by boiling. No news had spread among the others; he had ordered the healers to keep it quiet. He avoided Carla, for he wasn't confident of his ability to close his mind to her and he knew she would suffer terribly once she learned that Peter might be in danger. When it was time for supper he busied himself with the rest of the shuttle's payload, telling her that it must be put in storage before dark.

Back in the infirmary, he found Kira sponging Peter's face with cool water. "Has he been conscious at all?" he asked her.

"Off and on. But he's out of his head when he comes to. He doesn't know what he's saying." She frowned and told him firmly, "Get some sleep, Jesse. I'll see that you're called if there's any change."

"I'd rather stay."

"No—you mustn't!" He sensed a strange urgency in her that he had not felt before.

"Kira," he said, "don't try to hide anything from me. I'm in charge now. I have to know the worst, so I can deal with it. Whatever happens."

"Of course you do, that's not why—" She broke off, evidently regretting what she had been about to say. He could draw nothing from her mind.

A terrible thought came to him. "Is there any chance he might die—like Zeb?" he asked softly. Kira had explained when Zeb was fatally stricken that the unconscious mind controlled life and death—that as long as medical treatment didn't interfere, people died from organ failure when living became a burden to them. To be without legs, without prostheses on this world where there was no hope of even a wheelchair . . .

"Zeb was ninety-four," Kira said, "and had no mind training. His life was behind him. Peter's goals lie ahead."

In the night when he was awakened, it was not to Peter's side that Jesse was sent but to Claire's. "She's got a fever," Susan told him when he arrived, "and I can't tell what's wrong. I'm a gynecologist, after all. This is outside my experience."

Fever. Oh, God. If the virus was contagious after all . . . But Claire had not been near Peter. She had not moved from the mattress where she now lay.

Helpless, he stood by while women sponged her face. "Peter," Claire cried out suddenly, "hold my hand tighter! I can't see you anymore, I'm falling. . . ."

"Her temperature's rising fast," Susan said desperately. "You'd better wake someone to relieve Kira, Jesse, so she can leave Peter long enough to look at her."

But when he got to the infirmary with Olivia, Peter was worse. "He's delirious," Kira said. "He's been talking to Claire, of all people—begging her to come back. In his mind he's in the past, I guess, in the starship when she hadn't awakened from stasis—"

"No," said Jesse, horrified. *Peter!* he cried urgently. *Oh, God, Peter, don't go after Claire now! It's too risky! We need you more than she does. . . .*

Kira picked up his thought and in dismay, joined the plea, clutching one of Peter's hands while Jesse gripped the other. *Please, Peter, stay with us—you're needed here. . . .*

Abruptly, Peter's body sagged and he opened his eyes briefly, his face a mask of resignation and sorrow. "I . . . lost her," he murmured. "Ian told me to let her go."

A few minutes later Susan came to tell them that Claire had just died.

28

"THANK GOD HE'S unconscious again," declared Jesse. "We mustn't let him find out until he's recovered." Peter would be devastated by losing another of his former patients.

"He already knows, Jesse," Kira said sadly. "He knew before we did, at the moment their contact was broken."

"Was he really in touch with Ian's spirit?" Jesse wondered. "Or was it just illusion, as he said when we saw Ian on the night we escaped from the Island?"

"You might call it that," Kira said. "It certainly wasn't a ghost or a message from beyond the grave. But I think he did actually see, or hear, Ian. The brain interprets input from the unconscious mind in the form of images, just as if it were receiving them through the senses—it has no way of distinguishing. That's why throughout history some people believed they'd communicated with spirits, or even that they heard the voice of God. Subconsciously, Peter was torn between saving Claire and his responsibility to the colony. Ian would have said the colony must come first, and underneath he knew that."

"How could he have saved Claire? How did he even know she was sick?"

"Psi connections are stronger outside of normal consciousness, as you know, Jesse," Kira reminded him, "especially when people are under stress. Claire was disturbed. She couldn't face the thought of Peter not being there to rely on, and so she retreated from her body and sought him with her mind. He was . . . elsewhere, too, because of the fever, and sensed her call. He tried to bring her back to reality because he felt responsible for her."

"But how did she catch the virus?" Jesse protested.

"Physical conditions can be shared by psi, just as you can telepathically feel another person's physical pain. People sometimes develop actual wounds that way. And as we all know now, body temperature can be affected by thought. When Claire tried to draw on his mind as she had before, her own mind absorbed his fever, even though no virus was present in her body."

"If she experienced only what he's experiencing," Jesse whispered, aghast, "then for him too it could be fatal—"

"Claire lacked Peter's will to live. He's much stronger than she was, and far better equipped to survive."

Yet the fever showed no sign of diminishing. The day passed and then another, and Peter's condition did not change.

Jesse, frozen with dread, did his best to keep up the Group's spirit. Everyone knew where they stood, now;

Claire's death had made it impossible to hide the fact that Peter was also dangerously ill. It could not have been hidden much longer in a telepathic society in any case. And in fact, the futility of planting new fields could not be concealed from telepaths, either; he'd been deceiving himself to suppose that it could. No one spoke of it aloud, but it was obvious that they were losing hope, and work on the stone huts slowed to a standstill. When they were subsisting on such short rations it was easy to give up the effort.

A robot had been diverted from the leveling of farmland to the creation of a cemetery. Group members were accustomed to shrouding bodies for burial, which had been part of their undercover work on Undine; so they had no difficulty with Claire's. But the idea of earth burial was foreign to them. Undine had no cemeteries. The bodies they'd saved from stasis had been consigned to the sea. Jesse had seen to it that the grave was dug deep, but even so, when people gathered around he'd sensed their revulsion. The thought of a dead body remaining there, decaying where it was in theory as identifiable as in the Hospital's hated Vaults, did not bear thinking about.

He'd led the simple graveside ceremony, as was expected of him. Lack of refrigeration having left no alternative to holding it at midday, there was no protection from the merciless sun. The participants could adjust their own temperature but had no control over that of the body, which was encased only by a thin fabric shroud. Heat scorched Jesse's shoulders and shimmered off the newly-cleared ground. Not only was there no water, there were no candles to float, as was traditional, above the burial site. Nor, to his private dismay, would there be any sort of headstone. It had been decided that graves would not be individually marked; instead, there would be a single stone monument with name plaques like those in the underwater cave used as a memorial on the Island. Hari's name would be the first after the stasis casualties, Claire's second . . . oh, God, Jesse thought, would Peter's be next?

On the second night after Claire's death, standing vigil again with Kira, he voiced a worry that had been growing. "Did his attempt to reach her . . . weaken him?" he asked. "I don't mean just emotionally—does being out of one's body, as you all claim literally happens, take a physical toll?"

"It can," Kira replied. "He is experienced and adept at maintaining his body's well-being while his mind is detached, but he can't do it while semiconscious, any more than he can control his pain." She and other healers had been relieving the pain of the amputations telepathically, as Jesse had done on the ledge. "Peter takes on too heavy a load; he always has. He won't admit that the strain's sometimes more than he should try to bear. When he's not fit to judge rationally his instinct to protect the weak takes over—and now, with the whole colony in danger of starvation—"

"Surely no one's told him about that!"

"Not specifically, but did you think the general despair could be kept from him when he's so sensitive to psi on the unconscious level? Those of us in direct contact with him have tried to close our minds, but by this time it's been unintentionally broadcast by everyone else."

Yes, of course, Jesse realized. The initial confidence was fading, and Peter, the only one who could have revived it, was being weighed down. The colonists' ability to deal with fear made things worse, not better. They had pledged in the Ritual not to be ruled by fear, and were practiced in setting it aside. The Group had been founded on the principle that death was not evil when it came naturally. They were appalled by Hari's untimely death and Claire's, and deeply stricken by the possibility of Peter's. But insofar as they considered their own, they looked on it as the natural and unavoidable result of eventually running out of food. They didn't dwell on it—but they saw nothing to be gained by struggling against it, either. They were resigned to what had begun to seem inevitable.

Even Carla was affected. "Maclairn hasn't felt right from

the beginning," she said sadly, when Jesse lay down on the mattress beside her. "When we were in danger on the starship, we thought that if we got to a new world everything would be great. That the risks and hardships wouldn't matter because it would be an exciting place, a place where we could build for the future. But it's never offered much promise. It's been—*deficient* somehow . . . drab, dry, even when we stopped minding the heat, and not just in a physical sense. And now that we know we've lost the gamble, it's not going to get any better. Even if we don't starve soon, we can never establish a real foothold here."

Jesse could not deny this. Nor could he reveal that underneath, he had never shared the general conviction that a new world would prove better than the old in any way other than its lack of a tyrannical government. But they were here. They would be here for the rest of their lives, whether that was a short time or a long one. The responsibility for their survival was his. He had taken it on when he agreed to command the ship that brought them here, even before his failures led to the choice of a particularly bad site—long before it became a matter of perhaps having to go on without Peter. He could not let them give up.

"Think of the baby," he urged Carla. "Think of Kel! We can't let him feel as low as we do—Kira said it matters what a child senses in the womb—"

She burst into tears. "I know," she said miserably. "I know, yet I can't help it! I want to give him happy feelings, but I can't! We can control our bodies' reactions but we can't create joy out of nothing. . . ."

He held her close, unable to offer anything more than his love for her. After a long time they went to sleep.

Around midnight a voice roused him. "Carla!" Olivia was there, shaking Carla awake beside him. To Jesse she said, "Peter is delirious again. He's calling out for Carla, and Kira says she must come."

Carla, stunned, was pulling on her clothes. Jesse rose, saying "I'll come, too."

"No!" said Carla. "Please don't, Jesse. Please let me go by myself."

Bewildered and hurt, he stood back and let her go. Why did she not want his support? Why had Kira sent for Carla alone, and not him?

She was gone the rest of the night. When they met before dawn for breakfast, she was silent, and he made no attempt to question her. It was best, he decided, to let things ride.

But he could not allow the others to sink into lethargy. Calling on the remote viewers, who were stunned by the death of Hari and seemed more detached from real life than ever, he asked them to start seeking sites for irrigation wells. "We won't try to cultivate more land than we can irrigate," he said, "which means that unless we can figure out some solution, we can grow only a small grain crop, not enough to last from one harvest to the next. No vegetables, no fiber for fabric—and of course no trees. But if even a little rain falls, there's a chance we can keep from starving."

There were protests. Some felt it might be possible to bring rain again, considering that it wouldn't matter now if the valley flooded. Most believed that would be asking for trouble. Yet hardly anyone thought it was worthwhile to expend energy on digging wells and planting fields on the unlikely chance that natural rain would prove sufficient. They were not even sure that building stone huts now made sense, until someone pointed out that whatever happened, the addition of over a hundred crying babies would make shelter living intolerable.

Jesse listened to everyone's arguments, then made plain that he was Captain. "In space, the Captain calls the shots," he declared. "In effect, we're still in space. We're mere emigrants, stranded on an unopened world—until we can grow our own food, we have not established a true settlement. Even if Peter were able to take charge, he wouldn't expect me to quit my job."

"Ian trusted Jesse to be Captain, as we acknowledged

when we accepted his decision about stasis," Reiko reminded them. That, of course, settled it. Their reliance on Ian had always been the basis of the Group's unity. Besides, they wanted someone to lead them. Someone to say that their seemingly-hopeless situation was not hopeless after all, that they would awake as they had from the near-death of stasis to find themselves on the threshold of a new life.

They would not contest his orders again, Jesse saw. He alone would be torn, wondering if those orders were wise.

29

THOUGH SEVERAL HEALERS were taking turns caring for Peter, Kira was with him most often, allowing herself the barest minimum of time to eat and sleep. That afternoon when Jesse came to the infirmary, he suddenly noticed how tired she was. "You were up last night along with Olivia," he recalled. "You can't have slept since the night before."

"I'm okay, Jesse. Ingrid's coming at supper time; I'll be fine until then."

Kira was over a hundred years old, and she was pregnant. "You should rest," he said. "Go and lie down, and let me stay with Peter. I can manage his pain if he wakes—I did it for Zeb, after all, and I'm closer to Peter than I was to him."

"It wouldn't be a good idea," Kira hedged, not letting him sense what she was thinking.

"Why not?" Jesse exclaimed in surprise. "You've told me in the past that Peter needs my support."

"He doesn't need it when he's not in conscious control of his emotions. Your strong telepathic bond would lay them open to you—"

"There is nothing he could feel that would make me think any less of him," declared Jesse, remembering that twice before, briefly, they had shared thoughts at a time when Peter was weakened. Kira knew how deeply the amputation had affected him; she must be afraid that he'd be crushed if Peter dwelled upon it, as in his semiconscious state he might. He did not want protection from that. His debt to Peter as well as their friendship required that he stick by him through every possible ordeal. Unhesitatingly, he pulled rank on Kira and insisted that she leave.

In late afternoon the air in the small, cramped infirmary was stifling, and Jesse was worn out. The hardest thing, apart from the horror of seeing the once-invincible Peter in such a state, would be keeping his own mind free of despair, he realized. Without Kira's presence to distract him he could not do so, yet if he let their minds blend Peter would feel everything he was feeling—even beneath the level of consciousness he would. Still, Peter had seen the flood and must already know what lay in store for the settlement. Facts could not be hidden from him. It would only be necessary to avoid triggering strong emotion about them.

As Jesse bent over the cot, Peter woke briefly and recognized him. *Jesse . . . I owe you my life, Jesse. . . .* He slipped back into semi-consciousness, suddenly overwhelmed by pain he had not the energy to counter. For a moment Jesse, too, was overwhelmed by experiencing it. He had not expected it to be so bad—the stumps had, after all, been healed. He suddenly recalled having heard once that the pain of amputated limbs never ended, that phantom pain was felt in them long after they were gone. Quickly he extinguished the thought. It was not what Peter needed to sense.

He focused on turning off their suffering. Within moments the sensation in his legs ceased to matter, as it had on the rock ledge; but Peter stirred. *I've got to get up now, I'm needed . . . Ian said everything would depend on my strength. . . .* To Jesse it seemed like his own thought; the mind transfer he'd initiated for pain control worked both ways. All that was presently in their minds was shared. He surrendered to it, letting Peter's thoughts predominate, almost glad to escape into what he now perceived were memories.

He was with Ian. With Ian he felt secure, self-confident—Ian made everyone feel that way. He saw Ian not as he'd been in extreme old age, but earlier, back when he, Peter, was a medical student, not long after his recruitment into the Group. Ian was already over a hundred years old, but no one who didn't know that would have believed it. He was strong, virile, full of life. He was the father that he, as a crèche child, had never known.

Ramón, his best friend, felt the same, and so it was as if they were truly brothers. The hours they spent at the Lodge were the center of their existence. Hours of active fun—diving, sailing, flying—but even more, the mind training, the joy of gaining the powers latent within them that Ian taught them to harness. And better yet, evening hours by the fireplace when they spoke of all the things that no one in the city dared speak of, or even cared about. The wrongness of the Med government. The burden of resistance Ian trusted them to take on. It wouldn't be easy to work as doctors under a system they despised, but Ian maintained that they could handle it. That by using such a cover role, they could save people who would otherwise be doomed to needless suffering. And beyond that was the vision, the shining vision of a new world that Ian warned could not exist within their lifetime, not unless a miracle were to happen, but that symbolized their deepest conviction—their belief in the ongoing evolution of humankind. Sharing this with Ian and with Ramón was all that had ever mattered to him. . . .

No, not quite all. Not even close. What mattered even more, for a time, was Carla.

She came to the Lodge one gloriously sunny morning, a new recruit, and from that day on, his life revolved around her. Carla, glowing in the firelight, joining in the camaraderie of the Group and seeming more real to him than any other but Ian. Carla, her dark hair blowing in the breeze as she stood on the dock waiting for his seaplane to land. Carla swimming topless, as did all the women on the Island . . . but he could not bear to remember now what he'd once been free to feel. He had not let himself think of it after she'd slept with Ramón, much less after she and Ramón were married.

Ian had sensed his longing for her, of course, and had felt sorrow that would have been inescapable whichever of them she had chosen. He had mentioned it only once. "It may always hurt," he'd said, "but it would have hurt worse if you'd let it affect your friendship with Ramón. That you're truly happy for them tells me that you'll come out of this okay."

Carla and Ramón, then, the three of them a bit awkward together until Lesley had come along. For many years after that, the bright years of their youth, the four of them were inseparable. He had never told anyone that Lesley was merely the woman he'd settled for, that he'd married her on the rebound from a hope he'd had to abandon. He had loved her. He had not allowed himself to be aware that he loved Carla more.

Until the tragedies: first Ramón's execution, the long years when seeing Carla's grief was worse than seeing them together had ever been, and then the sailing accident when Lesley had died in the storm. He had done everything he could to keep her from drowning. When that proved impossible, he had risked arrest for murder by sinking the boat to keep her body out of the Vaults. But during the dark hours he'd spent afloat in the bay, waiting for rescue, he had not cared if he lived or died; for he'd feared that underneath he was glad about it, glad that he and Carla were now both free.

After nearly five years Carla was still grieving for Ramón. It was past time for her to break out of it, and he could now offer her more than the comfort he'd tried to provide over the years. He knew she cared deeply for him. After a decent period of mourning for Lesley he would speak. He was on the verge of speaking when, beyond all expectation, the long-desired miracle had happened—the awesome, incredible chance for them to escape to a new world.

But that chance depended on Jesse. On the immediate recruitment of Jesse, who had no compelling reason to join the Group. With anguish Peter relived the moment in which he realized that there was only one motivation powerful enough to see Jesse through the ordeals that recruitment demanded. . . .

"It's the answer, of course," Ian said, in wonder at the fate that had brought them not merely a Captain, but a man who had stirred Carla's frozen heart. "But have you the strength, Peter? To give her up a second time, to live the rest of your life in a small colony where you'll see her daily and watch her bear another man's children?"

"It won't happen that way unless she wants it to," he replied, "and if she does, I'd not stand in their way in any case. What I want is for her to be happy."

Yet he was aware Carla wouldn't have followed through on her attraction to Jesse if he, Peter, had not asked her to. She hadn't known what was at stake; he'd told her only that Jesse would be better off in the Group than stranded at loose ends on Undine. He'd been torn, needing Jesse's commitment yet hoping her relationship with him might prove temporary . . . and then during those first days Jesse spent on the Island, he'd sensed that it was forever. That he could never hope for her love again. In the light of what had been gained he did not regret the sacrifice. All the same, the cost would be high in the years ahead. *Carla, dearest Carla, I love you enough to want your happiness, but I can never love anyone else . . . this time I won't make the mistake I did by marrying Lesley. . . .*

Oh, God, Jesse thought, jolted out of Peter's memories. Oh, my God.

Peter had never intended for him to know. Kira, aware of that, had done her best to keep him from finding out. Now he must guard his thoughts, as Peter had guarded his while well and strong—but the tragedy of it would always haunt him.

Peter, who had seemed supremely at peace with himself, who had been admired and even envied by everyone who knew him, had all along been living with the loss of the one thing apart from a new world that he had ever really wanted . . . and now he'd lost his mobility too. If he recovered from the fever he would be alone, crippled, for the rest of his life. He would devote himself to the Group and would be loved and honored for that devotion, but as a man he would never find happiness. Certainly not with Edris—that relationship was merely for expediency. It had never brought him joy.

And he, Jesse, was responsible for both of Peter's losses. Not through any fault of his, not even unnecessarily, but nevertheless he had first taken Carla from him and then cut off his legs. Would I have been willing to endure the test for mind-training aptitude without the prospect of Carla's love? Jesse asked himself. Probably not. Peter had chosen wisely, considering the compelling need for a starship captain. That did not make it any less sad for him.

Stunned, stricken, Jesse waited anxiously for Olivia, knowing he must depart before Peter came fully awake. He would need time to adjust before contact with him. Before contact with Carla. Did Carla know? Of course she did; this was what she had been hiding. Looking back, he was sure she had not known on Undine. She had believed Peter's feeling for her was brotherly, nothing more. It must have been soon after coming here that she'd found out—even during their night in the shuttle, a corner of her mind had been inaccessible. Now, with Peter doubly burdened, her grief for him was too great to be buried deep enough.

Peter had called out for her when he was delirious. He had thought only of her when he believed he would drown. Conscious, he would hide his feelings again, but Carla would be aware of them and he, Jesse, would be aware—and, he realized, it would come between them unless it was acknowledged. But what could he possibly say to her?

30

HE DID NOT, of course, let Kira know what he had learned. But, aware now of Peter's buried sorrow, Jesse was more disturbed than ever about his prolonged unconsciousness. "There's got to be something more we can do," he insisted when he saw her the next day. "We can't just rely on hope indefinitely."

"No," Kira agreed. "Hope's not enough. If he's no better by tomorrow, we may need to call the Group together to pray for him."

"*Pray* for him?" He had always known that Kira's views were closer to traditional religion than his own, although this was more often implied than discussed openly. In the silent pause during the Ritual people were expected to do whatever was most meaningful to them as individuals. The Group was officially neutral on the subject of prayer.

"Jesse," Kira declared, "it doesn't matter what word, or what metaphor, is used for it. Long ago on Earth scientific studies showed that prayer sometimes did heal the sick, which confirmed what countless cultures have believed since the dawn of civilization. But that doesn't mean what happens must be interpreted as formal religions interpret it. All we know for sure is that it's a result of the mind powers latent in everyone, the same powers we in the Group aim to foster. Direct healing, what I and other healers do, is one form of such power. Reaching out in our minds toward something higher than ourselves is another. Many of us have been praying privately all along, of course—but to join together would increase our strength."

"Are you saying this might actually have an effect on the virus that's attacking Peter?

"Possibly, if we are focused enough—or at least it could augment his will to live. And I think it may be our only option now."

Rainmaking had once been viewed as prayer to rain gods,

he reflected. Peter had even suggested that some people might choose to think of it as prayer. "But we can't have the Ritual," he said. "Peter is the only one qualified to lead it."

"It's not necessary to handle fire to combine mind power," Kira said. "That's simply our symbol, as offerings to gods or spirits were symbols to traditional groups."

Jesse lay awake thinking about it after he went to bed. He closed his eyes and reached out with his mind and knew that the only thing important now was that Peter must live, he would do anything, no matter what it took, to help Peter live . . . and he knew that this was more than just wishing, that there was indeed power in it, and if it was shared by all of them at once, the power would be magnified. And he understood that this was why religious ceremonies had been meaningful to people on Earth for thousands of years. When morning came he would order the making of more tapers, he decided. They could not touch fire without Peter, but they could hold tapers, three hundred sparks alight to fire their hearts. . . .

At breakfast he presented the idea to the others, letting it pass unspoken from mind to mind among them, and asked them to start twisting grass for tapers. The day passed slowly, with no change in Peter's condition. At dusk the Group gathered once more in the assembly ring; Kira left Olivia with Peter and came to lead the healing rite. Carla came late, after he'd joined Kira on the dais, and did not sit in the front row. He knew she must have been with Peter again.

He tried to forget that she was not beside him, as she had been in every other Group rite he had ever attended. He focused only on Peter, on his feeling for Peter, as Kira said, "We must put worry about the future out of our minds now. We must think only of him, visualize him strong and well, as we've known him and loved him . . . visualize him as we visualized Ian that night aboard the starship. As you light your taper, picture Peter beside you, imagine holding out your hand to him in flame. . . ."

This was like all the other psychic powers, Jesse realized. It would not work unless he was willing for it to fail. Just as touching fire demanded willingness to be burned, he must commit himself fully without fearing the consequences of failure. Some called it submission to the will of God, Kira had said when he'd protested that he couldn't become willing to let the shuttle crash. And so yes, if you used that metaphor, it was a form of prayer. It was not fatalism, but a surrender of conscious control in order to set your unconscious mind power free.

He concentrated on visualizing. *Peter, as he'd first seen him, extending his hand in welcome as they were introduced in Carla's apartment . . . in the swimming cove at the Lodge, smiling, daring Jesse to face his childhood fear of water, supporting him during his first scuba dives . . . and of course, as mind-power instructor, inspiring absolute trust even as he subjected Jesse to overwhelming pain. The joy of shared emergence from that pain. Peter on the night of the firewalk, stepping onto the glowing coals and encouraging him to follow. His first Ritual, with Peter probing his mind, wordlessly assuring him that no harm would come to him during the timeless moment when their hands touched in fire. Peter coming to him in the Hospital, injecting him as he was forced to do, yet calming him, helping him to bear what neither of them had thought could be borne. . . . Embracing him before the Council after he was freed, on the night he revealed that Ian had counted on him to take them to a new world . . . aboard the starship, convincing the Group that they must take the risk of dying in stasis as he, Jesse, had ordered. . . . And then Peter at his side in the shuttle, becoming his eyes when sleep overtook him and there was no chance that they could survive without their bond. . . .*

So many memories, and not his alone, for with his were mixed those of all the others who had been helped by Peter and cared about him. Their minds meshed in an outpouring of love and longing, their sorrow over Peter's crippling now overshadowed by the desire for him to live. For the settlement to go on without him was unthinkable. *Live, Peter, live! If there is any pattern in the universe, any justice in the fate you've placed faith in, then it can't take you from us....* Jesse knew beyond question that he would do anything, make any sacrifice, if only Peter's life could be spared.

And as he realized this, he knew what he must say to Carla.

The tapers burned down quickly, but the focused emotion lasted. He lost track of time. Not until he found himself walking with Kira back toward the Commons did he come fully alert. "We weren't just touching each other's minds, Jesse," she was saying confidently. "We reached something beyond." He nodded, wondering how long they would have to wait to know whether that had done any good.

It didn't take long. Olivia met them at the door to tell them Peter's fever had broken.

They would never know just how it had happened, Kira said. Peter's immune system might have overcome the virus without help, or the power they channeled to him might have enabled it to do so by influencing his unconscious mind. Or they might have had a direct PK effect on the virus. Or perhaps, touching something greater than human minds had turned the tide....

It would take a good many days for him to recover, she warned. The virus had further weakened him before he'd recovered his strength after the amputation. It was still essential for him to sleep most of the time, and above all not to worry about the colony's future. "If I let him come fully awake he'd try to take charge," she told Jesse. "He mustn't be burdened with our food problem too soon."

But for Jesse, the burden had been lifted. Reason told him that their doom was as sure as it had been while Peter lay dying, yet inside, he could not help feeling that Peter's presence would make a difference.

At bedtime, when their turn for private quarters had come around again and Carla once more hesitated, Jesse pleaded, "Please, Carla? Just to talk, if that's all you feel like doing. We need to talk."

The huts were not yet wired for lights; they took a battery-power lantern. It was cold, of course. There were several blankets piled on the mattress that lay on the leveled floor. Carla threw one around her shoulders as she sat down on it, not undressing. "I—I'd rather wait," she said unhappily. "I haven't been feeling well today, the baby—"

"Carla," Jesse said. "You don't need to make excuses anymore. It's okay if our minds merge. I sat with Peter while he was feverish, and a lot came through to me. I know."

"You *know*?" He could feel her astonishment. *You can't mean what I think you do. Peter wouldn't have let it slip out, not even telepathically—*

"He wasn't fully conscious. I didn't mean to invade his privacy, but he was in pain and I relieved that, and because I'd had close mind contact with him before, I couldn't help picking up his memories. He doesn't know it happened, and I won't tell him, of course. But you needn't guard your thoughts from me, dearest. Not ever again."

He reached for her and she came to him, snuggling against his chest. *Oh Jesse, I didn't want you to know! Not that I thought you'd be jealous—but you'll suffer over it the way I do. I knew how much you care about him. I love you too much to have you suffer, too.*

Jesse did not answer, but simply pulled the blankets over them; and before long their clothes were off under the blankets, and their minds blended even before the joining of their bodies. *Nothing, nothing will ever come between us,* they realized simultaneously. For a long time they lay together, knowing that nothing could.

But now it was Jesse who withheld one corner of his mind, for there was something he had to say to Carla, and it had to be said in words. He did not want there to be any misunderstanding.

"We're on a new world," he declared as sunrise brightened the curtain covering the hut's open door. "The old world's rules don't apply here. Perhaps among telepaths they never did. Neither of us wants Peter to be more unhappy than he's now bound to be, and I think you feel more for him than for a brother, Carla."

She stared at him, bewildered, as he went on, "If there is anything you can do in the years ahead to ease his loneliness, I want you to do it. Anything—do you understand?"

"Jesse! You know I wouldn't!"

"I know you wouldn't do it behind my back, and that *he* wouldn't. I know you would never hurt me. But don't you see, Carla, love isn't something that must be taken away from one person if given to another. Not the kind of love we in the Group have, the love that's founded on something more than just sex. The love you have to give is infinite. I will not be hurt if you love Peter, because I know that won't lessen your love for me."

He knew, and sensed that she knew, that he had not said this out of generosity, as if he were offering to share something that was his. There was no possessiveness in the bond that formed between telepathic couples. It was a commitment not to renunciation of all other feelings, but to the permanence of a link without which neither partner could ever again feel complete. Marriage on Maclairn involved neither legalities nor vows because there was no need for them.

As she nestled in his arms, moved to tears, Jesse too felt relieved and thankful. What he'd first deemed a sacrifice was no sacrifice at all, for he would lose nothing by it. He and Carla were bonded. They would not be any less bonded if she also bonded with Peter.

31

ONCE PETER WAS fit for it, he underwent surgery to remove the bone splinters and to equalize the length of his stumps. He was now able to manage the lingering pain, but someone was always within call to help him move around. Kira ordered the caregivers not to discuss the colony's problems with him yet, and he, realizing this, acquiesced. He no doubt drew much from their minds, emotions even if not the thoughts they were shielding from him, and, Carla knew, he was not blind to the situation in any case. Was he as resigned to despair as the rest, or was he buying time in the hope of finding the solution that everyone, against reason, longed for him to offer?

She was no longer hesitant about being alone with him. She had no intention of telling him about Jesse's suggestion, for if she did, she might be tempted to act on it, and Jesse's unconscious feelings might be less objective than he himself realized. But it had set her free of worry. Both Peter and Jesse would grieve over what could not be helped, probably for the rest of their lives; and she would feel sorrow for them. Yet she need no longer fear hurting either of them merely by allowing her feelings to surface.

Time passed with people going about their work as usual, pretending that it was leading somewhere. The hut-builders tired more quickly than in the past and spent more time resting in the shade, but if it reoccurred to any of them that the need for huts might prove short-lived, they kept it to themselves. Nobody complained about the scant rations, though each day unprecedented twinges of hunger reminded them that planting a new crop was urgent. It also reminded them that there would probably be no harvest. Peter's life had been spared, but for how long?

A room was built for Peter, since the infirmary was needed for general use and in any case was not large enough for permanent quarters. Without mobility he could never live in a stone hut. All he could manage to do by himself would be to transfer between his mattress and a chair, using overhead handbars. Everyone agreed that he should have a home indoors next to the neurofeedback lab where he'd be working, and that a handbar should connect the two. Kira announced that she would remain his chief caregiver even after her child was born, so a room for her was built be-tween Peter's and the infirmary. Thus one whole end of the Commons was partitioned off for the four compartments, using materials gleaned from the wreckage of the ill-fated large shuttle.

"Isn't Edris going to care for him?" Reiko asked when this was first proposed to the Council. "Considering that she's carrying his child—"

"Peter has sent Edris away," said Kira. "He won't hear of her devoting her life to him. She is young, and he says she deserves a normal marriage."

"And she accepted that?" It was like Peter to sacrifice even the solace her love might provide, but no one had thought Edris so shallow as to desert him.

"He didn't give her a choice. He wants his child raised in a home like everyone's."

"But not your child?"

"That's different," Kira pointed out. "My child won't have a typical upbringing anyway. I'm over a hundred years old, and Ivana won't have a dad wherever we live."

After much discussion, it was reluctantly agreed that there was no way to construct a wheelchair for Peter. The starship contained no wheels, or anything of which they could be made with the tools available. The best Jesse could do was to bring down the Captain's chair from the bridge, which was comfortable though stationary. It was fastened to the deck and hard to detach—and even harder to make por-table, as like all starship seating it had been designed with a pedestal rather than legs. But appropriate materials were found to make a base for it.

"It's not as if he would ever have to live alone," Reiko said. "There will always be plenty of volunteers to carry his chair from place to place."

That was certainly true, but Carla knew that Peter would hate being dependent. He would especially detest imposing duties on others through his inability to visit the outdoor privies. She also knew that he would accept his situ-

ation with grace. At least he need never fear becoming a
burden. The Group members would vie for the opportunity
to do what they could for him.

There were no other chairs in the shelters except two
armchairs in the neurofeedback lab, which had also been
brought from the ship. The pods had contained folding
benches for the dining tables; elsewhere people sat on the
floor on mattresses ripped out of the starship's cabins, an
arrangement that seemed natural because there'd been only
floor cushions around the central fireplace at the Lodge.
Several spare ones were placed in Peter's room, as it was
decided that henceforth the Council would meet there.

Each afternoon, now, the women gathered in the Commons while Susan and Kira prepared them to experience
childbirth. The physical aspect of it—labor, the breathing,
the ways in which they could help each other—was easy to
grasp; of course they already knew how to deal with pain.
What was more frightening was Kira's emphasis on the fact
that even now, before the births, they were responsible for
their babies' emotional well-being—and that from the beginning, baby care would involve more than cuddling, feeding and diapering. The telepathic connection established in
the womb must be fostered, not broken off as it was among
outsiders with no conscious psi powers.

This was not merely because of the goal to base their
new culture on psi. It was necessary to the children's health
in an environment where no medical care would be provided.
"And the hardest thing," Kira said, "will be holding back
when we're tempted to help too much. Babies can't learn to
function without the normal discomforts nature provides—
hunger, thirst, the urge to eliminate, sometimes sickness or
even pain. If we were to telepathically suppress unpleasant
sensations before the kids had a chance to learn what they
mean, they'd grow up not knowing how to meet their physical needs."

That was all very well to say, Carla thought. But they
might not grow up at all. Each time she felt the child move

within her, dread struck her anew. What would happen when her baby was literally starving? There being no milk from animals available, he would have to be breastfed for at least two years. What food they could grow would not last that long. She would slowly starve, and her milk would dry up ... and would Kel die first, or would she? How could she nurture him properly, knowing what lay ahead of them?

Early on the morning when digging of the new wells was to commence, Arwen, who as the most gifted of the remote viewers was in charge of the dousing effort, came looking for Jesse in their sleeping shelter. Carla had long ago gotten used to intrusions of this kind; Jesse's advice was sought on every detail of construction activity. She hated seeing him weighed down, and yet only his acknowledged leadership was keeping the settlement going. Of course he must have the last word on placement of the wells.

The plan had been to put them at the far edge of the newly-cleared land, but Arwen, evidently troubled, now said they should be on the canyon rim. "Kwame won't listen to me," she said desperately, "and he's ready to start digging. Please, Jesse, tell him I know where they belong!"

"Isn't there water on the other side of the fields?" Jesse asked, puzzled. "The land slopes down toward the canyon. There's not enough of a grade to matter much, but it doesn't make sense to do any more pumping than we have to."

"I've *seen* them," Arwen insisted. "We can reach ground water on either side, but I've seen wind pumps rimming the canyon."

Jesse and Carla exchanged glances. *She saw evidence of our settling here*, Jesse recalled, *so I went along with that. And it was wrong. God knows how much better off we might be if I'd picked the other potential site.*

But Jesse, Carla reminded him, *she also saw the flood before it happened.*

True. If we'd listened to her warning about the flood. . . . They couldn't have prevented the flood by believing Arwen, but Peter might not have been trapped by it.

Either we trust the guidance of psi, or we don't, she declared. *And if we don't, why did we come here in the first place?*

That's what I decided about the site, he agreed. *I guess I've got to stick by it, because if we don't even try to do what we came to do, what's happened to us is all for nothing.* He went with Arwen to order the moving of the wells.

Not long after that, Peter called the Council together. "It's time for us to talk," he said.

As they settled on the floor mattresses surrounding his chair, Carla knew that he was his old self again. There was no longer any need to worry about whether he could take charge; they were all looking up to him in more ways than the literal one. With a blanket over his lap, his leglessness was forgotten.

Briefly, Jesse reported on the situation with the wells. "The change in plans will delay planting," he said. "And we'll have to raise the water into holding tanks, because it's not going to run uphill into the furrows. If it weren't that we can't irrigate much land anyway, I'd have overruled Arwen, but since it's only a gesture to keep up morale—"

"We don't need to rely entirely on irrigation," Peter said. "We know how to make it rain now."

Everyone stared at him, surprised. "Are you seriously saying we should try it again if we face another drought?" Carla protested. "Bring rain again, in spite of what it has cost us, cost *you?*"

"Yes, I am. We know it's possible, and we know where we went wrong. Maybe we'll fail again. But if we give up, we'll have failed in a wider sense."

"I suppose that's true," said Kira slowly. "We can't renounce the use of psi when it was the main goal of establishing a colony."

"Is trying to control nature right, though?" Teresa questioned. "Maybe we're not meant to subdue new worlds—"

"That's what some people thought about every step in human progress," Reiko reminded them. "Everything from the building of factories to the development of space travel, and probably long before. Unless you're willing to say humans should have remained cave-dwellers, you can't say it's wrong to keep finding new ways to control our environment."

"Maybe," Teresa conceded. "But look at how some of those developments messed up Earth. A line has to be drawn somewhere."

"No, it doesn't," Peter said. "Mistakes are the result of being in the learning stage. Backing off does more harm than good, as the situation on Earth clearly shows. The only way to avoid long-term damage is to move ahead."

"Once a means of meeting human needs exacts a higher price than can be justified, it should be superseded by a better one," Reiko agreed, "and the better one generally isn't gained without cost. History is full of examples where old assumptions held sway for too long."

"Which is what the trouble was on Undine," Kira said. "The Meds clung to outgrown ideas about achieving health until they were literally preserving bodies in stasis—an apt symbol, perhaps, of refusal to press forward."

"From the beginning," Peter said, "our aim has been to utilize human mind power alongside technology—not just for preserving our health, but in ways we can't foresee. Rainmaking is a step in that direction. It doesn't mean we're going to abandon wind pumps, any more than we're going to abandon the robots or the power receiver or the comm satellite. Developing the full potential of our minds will be a long process and if it costs us our lives, we won't the first to die in pursuit of human advancement. I am not as sure as the rest of you that we're doomed to starve, however."

"You really think we can control the weather, Peter?" Kwame asked.

"Maybe. I also think we might not have to, at least not very often. There's bound to be natural rain eventually." He paused, silently appraising them. "And meanwhile, there are other steps we need to take if we want to survive."

"What, Peter?" Carla asked.

"To begin with, haven't any of you realized that since we can consciously control our own physiological responses—our heart rate, biochemistry, and internal temperature—we can also control our energy metabolism? There are records of yogis and others who fasted for religious or political reasons going many weeks without food. We can live on much shorter rations than you've been figuring."

Skeptically, Dan protested, "Don't people who refuse to eat die from malnutrition?"

"Yes, if it's done for unhealthy reasons. As a psychiatrist I treated anorexics whose lives would have been endangered if the Meds hadn't force-fed them. But fasting is quite different from anorexia. An anorexic has a distorted body image and wants to be thinner, subconsciously as well as consciously. The influence of mind on metabolism works in the wrong direction. In our case, it can be used to conserve our bodies' resources. We'll develop a neurofeedback pattern for that, and of course you'll be shown telepathically, as you were for temperature control."

"It's a nice theory," Kira said. "But the other skills were originally taught to us by Ian. You and Hari and I got them from him and passed them on to the rest of the instructors. Can you figure this one out from scratch?"

"Ian did teach it to me," Peter said. "I went without food for several weeks once, when I was young. For a while he considered including metabolic control in the normal training program for new members, but he decided against it because he wasn't in constant contact with everyone. There's some risk attached to fasting if it isn't supervised. Also it's closely associated with asceticism in most people's minds, and that's something the Group has always discouraged."

"He wanted us to focus on skills with practical value," she agreed.

"And now it's got plenty of that—which, incidentally, Ian knew that it might when he and I first discussed the idea of colonizing a wilderness world."

"You mean we're just going to stop eating?" Kwame inquired.

"Nothing that drastic, at least not for more than few days. We have to work, and activity requires fuel. But we—that is, the men—can do with one small meal a day. The women can't, because they're all either pregnant or soon to be." Peter smiled. "Don't look so glum, guys! You won't find it hard. In fact it may be too easy; that's where the risk lies. Because you normally decide what to eat consciously, there aren't the built-in safeguards that protect you while you're learning to control unconscious processes. There's a danger of eating less than your body needs before you've mastered the skill of balancing food and energy. So you'll have to be monitored by a healer to make sure no damage is occurring."

For a few moments there was silence while everyone contemplated this. Then Jesse said, "Peter, all this is great—we're better off trying to avoid starvation than believing we don't have a chance. But the fact, which I'll state here to the Council but not to everyone, is that we don't. We can stretch the food and maybe harvest a little, but we can't provide for an expanding population, not even for one generation of kids. The plateau isn't large enough. It wouldn't be, even if it all could be watered. With the valley, we might have made a go of it eventually, but without it that's impossible. I let you down—the site I chose isn't adequate."

Carla's heart ached for him. What he was saying was true, of course. Peter would deny it; he knew Jesse was prone to self-blame and would not let him take responsibility for the colony's failure. But they all knew underneath that it was going to fail.

To her astonishment, Peter nodded. "It's not the sort of place we counted on," he said seriously, "and it's time we faced that. Either we get back on track, or we die."

32

"THERE WILL BE a memorial for Hari and Claire this evening," Peter announced, "and afterward I will say what must be said to the Group as a whole." He hesitated, as if he'd intended to elaborate but had thought better of it. Then he continued, "But I'll say some of it here and now. We are the leaders. It's important to understand what we're up against."

Turning to Jesse, he said, "Your choice of site wasn't a mistake—given the information that was available to you, it was the right choice. But we didn't follow through. We didn't make enough effort to learn about the environment we're stuck with."

Jesse nodded, chagrined. He was the only one of them who'd been educated on Earth, yet he hadn't done much more than teach them to survive desert heat. He had been too busy retrieving equipment from the starship to give thought to the climate's long-term implications.

"We weren't wrong to try rainmaking," Peter went on, "but we should have studied meteorology beforehand—even elementary knowledge of Earth's weather would have told us what causes flash floods. Now we are farming in the way it was done on Undine. It seems obvious that it's the only way. It fits the supplies and instructions given to us in the pods. But agriculture existed for thousands of years on Earth in many different cultures. Were they all alike, or is it possible that some had ideas that might be useful to us?"

"There were dry regions on Earth before the widespread use of irrigation," Reiko said thoughtfully. "Did nonindustrialized cultures rely entirely on rainmaking, or did they have some forgotten way of dealing with drought?"

"It would be wise to find out," declared Peter. "That's what the knowledgebase is for, and we haven't been fully utilizing it. It's not enough to learn the skills we've expected to need. Let's have some people read up on agriculture—not just modern methods, but the ones used in ancient times.

Another thing—Arwen has viewed wind pumps in a place where it doesn't make sense to put them. There's got to be a reason for that. To say we put them there just because she foresaw them would be circular reasoning. I suggest that we look for some clue."

"Are we sure there *is* a reason?" Kwame asked. "Maybe it was just a dream."

"Arwen is exceptionally psi-gifted," said Peter. "In fact, I think we should ask her to take Hari's place on the Council. His outlook was different from the majority's, and should be represented."

"That's fitting," said Kira, "especially since the child she's carrying is his."

At their nods, Peter went on, "Our ignorance has cost us, but our greatest failure is something else. We've lost sight of what we stand for. The emotional ambience in the Group right now is deadly, friends. It's enough to defeat us even if we don't starve."

There were murmurs of protest. "I think people have been holding up remarkably well, considering the circumstances," Jesse protested. "Certainly they're calm about it. Nobody's giving way to fear."

"Yes, they are. All of us have been, me as much as anybody, in spite of the pledge we've made in the Ritual to support each other. I succumbed to illness—"

"God, Peter! You were hit by an alien virus! You can hardly blame yourself for that."

"It's not a matter of blame, but all the same I got sick in violation of our most basic precepts. It was known as far back as the twentieth century on Earth that the mind affects the immune system. There are pathogens so toxic that no one's mind can overcome them, but the virus that attacked me isn't that virulent. If it were, we'd have an epidemic by now."

"Peter, like the rest of us you're only human," Kira said. "Your injury put you under tremendous stress. We're not pledged to become supermen."

"We're pledged to live by the principles Ian taught us. Yet I was so absorbed by the needs of the new recruits and the traumatized members I felt responsible for that I didn't notice what was happening to the rest of you. Then, when I woke up in the infirmary and realized how hopeless you all were beneath the tranquil facade, I couldn't pull myself together to deal with it. The virus allowed me to close my eyes."

"No one expected you to deal with the situation," said Dan. "Not when—"

Breaking in, Peter continued, "I've had a lot of time to think now, and I know things got out of hand long before the flood. We were—disillusioned. We came here after weeks of anticipation, expecting our new world to be wonderful, a great place to live even though we'd have to give up comforts and work hard, and when we found it's not—that in some ways we even miss Undine—something in us faded."

They stared at him, letting this sink in. They had all felt it, without daring to acknowledge it often. "What held us together on Undine was rebellion against the Meds," Kwame said slowly. "Now that that's gone, we've been—adrift."

"And there's no going back," said Carla in a low voice. "I don't mean back to Undine, I mean to feeling the way we did before. Before—stasis."

"Did stasis do this to us?" Reiko wondered.

"Probably," said Jesse grimly. "And having to land so fast while we were still debilitated from it didn't help, either."

"Going into stasis amplified the effect," Peter said, "but not physically. What we've been feeling here is the abrupt loss of a supportive psychic milieu. Remember, we've always known that the collective unconscious doesn't extend across interplanetary space. That's why on Undine we couldn't draw on the metaphors that have traditionally upheld people on Earth. But at least we were part of something larger than ourselves, a world with a framework to which we were oriented, even though we weren't happy with the government and, as Kwame says, were united by resistance to it. We are very few here, and we are alone."

"I did feel fear, underneath, even before the crop was destroyed," confessed Teresa miserably. "Not of danger, not of dying soon . . . I didn't know what I was afraid of."

"That was the result of psychic contagion," Peter said. "Some of our people never really wanted to be stuck on a new world—they came only because they were needed, or because they were unstable and needed the Group's support. They were the first to falter, but all of us felt insecure for one reason or another. Our individual doubts and worries have been feeding on each other because we haven't faced them squarely. We've ignored the first declaration of the Ritual—the statement that it's *unacknowledged* fear that destroys."

"Psychic contagion?" Jesse questioned. "You mean unconscious telepathy, like what I caused when I first reacted to the crawlies?"

"Yes, except that everyone contributed to it in one way or another," Peter said. "Fear is a normal response to stress. Through our mind training we've learned not to let it harm our bodies. But it's still there, in our unconscious minds, whether we're in actual danger or not. On Undine our natural fears were symbolized by the stasis vaults—that symbol was a useful outlet for them, which was why Ian fostered it. But aboard the starship we overcame that fear. Stasis holds no terror for us now. So what's to be afraid of here?"

"Starvation," said Dan.

"No. The trouble started before we had reason to think we may starve."

"Dying in general, then, simply because this is a strange environment where we haven't known what might happen."

"The unknown, yes. But not of dying, at least not consciously. We're conditioned against that fear because on Undine we fought against society's denial of death. Now that there's really some danger of it happening in the near future, nobody is going around in terror of dying—on the contrary, most of you are so resigned to it that you're ready to give up."

"That's true," Jesse agreed. "I noticed that some time back. I've been trying to get people to fight for survival, but they just—go through the motions."

"Well, we've always held that there are worse things than death," Teresa said.

"What things?" Peter persisted.

"Oh . . . I see . . . on Undine it was stasis. And so now I guess I can't put a name to it."

In a low voice Carla said, "Neither can I. I wonder sometimes . . . what we're doing here, so far away from all the settled worlds . . . just living, not very comfortably to be sure, but even if we had everything we could want, what's the *point*? I don't mean we'd be better off on Undine . . . I'm glad we escaped from there . . . but for what?"

"What is anybody doing, anywhere?" Kwame said. "It's no different for us than for others, except we've got reason to wonder. Most people just take living for granted."

"It *is* different for us," Peter said, "because of what I just mentioned. We don't have the psychic support of a vast civilization to serve as an anchor. We're cut off not only from physical contact but from unconscious psi contact with the rest of the human race—and that's scary."

Why was Peter stirring this up? Jesse wondered. Rousing these thoughts would only make people feel worse. On the other hand, the Group had never shied from disturbing thoughts. His first week on the Island, when they'd made him confront his dismay at the thought of dying slowly in old age and had revealed the risks they were taking to save old people from the Vaults, he had been impressed by their courage in speaking of such things. Gradually, he had understood that it was what set them free to enjoy the good times. Peter's right, he thought. Somehow we've changed, lost our way. . . .

"A sudden break with a planet's collective unconscious

has inescapable effects," Peter pointed out. "We're facing a challenge no human beings have ever met before, except perhaps on starships adrift in space without hope of return. No colony on a new world has ever been as small as ours, or as isolated. Jesse is less vulnerable than the rest of you; he's used to being in space, and he has never relied on the backing of any world. Still, as a spacer he was supported by the culture of Fleet, knowing he wouldn't be separated from humankind forever. And even so, he tended to be depressed. You all realize, don't you, that we're experiencing what the Meds on Undine—or Earth, for that matter—would call clinical depression? We'd be drugged senseless for it if we were in their hands."

"Well, we've escaped that, anyway," Kwame said, trying to smile, "which is a good reason to be glad we're here."

"Our goal was to escape the Meds' authority," Dan agreed. "But now that we've achieved it—what's left?"

Peter's smile was genuine. "You put your finger on it," he said, "as Carla did a moment ago. Human beings can endure just about anything—danger, deprivation, sorrow, even torture—as long as they see meaning in their lives and a goal that will lead somewhere. When they don't, depression sets in. This was occasionally recognized on Earth, but most doctors bought into the claim that depression is the result of biochemical changes rather than the cause, a theory that led to far more suffering than it relieved."

"It created a market for drugs," Kira said bitterly. "From the Meds' standpoint it was a spectacular success."

"But Peter," Reiko pointed out, "we do have a goal! We came here to establish a more advanced human culture, a culture based on psi."

"And are we doing that? Or are we doing just the opposite by letting the lack of a worldwide collective unconscious rob us of roots, while allowing unconscious telepathy among ourselves to spread gloom?"

There was a moment of shocked silence. Breaking it, Kira said, "Dear God. We thought a better culture would create itself once we no longer had to hide our powers. But you're saying that they've been working *against* us."

"They have," Peter admitted, "and that shouldn't have happened, because it was my job to stay on top of the psychic situation here. It's not too late to turn it around—but we can't afford to waste any time. It goes without saying that we don't want our kids born into a world where everyone's resigned to an early death."

"The babies!" Carla gasped in horror. "Are they suffering from depression, too, because of their prenatal psi bonds with us? I've tried so hard to project positive feelings to Kel, but I just *couldn't*—"

"You can't project what you don't feel," Peter said. "Yes, the babies are already affected, and that's why we have to act soon. Otherwise they won't thrive, and what's ahead will be much more painful for us, seeing that, than it will be if their lives are merely short. And of course if it turns out that we *don't* starve, it would be a terrible thing to have produced an emotionally-warped generation."

"But what can we do?" Teresa whispered. "There's no way to force ourselves to feel differently."

"No," Peter agreed. "Any attempt to force feelings by willpower would mean repressing our genuine ones, which would simply make matters worse."

"Then what's the solution?" Jesse demanded. "You didn't start this conversation just to tell us what we've done wrong, Peter."

"What was the first thing you learned in the Group, every one of you, when you were taught how to stop suffering from physical pain?"

Jesse said slowly, "To alter perception. Not to deny feelings, but to experience them differently."

"Are you saying we're supposed to alter our perception of the mess we're in?" Kwame protested. "How is that possible?"

"The answer can't be reached by reasoning alone," Peter replied. "It must be felt. I can point the way, but I need your support. I need all of you to back me up, starting to-night—to share the truth with the others instead of shrink-ing from it. To help me convey feelings the rest of the Group needs to grasp."

He will use his telepathic power, Jesse realized, commu-nicating the thought to Carla. *He'll mesmerize people, as he did when he talked them into hijacking a starship, and later into stasis. Or for that matter, as he does every time he leads the Ritual.* And then with sadness he thought, *Oh, God, the Ritual—with Peter crippled, can we ever hold it again?* There would be no more initiations until their kids reached ado-lescence, but there could well be a need for rainmaking be-fore someone else could become qualified to lead fire han-dling.

"We'll weep not only for Hari and Claire but for our-selves this evening," Peter said. "But I hope we can move beyond that, and regain the vision that led us here."

33

AT FIRST IT was assumed that the memorial would be held in the Commons, as the one for those who died aboard the starship had been, so that Peter could participate. But he insisted on being taken to the assembly ring. "There will be no special accommodations made for me, now or ever," he maintained. So Jesse and Kwame carried him to the settlement's motorized cart, which they drove all the way onto the dais as a platform for him to sit on. The Council members sat around him, ready to provide whatever physi-cal assistance might be necessary.

"And whatever telepathic backup he's expecting from us," Reiko reminded the others. "I can't imagine what we're supposed to convey to the Group, but no doubt he'll make it clear when the time comes. Or perhaps . . . he just wants insurance, in case—"

In case he finds he can't focus their minds, Jesse thought

grimly. In case their reaction to his leglessness proves too distracting.

Oh God, I can't bear to watch this, Carla cried silently. *To think of all the times he's inspired us—standing tall for us to center on, strong and whole, embodying vitality. . . . It can't be the same, Jesse! It's one thing when we're on the floor in his room, but here, with everyone looking down at the dais—* She broke off, remembering that the sight of Peter's maimed body was more painful for Jesse than for anyone else.

I don't see how he could alter our perceptions even if he could still stand, Jesse confessed. *But we've got to assume he knows what he's doing.*

In anticipation of the occasion, more tapers had been braided and more torches made—enough for several gatherings, since it had become apparent that they might be needed in the future on short notice. The gatherings were becoming an essential focus for the Group, Jesse realized. With confidence now faltering, only the enhanced telepathic bond produced by a full assembly might sustain it. Was that all Peter had in mind—the cementing of that bond? If so, they would indeed need more such assemblies during the dark time to come.

Although the Group's memorials usually had no music apart from singing, Peter had asked Erik to set up the speaker system as they did when gathering for the Ritual. Familiar recordings had been among the electronic files brought from Undine. The soaring, stirring synthesized music that had so often thrilled Jesse was not now being played, however. What he heard in the background was heartbreakingly sad, appropriate to be sure for a funeral, but he couldn't help wondering why Peter, knowing how depressed they already were, had not seen to it that something brighter was chosen.

The sound faded, and the traditional rite began, with Peter speaking as usual through a wireless mike. Jesse sympathized when he eulogized poor Claire, knowing he'd blamed himself for the starship deaths and would see hers as even more directly attributable to him, if in fact he believed he should have thrown off the virus. For the first time, Jesse grasped the truth of what Peter had told him about guilt being felt by everyone. Of course no such feelings were warranted in Peter's case, even if in theory he could have avoided the tragedy! And then Jesse wondered, was it true that they weren't warranted in his own? Had it been merely fate, and not his error, that had stranded them here at a site that could not sustain their lives?

After his eulogy for Hari, Peter called on Arwen, too, to speak of him, and afterward proposed that she take over his Council role as coordinator of psi research. This was quickly approved by voice vote, and she remained on the dais with the others. When the last song had been sung and the tapers had gone out, the assembled people started to leave, but Peter called them back.

"There's more that needs to be said," he declared. "That we're grieving now for Hari is unavoidable and right. But I sense more gloom here than mourning for him. I sense fear that his death was meaningless. I sense a feeling that we're stuck in a bad situation with no way out. And that is *not* right."

Jesse and the rest of the Council exchanged glances, frowning. Though they had known this was to be openly discussed, it seemed risky. Peter's optimism in the face of his loss would be admired, but could hardly be shared. How could he claim that the future would be anything but bad, if he forced everyone to confront it?

Peter proceeded to explain the practical ideas he'd offered to the Council earlier. The possibility of controlling their metabolism to require less food. The justification for more rainmaking. The search for information about ancient ways of dealing with drought. But the fact that these measures wouldn't be enough was not lost on anyone. Reason told them, once they thought about it, that there simply wasn't enough farmland. They might live, but an increasing population could not. And Peter must be aware that they knew this. What he'd said was only a prelude to whatever he was planning.

I think, Kira confided to the Council, *that we're about to experience the dark before the dawn.*

Yes, thought Jesse suddenly. That was the principle behind all the transformative lessons. Feel fear or pain, accept it, and then discover that it truly didn't matter. There had always been a dawn, always a high after intense stress, even in such trivial situations as the immunization to the crawlies. Despite himself, in defiance of all logic, he was beginning to believe that Peter might pull it off again. . . .

The slow, sad music resumed, first barely audible, then swelling. Peter began to speak of Undine. "We longed to get away from tyranny," he said, "and we succeeded. But we paid a high price—"

In the front row of the ring, Greg rose and declared, "We don't regret that, Peter. None of us think the price was too high. It was right to resist, to gamble on reaching a better world."

"Of course it was. But there's no shame in sorrowing for the things we lost. This is a dreary world, compared to Undine. It was a golden world seen from space, but the gold is only dryness, only bare rock and soil we can't bring to life. Our crops may shrivel and die, and we with them. While on Undine the sea is still vast and blue, dotted with green islands. . . ." *And on our Island, the green woods are flourishing again around the ruins of the Lodge . . . and the water laps against the beach of the swimming cove, and it's clear beneath the rock we dove from, but across the bay, near the cave we could reach only by scuba diving, it's green with sea life . . . and the air is cool, you can expose your skin to it, feel it soft and moist around you . . . and planes still fly over the sea, soaring, free. . . .*

He was no longer speaking aloud; the images surged through the assembled minds, clearer than mere memory yet unreachable. It was agony. Jesse, who had lived on Undine only a short while, found that he was as profoundly stricken as everyone else. *My God*, came Carla's thought, *we're* homesick! *Homesick for Undine! I never admitted that to myself, it was so foolish, I'd wanted so much to leave . . . I guess I just pushed it down inside, into a place I didn't dare go. . . .*

They must not fight the sorrow, Jesse knew. The Council must enhance the imagery with all the telepathic power they could muster, backing Peter's as he had asked. What they were feeling now was what everyone had felt all along, and had hidden from, letting it spread from mind to mind at a deep unconscious level. No wonder they'd all been depressed. Even he knew enough about psychology to understand that buried feelings hurt more than those that were allowed to surface.

It went on for a long time. Peter spared them nothing; from images of Undine's beauty he went on to urge recall of happy times around the Lodge fireplace, and then the faces of families and friends—outsiders—who'd been left behind. There were no dry eyes in the assembly, and some people had given way to sobs. When the tears had subsided, Peter took up the mike again.

"We never imagined," he said, "that we'd get to a new world and then *not like it*. We were thrilled by the idea of going into space. Yet we never saw space—the starship had no viewports, we slept through most of the trip, and many of us landed here at night. There are seas on this world, but we've never seen them and probably never will, since the shuttles are too precious to risk on sightseeing trips. We've seen one small plateau covered with rocks, one canyon that's now a shambles, and a view of bare, unreachable mountains. The climate is terrible, the food is unappetizing even when there's enough of it, and it's hard to stay clean without plumbing. And we're weary now not only from lifting stones, but from hunger. Don't try to pretend that you're enjoying this place. The more you lie to yourself, the more you'll be dragged down by the disappointment."

"What good does he think it will do to tell it like it is?" Teresa murmured, but Kira whispered back, "Don't worry, he knows. Just watch—if he offers a straw of hope now, people will grasp at it."

"It has been declared that we probably won't be able to survive here," Peter went on, "and nobody seems to be resisting that verdict. It's easy to resign yourself to death when you're not consciously afraid of dying and it doesn't look as if the place you're stuck in will ever let you enjoy living. The old saying "I'm so homesick I could die" has a basis in human psychology. What's more, if there's no likelihood of achieving anything important by living, what's the point in struggling? Starving to death might be convenient, since we in the Group can't condone suicide."

There was a shocked gasp from the audience. Then Bernie, stepping forward, spoke out. "I trust that's irony, Peter, but even so—you can't think that we wouldn't make every effort if there were any chance at all—"

"But are you God, Bernie?" Peter retorted. "Are any of you as wise as gods—wise enough to be sure that Ian's vision and Ian's sacrifice meant nothing, that no chance of its validation exists?"

"Ian wasn't God, either," Bernie said. "Yes, he gave his life to buy us the chance to leave Undine, but he knew it was a risk. He was well aware that we might fail."

"Everything's a risk. To say it isn't would be to accept the notion of predestination. But Ian *believed* we would accomplish something here, not just that we'd escape from the Med government, but that we would make use of our mind powers to create a new kind of society. If we deny all possibility of it we're dishonoring his memory."

"I don't agree," Tomas argued, rising beside Bernie. "We all honor the memory of Ian. You drew on that when you persuaded us to emigrate, and again when you got us to go into stasis. It won't work this time, because above all, Ian valued honesty. He wouldn't have said we should close our eyes to hard fact."

"Nor would I," Peter pointed out, "as I've just now demonstrated. But he wouldn't let us close them to our inner faith in a destiny, either. Think of all that's happened that points to it—the synchronicities. Jesse being stranded on Undine just at the time we needed someone who could take us away. Ian's dreams, without which he wouldn't have acted to save Jesse as he did. The ship having stasis facilities, the last in existence to retain them. Our successful landing after almost—but not quite—running out of air, which was a closer call than most of you realize—"

"We don't all have the faith in destiny you do, Peter," Tomas said sadly, glancing at the faces around the ring. "Not in the face of knowledge that our food supply can't be replenished."

Peter raised his voice, his eyes penetrating the crowd despite the deepening dusk. "Yes, you do," he said. "You have faith in the future, even though it's suppressed by what you think you know. I'm sure of that because I've felt the evidence."

"Evidence? What evidence?" Jesse burst out, too surprised to recall Peter's plea for backing from the Council. It seemed to him that faith on the part of the Group had been notably lacking.

"Not long ago you all gathered in this place to pray for my recovery," said Peter. "Whether those prayers, if you perceive them as prayers, reached any power beyond our understanding is something none of us can know. But they reached *me*. I'm telepathically sensitive, after all, and I could hardly have failed to sense what was in so many focused minds, even while I was unconscious. It's clear that you all believed, and were aware that you believed, that whether I lived through my illness *mattered*."

"Of course it mattered!" Reiko said. "How could it not? Did it surprise you to know we care about you?"

"No—but you see, you couldn't have felt that my recovery mattered if you'd been inwardly convinced that we're all going to die soon anyway. You knew as much about the food situation then as you do now. You knew I was crippled and might not be fully functional for a long time, if ever. What difference would it have made if I'd died a little ahead of everyone else?"

"It wasn't a matter of logic," Kira declared.

"No," Peter said dryly. "Faith never is."

Stunned, everyone stared at Peter. "We've been out of touch with our inner selves," he went on, "and so we've lost sight of what being in the Group used to mean to us. It will help to be honest about our feelings—both the sad ones and those that may seem like wishful thinking. Those we're afraid to acknowledge because we think we couldn't bear another disappointment."

"We've shut out hope to escape the pain of finding it false," murmured Carla.

"And that's a costly anesthetic," Peter said. "It won't do any real harm if we bet on optimism and lose—but betting on despair would be a sure way to rule out any chance of becoming all we can be."

34

THE MUSIC SWELLED again, no longer heartrending but exhilarating. The Council broke into smiles, aware of an abrupt change in the psychic atmosphere of the gathering. As always, Peter's skill in projecting emotions had transformed fear into confidence, impossible though that had seemed only a few minutes ago.

Jesse rose and prepared to move the cart from the dais. But Peter was not ready to leave. He softened the music, which they now saw he'd been controlling with a remote, and motioned them all to sit down. Then suddenly he threw off the lap robe that had concealed his body's mutilation, and ignoring the murmurs of dismay, began speaking again.

"There's another thing," he said. "Some of you have been questioning whether we should have come here because

anywhere else, I could have had bionic legs or at least prostheses. Have you forgotten why we opposed the Meds? Have
you forgotten the most fundamental concept we believe in,
that the mind has primacy over the body? Good God, people,
there's nothing wrong with my mind! I still have the powers
I've always had. Our goal has always been to prove that the
mind controls health and well-being. If my living without
legs can't contribute to that goal, then it's true we shouldn't
have come—because we don't believe what we've been saying in the Ritual unless we believe it unconditionally."

The assembled people drew breath. Some of them bowed
their heads, shamefaced. "I—haven't looked at it that way,"
Carla admitted.

"I have," Kira replied quietly. "But it had to come from
Peter himself."

"We can't achieve what we came here to achieve unless
we do look at it that way," Peter said. "It's all for nothing if
we fall back on traditional premises the first time our own
are challenged. Don't you see, physical survival isn't enough.
Even with a bountiful harvest, without rejecting the Meds'
scale of values we'd end up worse off than if we'd never left
Undine."

"If the power of our minds isn't what matters most, we
might just as well have stayed home," Kwame agreed. "You
needn't worry, Peter. We won't waver again."

"I'm glad to hear it," Peter said. "And I'm going to ask
you to prove it. We are going to hold the Ritual here and
now, the full Ritual with the pledges of commitment, and
afterward we will have no more doubts about the rightness
of settling this world."

"Peter, you can't!" Carla burst out. "It's too dangerous
for you—"

"If I can't, it means one of two things," declared Peter.
"Either all we've been working toward is invalid, or I'm not
fit to be your leader. If I'm not, it's best that we find out."

That was why he hadn't warned them ahead of time,
Jesse realized. He had made it impossible for them to pro-

test, for they knew that such a statement to the assembly could not be withdrawn.

Reiko frowned. "It's not just the risk to you, but the logistics of it. How can we position a torch between us when you're sitting down?"

"Well, I expect I can find a couple of volunteers to hold me upright."

"On something to raise you to the height of the others," Kwame suggested.

"No," said Kira. "We will kneel for the Ritual from now on, so as to be on the same level as Peter."

The Group waited with growing tension while more grass tapers were distributed and someone prepared the torches from which to light them. The Council formed a double semicircle, the three men facing Peter, the women, who because of pregnancy could participate only telepathically, behind them. "Without both Hari and Kira, you're going to have no one with much experience touching fire with you," Reiko protested. "You've always said that's not safe."

"I won't have a novice to protect, either," Peter pointed out. "And Jesse has done this quite often by now."

Jesse nodded. It was of course essential that he take part. But having little aptitude for the paranormal himself, he had always relied on Peter's strength, and he was not entirely sure that Peter was fully enough recovered to control the psychic forces involved. If it turned out that he wasn't, far more damage would be done than burns that could be healed, now that he'd staked his role as leader on renewing the people's faith in mind power.

Carla was still apprehensive. *Jesse, it's too risky for him to try it so soon!"* she protested silently. *Can't you stop him somehow?*

He has to do it, Jesse told her. *It's the only way he can retain people's trust—and his own belief that even without legs, he's a whole man.*

"Carla," Peter said. "Twice before you've served as torch-

bearer at times of crisis—will you do it once again? Please—
I need your support."

Striving for composure, she assented. He had left her
no choice. Jesse knew, as did she, that for her to refuse
would magnify his peril, perhaps even cause him to fail. Yet
the torchbearer's role was in some ways more demanding
than that of a participant. To hold the torch steady while
people you loved plunged their hands into it required full
confidence that they would not be burned, for any doubt
would be wordlessly passed on to them at the most crucial
moment of all.

Greg and Nathan came to the dais to lift Peter down
from the cart and hold him erect. As usual, he spoke at
some length before the lighting of the torch, reminding them
of the Group's aims and the kind of world they were committed to work toward. But this time he also spoke specifically of the crisis they were facing. "I for one can't believe
we've come halfway across the galaxy, only to be defeated
by the weather," he said. "But if we give up the principles to
which we've pledged ourselves, then we're already beaten."

Carla stepped forward with a torch lit from one of those
stationed around the ring for taper-lighting. Somewhat
awkwardly, the Council—the women as well as the men—
knelt. To his surprise it dawned on Jesse that this was
going to be challenging; the rough stone surface dug into
his knees and he realized that were it not for his near-auto-
matic skill in pain control, maintaining such a position
throughout the rite would make extending his arm to the
flame considerably more difficult than doing it while
standing.

"As we say the words of the pledges, make them happy
words," Peter urged after the customary period of silent meditation. "Remember that the Ritual is a joyous thing—remember
how it felt when you first heard those words and found that
you could pass your hand through flame unharmed."

The questions ordinarily posed to the novice, which had
been omitted in past Rituals when no new member was being

initiated, were answered by the Group in unison, either tele-pathically or aloud as each person chose:

"Do you by your own free choice commit yourself to live by the precepts of the Group?"

We do. The precepts included willingness to acknowl-edge fear; how could they have lost sight of that?

"Will you support fellow-members of the Group in all ways, even at the risk of your personal safety?'

We will. Not just through action, but through ongoing telepathic projection of hope instead of despair.

"Do you believe that your mind has power over the well-being of your body, and that it can protect or heal you from sickness, injury and pain?"

We do. And from hunger, even from near-starvation. . . .

"Are you willing to confirm your commitment by prov-ing your trust in that power?"

We are. It meant more, this time, than briefly touching flame. It meant trust in the colony's survival.

Then as the music surged and Carla lowered the torch, thrusting it horizontally with their reach, Peter began the for-mal declarations:

"Unfaced fear is the destroyer. We will acknowledge fear and accept it, we will go past it and live free.

"We will trust the power of the mind over all restric-tions, whether imposed from within or by the world outside.

"We will act always through volition, allowing neither internal nor external pressures to enslave us.

"We will support one another unfailingly in fulfilling this pledge.

"We believe that we are stewards of a flame that will illuminate future generations."

As he said this, Peter's thought was clear, and was passed among them all. This was the vision, the focus of the faith they had thought they'd lost. They were stewards. The flame that had drawn them to the Group must not be al-lowed to die. Maclairn was not merely an inhospitable planet whose lacks they were forced to endure—it was the hearth from which that flame would rise. And so they must live, to tend the flame and pass it on to their children.

"And we now seal our commitment with the symbol of the mind's power, which is fire."

He paused briefly, checking the readiness of the other participants, and then as fearlessly as he always had, he thrust his hand into the flame. Jesse, touching that hand with his own as the world merged with infinity, knew that Peter was all right. He would always be all right. Legs were a minor consideration beside the power of his mind to sustain him, and to enhearten the followers he inspired. *How could we have doubted?* Jesse wondered as he withdrew his hand, and Carla replied, *We forgot what's important. We forgot what it means to be unfazed by fire.*

35

IN THE DAYS that followed, hope within the Group was rekindled. Jesse was not sure whether this was because Peter had managed to alter their perception of the future, or merely because they had placed their trust in Peter. Everyone except Jesse and the new trainees had been brought into the Group by Ian, who—as Kira had once mentioned—had been the equal of the great spiritual leaders of ancient Earth. His death had been a blow from which they could not quickly recover. They had followed Peter because Ian had appointed him heir, emigrated to a new world because he had said Ian wanted them to, had gone into stasis aboard the starship because he'd convinced them that their regard for Ian's memory demanded it. Now, after the shock of almost losing him to crippling and near-death, their allegiance had shifted. From now on they would follow *him*, not for Ian's sake but because he had proven unshakable.

The Commons meal shifts were rearranged. All the men gathered before dawn for their single scant meal of the day. The women ate later, at noon and in the early evening, sparingly but no less than required to maintain the health of their unborn babies. "It goes without saying that fasting will be voluntary," Peter had said to the men. It also went without saying that "voluntary" was a mere formality in this case, Jesse thought, for no one would intentionally violate a rule presented as part of the Ritual commitment to use mind power. Nor would anyone choose to eat more than a fair share when food was scarce.

Each of them, immediately preceding the scheduled neurofeedback session in which the volitional alteration of metabolism would be taught to him, was asked to fast totally for three days. The skill would be easiest to learn, Peter explained, when the body craved nourishment. "Doesn't fasting lead to altered consciousness, Peter?" someone asked when this was first discussed. "Historically, it was one of the techniques employed by shamans and mystics."

"That's true. It's not what we're seeking and in any case, we already know how to choose what kind of altered state we want to be in—we've learned through neurofeedback to enter states the ancients needed fasting to attain. But if it happens spontaneously during the initial training phase, no harm will be done."

This revelation worried Jesse far more than the prospect of being hungry. He'd never liked the idea of altered states and he knew there were more than had been taught to him as a necessary part of his mind training. So far he had not experienced disorientation or seen visions or slipped out of his body, as Hari and perhaps others had during rainmaking, and he did not want to. The mere thought repelled and frightened him.

He soon found, however, that hunger had a greater effect on his mind than on his stomach. Despite determined resistance, he began to feel . . . detached. He couldn't shake himself back to his normal focus on work. And then on the third night he woke in absolute terror, looking down at the mattress on which he lay as if seeing it from above, seeing his own body, and then as he turned away to shut out that sight, drifting across the sleeping shelter and out through a dissolving wall into the black night. . . .

In desperation, he sought a firm hold on the reality his life had been built upon. He must not panic. He was sane enough to know that panic would destroy him. He felt no physical symptoms of it yet—no racing heart, not even cold chills—but that was because he felt no connection to his body at all. . . . And then he remembered something Kira had taught him long ago on Undine. She'd said that because he had learned to enter specific altered states, he was vulnerable to slipping into other states spontaneously. She'd shown him a mind-pattern for overcoming the fear that might arouse in him. Grimly, he visualized it, and the strange perception ceased abruptly. But only gradually was he able to calm himself afterward.

That day he went through the neurofeedback training for metabolic control. Having had plenty of past experience in matching his mind-pattern with an instructor's, he mastered this one quickly. His hunger literally disappeared. It might be difficult to maintain the new mindset continuously when no feedback was available, and he realized that Peter's warning about its becoming too easy to ignore his body's needs made sense. Once used to fasting, he'd heard, people didn't feel hungry anyway. The trick of doing with less food lay in consciously lowering metabolism, not mere immunity to hunger. He didn't doubt his ability to achieve that.

But to Peter, before leaving the lab, he confessed other doubts. "You all seem not to mind this out-of-body thing," he said. "I—I suppose I ought to learn to do it. It started to happen to me last night, and I pulled back. Am I a coward, Peter, or do I just lack aptitude?"

"Feeling repelled isn't the same as cowardice," Peter said, "and there's no need for you to explore this particular phenomenon if you've no desire to. It occurred not only because you were fasting but because others were—people who welcomed the experience—and fasting, like other stress, enhances telepathic sensitivity. You unconsciously picked up a mind-pattern you weren't ready to deal with, a harmless one that has been quite common throughout human history."

"But doesn't it occur with near-death experiences—NDEs?"

"Yes, but it's by no means confined to them. You were in no danger of getting stuck in it like Claire or Hari, you know; both of them, for different reasons, went too far and were tempted to stay too long. Assuming that your body isn't near death to start with, if you want to get back you can always do so instantly. Someday, if you ever have reason to pursue this, you may be glad to have found that it's possible for you. Otherwise, just let it go."

Inwardly relieved, Jesse put it out of his thoughts and got on with his job. But something nagged at him. His telepathic awareness continued to increase and he sensed that the Group felt on the verge of a breakthrough they had no real reason to expect—as if a deep spring had been tapped but had yet to burst through into the surface. Was it just that they were no longer denying faith, he wondered, or was psychic intuition in some way responsible?

The wells had been dug and a part of the plateau cleared for planting, no more than it would be feasible to irrigate. The time had come to plow and fertilize the land. Yet Jesse held back from giving the go-ahead, inexplicably uneasy about it. Once their limited supply of soil nutrients had been dispersed, there would be no way to replenish it. They would never be able to prepare a third set of fields. Was he sure that he'd chosen the best location? Peter had placed him in charge and he knew he mustn't be hesitant. He didn't know what had come over him—his normal tendency had always been to act fast when action was called for. Still the positioning of the wells still bothered him. Peter had advised looking for a reason why Arwen had seen them on the rim of the canyon, and no reason had yet been uncovered.

He did not see how irrigation could work unless they

built water towers. They wouldn't need to be high, as the slope was not great; materials could be scrounged from the starship to raise them. Holding tanks would be harder to come by. They might need to accumulate water to build enough pressure for filling the furrows. Kwame was doubtful that this could be done. Yet there had to be a way, since there was simply no land near the wells other than the area already chosen. He supposed he should forge ahead, trusting that the way would be found, as they couldn't afford to waste any more time . . . even though his instinct told him something was wrong. Perhaps it wasn't instinct. Perhaps he was merely afraid of making another disastrous mistake.

Tomorrow he would have to quit stalling, Jesse decided as drifted into restless sleep. He woke in the dark with Carla shaking him. "Jesse! Jesse . . . I think it's time."

"Time?" Confused, he mumbled, "Time for what? It's nowhere near morning—"

"For the baby. Get Susan—she can tell for sure."

"The baby? Oh, my God." He jumped up, pulling on his clothes. They had not expected this for at least another week. On nearby mattresses, others had awakened; several of the women gathered around Carla, excited and happy, ready to help her to the infirmary if her labor was in fact beginning.

Fumbling with his phone, Jesse called Susan, who slept in a different shelter, only to be told that she wasn't free. "I'm with Kira," she said. "Kira's gone into labor early."

God. It was too soon for Kira; her baby would be premature. Were they even equipped to care for premature babies? Considering her age, it would be a high-risk delivery and Susan would have to stay with her. Because of the possibility that several women would be in labor simultaneously, a few of them had been trained to serve as midwives. Where would they take Carla if the infirmary's bed was in use? Kira would soon need her own room to care for her newborn; Peter couldn't be evicted from his. Yet they would hardly deliver a baby in the main room of the Commons, much less on a floor mattress in the middle of the very crowded public sleeping shelter. And at night the stone huts were too cold.

A shuttle. It was the only suitable place—it had light and warmth and power for heating water. Whatever couple was using it at present would have to be turned out.

He hurried to the infirmary to pick up supplies and found Olivia there with Susan. "There's nothing to worry about, Jesse," Susan said. "It will be an easy birth, completely natural. Carla's healthy and I checked her only yesterday." She had used her healer's sense to do that, Jesse knew, not just physical examination. All the same, he was tense with apprehension. He had never known Carla's exact age, but she must be near forty, considering the length of time she'd been married to Ramón. What if it wasn't easy, what if some problem arose and Susan could not come?

Olivia, after calling Ingrid to help, went with him; the three of them took Carla to the shuttle in the motorized cart. Walking would be okay at this stage, Olivia said, but not in the freezing air; in the cart she could be bundled in blankets. The cart also brought mattresses, which he piled to make a bed for her. He covered them with a clean sheet and she lay back on it, grimacing at the contractions, which were by now coming only a few minutes apart.

He had been warned that labor would last a long time. He hadn't foreseen how interminable that time would seem. Carla knew how to turn off pain, of course, so he'd somehow thought she could simply relax and wait while her body did what women's bodies were meant to do. He had not had any real conception of why it was called "labor." After some hours, when he thought it must soon be over, the contractions intensified and Jesse rushed frantically to her side. In vids women didn't writhe and pant and grunt; they didn't fall back, sweating, exhausted, only to be overcome again by one spasm after another. *Carla . . . oh, Carla, what's gone wrong?* he pleaded. *Can't this be stopped?*

Nothing's wrong . . . it's not supposed to stop! It's sup-

posed to keep on getting worse! That's the only way the baby can come out. She was too breathless to speak aloud.

But can't I do anything to help you?

Just stay with me, Jesse! Hold my hand!

As he clutched it, their minds merged as they did during lovemaking, and he felt what she felt; there was no division between his sensations and hers. Though she was not suffering from the pain, it was there—a terrible cramping pain surging through his body—and he too had to maintain control of it, as if it were his own. For thousands of years on Earth women had gone through this, he reminded himself. How had they ever endured such an experience?

Olivia and Ingrid too stood beside Carla, bathing her face with cool water between her contractions. Despite their instruction from Susan they were uncertain about what to do, Jesse realized. They were as stunned as he was by the reality of facts they had known only in theory. On Undine childbirth occurred only in medical settings, with women heavily drugged, and no one there had had any other experience with it for generations. Probably the knowledge of how to cope was absent from the collective unconscious Peter was always talking about.

Jesse . . . stop worrying! Carla pleaded. *It's not good for him, he's scared enough as it is. . . .*

He? What—

Kel. Did you think he can't feel anything till he suddenly breathes air? Being born is scary, it must be—his head's being pushed hard now, and he can't know what that means. It hurts, *Jesse! I'm trying to reassure him, and you're not helping.*

God, Jesse thought. It had not occurred to him that the baby would perceive his own birth, aware though he'd been of the unconscious telepathic bond formed in the womb.

"There's been speculation about it since the early twentieth century," said Olivia, sensing his thought. "They didn't know about the telepathic element, of course, but quite a few psychologists believed babies suffer trauma during birth and that if anything violent happens, like the use of forceps, it can affect them the rest of their lives."

"But that's terrible! You mean all through human history kids have started out scared and hurting, never understanding later on what had traumatized them?"

"Well, it's natural, like all the other unpleasant facts of life," said Ingrid. "What hospitals did made it worse, though, which is another reason why we chose not to have children on Undine. Here, mothers can offer comfort, at least. Kira talked to us about it in the women's meetings."

Abashed, Jesse merged his mind again with Carla's, projecting calm and courage as best he could. She was not concerned about her own sensations, he realized. She was focused on their son's. But if she'd been suffering, screaming, like the women in historical vids, the child would have felt her agony. We *are* making progress here, he thought. Our mind powers do make a real difference.

From time to time Olivia reported to Susan by phone and was told that things were progressing normally. Ingrid helped Carla take off her clothes. She was pushing now when the contractions came, but when they eased and the pain became burning, Olivia told her to stop. "Pant, instead," she instructed. "You want the birth to be gentle on him." Then, to Jesse, "Come and look—you can see the top of his head now."

Jesse moved to the foot of the bed and watched in awe. *Oh Jesse*, Carla cried out to him, *I wish I could see too! What does he look like?*

It's too soon to tell, he's face down. But you can *see, you know, if we merge our minds. . . .*

At that moment Olivia's phone rang. "Susan needs me right now," she told them. "Kira's in trouble, and she's got to do a C-section."

"But the delivery," Ingrid protested. "I may not be able to manage alone—"

"Jesse can help. There's no danger, but for Kira there is."

"Go, Olivia," Carla whispered, barely catching her breath. "Hurry!"

There was no alternative; Olivia was the Group's only trained nurse, and to attempt surgery without a nurse's assistance would be risky. Ingrid took charge. "Wash your hands again, Jesse," she instructed. There was a pan of heated water on the pilot's console; quickly, he complied.

"Get a clean towel and be ready to take the baby from me," she said when he returned to the bed. "Be careful— he'll be slippery."

Her hands were gently supporting Kel's head, now fully visible and turned to one side. Jesse could see his face. As he watched, the shoulders emerged, and then the body. *Oh, Carla, he's perfect! Our son . . . and he doesn't look traumatized, he looks content. . . .*

God, Jesse, he shouldn't be too quiet! Make sure he's breathing!

In terror, he bent to receive the child, and as he did, Kel took his first breath. Jesse held him while Ingrid wiped him gently. "Put him on Carla's breast right away," she said. "That's the best place for him to stay warm."

"Don't we have to cut the cord?"

"No, not till it turns white. He might even start to nurse first—if he does, it will lessen Carla's bleeding."

"Bleeding?" he asked, dismayed. "She can control that, can't she?"

"Of course, if it's excessive, but she's got other things on her mind. Some bleeding with the afterbirth is normal. I'll take care of that; you tend to the baby."

Carla, with Kel nestled against her bare body, was glowing with joy. *Jesse . . . I never guessed how it would feel . . . I was happy knowing he was coming, but I never imagined what it would be like to touch him, hold him. . . .*

The experience was overwhelming for all three of them, Jesse thought. If babies were aware of birth, what must it be like to emerge from the womb into a bewildering new environment, full of frightening sights and sounds? Of course he belonged on Carla's breast! How would they ever dare take him from it?

Facing a strange new world is part of living, Carla told him. *That's the first thing babies learn.*

Yes, Jesse realized. But what sort of world had they brought him into? A harsh world, where he might not even survive. . . .

No! They'd make it a *good* world. Somehow, someday, for Kel's sake and the sake of the other kids, they would turn Maclairn into the kind of place they'd imagined. They had to believe that they could, because if they lacked faith Kel would know. He was sensing Carla's thoughts right now on a nonverbal level, and perhaps his, Jesse's, too. They owed him a good start. For now, that was all that mattered.

Jesse knelt by the bed with his arm around Carla, aware not of what was still happening in her body, but only of their love for Kel and for each other. For a long time he stayed there, until Olivia returned with a sterile knife to cut the umbilical cord. Dazed, he looked up, recalling with a rush what had taken her away. "Kira?" he asked.

"She's fine, already healing herself from surgery. She has a healthy daughter."

"That's great."

"Kel and Ivana were born at about the same time," said Olivia. "We'll never be sure which of them was delivered first, but Kel is older because Ivana was premature."

The oldest of the new generation. What might that mean, in the years to come?

"And Jesse," Olivia added, "as soon as Carla's okay, you need to come and talk with the Council. Peter says they've found a better place to plant our crops."

Part Four

36

ON KEL'S THIRD birthday Jesse and Carla took him down into the canyon to play in the pond. There were no crawlies at present and the shallow water, warmed by the late afternoon sun, was a delightful surprise for him. He'd bathed in the stone cisterns fed by the irrigation pumps on the canyon rim, of course, as they all did. But with water scarce and precious, he hadn't known so much of it could exist in one place.

As they sat on the bank watching him, Jesse looked up at the stepped narrow terraces covering what had once been a steep slope, now striped with green against the yellowish rock of the retaining walls. What fools they'd been to think the settlement's site wasn't suitable for agriculture! Bound by unexamined assumptions, they had believed farms must be flat like those on Undine's islands, none of which had any land much above sea level. Like the farms of North America on Earth, an image so deeply embedded in its predominant culture that even he, though born on Earth, had been unaware of how crops had often been grown in other parts of that world.

It had not taken them long to learn better, once they began to study the knowledgebase. Teresa and Reiko had been the first to discover pictures of ancient Inca terraces in Peru, a revelation so overwhelming that they rushed to show

Peter before it occurred to them that these might not be as unique as they first looked. Later, they'd found that terraced agriculture had been common on many of Earth's continents—even among the Hopi and other tribes of the American Southwest, the very people whose rainmaking customs Hari had described. Hari, the anthropologist, would have known, of course. But Hari had died before the river valley proved unusable.

The advantage of terracing lay not just in the addition of more land to plant. Its main purpose was to cope with drought. Water sank into terraces instead of running off to erode the soil and be wasted. Where it rained infrequently, or as on Maclairn, hardly at all, there was no other way to use precipitation effectively. Wells could supplement rainwater—but only if they were placed on the rim above the top terrace, where Arwen had seen them, so that irrigation could rely on gravity.

The disadvantage of terracing was the amount of manual labor it required.

The ancients had built their terraces over many years—many generations, in fact—in some cases using large gangs of conscripted workers. And they hadn't needed to produce a crop right away to avoid starvation. Jesse, when he'd gotten over his first excitement at the discovery of a potential means of doing so, had been quickly deflated by the thought of how impossible it would be to create such terraces soon enough.

But the ancients had had no tools except pointed sticks. They'd had no way to transport anything other than by carrying it, sometimes with the assistance of pack animals. The colony had robots to grade the slope and dig irrigation ditches and move rocks into piles at the appropriate levels for the retaining walls. That part was completed within a few weeks.

The actual building of the walls had to be done by hand. Work on the beehive huts had ceased while all the settlers, except women in late pregnancy or not yet recovered from birthing, had labored on this higher-priority stonework.

They'd worked in the heat of the day, to which by this time they were inured, until their hands were raw and their muscles strained, heedless of the exhaustion intensified by hunger. Healers had monitored them; no one was allowed to eat less than enough to meet the work's demands. Mothers, of course, took breaks to nurse their infants, which they kept with them on cradleboards made of woven rushes. No one else paused more than a few minutes at a time.

And then, once the walls were in place and the robots had finished plowing, fertilizer was spread by hand, the spreader attachment for the robots having been lost in the flood. After that had come planting—also by hand—and in due course, harvesting. They'd been able to build only the minimum number of terraces needed to produce one crop, enough to feed the adults. In succeeding cycles more were added. By the third harvest it was possible to start giving small amounts of solid food to the children, who in any case would nurse through the toddler stage, a custom traditional in some cultures on Earth though unheard of on Undine. Jesse was not sure how soon the adults could return to eating as much as had once been considered normal, if they ever could. It wouldn't be soon, for the needs of growing kids would take precedence and in time there must be a fiber crop too, for clothing. But by now, they had forgotten what it was like to have full stomachs.

There were no noticeable seasons in the colony, as it was near the equator and there wasn't much tilt to the axis of the planet in any case. Therefore, for convenience in figuring kids' ages, it had been decided to adopt an annual calendar based on Earth Standard years, Maclairn's long astronomical year being irrelevant to crop cycles or anything else of significance. Ten-day weeks were retained, with a short week at year's end. The crop cycles were staggered, with different stages of growth on different terraces for maximum efficiency, and since the genetically-engineered grain grew faster than natural strains, each cycle took considerably less than a year to complete.

The huts had been completed now and all families with children were living in them. At least they were sleeping there; cooking facilities had not been installed, since the imported rations were gone and there was nothing to cook besides porridge and unleavened flatbread, which was most efficiently prepared in the Commons kitchen—though most people had alcohol burners for warming leftovers. The powered grain mills contained in the pods were small, so flour was ground as needed rather than in large batches. Someday, Jesse thought, we'll have vegetables and sugar beets— and chickens, when we can feed chickens. Chicken embryos were still stored aboard the starship. He rarely visited the starship now; he was too tired after a day of stonesetting or farm work and in any case, they had retrieved everything immediately useful.

He smiled ruefully, thinking of how they'd originally thought modern settlers needn't expend energy on manual labor. It had become evident that on Maclairn, this way of life would be permanent. The mining and industry so essential to the colony hadn't even been started. Perhaps, when the kids were old enough to help farm, some adults would be able to begin on it. Meanwhile, time not devoted to labor or craftwork was spent in study—not only of the techniques they knew it would require, but of everything else they could learn from the knowledgebase about Earth's various cultures. They would not make the mistake of neglecting to be thorough again.

To be sure, they did have a few free hours now, hours to devote to the children. One of the ironies of their new life had been the fact that after remaining childless on Undine in protest against its crèche system, they had been forced to centralize childcare. All the adults, excepting only Peter and Kira, were needed on the farm. Kira, who due to age had never fully recovered her strength after Ivana's birth, had taken charge of the kids, assisted by mothers of newborns—there always were some, for by this time a lot of the women had borne two children. Once enough people had moved into huts, one of the prefab shelters no longer needed for sleeping had been converted to a nursery and playroom. Separations weren't as long as on Undine, since mothers came in to nurse toddlers too old for cradleboards and parents cared for their own kids at night. But there had been no family outings until now, with the ninth crop in the ground; and so today, Kel's birthday, was a special occasion.

Carla was pregnant again. She was carrying their second son, named Tarin after Kira, whose former surname had been Tarinov. Her due date was drawing near; Jesse had hated to see her tiring herself out planting grain and was glad that job was finished for the time being. He, like most of the other adults, would begin work tomorrow on the retaining wall for a new terrace. But Carla would retire temporarily to making pottery, which she would sell to individuals rather than being paid the hourly credit people received for work benefiting the colony as a whole. Clay was plentiful and the supply pods had contained a powered kiln, so dishware was one thing the settlement was not short of; but now that so many kids had reached the toddler stage there was a pressing need for more potties.

Of course, Carla was still responsible for computer maintenance, in addition to studying up on the future maintenance of the robots. This had required little of her time, as the computers, both the server for the textreaders and those in the neurofeedback lab, had been running smoothly; no new programming had been needed. But the ability to troubleshoot was a mainstay of the colony as far as the future was concerned, so she had been training apprentices from among the Group's other former hackers whose computer skills were more limited than hers. And there was always the chance that an emergency might occur. "We really shouldn't both have come down here today," she said to Jesse. "There've been some glitches in the datalink lately and since phones don't work in the canyon, the only way I could be reached would be through you."

"Peter might reach you if the need was pressing," Jesse

said. "He's pretty good at it by now." Peter's already-strong psi skills had been developing further, almost as if his physical handicap had caused them to compensate. And now that the more critical goals of neurofeedback training were out of the way, he'd been teaching long-range telepathy to others, using the mind-pattern Jesse had recorded the night of Ian's funeral. So far, no one had used it over distances as far from the settlement as the bottom of the canyon; but he suspected that Peter could. At least with Carla he could, considering the emotional link between them.

Jesse was not sure exactly what that link involved, only that they were not—and never would be—lovers. Just once had she spoken of this, aware that he was puzzled because as far as anyone knew, Peter had had no relationships since being crippled. "I know he's not going to fall in love with anyone else," Jesse had said, "but there are women who'd be happy to bear him a child." His son by Edris had not been told who his biological father was; Edris had recently married a man who'd just turned eighteen and they planned to have a large family. Peter had a number of IVF children, whose progress he privately observed; but their genetic identity had not been revealed even to their mothers.

"Peter can still have children by artificial insemination," Carla had said.

"Well, yes, but why limit it to that? Not having legs should make no difference, he's surely aware that some of the unattached women are attracted to him." Long-term abstinence from sex was rare in the Group; no one felt there was any virtue attached to it. The sexual enhancement of telepathic intimacy was too highly valued to be set aside.

'Oh, Jesse—I thought you knew. You said you'd been with him in his mind, so when I found out, I thought I'd misinterpreted what you said to me."

"Found out what? I shared only some memories, not his whole mind."

"Jesse," Carla said sadly, "Peter was—injured, when the rock slide fell on him. There was nerve damage, you know, that Kira thought might improve someday. So far it hasn't. He doesn't talk about it, but we're so close, I couldn't help sensing—"

"Oh, my God." To think that even this had been taken from Peter, on top of everything else he had lost, was past bearing.

Yet Peter had retained his unquenchable spirit, which continued to inspire the Group, and for the most part people were happy. The work was hard, the amenities few, and Maclairn had not been transformed into the paradise once unrealistically expected; still the freedom from fear they'd achieved on Undine had returned. There was no tyrannical government telling them what it thought was good for them. They were successfully maintaining their health through mind control; the warm fellowship between them was flourishing; and the kids were a joy. Most of all, they'd regained their belief in the goal. At the completion of each harvest— seven times now—it had been reaffirmed in the Ritual, not out of despair but in thankfulness, in addition to several occasions on which the Ritual had been held for rainmaking. No one now doubted that the colony would survive and someday thrive.

Many, in fact, had begun to envision ambitious plans for improving its setting, driven largely by the desire to be near water. Stone cisterns had been built at each of the irrigation pumps, allowing the water flowing down to the terraces to be first used for bathing and laundry. But these were not deep enough to swim in, and swimming—a favorite recreation on Undine—was greatly missed. It was not long before someone pointed out that if only there were a way to build a dam, the canyon could be turned into a lake. It flooded periodically, though not as disastrously as after their first attempt at rainmaking, and it was a pity to let all that water go to waste. A lake would do much more than provide a place to swim. Water could be pumped up from it to irrigate the lower terraces, and it would become possible to grow not only more crops, but trees.

With great enthusiasm, Kwame and several others had studied the images from the orbital survey and had determined that damming the river would be quite feasible from the geologic standpoint. Some distance downstream from the settlement the canyon narrowed; all that would be necessary would be to blast the rocks on both sides. As the cliffs were not as high there, no danger of the water rising too far would be created—in fact, calculations showed that the shoreline would come just below the lowest terrace, where it would make a nice beach. Unfortunately, there was one catch. There were not enough explosives available to do the job, even apart from the need to save the existing supply for mining operations. And anyway, no one knew enough about dam engineering to place explosives effectively. So the lake remained a pipe dream. But it had become a symbol of belief in their site's future potential.

What a strange turn his life had taken, Jesse reflected as he watched Kel splash at the edge of the pond. All those years in space, empty years compared to the few since then . . . and he now had more responsibilities than he'd ever had during his career as a starship captain. He still felt uneasy about his competence. He still sometimes woke in the night with pain in his back and lay awake beside Carla, wondering how things would have turned out if he hadn't made that one small astrogation error, if the starship hadn't run low on air and they'd been able to explore Maclairn before settling. But he had come to terms with that. He was living as he supposed almost everyone lived, on Earth or Undine or on countless other colony planets—doing his job as best he could and not worrying too much about what couldn't be helped. He rarely recalled that Group membership promised resistance to the physical effects of aging, and that Peter had said he would need more training to gain that benefit.

"We'd better start back," Carla said, picking up the bundle of rushes she'd gathered for basket-weaving. "It's almost suppertime, and it's our turn for a Commons table tonight." The men, too, ate twice a day now, but instead of meal shifts, porridge and flatbread were served buffet-style and some took it back to their huts.

Jesse got to his feet, heading toward the pond, but Kel was already running to them; Carla had called him silently. Jesse frowned. "You shouldn't, when he's within range of your voice," he reminded her. Kel, like many of the Group's other children, had been slow in learning to talk. It had taken awhile before it dawned on the adults that this was because the kids' telepathic bonds with their parents had been so strongly encouraged that they felt no need to communicate vocally. Speech could not be allowed to die out in a psi-based culture; it was essential not only to reading but to the framing and communication of complex ideas. Now, everyone realized that like the skills for volitional control of the body, telepathic conveyance of concepts, as distinguished from emotions, must wait until the kids were older. But it was hard for mothers to break the habit. Kel was a contented child because his every need had been sensed and met from earliest babyhood, and Jesse knew it was painful for Carla to ignore his wants until he expressed them aloud.

There would no doubt be other problems in raising psi-gifted children that no one had yet anticipated. The group had known they'd be experimenting, feeling their way. Peter, perhaps, guessed more of what might lie ahead than the others did, for he seemed troubled at times. He planned to take direct charge of the kids' education when they were ready for school. Reiko would design the academic curriculum, but the most vital aspect would be the mind training, and the methods employed with Group recruits would need adaptation for use with the young. Jesse hoped they would not be too rigorous. Peter tended to ask a bit more of people than they could easily deliver, and while this was effective with adult volunteers, the thought of Kel being subjected to it in childhood was more than a little disconcerting.

For now, at least, he was happy and carefree. Jesse and Carla took his hands and together they climbed the trail to the plateau, glad it had been such a good day.

37

ONE REASON PETER was content not to be a dad, Carla realized, was that from the beginning he had served as a foster-father to Kira's daughter Ivana. No matter that he was far younger than Kira herself; the ages of adults were unknown to the children and would have been meaningless to them if revealed. Genetically, Ivana was Ian's daughter, and Peter had looked upon Ian as a father—which technically would make him her foster-brother. But since his room was adjacent to Kira's and the two formed, in effect, a household, Ivana felt toward him as the rest of the children did toward the adult men in their families. The Group had decided that the title of Dad would be used only for a man who was Mom's partner, and that others viewed as relatives would be called Uncle. Ivana adored her Uncle Peter and the love between them was mutual.

The strength of this bond was amplified by the fact that they were both powerful telepaths. Not surprisingly considering her inheritance of genes from Ian and Arwen, Ivana was an exceptionally psi-gifted child. Even in infancy she had sensed not only Kira's feelings, but those of everyone else around her. As she grew old enough to understand ideas, she sensed thoughts, too, and would have gained the ability to speak even later than the other toddlers if Peter hadn't insisted that she talk to him. Once able to express herself in words, she did so no more often than it was demanded, though she quickly acquired skill in the use of language. She had a way of gazing silently at people with a dreamy expression that would have seemed eerie had they not been telepathic themselves.

Ivana was especially attuned to Carla's mind because during her first few weeks of life Carla had breast-fed her along with Kel. Kira, despite reluctance to admit that age had anything to do with the ability of a healthy woman to bear children via IVF, hadn't had enough milk. There was no alternative to a wet nurse, and Carla had been the only one available. After other women had given birth, however, Kira had asked that Ivana be nursed by someone else.

"But why?" Carla protested. "I don't mind nursing two, really I don't. And it would be nice for Kel and Ivana to be close companions from the start."

"Yes, but not as close as siblings," Kira answered.

"Whyever not?" She and Jesse had assumed it would be natural, considering that Kira was among their dearest friends.

"They're the two oldest," Kira had said, "and they're likely to develop an affinity for each other whether or not they do as babies. Carla, do you really want to rule out the chance that your future grandchildren might carry Ian's genes?"

"Oh—I never thought of that!" If Kel and Ivana were raised together, for them to be sexually involved when grown would be taboo under the definition of incest to which the Group adhered. Yet they might easily fall in love. A union between them would, of course, please her—and it would please Peter if her son, his namesake, became as much his own as his foster-daughter was. Kira was right; that possibility should be left open.

By now, at the age of three, Ivana had begun to display psi powers besides telepathy. Even as a toddler she was able to heal herself quickly of the minor cuts and bruises all children experience. She had not been taught to do this. The Group had a strict rule against teaching volitional body control to the children prematurely, before they could understand how bodies normally function. Ivana had simply absorbed it from Kira and Peter through her access to their minds.

She did not appear to suffer from pain, either, and when this first became apparent it worried Peter. "There were rare cases of children born on Earth without pain receptors," he'd told the Group, "and it was a serious handicap. Often they died. They couldn't learn to protect their bodies from injury— they were unaware of burns, broken bones, and dislocated joints, for instance. Sometimes they even stuck things in their eyes, or chewed off their own tongues or fingers. Physical suffering exists for a reason. We have learned how not to mind pain and how to relieve it telepathically in others, so we'll be tempted to ease it in our kids. But we must not do so except when it's unduly prolonged. We mustn't deprive them of the ability to discover what signals from their pain receptors mean."

Ivana had reacted to pain during her first two years and she evidently still felt the sensation, for she was careful to avoid damaging her body. Yet like the trained adults, she wasn't bothered by it. Other kids cried if they fell and bumped their knees; Ivana just picked herself up, smiling cheerfully. When she accidentally touched a hot pan of steaming porridge she withdrew her hand fast, but seemed more surprised than distressed, and she paid no attention to the resulting blisters during the minutes before they healed.

"It's uncanny," said Kira. "Indifference to pain is a learned skill; it's never been easily acquired even by the most talented of us. Ian himself had to learn before he developed our teaching methods. So it can't be inborn, and I swear I haven't cheated by passing it on to her telepathically. In any case, it takes severe pain to evoke it initially, not just childhood hurts."

"Maybe it happened in the womb," suggested Carla. "You used the skill for hours during her birth, after all. Perhaps she picked it up."

"All the rest of you used it during labor, too," Kira pointed out. "Yet your kids react to pain normally."

"Yes, but you and Ivana are both exceptionally strong telepaths, and as an instructor you're used to projecting skills to others. Besides, you had a Caesarian—you were controlling surgical pain, not just the pain of labor."

"That's true," Peter said, frowning. "It could account for the necessary state of consciousness being familiar to her. But it doesn't explain how she's able to switch into that state. Altering consciousness is an act of volition. Barring the use of drugs or other external stimuli, it doesn't occur spontaneously in a normal person. And Ivana shows no signs of mental instability."

On the day after Ivana's third birthday, which was also Kel's, Peter took her to the neurofeedback lab for the first time. Primitive neurofeedback using less sophisticated input than the Group's had been tried with children on Earth as far back as the twentieth century; computer graphics in the form of games had been employed. Carla had begun programming something similar in anticipation of getting the kids used to the equipment when they reached four or five, so that they would have a jump start on the mind training that would come later. But that program wasn't ready yet, and in Ivana's case Peter wanted to find out if she was somehow already able to control states of consciousness. This required using the symbolic representations of brain function that the Group called mind-patterns.

Kira, as an experienced neurofeedback instructor, assisted during the session. Because she wanted to stay where Ivana could see her, she brought Carla in to operate the computer, which was behind a screen. "You're going on dual, Peter?" Carla asked when he told her what software to set up. "Surely you're not going to start teaching Ivana to match mind-patterns at this stage."

"No. She'll have the lead role and I'll follow, so that we can make a game of it, as if we were matching for fun."

Carla was puzzled. This was something Group members often did when the lab wasn't otherwise in use. But in the game, various states of consciousness were familiar to both participants; the aim was to score points by instantly following a partner's lead. Ivana, presumably, would remain in normal consciousness, so both mind-pattern displays would match to start with, and would not change.

Kira attached the sensors to their bodies and adjusted the helmets, reassuring her daughter telepathically that this strange new experience was nothing to be frightened of. But when she brought out the electronic armrest and at Peter's nod, strapped Ivana's arm into it, Carla gasped in dismay. *Peter, you're not going to use neural stimulation on a three-year-old child!* she exclaimed, horrified.

At a very low intensity, yes. We have every reason to think it won't bother her. If it does, I'll turn it right off, of course. I'll be in telepathic rapport with her, so I'll know instantly.

Kira . . . you've consented to this?

I trust Peter, Kira replied silently. *Even if it hurts it'll be no worse than giving shots to kids, as the Meds do. But I don't believe she'll mind it, and we need to find out why.*

Carla cringed. She couldn't imagine letting such a thing be done to Kel. And yet in due course, when he reached adolescence, it would be done at high intensities that *would* hurt, and he would have to gain immunity to that, as they all had, in order to take his place in the Group as an adult. They had been so eager to pass their mind powers on to kids— but had any of them imagined how it would feel to be a parent, knowing what was involved in acquiring those powers?

She hadn't been present when stimulators were used since her own long-ago training sessions with Ian, for she was not an instructor and pain management was never practiced during recreational neurofeedback. The thought of watching disturbed her. Peter and Kira might be sure Ivana wouldn't suffer, but they'd had long experience in the training of frightened recruits, beside which a brief taste of mild pain might seem literally like child's play. It was true that even if Peter had misjudged, this test would be no worse than shots, and yet in principle it was different.

"We're going to play a game," Peter said to Ivana, leaning toward her from his immobile chair. "It's a game grown-ups play, but you can play it with me just this once, to celebrate your birthday."

"Okay," said Ivana with enthusiasm.

"Look at the colored picture on the wall," he went on. "It's created by what's happening inside your head. Next to it is a picture created by what's happening in *my* head. Let's see if I can make my picture the same as yours."

This was the reverse of the training procedure. And Peter, knowing that Ivana would be unable to match with him even if it occurred to her to try, was starting out in a state of consciousness far beyond her experience so as to have a different pattern to change from. The dual patterns filled the wall, huge multicolored moving shapes of startling beauty. Ivana watched, fascinated. She was clearly unafraid; there was no trace of the characteristic breaks that would have shown impending panic. After a few minutes, when she turned her attention to Peter's pattern, he gradually let it settle into the same form as hers, signifying normal everyday consciousness.

The concept of control via the mind did not have to be explained to Ivana; she grasped it nonverbally from Peter and Kira, so that she didn't doubt he had produced the change by thinking. "You did it, Uncle Peter!" she exclaimed. "Can I do that too? Can I change the shapes on purpose?"

"Not till you're a little older. Only grown-ups can do that. But the colors or the shapes in your pattern might change when you don't expect them to. If they do, you can watch me change mine again." To Carla he said silently, *switch to black and white.*

She did so. "Oooh, like the clouds!" Ivana said. She had seen clouds only once in her life, a few weeks ago when it had actually rained. Everyone had been thrilled and excited, including the kids, who who'd been astonished to see water fall from the sky. She thus wasn't dismayed by the sudden loss of color in the pattern; she assumed the billowing gray shapes came from her memory.

"Sometimes when patterns change color, people get scared or uncomfortable," Peter warned. "If that happens to you while we're playing, you must tell me right away so I can stop the game."

"Do I have to tell you out loud?"

"No—you can tell me in your mind if you'd rather. But do it fast, okay, Ivana?"

"Okay."

Back to color, Carla, Peter commanded. *And be ready to switch to stimulator mode when I tell you.* In that mode the color, instead of being a component of the pattern itself, was a monochrome showing the intensity of the stimulus. Reverse spectrum order was used so that red would indicate the maximum level of pain human receptors could register. Most people could not tolerate anything above green without training. Jesse, she'd been told, had made it almost to orange when his aptitude for the training was being tested—but he'd been a hardened Fleet officer, after all. On average, recruits began to falter somewhere in the blue range.

Now! Peter ordered. Carla drew breath and hit the enter key. This in itself did not initiate stimulation—Peter did that with his remote—so for a moment the feedback display was gray again. Then it turned to soft violet. Ivana's pattern spiked briefly but settled into its regular form. "Uncle Peter, I have to move my arm," she said calmly. "It's touching something bad, it might get hurt."

"It won't get hurt as long as I'm here watching it," Peter said. "But if you *feel* hurt, be sure to tell me." To Carla's amazement, he raised the intensity so that the violet shaded into blue.

Ivana didn't react—but her feedback pattern did. Abruptly it morphed into the pattern familiar to all of them, the pattern for the state of consciousness in which pain didn't matter. For a few moments her face remained frozen in its dreamy expression, and Carla could tell she was communicating silently with Peter, who had quickly matched his own pattern to hers. Then she broke into a joyous smile.

"I did it too!" she burst out. "Mom, Uncle Peter, I changed the picture when I turned off the bad feeling! Isn't that like doing it on purpose? You said only grown-ups could—"

Slowly Peter replied, "Well, usually only grown-ups know how to turn off the bad feeling."

"Is that why Kel and the other kids can't do it and I have to do it for them?"

Dear God! Kira exclaimed. *She's already a natural healer!*

Peter, stunned, turned off the stimulator and the feedback gradually returned to normal. "Do you do it for them often, Ivana?" he asked.

"Just when they hurt themselves and I'm there. If I'm not there they cry. Sometime I hear them cry in my mind and I'm too far off to help."

I suppose it's not surprising, Peter said silently, as Kira removed the helmet and sensors from the child. *After all, on top of having Ian's and Arwen's genes, she was exposed to the healing process while in the womb—you were using it on other people all through your pregnancy. Her ability to pass on pain relief telepathically is understandable. But I still don't see how she learned to switch from one mode of consciousness to another. A child's pain from minor mishaps just isn't intense enough to trigger it in someone who hasn't done it before. If it were, it would defeat the purpose for which pain receptors evolved.*

Ivana, sensing his question, seemed bewildered by it. "I learned from you, Uncle Peter," she declared, as if stating the obvious.

"From me? I never taught you that—it can't be taught except here in the lab where I teach the grown-ups."

"But it happened when *you* felt bad," she protested. "Every time I heard you cry in your mind and then stop. After awhile I could do it by myself. Why did we do it backwards with the pictures, as if you had to learn from me?"

"Oh, Ivana." He held out his arms and she rushed to him, climbing into his lap and snuggling against his chest. Peter would never again be without love, Carla realized. Though one form of it had been taken from him, another now claimed his heart. She and Jesse would no longer have to grieve over his loneliness.

Later, after Ivana had been sent out to play, they talked about what she'd revealed. Peter still experienced phantom limb pain, and probably always would. It wasn't a big problem because whenever it struck him he switched into the state of not minding. But in the instant before he switched, he involuntarily broadcast agony to anyone sensitive enough to pick it up. The strong telepaths in the Group were used to this and, knowing he'd be okay in a moment, they ignored it. Ivana, however, had begun at an early age to share his pain, as healers always did; and their emotional closeness had kept her in rapport with him on a nonverbal level while the switch occurred. She had been carried along with it. Then, having learned how it felt to turn off severe pain, she'd instinctively applied that knowledge to her own trivial hurts and those of other children.

This was exactly the way they'd all learned in the lab, Carla realized. The instructor, using dual stimulators as well as dual sensors, induced pain both in himself and in the trainee, then initiated the mental switch, telepathically demonstrating how it was done. Adults needed feedback to master it. But adults expected it to be hard; they knew most people can't turn off pain by thinking. Ivana hadn't known that. She had simply done what Peter was doing, no more afraid than he was, because she loved and trusted him.

"Children might be able to learn it younger than we've been assuming," Peter said. "I think, though, that we'd better hold off until they reach puberty, even with those who have enough latent healing talent to acquire the skill vicariously. Besides, when learning isn't spontaneous it demands motivation. The only sure motivation for the average kid is the desire to become an adult."

"The puberty rites of primitive cultures made good sense," Kira agreed.

"Yes, and in some cultures puberty rites involved not only endurance of pain but altered consciousness—spirit visions, and the like. Such rites may be the best framework for teaching many of our skills. Meanwhile, we need to keep a close watch on Ivana. If she tries to deal with anything worse than playground accidents, she may get in over her head, and besides, right now we don't know what other exceptional talents she may have."

There was a knock on the door, highly unusual since interruption of a neurofeedback session was one of the few things flatly forbidden in the colony. "Carla, are you finished in there?" called Erik. "I saw Ivana come out, and we need you. There's something wrong with the datalink—most of the textreader screens are displaying garbage."

38

WHEN JESSE LOOKED up from the terrace where he was working on a new wall and saw Carla standing on the rim, he knew right away that something was seriously wrong. She was normally too busy with her own work to seek him out during the day. *Jesse, I have to talk to you*, she called silently from above. *We've got a problem with the commlink.*

The commlink. That, of course, explained why she wasn't using her phone. A sick feeling rose in him. He'd feared for some time that their luck with aging technological devices had lasted too long, that they were overdue for a failure of some sort. The colony's survival depended on the robots, the power receiver and wind turbines, the shuttles, the comm satellite and uplink, the knowledgebase and other computers, and of course the starship's AI in addition to the AI that controlled all this other equipment. Sooner or later something would give out. They had gambled that it wouldn't happen before they had learned enough, and established enough industry, to make repairs. But so far they had been too busy building terraces and cultivating them by hand to devote time to preparing for the future.

He left work and climbed to the settlement, aware that Carla was more upset about her computer work than at any time in the past. After talking with her, he shared her dismay. The phones were useless; the linked textreaders displayed garbage; the main knowledgebase station was down. Only the self-contained computers and personal datakeepers were functional. Erik had checked the uplink and found nothing wrong. That meant the comm satellite itself was failing. But any ordinary failure would have been repaired by a service robot sent out by the starship. The satellite's offline status would have been displayed. A problem the robot couldn't fix probably couldn't be fixed at all, considering that no member of the Group had any knowledge of satellite technology. And in any case, nothing could be done without going up there in a shuttle and examining it.

The comm satellite had been placed in orbit, and was periodically maintained, by a fully-automated subsystem of the starship's AI. *Mayflower XI*, not having been intended for long-term support of a new colony, did not carry a spare. Either they could repair it in place, or they would lose the datalink entirely.

"It's not as if we depended on it for survival," Teresa said, when the Council met in emergency session. "We don't really need the phones now that we're learning to communicate telepathically over distance. We could probably do without them anyway. And enough material has been downloaded to keep us busy studying for a long time—it's backed up locally, isn't it, Carla?"

"Yes, of course, but you don't understand!" Carla exclaimed. "We're not just talking about our current needs—it's a matter of what will be needed in the future."

"It is," Peter agreed. "But let's postpone this discussion until we know how bad a failure we've got. Have you a way of checking it out from the starship, Jesse?"

"I can tell whether the satellite's orbit has decayed. If so, the starship AI should already have signaled a correction, but I might have to initiate that manually. Beyond that, if the service robot isn't functional, I can determine whether the satellite has power. I hope it doesn't, because that would mean I'll just have to dock with it and replace the storage battery. But if it's still powered and is sending bad data, it will have to be looked over by someone who knows more about electronics than I do."

"Erik?"

"He's the only one qualified, yes. The trouble is, Erik has never worn a spacesuit except to cross the shuttle bay. He can't possibly do an EVA."

There was no one capable of an EVA except himself. And, Jesse thought ruefully, even he had not walked in space since his cadet days at Fleet Academy. It was not something the crews of freighters needed to do. Probably his training would take over once he got outside the ship—but it would normally require two people just to capture a comm satellite for battery replacement, not to mention getting it into the cargo hold where it could be examined.

Peter, grasping this thought, said, "You'll have to train someone before you can try it."

"That's too risky!" protested Dan. "We can't afford to risk Jesse, or anyone else with specialized skills."

"We can't afford to lose the datalink," Peter said soberly. "Our long-range goal can't be reached without it. But as I said, let's take one step at a time and try to get the link back before we worry about that."

"I'll volunteer to spacewalk," said Kwame enthusiastically. "I always wanted to, even back on Undine when I hoped I'd be chosen to work on its power satellites."

Peter shook his head. "It's true enough that we can't risk *you*," he said. "You're the only one capable of maintaining our power supply, on which even our current survival depends."

The shuttle pilots were the only logical candidates, Jesse knew. Besides flight experience they were used to working in spacesuits, since they'd helped him retrieve stuff from airless decks of the starship. The next morning Anne and Bernie went with him to the ship while Viktor remained on the ground, in accordance with the normal policy that one pilot and shuttle must always be available in case a rescue should be necessary. He had not intended to take Anne, as she was nursing a two-year old child, but she was so eager to spacewalk that he gave in to her. It was true that she was by far the most agile of the three and the most fearless, as well the most experienced in space. Her daughter was old enough to get along all day on solid food; if she didn't mind leaving her in someone else's care, far be it from him to argue.

It had been some weeks since Jesse had visited the starship, and as soon as he entered from the shuttle bay he noticed a difference that he couldn't quite put his finger on. It was eerily silent—but it was always silent, after all, when only he and one or two helpers were there. To his dismay he found that his nerves were on edge. Well, he'd gotten used to outdoor labor, now; he wasn't the same person as the Captain who'd spent most of his life confined in the artificial environment of a ship. And he was deeply worried about the coming repair mission. It wasn't surprising if he no longer felt comfortable on *Mayflower XI*.

When he got to the bridge all thought of undefined strangeness was driven out by the alarm lights on the board. There had been no previous alarms in all the time since their arrival at Maclairn. Now there were three blinking furiously at him. The air quality alarm was puzzling—most of the ship was unpressurized, so the AI should not be monitoring air quality except here on the bridge, where there was obviously nothing wrong. Even more surprising was the sewage system alarm, as hardly anyone had made use of the ship's heads in the years since the passengers disembarked. He hoped there wasn't a glitch in the alarm system, which he lacked the expertise to troubleshoot.

The third alarm was for the nonfunctional link to the comm satellite, which of course he'd expected. Examining the readout, he saw that the satellite was in a stable orbit and the maintenance robot had been sent out, but that no communication had been received from it after it reported a successful launch. Had the robot itself failed, then? That would explain the trouble—but it was strange, because it would have started with a full power charge and if its trajectory after launch was correct, there wasn't much else that could go wrong before it rendezvoused with the satellite. It wasn't an autonomous service spacecraft such as those that maintained the hundreds of satellites orbiting a settled planet. As a component of a minimum-capability emergency comm system, it had no AI of its own and was designed to operate under the control of the starship, which by means of feedback from it would determine which satellite module needed replacement.

Apparently, the robot had gotten lost. Jesse could think of no way this could happen other than its being hit by space debris, which was a million-to-one shot considering its small size, but nevertheless conceivable. Oh God, he thought. Their so-far-amazing streak of luck had finally run out.

With some difficulty, he located the robot's storage bay and brought out samples of all the spare satellite modules he could find. Hopefully, *if* they could capture the satellite and *if* they could open it up, the starship's AI would signal where the trouble lay; if not, they might have to try one module at a time, or possibly replace them all. He tried not to let himself think of what would happen in the future. No satellite component could last forever; all had limited lifetimes and someday the link would fail again. Even if they could learn how to repair it, what about the next generation? The starship's AI wasn't immortal, but unlike the devices under its control, it could for all practical purposes be relied on to serve their descendants. Were they to be defeated by something so minor as a bit of space debris?

Nothing could be done until Anne and Bernie had been given some EVA training. They suited up and he put the shuttle into orbit, at first merely to accustom them to zero-g, which they had experienced only briefly—the starship, of course, had artificial gravity and the shuttles were normally under power during most of the trip to and from the surface. Then, one at a time with the other at the controls, he took them outside, well-tethered and under orders not to let go of the handholds. It was immediately obvious that Anne had the most aptitude for it. She moved so confidently that it seemed she wouldn't have much left to learn. All she'd have to do would be to help him grab the satellite and pull it into position; she would not need to perform any skilled work.

They could get by with just one more practice session, he decided. The next day, before leaving the starship, they loaded the spare modules aboard the shuttle so they could set out directly from the surface on the following morning, and he programmed the starship's tracking system to guide him to the satellite's position by remote. As he left the bridge, the lights flickered. A bad omen, he thought. And then he realized that this was what had seemed different—the lighting. It was not quite as bright as the level at which it was normally maintained. But the power couldn't be failing. There would be plenty of power for some years yet, and in any case no power alarm had appeared.

That night he said to Peter, "Anne's a natural, just as she was for piloting. There's no question but that she's the best choice for the mission. Yet she's a mother, Peter. Is it right for us to put mothers of young kids at risk?"

"Well, mothers have been serving in all capacities for some centuries now, even in the military," Peter said, smiling.

"Not when their kids were dependent on breast-feeding," Jesse said, thinking that he couldn't imagine not being troubled by even a brief separation between Carla and Kel. "And not when telepathic bonding has been encouraged as it has been here."

"No," Peter agreed, "but when we decided to encourage it, we knew there'd be a price. The stronger the bond of love, the worse the consequences if forced separation breaks it—that's how it is everywhere, for adults and children alike. Yet total dependence of one person on another, to the exclusion of all other values, is never healthy or right. Anne loves her child, but she's entitled to a life of her own. If we denied her that while pushing for population increase, we'd be building a society in which women were little more than slaves."

"I suppose that's true."

"It *was* true on Earth in all too many cultures. It's one of the things that's been outgrown, and hardly a situation we want to bring back."

"Peter," Jesse said hesitantly, "I have a bad feeling about this mission. Something's nagging me. I know I've been afraid I'll mess up again—but this is more than that. It's more like the time I held back from cultivating the land above the wells."

Peter frowned. "Your instinct was right that time. We'd have been wiped out if you'd given the go-ahead; we wouldn't have had fertilizer for the terraces. But you had no objective reason for apprehension then, whereas now it's natural for you to worry. I don't think we have grounds for calling it precognition."

Precognition? Of course it wasn't, Jesse told himself. He didn't have any psi capabilities beyond those he'd been specifically taught to use. His sense of foreboding now was just nerves, surely.

When morning came he and Anne, wearing full spacesuits, took off without incident and through communication between the starship's AI and the shuttle's, caught up with the satellite on their third pass around Maclairn—it was, of course, in a geosynchronous orbit above the settlement, so could not be approached directly. Jesse saw it from a distance, a bright dot against the blackness of space, and prepared for rendezvous. But as they approached closer, he gasped in dismay. "Oh, God," he burst out. "It's done for, Anne. We can't save it."

"What? Oh, I see—there's already something docked with it. Is that the robot? You mean the robot tried to repair it and failed?"

"It failed," Jesse said grimly. "It's not docked, Anne. It crashed into the satellite, destroying a good part of it. They're jammed together, and trying to retrieve them wouldn't buy us anything. The commlink's gone for good."

"I thought AI-controlled spacecraft didn't crash."

"They don't. Not in space where there are no unpredict-

able influences on them." He was chilled by the implications. The satellite had maneuvering capability, but like the
robot it was under the starship's control. Though there was no
way to know which had misfired its thrusters during the docking, most probably the robot had come in too fast. No collision
with space debris could have caused this; if it had been knocked
off course or failed internally, it would have missed the satellite entirely. So the data sent to it had been wrong. The speed
had been miscalculated or else there had been a glitch in the
transmissions. Either way, *Mayflower XI*'s AI was becoming
unstable.

Sick to his stomach, Jesse remembered the false air
quality and sewage alarms and the flickering, not-quite-
bright-enough lights. The starship's AI was an integrated
system. If it was failing, any component might fail. They
could no longer trust it. The loss of the satellite link paled
beside this larger threat to the colony's future. They had
counted on the starship being available until the antimatter for its power system ran out—now they might have only
weeks to retrieve everything that might be needed for generations to come.

In silence, he unlinked the shuttle from external control and gave full control to its own AI, ordering a return to
low orbit and rendezvous with the starship. They could accomplish nothing here. They had best spend their time running a
thorough checkout of *Mayflower XI*'s present status.

Looking back later, he could not recall what had gone
through his mind during the brief flight to rendezvous. He'd
been preoccupied, and automated docking with the starship
was by this time so routine that he wasn't aware that it was
imminent until the shuttle bay's doors were gaping open
ahead of them and they'd started to pass through.

And then, the screech of grinding metal and the jolt of a
blow from the left as his seat was thrown sideways came so
fast that they scarcely registered in his mind before he recognized the now-stationery barrier in front of his face as a piece
of bay door. Not until then did he grasp the fact that the

ship's AI had tried to shut those doors prematurely, before the shuttle was all the way inside.

If he hadn't been wearing a spacesuit in anticipation of an EVA, he thought dimly, he would be exposed to vacuum now; the shuttle's hull had been torn and its cabin had decompressed. It was lucky that he and Anne hadn't bothered to take their helmets off. . . .

"Anne! Anne!" Jesse cried out, coming suddenly alive to the situation. The door from the other side might have hit her, she might be hurt. Unstrapping his seatbelt he attempted to rise, seeing that she was limp beside him, slumped against the center pilots' console.

She didn't respond. In shock, he saw that she'd been leaning forward; her helmet had been cracked open by the thrust of the sliding door. Anne was dead.

39

FOR A LONG time Jesse was unable to move, unable to imagine what to do. Then he realized that while the shuttle's air-lock couldn't be pressurized, there was no pressure in the cabin either, and so the hatch might be operable. He managed to open it, get out, and clamber over the top of the shuttle into the airless bay. Staggering to the manual control for the bay doors, he cranked them back. He was not sure they could be closed again even if the shuttle were clear of them, and he did not intend to find out. He left them on manual. Obviously, the AI could not be trusted for any function whatsoever, now or ever again.

Trust it or not, however, he had no choice but to use the automated airlock to get from the bay into the ship itself. After removing his helmet but not his suit, he made his way to the bridge and collapsed onto a stool, the Captain's chair having been removed long ago for Peter's use. The lighting was dimmer than ever, but the LEDs of the voice comm were still on. After a while he mustered the courage to call the settlement, praying Carla would not be the one to answer, and insist on speaking privately to Peter. There was no commlink to the starship in Peter's room so they had to patch through a connection to his phone, and by the time it was ready the ship was on the other side of the planet. While he waited to come back into range, Jesse rehearsed in his mind what would have to be said.

Peter took the news calmly, of course. Someone who didn't know him would have assumed he felt no emotion. But Jesse didn't need telepathy to be aware that he was as deeply stricken by Anne's death as he himself was, and that the loss of the satellite and starship was a devastating blow to him.

"It's too dangerous for Bernie or Viktor to come up here," Jesse said, finally getting to the point that he knew would be the hardest to make. "We don't know what will fail next. You can't risk their lives, or another shuttle either; you will need the two shuttles that are left to explore Maclairn in the future."

"I thought your shuttle was badly damaged."

"It is," Jesse admitted. "I am expendable, Peter."

"No, you're not." There was a pause. Then Peter said, "Human beings have always risked rescuers to save someone who is stranded. Of course we will send Bernie—it would be unthinkable not to, even apart from how we all feel about you. But besides that, we can't give up on the knowledge-base."

"The colony can survive now without it. People are adapting. They can get along without the things we expected to gain in the future—both the knowledge and what we haven't yet retrieved from the ship."

"Access to the whole of human knowledge is vital to our goal," Peter declared. "But we'll discuss that later. I'll hear no more argument now, Jesse. Bernie will pick you up."

"He can't get into the ship," Jesse protested. "Even if I can move the damaged shuttle out of the way, he doesn't know how to dock. None of the pilot trainees have ever taken manual control in space; they learned only to land on the surface. Docking is—was—a fully automated maneuver, and now we can't trust the AI to handle it."

"There's got to be some solution," Peter declared.

With his initial shock wearing off, Jesse was beginning to think clearly. "Well, the shuttle may be able to fly," he said. "Not in the atmosphere, but I guess it could rendezvous. The second shuttle can be put into a stable orbit; I suppose I can talk Bernie through that on the comm."

"Okay. He'll be there in a couple of hours. In the meantime, do what you can to secure the ship and gather up any stuff you feel should be retrieved right away."

Mechanically, Jesse did so. The ship no longer seemed a shelter from the hostile environment of space. The AI failures had apparently been random, and for all he knew, the oxygen level might drop next. For his entire adult life until his grounding on Undine, he had lived aboard starships and given little thought to his surroundings. He had no more doubted the AI than Earth-dwellers doubted sunrise or the natural pull of gravity. Even when he was Captain, a system-wide malfunction of a starship's brain had been outside the realm of conceivable emergencies he was prepared to deal with; there had been experts aboard to whom he would have handed such a problem if it had occurred. Now he felt helpless.

Well, whatever happened to him personally shouldn't matter to him, he thought grimly—after all, he had just volunteered to be left to die here. He'd known underneath, he supposed, that Peter would insist on a rescue. Yet he'd been willing to forgo it, rather than subject more people to the deadly whims of an AI system gone mad. He was still Captain. A captain went down with his ship—or at the very least, did not allow passengers to board if it was not spaceworthy. He would not bring anyone else here, whatever Peter wanted retrieved later on.

Chickens ... the settlers couldn't survive forever on

grain alone; once the nutritional supplements provided by the pods were gone, they would need meat. He must take the chicken embryos to the surface with him. There'd be no way to store them for more than a few hours in portable cryogenic tanks, so they'd have to incubate them and devote a portion of the harvest to feed. Perhaps they should have done so sooner; the eggs might compensate for smaller servings of porridge. . . .

He was thinking about chickens because he did not want to think about Anne.

Logic told him her death hadn't been his fault. He was not responsible for any of the equipment malfunctions; they were outside the scope of human error. But he had chosen Anne for the mission. Not that he wouldn't have grieved if Bernie or Viktor had died, but Anne had a daughter still nursing. Someone would wet-nurse the child until she was completely weaned, of course, but no one could take the place of the mother with whom she'd been telepathically bonded. What was it Peter had said? The stronger the bond of love, the worse the consequences if forced separation breaks it. If Peter had taken him up on his offer, what would have happened to Kel—and to Carla? He had not let himself consider that, had not realized the magnitude of the relief he'd felt at Peter's decision, not for himself but for their sake. . . .

Anne had been so eager for the spacewalk, the EVA she'd never had a chance to make. She had loved space . . . she'd happily risked her life long ago on that first solo shuttle trip she'd undertaken when they arrived. She had shown skill, been praised as a hero—only to die pointlessly from the random failure of technology in which she'd trusted. What sense was there in that? What could Peter, who believed in fate, possibly say about it? Hari, at least, had died while actively saving a life. Anne had died for nothing.

Jesse shivered. He knew he must fly the second shuttle into the bay himself after rendezvousing with Bernie. He felt shaky inside at the thought of approaching those bay doors again, even though they were no longer connected to the

AI. But that was precisely why he would have to do it. If he didn't, he might not have the nerve to come again. Besides, the more cargo he took now, the less need there'd be for future trips when conditions on the ship might have gotten worse.

Scanning the control panels surrounding him, he began to consider what AI functions could be shut down. The fewer left on automatic, the better; perhaps if he lightened the load on the system the essential ones would be less prone to fail. Life support had already been turned off to the living quarters. Satellite maintenance was now superfluous, of course, and imaging could be dispensed with; they'd already downloaded plenty of images of the whole planet. But they still needed power....

Power! Oh, God. He could not leave the power beam operative—it might not communicate accurately with the receiver. A small miscalculation in its targeting might fry the whole settlement. They had expected beamed power to last for many more years, but the danger was now too great. His hand trembling, Jesse threw the sequence of switches to take it offline. From here on out, wind power would have to do.

There was one more thing that must be taken care of immediately. A decision must be made about Anne's body. Whereas it would be possible to take it down to the surface, the earth burial of Claire had been upsetting to people, and no facilities for cremation had yet been developed. They had not liked the thought of the ship's converter much better, and in any case the converter had been turned off. There was only one fitting means of disposal, Jesse knew. He would not even consult Peter about it. He would leave the body in the damaged shuttle until he was clear of the starship, and then he would send it out through the airlock, as was customary aboard small ships in Fleet. Anne would float free in space after all.

The digits of the chronometer on the console in front of him changed slowly. Was even timekeeping affected by the

AI's malfunction? Jesse wondered. Surely the minutes couldn't really be that long. To his chagrin, he found that his watch matched the display. It was he who was misjudging the passage of time, unnerved by the emptiness of the ship and the silence and the knowledge that at any moment some new breach of *Mayflower XI's* integrity might occur.

At last Bernie's voice came over the comm, and Jesse, absorbed in instructing him how to program his ship to orbit, found himself back to normal. He returned to the shuttle, which had nothing more wrong with it than the gaping slashes in its hull, and took it outside, leaving the bay doors open behind it. Rendezvous was an easy maneuver that involved no manual control. The commitment of Anne's body to space went smoothly, though the fogging of his helmet from tears obscured his vision until he was inside Bernie's shuttle and could remove it.

The damaged shuttle, he decided, must be saved in case parts were ever needed to repair the other two. As it could not be taken into the atmosphere, this meant tethering it to the hull of the starship, which involved a more difficult EVA than the one originally planned. Fortunate though it was that Bernie had been introduced to spacewalking, Jesse disliked exposing him to risk. It was not like commanding fully-trained Fleet officers who'd chosen space careers.

The Group had never fully grasped the dangers of space. Its members had been passengers, not crew, in spite of the jobs they'd taken on, and he had felt uncomfortable about that from the beginning. Seven had died in stasis, one on a futile shuttle mission—not to mention the close call for the rest when they'd nearly run out of air. It was just as well, Jesse thought, that from now on there'd be no more space flights for them. Maclairn offered challenge enough, and life there could be made good.

40

THE COUNCIL GATHERED in Peter's room that night, stunned and bewildered. They listened to Jesse's report in silence. "We knew it was an old, obsolete ship," he reminded them. "That was the only reason we could afford to charter it. We gambled on it, and we were incredibly lucky for a long time. Its aging AI not only got us here, it kept us alive in stasis! We can't really complain that it's failing now, when our need for it is past."

"We still need it," Kwame protested. "There's a lot of stuff up there we can't utilize until we have manufacturing capability—not to mention the power beam. You shouldn't have shut that off without warning me, Jesse. It's got to be turned back on for brief periods at least, if not now, then later so we can establish the industry to build more genera- tors. The wind turbines we have now can't do any more than power the settlement."

"It can't ever be on again," Jesse declared. "It's too dan- gerous when we can't rely on communications between the ship and the receiver."

"The idea of establishing heavy industry is a bit unrealis- tic anyway, isn't it?" said Dan. "Sure, we thought in the begin- ning we'd do that someday, or our kids would—but that was before we had any idea of what the conditions would be on this planet. Whatever mining we manage to do will always be on a small scale, even if eventually we can stop devoting our full time to raising food."

"I'm not sure we want an industrialized world," said Teresa. "We've found a different way of life now. The work's getting easier and someday we'll have more food and more leisure—what else do we need? Not factories, surely."

"No," Arwen agreed. "We came here to build a culture based on psi, not to duplicate what the other colonies have. The kids are content, and they'll be happier keeping what they grow up with than they would be if we kept pushing for more."

"But the knowledgebase," protested Carla. "We depend on the starship for access to knowledge. If we've lost the satellite we can't have a continuous datalink, but we've at least got to maintain a direct link that works while the ship is overhead."

"Why?" Teresa asked. "We've already downloaded all that's important to us."

Appalled, Carla burst out, "All that's important? What about science, philosophy, art—all that humanity has achieved in the past that must be passed on to our kids to feed their minds, even if it has no practical use here?"

"Knowledge of humankind's achievements is indispensable to new generations," Reiko said. "And some of it's practical, too—don't forget that we'd have starved if we hadn't searched the knowledgebase for facts we had no idea were there."

"That may be true," Jesse said, "but we're not being given a choice. The knowledgebase is intact now, but as AI failures progress, the computer system will go down too. The ship's internal power system is already fluctuating. We're going to lose data access, and the sooner we accept the situation, the more we can preserve before it happens."

"We can't preserve more than a fraction of it by downloading," Carla said in dismay. "We don't have enough data storage facilities, and our self-contained computers couldn't handle the load even if we did. The ship's servers are huge, Jesse. All the knowledge human beings have recorded since the beginning of history, and all of it duplicated for backup—have you any idea of what that involves?"

"I do, but facts are facts," Jesse said. "I know how much it will hurt you to lose that system—computer work has been your life—"

"The servers are huge, but they're discrete devices like those at the university, aren't they, Carla?" said Reiko. "They're not built into the ship itself?"

"No—the computer system is installed like any other large one, except for being secured so it won't float around during zero-g. It's not as old as the starship; it was modernized somewhere along the way."

"Then can't it be brought down here and installed in one of the shelters? We don't need them all for sleeping anymore."

"Yes!" Carla said, brightening. "Yes, it'll be a big job, but we can do it!"

"Too big a job, I think," said Dan. "It would mean a lot of work adapting the shelter, and careful handling during the shuttle trips—and we've got just the one motorized cart for surface transportation."

"Most of the components aren't heavy," Carla said. "We could use the stretcher."

"We can't spare people from the farm," Teresa told her. "The retaining wall for the new terrace is barely started."

"Teresa," Carla protested, "we don't need another terrace right now. We can live on short rations a while longer; the knowledgebase is much more important than what we eat."

"That's not the main problem with the idea," said Jesse. "I'm no expert, but I do know I couldn't just pick up computer parts and carry them off without a planned shutdown. It's not merely one switch to throw. And I don't have any idea how to identify the components, let alone how to safely dismantle the system. Neither does Bernie, assuming I were willing to let him go back up there, which I'm not."

"Well, of course you couldn't do it," Carla said. "I'll have to go myself."

"Oh, no, Carla. That's absolutely out of the question," Jesse stated firmly. "I won't let you take the risk."

"It's not up to you," she retorted. "I'm in charge of all computer work on this world."

"And I'm Captain of the starship. Nobody boards without my consent. Besides, you're too far along in pregnancy."

She nodded. "That's true. I couldn't go until after Tarin's born, and not for the first few weeks after—he'll need to nurse too often. But it will take awhile to convert the shelter anyway. The starship will still be there when I'm free."

"It may not be. God knows what may have happened to it by then; a ship without a functional brain can't be trusted—"

"You're talking as if we'd already decided to build a high-tech society," Teresa put in. "It was one thing to have the ship in orbit, in case we needed something from it—but to put forth all that effort to bring advanced technology here, when it doesn't fit in with the culture we're creating, the one we're finally starting to be comfortable with—"

"And when it will probably be wasted effort," Dan said. "However much work we do toward that goal, we're never going to catch up to other colonies."

"Which is just as well," said Arwen intensely. "Let's keep this a natural world! We left Undine and its technology behind. Peter has more reason to regret that loss than any of us, yet he believes it will contribute to the enhancement of our psi powers—"

Peter had been uncharacteristically silent throughout the argument. Now he said, "You're all forgetting something. We didn't come here just to escape from the government we didn't like on Undine. We didn't come just to develop psi in ourselves and our kids, either. We came to move human evolution forward."

"Yes, of course," Arwen said. "That's what developing psi powers does."

"No, it doesn't—not in itself. There have been people throughout history who developed advanced psychic abilities. They had no effect on evolution; history passed them by. They were ignored because psi is rejected by the vast majority, who fear that if it's allowed to spread it will lead to a fundamental change in life as we know it. Those groups didn't have the opportunity we do because they didn't possess, or at least didn't use, the technology to maintain a civilization at the level humankind had reached. They turned back from it—and as a result their contemporaries were able to ignore them, write them off as exceptions, instead of integrating their advances into society as a whole. And that's what will happen to us if we give up and revert to older ways of living."

"But we're isolated," said Jesse. "We're not going to be judged by anyone until generations from now, if and when the information about this world that you transmitted to Ian's friend on Earth is decoded by his successors and they come to find us."

"They'll find a backward society, not an advanced one, if we don't regain technology equivalent to theirs by then," said Carla. "And that will defeat our purpose."

"The long-range goal has always been to demonstrate that psi and volitional mind control can improve people's lives without lowering their standard of living," Reiko added. "We're aiming to move forward, not back. Even if some individuals prefer a simpler lifestyle, it's contrary to human nature not to keep on progressing. And we can't progress without the store of human knowledge accumulated in the past."

"This colony has been founded to serve as an example," Peter said. "Our hope is that those who discover it in the future will see it as a place to be emulated, not simply studied by anthropologists. A place they can't pretend doesn't exist on the grounds that psi isn't something modern science-oriented cultures believe in. This is what we mean in the Ritual when we say we are stewards of a flame that will illuminate future generations."

Oh God, Jesse thought. If he brings the Ritual into it, all argument is finished. "It's a little early to worry about being an example to posterity," he pointed out. "Right now, we've got plenty of more immediate problems to be concerned with."

"I had hoped not to raise the issue this soon," Peter agreed. "I knew it would arise when we began educating the children, but I wanted to hold off until then. Unfortunately, fate has forced us to act. If we lose the knowledgebase now, we lose it forever."

"We'll still be an essentially technological society," Dan said. "We have electric lights and heating and personal computers and wind turbines to power them. We have the robots."

"But without the industrial facilities to produce more, they won't last, let alone serve an expanding population," Kwame pointed out.

"Would that really matter?" asked Teresa. "Do we really need any of those things?"

"We do if we care about women's freedom," Reiko said. "The only thing that allows us to aim for population increase while maintaining gender equality is the fact that technology reduces the work that raising children would otherwise require."

"And unless there's access to greater knowledge and an effort toward progress, we won't have any technology in the next generation," Peter added. "It will be mere magic to our grandchildren. They won't know how to maintain it and they won't see the point in struggling for a better life than they're born into."

"I don't see it, myself," said Teresa. "We're making them happy here. We overcame our own depression, and we're getting along fine now. We've adapted."

"The danger," said Peter, "lies in adapting too well."

Jesse stood up. "This discussion isn't accomplishing anything," he said "You don't understand our situation, Peter. *Mayflower XI* is dying. Its life support system may go crazy at any time. The artificial gravity may function unpredictably. Even the antimatter power generator could pose a hazard if its AI controller fails. One person has been killed already—"

"The knowledgebase is worth the loss of lives, if things should come to that, though now that we're warned I hope we can retrieve it safely."

"We can't retrieve it at all. As Captain I won't allow anyone but myself up there, certainly not Carla."

They faced each other, the tension in the room growing. They had never disagreed before except about going into stasis, Jesse reflected, and that time, Peter had ultimately acknowledged that in matters concerning the ship it was the Captain's place to command. Peter, on the other hand, was the undisputed leader of the colony. He had never been a dictatorial leader. But he had never been opposed on any issue he felt strongly about, either.

Arwen said, "Shouldn't this decision should be made by the Group as a whole? We're not going to agree here, and it's too important to be left up to nine people, anyway."

"The Group should discuss it," Peter agreed. "But I will not put it to a vote, not when it's a question of the fundamental reason why Ian wanted us to found a colony."

In turmoil, the Council adjourned for the night and went to bed.

41

ALONE IN THEIR hut, with Kel sound asleep on his mattress beside theirs, Jesse and Carla continued to argue. "I'm not going to take you up there," Jesse insisted. "The ship killed Anne. I can't risk letting it kill you, too."

"Do you think I like the idea that it might kill *you*?" she demanded. "You're going up again yourself, aren't you?"

"It's my job. And I don't plan to go any oftener than I have to."

"It's *my* job to maintain the computer system. I won't let you stop me from doing it."

"If your own safely doesn't matter to you, think about Kel and Tarin," Jesse retorted. He was inwardly aware that this was the same discussion he'd had with Peter about Anne. When it was the woman he loved, the mother of his own kids, confronting it was less easy.

"Oh, Jesse. I do think about them. I think about the legacy we've got to give them and those who succeed them. I don't want them to be deprived of the chance to move humanity forward."

"Neither do I, Carla." He paused, wondering if this was entirely true. Kel was a happy, carefree child. Mightn't he be more likely to remain happy if he never had to learn about all the things his world was lacking? If the kids were exposed to the knowledgebase, taught that it was important to regain the technology people had on Earth, they'd spend their lives striving for something their generation could never achieve. . . .

It was just as well, perhaps, that there'd be no need to worry about that. "It's not up to us," he said. "I'm responsible for the starship, and it's unsafe. I won't take people there on the very slim chance that we might be able to dismantle the computer system successfully and reinstall it in a flimsy prefab shelter—least of all you."

"Jesse . . . if you don't care how I feel about it, at least don't do this to Bernie."

"Bernie? Don't do what to him? He hasn't any special interest in the knowledgebase."

"Don't make him choose between his respect for you and his loyalty to Peter. You're not the only shuttle pilot anymore, and Bernie will take me to the starship if Peter asks him to."

"God, Carla! You'd defy an order I give as Captain? Does your computer work mean that much to you . . . or is it Peter? Is that it? I suppose, because you love him—" *I suppose because you love him you believe he can't be wrong, or maybe you don't care if he's wrong, you'll stand by him anyway. . . .*

Oh, Jesse. Her face went white, and Jesse was immediately stricken with remorse. How could he have said such a thing? What had they come to, if he could even consider using her love for Peter as a weapon? Long ago he'd resolved that never, never would he let her think he viewed Peter as a rival. He reached for her, but she drew away, crushed, and her mind was closed to him. The damage had been done.

The next day the Council met again and went over the same ground. Jesse's heart ached for Carla and also for

Peter, who was encountering opposition for the first time. Group members had pledged in the Ritual to support each other; never before had there been an occasion when there was conflict over whom to support.

Peter's opponents—Arwen, Teresa, Dan, and Jesse himself—had talked to others, and it was apparent that their feelings were widespread. People were more concerned about their own lives and those of their kids than about a hypothetical situation that might arise in the distant future. How did they know Maclairn would ever be found? Ian and Peter had planned for it to be, but whether descendants of Ian's friend on Earth would care about contacting an ancient, secretly-established colony was, to say the least, uncertain. Meanwhile, the colony had managed to pull out of the worst of the hardships of starvation. Its people had finally gotten settled in huts, which offered privacy and reasonable comfort after the floor of the crowded shelters. They'd become used to manual labor and were not eager to have their contentment with it shaken. They did not want to think about the things they'd given up, which emphasis on the knowledgebase would inevitably bring to mind.

Moreover, the faction once led by Hari, whose members normally stood apart from everyday affairs while pursuing a mysterious inner life, suddenly became vocal. They had never wanted a high-tech lifestyle. They had, some now admitted, joined the Group in the first place because they perceived it to be anti-tech—though they had made as full use of its neurofeedback facilities as anybody else. They had come to Maclairn reluctantly but had found it more to their liking than they'd expected, largely because of the very things the others saw as deprivations. To them, high technology was something to be outgrown.

"We're moving past reliance on machines," Arwen declared. "Isn't the power of the mind what we've always believed in, Peter? Isn't its primacy what we're aiming for?"

"The mind has many powers," Peter replied, "and humankind needs to use all of them. Psi and mind control couldn't have been allowed to distract us until we had the technology to expand beyond Earth; if it had, our species would have died out. Now we can integrate them into civilization. But for the pendulum to swing the other way would be reversion, not evolution. Evolution means moving forward on all fronts."

That was true in theory, Jesse acknowledged. But there was no assurance that the colony could ever move forward technologically, and the risk attached to preserving the option was even greater than he'd first seen.

The starship now posed a threat to the colony, a greater threat than the harm that might befall those who boarded it. He turned cold at the possibility that occurred to him. The ship would still be accessible after Tarin's birth, Carla had said yesterday, and he had casually replied that it might not be. He'd failed to pursue the thought of where it would be if it was not in its present low orbit.

The orbit was maintained by the ship's AI. If the AI could no longer guide a robot to the satellite accurately, it could not be counted on to manage station-keeping for the starship itself. A random failure in firing its thrusters was as likely as any other glitch. Its orbit might be allowed to decay—or the ship might be thrown into a trajectory that would send it to the surface. In either case, it would collide with the planet.

A direct hit on the settlement was, of course, extremely improbable. But that was not the major worry. The destruction produced by the crash would be the equivalent of a meteor strike, perhaps even worse. Although the starship was small compared to the ancient meteor that had killed off Earth's dinosaurs, it contained enough stored antimatter to power it for many more years. Wherever it hit, the force of the explosion would be past imagining.

If it happened anywhere in the region of the colony, the dust raised would block the sunlight, perhaps for a long time. It would get dark and cold. The crops would die. There might be acid rain. These potential disasters had been discussed fearfully on Earth long before the capability of deflecting meteors had been developed. Now, of course, they could be averted there. They could not be averted on Maclairn if *Mayflower XI*'s orbit became unstable.

To Peter privately, he explained this, not wanting to scare anyone else unnecessarily. He felt sure that it would override any desire to keep the ship around until Carla was free to supervise retrieval of the computer system. But Peter was not swayed. "Fate sent us here," he said. "We've survived crises that logic would have said we couldn't survive. Have you no faith in our destiny, Jess? Aren't we obliged by what's past to keep striving toward that destiny?"

Anne's memorial was held that evening. Beforehand, Jesse feared that Peter might seize the opportunity to sway the Group's emotions. After all, he had used Ian's memorial to inspire them to emigrate and Hari's to lift them out of despair. "We all know what will happen if he mesmerizes them with mass telepathy," he said to Kira, trying to hide bitterness. "Peter is my closest friend—I never thought a time would come when I couldn't support him. But he's not acting in our best interests, Kira. He's always been more of a visionary than a realist, you know. I suppose you can't see that—you're taking his side."

"I'm not sure I would be, if it weren't for one thing," Kira confessed. "I fear that in addition to the danger of losing lives, a futile attempt to regain a high-tech lifestyle might spread the colony's resources too thin. Still, I can't bring myself to oppose what Ian wanted."

That was understandable. She had loved Ian since youth and had borne his posthumous child. She was the swing vote in the Council, Jesse saw. Reiko and Kwame were solidly behind Peter on the importance of technology; Carla cared about nothing but preservation of the computer system. That made it four against four, so Kira's choice would be decisive if it were up to them.

But it wasn't. The Council had no legal authority under the charter. Its members, chosen for expertise in specific

fields rather than popularity, were tenured for life unless removed by a two-thirds vote of the Group. It was an
administrative rather than legislative body; the colony
had no laws, and expected to have none until a population increase called for adoption of a constitution. For all
practical purposes, the decision-making power lay solely
with Peter. Was it right for one man to have that much
power? Or did he in fact not have it except through the
support of the majority?

Peter didn't attempt to use telepathic persuasion at the
memorial. That was wise, Jesse realized, sensing the mood
of the Group. In the first place, the emotion about Anne's
death would have worked against his position instead of for
it; people were horrified, as Jesse was, by what the starship's
AI had done to her. In the second place, in the past he'd
been supported telepathically by the whole Council and all
the rest of the strongest members—he had channeled their
collective feeling. He could not do that when some were
against him. He was not the only powerful telepath, after
all. In particular Hari's faction, now led by Arwen, would
have joined to counter the conviction he tried to convey.

At the end, he spoke out in plain words. "You all know
the decision facing us," he said after explaining his argument for the sake of those who hadn't heard it. "This decision is too important to be made by counting opinions. The
colony can never become what it was intended to become if
we fail to preserve the knowledgebase. Perhaps we *will* fail;
that is up to fate. But we will not purposely let it go. I will
use any means at my disposal to persuade individual
members to do what must be done to save it. And if I
can't persuade enough people—if the effort is not made, and
the knowledgebase is lost—then you will have to choose a
new leader. I will not preside over the abandonment of Ian's
vision."

There was a gasp from the listeners. That he would go
this far had not occurred to anyone. Jesse and Carla looked
at each other in dismay, their quarrel forgotten. *He can't*

resign! Carla cried silently. *We couldn't get along without him . . . and he'd be destroyed, his whole adult life he's been preparing to lead the Group. . . .*

Jesse too felt anguish at the thought, and worse pain at the realization that it was his opposition that had brought Peter to this. It was true that the colony couldn't thrive without his inspiration; that had been proven long ago when he was ill.

But Peter wouldn't need to resign, of course. Unwilling as some people might be to accept his decision, they were even less willing to give up the leader on whom they'd come to rely. As always, he had known what must be done to win their allegiance.

Jesse couldn't help being glad; he cared too much for Peter not to be. Besides, ongoing dissention within the settlement would have destroyed the mutual trust that was its greatest strength. Yet the same time, he was determined to prevent any more pointless deaths—perhaps even Carla's death—aboard the starship, not to mention the cataclysm that might result if it fell to the surface of Maclairn. And if one man could decide for the Group unilaterally, so could another. It was time to take things into his own hands, and he knew what he would have to do.

42

MAYFLOWER XI COULD not be left in orbit indefinitely, as it could if its AI were reliable. Sooner or later, Jesse knew, he would have to act. And since he wanted to keep people from boarding anyway, there was no reason to delay. Nothing would be gained by procrastination.

He rose very early the next morning and took off in a shuttle alone, skipping breakfast and not speaking to anyone. Carla was still sleeping when he left the hut. Kel would wake soon and arouse her, and she'd wonder why he'd gone without a word. She would never forgive him for what he was about to do. That couldn't be helped; he was too deeply concerned about her safety to be put off by the prospect of her anger—or even by her pain. He knew she would be terribly hurt as well as outraged. That troubled him . . . but it would be no worse than what she'd meet if she tried to relocate the computer system, an undertaking that would have little chance of success even if he gave it his full support.

Peter would not forgive him, either. He would be devastated by the loss not only of the knowledgebase, but of the loyalty of a trusted friend. The enormity of the betrayal exceeded anything he could ever have expected from his followers, let alone from his deputy. Jesse himself would have to resign from the Council, he realized. That didn't matter, but the thought of Peter's suffering did.

The ship, when he boarded, seemed more silent than ever, and it was cold. The temperature control had failed. Was the computer system even functional, now? He stopped by the computer room and stared at it for a long moment. Its panel lights looked normal. He wished they did not; he wished he could say it had already been past saving. Could he lie about that? No, in a telepathic society lying was impossible. He certainly couldn't conceal a lie from Carla or Peter.

He should carry back one more shuttle load, Jesse decided. There was no point in wasting the cargo space. Besides, if he returned too early in the day he would be questioned immediately; there would be no grace period during which he could hide from people on the pretext of fatigue. It was hard to put his mind on what to take. He'd retrieved the chicken embryos and the specialized equipment for incubating them on the previous trip, along with what medical supplies he thought might prove useful in addition to those brought down earlier. All housekeeping supplies and detachable furniture had gone down long ago. So had all loose electronic devices. Replacing his helmet, he walked through the airless decks, which had been stripped clean. The Group had intended to eventually cannibalize the ship for construction materials, but he couldn't do that alone.

Spare parts for the two remaining shuttles might someday be essential, he realized suddenly. By himself, he
wouldn't be able to dismantle the damaged, tethered one,
but there were stores in the shuttle bay. He returned to it
and devoted himself to loading whatever he was able to carry
into the cargo hold. It was hard work, especially while wearing a spacesuit. He welcomed this; it left him no chance to
think.

Once he was finished, Jesse made a final inspection of
the ship. As he passed what had once been his cabin on his
way through passenger quarters, he looked back on the day
the Council had met there, the day he'd persuaded them to
go into stasis. *We were wrong to assume it's up to us*, Peter
had said. *Ian placed our lives in Jesse's hands, knowing full
well that in space, the Captain commands. . . .*

Ian had declared that he trusted him *in all things*, a
somewhat mysterious statement to which they'd eventually
given various interpretations. As he'd done often in the past,
Jesse relived the dream in which Ian had come to him telepathically, the dream where they'd walked together in space.
He recalled the foreboding he'd felt then—the knowledge
that Ian depended on him, the Group depended on him,
that if he gave in to pressure or fear or despair, Carla would
die. Had Ian's precognition extended even to this, years later,
when she and others were again in danger? Had he knowingly
trusted him to give up Peter's friendship, the Group's respect,
even the solidity of his relationship with Carla, if that was
what it would take to protect them?

Returning to the bridge at last, unable to put it off any
longer, Jesse pulled a stool over to the Captain's console and
began programming the maneuver he'd decided on. Once
more, he thought. If the AI could compute a trajectory
just once more, it would never need reliability again. It
wouldn't have to use the hyperdrive, of course. The main
drive would take *Mayflower XI* out of orbit, moving slowly,
leaving him plenty of time to depart in the shuttle before

it picked up speed and escaped from Maclairn's gravity, heading into the sun.

He was feeling dizzy. It was a good thing that the bridge was pressurized; if he'd been forced to wear his helmet sweat would have fogged it up. The board looked a bit foggy as it was, as if a sheet of frosted glass had fallen in front of his eyes. An emotional reaction, he told himself. He was a spacer, conditioned by Fleet; the death of a starship could not help but shake him. No captain could be calm about sending his ship to destruction.

The lightheadedness increased. It was hard to think clearly; the programming was complete, but perhaps he should wait a minute or two before he pressed Execute, give himself time to recover before trying to reach the shuttle. . . .

Suddenly the board disappeared and he was somewhere else, looking back on his own body as he had years ago while fasting. For an instant he felt terror—but then Ian was there with him, as in the old dream. *Jesse! I trusted you, Jesse, and you're about to betray me. . . .*

No! I'm betraying Peter, and maybe Carla—at least she'll interpret it as betrayal—but not you, Ian. You put their lives into my hands. I've messed up sometimes, failed sometimes, but I've managed to protect their lives. That was my responsibility, as Captain as well as to you. . . .

Oh, Jesse. Do you think their lives are all that matters? Ian's wise eyes penetrated him. *You risked your lives when you set off in an aging starship to reach an unopened world. Why did you do it, if only survival was important?*

For freedom. For the chance to live our own way, develop our full capabilities.

Just for yourselves? It was a lot of trouble to go to, if it's going to end there.

It won't end with us. We did it for our kids, our grandkids.

But not their grandkids. It's going to end sometime if they fall behind the rest of the human race. You'll be lucky if whoever discovers the colony doesn't tear down what you've built and take over the planet. That wasn't what Peter and I planned. We wanted Maclairn to light a beacon for future generations. A flame that could never be put out.

God, Ian, we'll never have the resources to equal Earth! Jesse protested. *We'll surpass them in mind power and that's all—we can't catch up in technology or science.*

Without the knowledgebase you can't, that's for sure.

Are you telling me we should stake lives on the slim chance of preserving it?

You're telling yourself, Jesse. I'm not really here, you know—

The blaring of an alarm horn jarred him back to reality. Groggily, Jesse searched for its source. He was back in his body and an insistent red light was flashing . . . the air quality indicator . . . it must not be a false alarm this time, for he was passing out. . . . His Fleet training kicked in as he recognized the symptoms of anoxia. The AI's regulation of oxygen level had failed.

Shaking, he managed to get his suit's helmet back on and adjust the air gauge. He almost hadn't made it. Another minute and he'd have been too far gone to save himself. How had Ian known?

But no . . . Ian hadn't come to warn him. Not about the oxygen. He had not been talking to a ghost. Peter had once told him, *Everyone's unconscious mind contains some image, some concrete symbol, that emerges as a source of deep wisdom—wisdom that comes from beyond the limits set by space or time. In my mind, and I think in yours, it takes Ian's form.*

Triggered by anoxia, the image of Ian had arisen from within—arisen because with his finger on the key to send the ship away forever, he had been aware underneath that his responsibility wasn't what he'd always thought it was. Right from the beginning he'd believed it was up to him as Captain to protect unwary passengers. When his astrogation error had led them to stasis and then to the choice of a poor landing site, he had agonized over his failure. He'd been determined never to put them in danger again. But that wasn't what Ian had wanted of him.

Ian gave his life to make you Captain! Carla had said when he'd convinced her to go into stasis. *He relied on you to do whatever it took to make his dream come true.* Not to keep them alive at any cost, but to fulfill his vision. Whatever it took—even if that meant risking both lives and probable defeat. If it was their choice to assume risks, it was no more his right to stop them than it had been the government's right to ban health risks on Undine.

Jesse's finger moved decisively from Execute to Cancel. Drawing deep breaths of reviving air, he wiped the planned departure from the ship's memory and turned to setting up a direct datalink from the knowledgebase to the settlement.

43

POSTPONING FOR AS long as possible the moment when he'd have to face Carla, Jesse took his time unloading the spare parts from the shuttle and moving them into the pods. Several men came to help him, fortunately not close friends who would have expected telepathic conversation. He did not want to talk to anyone. He did not see how he could bear the secret of his near-defection during the days and weeks to come.

He wasn't going to tell anybody about it. That meant closing his mind to full communication, something which, now that he was used to telepathy, would be hard to do on a long-term basis. Yet as deputy leader, he could not afford to lose the colony's respect. He surely would lose it if what had happened became known—Peter's supporters would despise him for having planned to destroy the starship, while opponents would consider him spineless for not having gone through with it. Respect was not what mattered to him. He would have been happy to resign from the Council. But if he did so, Peter would have to know why, and the one thing he was sure he couldn't endure was Peter's pain.

He didn't believe he could endure Carla's, either, but sooner or later she would find out. Reticence now might be interpreted as an aftermath of their quarrel, but the first time they made love, their minds would be fully open to each other. That could be put off for awhile because she was soon to give birth, he thought, dismayed at the realization that he felt glad. There had never been a time when he didn't want to make love to Carla. He hadn't believed that anything could come between them. That it was his own fault—that if he hadn't been stopped by oxygen loss he'd have done something she'd view as unforgivable—made it all the more intolerable.

Much easier was admission that he'd been wrong to oppose the computer relocation. "I've set it up so we can download directly from the starship instead of through the satellite," he told Carla when they met at suppertime. "It won't be continuous, of course, since the ship will be out of range much of the time, but it will be better than nothing until we can move the knowledgebase here."

She threw her arms around him, radiating joy. "Oh, Jesse! I knew you'd change your mind—I knew you couldn't really believe it's not important."

"Well," he said, "I got to thinking about what Ian would have wanted."

In the weeks that followed, work progressed on preparing a place for the computer system. Of the six prefab shelters, one was in use as the Commons and another as the children's playroom. It was decided to devote one of the rest to computer and biolab facilities; reserve one for the school that would be needed when the kids were older; and divide the fifth between a chicken house—for chickens couldn't survive the outdoor heat or cold—and a workroom for the spinning, weaving, and sewing that would start as soon as fabric crops could be grown. The sixth would continue to be used as living quarters for people without families.

The shelters were well enough insulated for housing, but a computer complex would require a more even temperature. A layer of stone was therefore erected around the outer walls to thicken them, and Jesse, swallowing his reluctance, began taking volunteers to the starship to tear out bulkheads that could be used to reinforce the roof. What the hell, he thought. He'd made his decision, and there was nothing to be gained by worrying about accidents anymore. Determinedly, he put the risks out of his mind. On days when he didn't fly, he labored on the stone wall, leaving himself no time free for thinking. But underneath the strain was wearing on him. Every time he boarded the ship he cringed inwardly.

It would have been different if he'd been convinced the work was leading somewhere. But now he felt anxiety on both counts. He feared the disaster that might result from keeping the ship in orbit; yet at the same time, having adopted Ian's goal, he wanted it to be honored and dreaded the failure he saw coming. Computer systems were delicate, despite the fact that those designed for starships were vastly improved over the primitive ones common on Earth. Even supposing that the AI held out long enough, the idea of inexperienced workers disconnecting many components, carrying them through the airless ship, loading them into a shuttle, and making a soft enough landing not to damage them struck him as totally impractical. And if they got that far intact, there would then be the difficulty of moving them into the shelter, installing them on makeshift shelving, and keeping them operative not just for years but for generations. Carla believed this could be done. She believed it, Jesse suspected, because she *wanted* to believe, and the others, most of whom had little technical experience, were taking her word for it. Whether or not the cost of maintaining her illusions proved high, she would be crushed when she ultimately lost them . . . and so would the rest, he as much as anyone now that he'd conceded that the knowledgebase was essential to fulfillment of the colony's purpose.

It was possible to hide his thoughts, but not, in a tele-pathic society, his feelings. In the effort to do so he became distant and withdrawn, and as time passed Carla grew more and more puzzled. Her initial happiness over his change of heart faded as she saw that he was conflicted. Jesse knew she was bewildered and hurt, yet he could not help himself. He held her, kissed her, just as he always had, but he dared not get far enough aroused to let her into his mind. It wasn't that he feared her anger; he would even have welcomed it. But she might not be able to keep the truth from Peter, and for Peter to find out would be intolerable. He could not let either of them suffer as they would if they knew how close he had come to defeating the colony's true purpose.

The only thing keeping the tension from becoming in-tolerable was the imminent birth of Tarin. Carla evidently believed this would restore their closeness, and while Jesse knew it wouldn't, he too looked forward to the coming of an-other child. It would occupy their full attention, and in any case, the kids were the one bright hope in what had become, for him, a dark view of future. What free time he had on the ground he spent with Kel, who was too young to grasp what troubled his dad and was therefore safe to communicate with. The love he could no longer convey to Carla he gave to Kel, and in Kel's company, briefly, he knew peace.

The colony's children were in a situation different from what they'd have known in any other society. In the first place, there were no older kids to look up to—Kel and the others born in the first year perceived only a wide gap be-tween themselves and the adults, without any concept of gradual growth. This would change when they reached the age to watch live-action vids and read stories, but in the mean-time they were completely ignorant of what lay ahead for them. In the second place, they had few toys. Some primitive dolls and bears had been made by stuffing fabric with straw, crude balls were formed in the same way, and small figures had been fashioned from clay. But the possibilities for play these offered were limited, and without wood, paper, or spare metal, little else could be fabricated. The kids weren't quite old enough for electronic games, and in any case there were only a few computers to play them on; the screens of personal datakeepers simply weren't large enough to hold a small child's attention.

Thus the coming of the chickens was a major event in the lives of the oldest. As the biolab wasn't ready, the chicken embryos had been incubated in the infirmary, which had been temporarily given over to the job. No one in the Group had any experience with chickens, but the process was not much like farming in any case; it was merely necessary to follow the downloaded instructions for hatching chicks without shells. These warned that a percentage of them would not prove viable. Enough live ones were produced to start a flock, however, provided they were nurtured very, very, carefully. Only a few people were allowed in at a time to see them, and the line was long—the adults, born on Undine where there were no living creatures except the poultry raised on inaccessible farm islands, found them as fascinating as did the kids. But Corrine didn't have the heart to keep the children away entirely. Accompanied by parents, they were permitted to watch but not touch.

Kel had never so much as imagined anything like living, moving chicks. That they could run around on their own astonished him. Jesse was appalled to discover this gap in his son's understanding—didn't all kids just naturally know what animals were? They did on Earth, even in cities where they hadn't personally seen any. After all, lots of kids Kel's age didn't have pets, yet they responded instinctively to pictures of dogs, cats, and ducks. "On Earth, yes," Kira explained. "But it comes from the collective unconscious, Jesse, the link that doesn't extend from world to world. Positive associations are passed on that way, just as negative reactions to creatures like the crawlies are. Everyone here except you grew up on a world without animals and so our kids haven't absorbed knowledge of them from us—and even you spent most of your life in space."

"Is it going to work that way with other things?" he asked. "Things everyone on Earth takes for granted?"

"Of course," Carla said. "That's why the knowledgebase is so very important, not only for regaining technology but for raising the kids to share humanity's heritage."

Oh, God. It would matter in Kel's generation, then, not just to posterity. He hadn't thought of it like that. He had been about to do even worse damage than he'd recognized. And yet they were probably going to lose the knowledgebase anyway. . . .

Ivana, too, was surprised by the chicks, but she caught on very quickly. Solemnly, she pointed to one huddled in the corner of the cage. "That one's hurting," she announced. "It doesn't hear me, I have to pick it up."

"You mustn't touch them, dear," Kira told her. "They might get sick if you touch them."

"But Mom, it's already sick! Let me make it well—please?"

Everyone stared as Kira reached for the chick. She and other healers had indeed helped a few of the hatchlings survive; when the trouble wasn't due to incomplete development, that sometimes worked. "You may touch it very gently while I hold it," she told Ivana.

Wearing her dreamy look, Ivana did so. After a long silence, she said, "It's okay now. You can let it go run with the others."

The chick scampered off, having gained vigor. *Kira, did you do that . . . or did she?* Jesse inquired, awe-stricken.

She did. We've known for a long time she can heal herself, but to heal a chick at the age of three . . . I—I'm not sure how far ahead of me she'll end up, Jesse.

In addition to the chicken embryos, the starship's cryogenic storage bank had contained fertilized fish eggs, which Jesse had brought along thinking fish might thrive in the pond. Cryopreserved algae for them to feed on were also provided, as it wasn't known whether native algae would be suitable. It was decided to use the largest and deepest of the cisterns as a hatchery to find out whether they could survive the climate and the mineral content of the water. So far, a good many fingerlings appeared to be flourishing.

"If we could have a lake, we might eventually be able to stock it with fish," Kwame said. He had never wholly given up the idea of damming the river, impossible though it was. Now, with the prospect of the shuttle flights coming to an end, he asked Jesse to get some aerial shots of the narrows from a lower altitude than the images obtained from the starship. For the sake of morale Jesse obliged. A group of enthusiasts poured over the photos, noting with regret that a dam would be entirely feasible if only there were a way to blast enough rock.

By the time the work on the computer room was nearly finished, Carla's due date was close. Jesse had planned to delay further flights until after the birth. But Tomas found it would be necessary to reclaim wire from the starship, for although enough electricity was being generated in the settlement to supply the computers, not quite enough new wire existed to route it there. Tearing it out of the passenger deck, to which all power had been cut off, was a major job, and Jesse did not want to wait any longer than necessary to begin it. So he enlisted several people familiar with wiring and took them up—only to be informed via the comm that Carla had gone into labor early. There was no way he could go to her immediately. He couldn't strand workers aboard the ship, and he couldn't bring them back before anything was done, thereby increasing the number of risky trips required. Carla was being attended by Susan, who assured him that she was fine and that evening would be soon enough for him to arrive. With raw nerves, he got through the day. When he landed the shuttle, people rushed to congratulate him. Tarin had already been born.

"It went faster than last time," Carla said to him. "It wasn't your fault that you weren't here." But they both knew that although it really was not his fault, it nevertheless made a difference. She had expected him to support her during

Tarin's birth, as he had during Kel's, and the prospect of
going through labor without him had dismayed her. Inevitably, she'd been unable to turn off the feeling of being abandoned. And so she'd asked for Peter, whose room was close
enough to the infirmary for his chair to be carried there, and it
had been he who'd held her hand, he who'd telepathically
shared both her ordeal and her ultimate joy.

Jesse cursed himself, cursed the task aboard the starship
that he had not wanted to do in the first place, and it didn't
matter that Carla was the one who most wanted that task to
be undertaken. It wasn't something either of them could view
rationally. He knelt by her bed and caressed the child on her
breast, the child whose emergence he had not seen; but the
intimacy they'd felt after Kel's birth was lacking. Carla's mind
was closed to him now, as much as his to her. He stayed by her
through the night, holding back tears, wondering if he could
ever heal the rift between them.

44

CARLA WAS SLOW in regaining her energy after Tarin's birth.
She knew she must get to the starship as soon as possible to
oversee dismantling of its computer system, but she didn't
feel up to doing anything beyond nursing the children. This
was something new to her—since her entry to the Group in
youth, she had never been sick. She had quelled any incipi-
ent illness before feeling noticeable effects. And that had
been true after Kel's birth, too. None of the women in the
settlement were disabled by childbirth; being experienced
in self-healing, they went back to their regular activities
within a day or two.

"I can't seem to pull myself together," she said to Kira.
"I don't know what's wrong with me."

"Yes, you do," said Kira gently. "You're troubled, so
troubled that you've stopped managing the physical effects
of stress."

"I guess you can sense it," Carla agreed miserably. "Oh, Kira, I love the new baby, and the computer preparation's almost done—I should be happy, even if Jesse and I aren't as close as we used to be."

"We've all noticed the change in Jesse. I don't want to pry, but—"

"Something's happened to him . . . he says he loves me, but he shuts me out of his mind. He doesn't even want to have sex! It's too soon after the baby, of course . . . but he acts almost as if he were thankful that we have to wait. And that's not all."

"No, he hasn't been himself even at Council meetings," Kira said. "He seems detached, and he barely speaks to Peter."

"I know." Carla hesitated, then burst out, "Jesse knows how Peter and I feel about each other. He's known for a long time, and it hasn't bothered him. He told me once— well, never mind. But he made it very clear that he wasn't jealous or hurt. Now . . . I don't know. Peter was with me when Tarin was born—"

"I wondered at the time whether that was wise."

"I thought it wouldn't matter by then. Jesse had already cooled toward Peter. I think he resents what he and I share, not the love between us, but how deeply we both care about preserving the knowledgebase. I believe he hasn't forgiven me for supporting Peter instead of him when they disagreed about it—he hasn't been the same since the night of the showdown."

Kira frowned. "I suppose that could be true, and yet I thought I knew Jesse pretty well, after our being in close touch telepathically during his mind training. It's not like him to resent a thing like that. Besides, he changed his mind about retrieving the computers. He's working hard to get it done."

"He told me he decided it was what Ian would want. He wasn't swayed by what *I* want, or even by what Peter wants. Maybe underneath he hated giving in to us. I've tried and tried to imagine what I might have done to hurt him, and I can't think of anything else."

"Carla," Kira said, "you know Jesse was, and still is, afraid for you—afraid to have you go to the starship after Anne was killed there. Perhaps that's all that's bothering him. Perhaps he's so scared of losing you that he's keeping a tight rein on his emotions."

Do you really think so? Carla queried silently. Kira didn't reply in words, but it was plain that she didn't believe that was enough to account for so great a change.

The day came when she felt well enough to proceed with the computer relocation. Jesse, having resigned himself to the inevitable, didn't protest when she told him she wanted to get started the next morning. But he seemed silent, distant, during the flight to the starship—since Viktor was in the copilot's seat she wasn't seated near enough for Jesse to talk to her anyway, but if things had been normal between them, they'd have conversed telepathically.

Carla had not been in space since her original night trip to the surface, so she'd never seen Maclairn from above. The view was awe-inspiring. She knew she should be thrilled by its beauty as the planet fell away beneath her and then, as they went into orbit, became a vast golden curve overhead, filling half the star-studded sky. But her eyes blurred and she could not see it clearly, thinking how much more she'd be enjoying it if Jesse's mind were in touch with hers.

Only Erik had come with them, leaving plenty of room for cargo; the most fragile computer components would be strapped into seats rather than placed in the hold. As they docked with the ship she saw the damaged shuttle tethered to it, and shivered. She was not immune to worry about the perils of this job, especially when she pictured Anne's death in that shuttle, with Jesse seated so close that he too might have been killed. But the job had to be done, and she was the only one qualified to supervise it. She couldn't afford to be nervous.

Most of the ship was now unpressurized, but as Carla

had had experience working in a spacesuit before the initial landing she wasn't hindered by it. The computer room had air, but Jesse insisted that they keep not only their suits but their helmets on—the air quality, he said, was unreliable and might deteriorate suddenly. For the first time she became aware that he might have had more narrow escapes than the one he'd told the Council about. He might have had valid grounds for his reluctance to let them come.

She set to work analyzing the system configuration. There was extensive backup memory, of course, and also backup servers; she was knowledgeable enough to identify the components by calling up an information screen before trying to physically locate them. Then, cautiously, she began the shutdown process. The system wasn't meant to be shut down; it was designed to automatically switch to the backup units if a failure occurred. Nevertheless, she managed to get the datalink offline without too much difficulty, so that Erik could disconnect the equipment associated with it and with Viktor's help, carry it to the shuttle. Turning off the computer itself proved harder. It took a long time and involved overriding many alarms. Finally, she deemed it safe for Jesse to cut the power to it from the bridge. Only then were they able to start dismantling the system, carefully noting the cable connections.

It was slow work, hampered by the difficulty of managing it with gloves. They could not possibly complete it in one day, and in any case, Carla insisted that the main and backup components should not be taken on the same flight. After landing, much time was consumed carrying various devices from the shuttle to the newly-reinforced shelter. There were plenty of people on hand to help but only one stretcher, so that many trips were needed, with Carla walking alongside to make sure that no mishaps occurred. Finally, exhausted, she stopped by the nursery to get Tarin and made her way home to the hut. Jesse wasn't there; by this time, he had picked up Kel and was off somewhere with him. Ruefully, she reflected that he was more eager to be with Kel than with her.

The next day they returned to *Mayflower XI* for the backup components. Jesse said Carla needn't go, since all computer parts had already been identified, but she didn't want them handled when out of her sight. She sensed that he was more troubled than ever, which was strange since this was the last day he would have to take anyone aboard. At the end he went to the bridge to check on something. "I'll be coming back one more time alone to—finish," he said when he rejoined them, and though she couldn't see his face through his helmet, the wordless pain in his mind flooded into hers. Was it hard for him to abandon space? she wondered. Hard to face the thought that since there was no more work to do aboard and the starship was unsafe to visit, he would be grounded for the rest of his life? But surely that wasn't something he'd mind telling her, if it was true.

At dusk, as on the previous evening, Carla sat alone in the hut nursing Tarin. "I promised Kel I'd take him to see the fish again," Jesse had told her. All at once Carla was stricken by an overwhelming sense of something wrong: a vague, formless, telepathic perception that she'd experienced only a few times in her life. *Jesse?* she cried in terror. *Jesse, where are you? Are you okay? Answer me, Jesse, please answer—*

Carla . . . oh God, Carla. I was responsible *for him. . . .*

Responsible? For Kel? God, nothing's happened to Kel?

He's safe now. But it was my fault, I lost sight of him for a minute. . . .

Clutching Tarin to her breast, Carla jumped up to search for Jesse, but he was already on his way to her. They met at the door of the hut. Jesse was holding Kel by the hand, and they were both soaking wet. Kel, she saw, was fine. Jesse was not. She could tell that he was on the verge of breaking down.

"I stopped to speak to Erik," he said, "and Kel ran ahead to the cistern. The next thing I knew he was in the water—"

"I fell in," Kel told her, not unhappily. "I tried to grab a fish. Dad jumped in and grabbed *me*."

"It was over his head, he could have drowned," Jesse said with remorse. "He's bathed only in the shallow cisterns, he didn't know this one's different. Didn't know what deep water is like." He buried his face in his hands.

Carla said quietly, "But he didn't drown. He didn't even get scared. You were there for him." Jesse, she knew, had developed a phobia about deep water when he fell from a pier at an early age. He had overcome it on Undine, had learned to enjoy swimming and scuba diving. But an incident like this might well have stirred memories.

"I can't rely on myself, Carla," he said slowly. "No matter how hard I try to stay on top of things, I end up failing, the way I did with the astrogation—"

"God, Jesse, you're not still worrying about that, are you? It was years ago."

"—then Anne died aboard my ship, and you might have died too. I can't even count on keeping my own son out of danger. Yet everyone's trusting me."

"I will always trust you. Just as Peter and the others do. As Ian declared that he did."

"But you wouldn't, if you knew—" He broke off, obviously in agony.

This was ridiculous. Jesse had proven himself trustworthy over and over again. As for Kel, he had just saved him through his ability to act fast in a crisis. But Carla saw that more reassurance now would not do any good. It would take Peter's skill as a therapist to get to the bottom of this, if Jesse could be persuaded to consult Peter, which was questionable.

"Get out of those wet clothes, both of you," she said, laying Tarin in his cradle and starting to undress Kel. As Jesse pulled off his shirt, she saw a gash on his arm she hadn't noticed at first. "Where did that come from?" she asked. "Why isn't it healing?"

"I must have scraped it on the stone of the cistern. I

stopped the pain and bleeding, that's automatic now, but my mind was on Kel—I didn't think about healing it." Somewhat abashed, he confessed, "I guess I'm still not used to having such powers."

"Let me heal it now," Carla said. She sat down on their mattress and held out her hand; the wicker stools in the hut weren't meant for relaxing on. Her heart ached for Jesse. He'd always been so strong, so reliable, despite tending to underrate his capabilities. Now his confidence seemed gone. God, she thought, is *that* it? Is he unsure that he even *can* make love?

When Jesse's arm was healed, Carla continued to hold it, hoping against hope that he might move closer. It didn't happen. After a while she set out some flatbread left over from breakfast; she was too tired to go up to the Commons for hot porridge. They ate in silence while Kel chattered on about the fish. Then, once the children were asleep, Jesse too went to bed, saying he'd had a long day. Carla joined him; she would have to get up frequently to nurse the baby, so the more rest she could manage now, the better.

She did not sleep. Late in the night Jesse began to toss and turn. By dawn she found to her dismay that he was burning with fever.

Oh God, Carla thought. The alien virus. The virus from which Peter had almost died. Kira had said it was waterborne, that it had entered through Peter's wounds. No others had gotten it in the years since then, but they had healed any cuts quickly, certainly before bathing. Jesse's gash had gone unhealed too long.

The phones no longer worked and she dared not leave the children while Jesse was unconscious. She could, she supposed, wake someone in a nearby hut; but that would mean delay. Carla did what her heart told her to do—she cried out in her mind to Peter. Though she had not previously tried to communicate over distance except with Jesse, she was sure Peter would hear. *Peter . . . Peter, help me! Jesse's sick, please send someone to help!*

Carla? What's happened, Carla? I know he's not been acting like himself....

It's nothing to do with how he's been acting, she told him. *He's feverish, he's got the virus.*

Oh, God. We knew he was more vulnerable to illness than the rest of us, but I didn't think he'd be exposed. I assumed we had time. . . . Well, stay calm. I'll send Kira over.

And men with the stretcher, Carla added. *He's not conscious—he's got to be moved to the infirmary.*

Edris came with them to take charge of the kids. Kira, when she arrived, was reassuring. "It won't be as bad as it was with Peter," she said. "Peter's body was weakened by the amputations, but Jesse is physically strong. There's no reason to think we can't heal him, though it may take awhile. Peter says he has been under great stress recently, that he needs time out."

"But the starship work is finished. The stress of worrying about it is over."

"Sometimes that's when people collapse. When they've been holding themselves together, and then suddenly let go."

"You're saying this is more than just the virus."

"I'm saying stress weakened his immune system, giving the virus a chance to invade. That's common with outsiders, you know. It's part of what our training aims to prevent."

"And Jesse was never fully trained," Carla said bitterly. "Peter's waited for years, when it should have been done before we ever left Undine."

"I'm sure he had his reasons." Kira paused and then added, "Peter believes Jesse is okay, Carla—in spite of having seemed different lately. He made that plain to me just now. He said to tell you to be patient."

"Peter doesn't know all of it. I haven't talked to him about the trouble between Jesse and me. He's the last person I could tell. It would—hurt him, Kira, considering that he gave up his own hopes for the sake of our relationship."

"I suspect he knows more than you think he does," Kira said. "Peter cares too much for his people not to be aware of everyone's problems."

"Maybe so. But he can't read minds that are intentionally closed to him." She was sure Jesse hadn't confided in Peter. When she'd suggested it once, he gotten terribly upset. Perhaps while feverish he wouldn't be able to close his mind, and in that case, as long as Kira didn't think his illness was serious, the accident might have been a stroke of fortune.

45

JESSE LAY IN the infirmary for many days. At first, his mind clouded by fever, he did not know where he was—he saw the blackness of space, and whirling lights, and the starship a dark shape against the glare, merging into the sun . . . and Carla was between him and the stars, weeping. *Jesse! Jesse, how could you . . . how could you destroy what you knew meant so much to me? When it meant so much to Peter? How could you kill our dream?* And he protested, *I didn't, Carla! I didn't do it after all!* But she reproached, *You wanted to. You would have, if Ian hadn't stopped you. You said you loved me, that you cared about Peter, but you'd have betrayed our trust in you. . . .*

He cried out aloud, "Carla! I tried not to hurt you, Carla!" *I love you, I can't bear for you to be hurt . . . I'd give up anything to keep from hurting you. . . .* She was there with him, holding his hand, her face close to his; and Peter was there also. And gradually he became aware that there was no reproach in their voices after all. The accusation had come from his own mind, for they didn't know about the plan he'd kept secret. *Jesse, I love you!* Carla kept saying. *I'll always love you, it doesn't matter how you've changed, what you've done or haven't done . . . please come back to me, Jesse. . . .*

Peter, too, was speaking in his mind, saying over and

over, *We care about you . . . there's nothing to worry about . . . nothing to blame yourself for. . . .* Jesse knew it was meant as comfort. But if it was not a mere delusion then Peter, unknowing, was making things worse than ever by the irony of his trust.

Time passed, and his mind remained too hazy to guess how much of it was passing. He was conscious of Kira pressing cool clothes against his face. Then later he felt that others were calling to him, many others: *Jesse! We're all pulling for you, we all care about you . . .* he was back in the Hospital on Undine, drugged, his mind being slowly destroyed, but he knew the Group would support him even after it was gone. . . . How could they? He had failed them. He had miscalculated, led them all into the emptiness of space, so far from any star that only the pseudo-death of stasis was left for them, and perhaps they would never wake. . . . Or was it on Maclairn that they were going to die? He had led them to a hellish site on a barren world . . . and their ship was dying, too . . . it would kill them, it would kill Carla, yet Ian said he must take that risk . . . but hadn't Ian said long ago that she would die if he lost courage? It was all mixed up. He could not sort it out. *Jesse! Jesse! We're counting on you, we want you back. . . .* But they *shouldn't* count on him! He'd tried to save them, and had almost destroyed their dream. . . .

He slept, then suddenly awoke to find himself floating. In dismay he looked down and saw his own body once again, sprawled on the mattress of the infirmary's bed. It was less frightening than it had been the other time. Was this death? he wondered. He had not wanted to die. But he was not sure he wanted to wake up, either—it was so much easier just to drift and not worry about what he needed to do. Not worry about how to protect the colony. He was too tired to worry anymore . . . someone else would see to it . . . he was back aboard the starship now, where he belonged, where he'd wanted to be since boyhood, and it was as he'd once imagined it would be, out among the bright stars. . . . He recalled the time he and Ian had walked among the stars. Ian had shown him a planet floating in space, a glorious golden world . . . he could see someone approaching him now; had Ian returned for him? Ian was dead, but perhaps out here time was meaningless. . . .

Jesse! Jesse! Come back to us! He moved forward to meet the man who was coming toward him. It was not Ian—it was Peter. Peter, strong and whole as he'd first known him, his tawny hair shining in the sunlight, young, full of life. And Jesse knew that he was not simply drawing this from his mind, as he had drawn the image of Ian twice in the past. This was happening. Peter had left his crippled body and had come for him as he had gone for Claire. He smiled and held out his hand, and Jesse reached for it, feeling no physical touch but knowing they were in contact. They met on a plane beyond the corporeal that was just as real as the one where they'd so often met in the flesh. *I'm here to bring you back to us,* Peter told him. *It's time to come home.* And Jesse responded, *Okay, Peter.* . . .

The next time he woke his mind was clear. Kira was beside him in the small room. "You're all right now," she said, "but you're weak, so don't try to get out of bed."

"What happened to me, Kira?"

"You came down with the alien virus. It wasn't life-threatening, but you were unconscious a long time. You'll be okay in a few more days."

He was glad to rest, glad to know the trips to the dying starship were behind him, except for one more that he was happy to put off. But he was worried when told that Peter's chair had been carried to the infirmary. Jesse perceived that although Kira had cared for his physical needs, it had been Peter who had healed his body in addition to the contact he'd made with his mind. How much had he revealed when he was raving from fever?

Carla might have heard something, too. She'd delayed starting the computer installation and stayed with him most of the time, nursing Tarin at intervals. He didn't know what he'd said while delirious, although if she was angry she didn't show it. They spoke casually to each other, avoiding telepathic rapport. He hoped she wasn't simply hiding feelings because of his illness.

On the third evening, after Carla had gone to pick up Kel, Kira pronounced him fit to get up. "You mustn't fly yet, or do stonesetting," she cautioned. "But you can go home as soon as you've been in to see Peter. He told me to make sure you don't leave before he has a chance to talk to you."

When he entered Peter's room, Jesse knew right away that he'd revealed nothing, for the warmth he'd always felt between them was still strong. Realizing that Peter expected it, he stooped and embraced him, determinedly shielding his mind from intrusion. It would always be hard not to be open with Peter, he thought with sadness. Their telepathic bond had been so good. With a rush of hope he recalled that Peter himself had managed to hide his love for Carla even while communicating wordlessly. Perhaps someday he too could learn to conceal without renouncing such communication entirely.

"It's good to see you, Jess," Peter said. "I've missed you these past weeks. I hope you understand why I had to take the stand I did about the computer retrieval. I don't blame you if you haven't forgiven me for rejecting your advice as Captain."

"What? Me forgive *you*?" Jesse was stunned. "There's nothing to forgive. I changed my mind about the retrieval, you know that. You were right, and I was wrong."

"But you were the expert on the status of the starship, and I pulled rank on you. I didn't give you much choice about how to respond." Slowly, meaningfully, he added, "Sometimes, when a person believes strongly that action is justified, it's necessary to forge ahead without regard to the feelings of friends—even at the risk of losing the friendship. You see that, don't you?"

Jesse's thoughts spun. Peter couldn't be implying what he seemed to be implying . . . and yet, unbelievably, he was.

He sensed it clearly, for though his mind was closed to Peter, Peter's was not closed to him. Aloud, Peter had worded what he said tactfully, but he had not been talking about his own action.

"You *know*, Peter?" he whispered. "You know I came close to ruining everything you and Ian worked for?"

"I wasn't trying to pry. When I went into your mind to heal you, though, I could tell that the virus wasn't the only thing making you sick. You attempted to shut me out, but underneath you longed to confess—and so then, telepathically, I knew."

"Oh, God. I didn't want you to. I never meant to hurt you—"

Peter smiled. "I'm not hurt, except maybe by your having judged me self-centered enough to think less of you for planning to do what you believed was best."

"But you'd given up so much for my sake, and trusted me to be your deputy . . . and you were willing to resign as leader rather than lose what I set out to destroy. How can you not see my defection as betrayal?"

"Because I know you wouldn't have gone through with it. I knew the day you took off in the shuttle alone, as far as that goes. It wasn't hard to imagine what you were thinking."

Incredulous, Jesse burst out, "Then why didn't you stop me?"

"By force? Send Bernie up there with enough men to overpower you? The colony couldn't have withstood the conflicts that would have led to. Besides, I wasn't very worried." He leaned forward in his chair. "I know you better than you know yourself, Jess. After all, I've probed you in the Ritual repeatedly, and on Undine I examined you twice under truth serum."

"And so you counted on my losing my nerve."

"No," said Peter, surprised. "I counted on your sense of values. I knew that when the chips were down, you wouldn't close the door on our chance to shape humankind's future."

"But I would have, if anoxia hadn't struck me just before

I executed the maneuver." He let it all flood into his mind, silently telling Peter the things he'd been fighting so hard to keep from him. "I don't deserve any credit for reconsidering," he concluded aloud. "I stopped thinking clearly and my subconscious impulses took over."

"Exactly. Under stress, you stopped rationalizing and did what you really felt was right. The anoxia contributed to your seeing the image of Ian, but you wouldn't have gone through with what you planned in any case."

"Why are you so sure I wouldn't?"

"Because I knew Ian had judged you trustworthy. And because you wouldn't have chosen a space career in the first place if you didn't have faith in the kind of future we're working toward. A starfaring civilization, always on the edge of human progress."

"I don't see what you mean," Jesse admitted in confusion. "What has my joining Fleet got to do with believing what Ian believed?"

Peter paused, framing his answer. "Jess, there are two fundamental attitudes toward how humans relate to the universe," he said. "Of course, most people don't adopt either one totally; the majority take a position somewhere in between. But they lean one way or the other. Either they believe it's our nature to keep gaining more knowledge and more control of our environment, or they feel we should live as simply as possible and make no attempt to control anything but our own minds."

"I guess space travel promotes increased knowledge," Jesse reflected, "yet developing our own mind powers is what the Group is for, isn't it?"

"It is—but not in the way some members think. Psi and mind powers are important, but by themselves, without development of other human capabilities, they are a dead end. That's one reason why scientists deny their existence. They sense that it would be a dead end to focus too much on them. The aim of the Group, from the day Ian founded it, has been to demonstrate that psi is *not* a dead end—that it can coexist with an advanced technological civilization. If we fail to do that, we'll accomplish nothing for humankind. All our efforts will be self-defeating, except insofar as they benefit us as individuals."

"So people like Arwen, who oppose the effort to regain high technology here, would end up decreasing the acceptance of psi instead of advancing it?"

"Ironically, they'd do just that. Whether or not someone personally admires nonindustrialized cultures, it can't be denied that if one with psi capabilities were discovered here, psi would get the blame for its backwardness. The notion that mind power and technology are alternative forms of evolution, rather than complementary aspects of it, would be reinforced."

"You mean the idea that one must surpass the other."

"Yes. There was a time on Earth, in the twenty-first century, when many people were against what they perceived as tampering with nature. A lot of them were the same people who advocated spiritual development. If they had prevailed, there would be no starships and therefore no colonies here or anywhere else, and Earth would be in ruins. They didn't, and there was a backlash that included even stronger opposition to mind powers than had existed previously, just as evidence for psi was finally gaining acceptance. Ian vowed never to make the same mistake."

Jesse frowned. "Peter, I'm not sure you talked enough about this in the Council meetings," he said.

"It would have fallen on deaf ears. The faction opposing me was composed mainly of people who joined the Group thinking that we disapproved of high-tech lifestyles. They interpreted our rejection of medical technology in that way, even though we objected only to its inappropriate applications—and even though our mind training depended on very advanced neurofeedback equipment. They overlooked the fact that survival on Undine itself would have been impossible without terraforming. Ian never did get Hari to understand our goals; that's one of the reasons why he and his friends saw no need for us to travel to another new world."

"But if you and Ian knew this, why did you urge them to come? Didn't you realize that they might make trouble?"

"Oh yes, we realized it—I've known all along that a showdown would come sooner or later. But psi-gifted people tend toward such views, and we need their gifts. Hari was a good man and his loss will hurt us. We banked on there being enough technology-oriented people like you and Kwame to counter the negative side of his influence."

"The last thing the Group needed was for me to be swayed by it," Jesse said grimly. "I was blind, Peter. You're right about why I signed on with Fleet. How could I have forgotten what used to be important to me?"

Peter looked searchingly at him. "Don't you know?"

"I—I was afraid," he admitted. "Not for myself—not physically, anyway—but I put my fear for Carla, for anyone who boarded the ship, above everything else."

"And so since it's always been your way to act fast in a crisis, your first impulse was to deal with the threat to them."

"I took too much on myself. It was no more my job to stop volunteers from risking themselves than it was the Meds' job on Undine to force medical checkups and outlaw dangerous sports."

"True, but it was natural for you to think it was. You were Captain—and precisely because you were a spacer, had learned over many years to depend solely on technology for survival, its failure frightened you more than it scared those of us whose reliance on it has been less direct," Peter pointed out.

"And I felt to blame for Anne's death," Jesse reflected. "I suppose that's why I unconsciously exaggerated the danger—to justify myself for not having kept her safe."

"Perhaps. Or it may have been just that you take your responsibilities seriously. You pay a high price for that, Jess, especially when they conflict—but it's a lot better than not feeling any obligation to people. It's why we know we can rely on you."

Thoughtfully, Jesse said, "I guess maybe blaming myself is part of the price. I fell apart when Kel almost drowned, it seemed like the last straw."

"Yes, because you'd let down your guard then—after weeks of tension, you'd been able to stop worrying about others. And then you saw that there'll always be someone to watch over."

"Is that why I got sick, Peter?"

"Only in the sense that it was stress, and prolonged stress makes nearly everyone sick, some much sicker than you were. Even before there's organic damage, it's normal for the body to demand time out."

"But in the Group we supposedly stay healthy."

"When we've had enough training, we do. Your immune system was weak because unlike most of us, you've never been taught to control the physical effects of your unwarranted guilt feelings. At long last, it's time we embarked on that. It's difficult, but not incompatible with the work you'll be doing now that there'll be no more space flights."

Jesse nodded. "There's just one left to make, to finish what I started. I have to send the starship away now, Peter. It does pose a hazard to us if its orbit decays."

"Of course. Do you think I haven't been aware of that all this time? I haven't liked it any better than you have, though perhaps I've had more faith in the workings of fate. Go with my blessing, Jess. *Mayflower XI* served us well, and to be vaporized in the sun will be a fitting end."

"I wish I had some of your faith in fate," Jesse declared. "I conceded that a gesture toward preserving human knowledge is important here, but that may be all it is—a gesture. Carla's optimism about keeping that computer system up may not be realistic, and even if she succeeds, we've lost our main power source. We may not be able to get industry going without beamed power."

"But Jess," Peter said, "if you had been *sure* we can't, your inner convictions wouldn't have come to you in Ian's voice. He represents truth in your eyes, doesn't he? How could your unconscious mind perceive advice you consider futile as coming from him?"

"You mean underneath, I believe something different from what reason tells me."

"That's what faith *is*," Peter pointed out. "A belief rising from within that belies reason."

Awed, Jesse nodded. He rose to go, feeling as always a stab of pain at remembering that Peter could not move from his chair. For a moment the image of him as he'd appeared while they were out of their bodies—Peter's own self-image—replaced what he was seeing with his eyes. That was the true essence of him; whether he had physical legs or not had no bearing on his identity as a person.

As he turned toward the door Peter added, "Jesse—you have to tell Carla, you know."

"God, Peter. I—I don't know what to say to her now. She'll be crushed—"

"No, she won't. As for what to say, it shouldn't be necessary to say anything. Just make love to her and your minds will merge—after all, that's why you've been letting her think you don't want to anymore."

He did want to. He had never wanted anything so much; striding across the clearing toward the hut, he wondered how he could wait until Kel was asleep. Carla rushed to meet him and her joy as he opened his mind to her told him he need never have feared that anything could come between them.

A few moments later Kira appeared at the door with Ivana. "Peter thought Kel might like to come with us to see the chicks," she said.

Alone with Carla, Jesse undressed her without speaking. *You'll learn something I didn't want you to know*, he warned. *I love you so much that I didn't want to hurt you. But I've hurt you worse by hiding it....*

Their communication after that was wordless, and he knew no words on the subject would ever be needed.

46

LATER THAT NIGHT, awake while Carla slept peacefully, Jesse pondered the task still ahead of him. It was necessary, and yet . . . so much wasted. So much power left in the ship, lacking only the means to put it to use. Since the AI could never again be trusted to control either the thrusters or the power beam, no further benefit could be derived from the antimatter engines, the pinnacle of the technology so far created by humankind. There was nothing wrong with the engines themselves and no shortage of fuel . . . what a pity to destroy them prematurely, when power was so badly needed on the ground.

Power. He sat upright, struck by sudden excitement. Power could be used slowly under control—or it could be released in one blaze of glory, as in an explosion.

Before sending the ship to its death, he could give the settlement a lake.

"It won't involve any risk," Jesse told the hastily-convened Council the next morning. No risk to the colony, anyway—he was uncomfortably aware he himself would be aboard the starship longer than he'd have to be just to program its departure. "We're too far from the narrows here for there to be danger of being hit with the power beam if my aim isn't accurate. The force of the blast will be no greater than if we used explosives—at worst it will cut a swath through a desolate region we'll never go near."

They examined the low-altitude photos again, which during the night he'd studied thoroughly. "I thought you've been saying the power beam isn't reliable," Teresa said.

"Under AI control, it's not. But it's got a manual override. It can be linked directly to the fire control system, which is separate from the computers we removed."

"The intensity of the beam isn't high enough to blast rocks into a dam," Dan protested. "All this time, we've only needed to avoid straying directly under it."

"The power level can be adjusted. The mechanism's the same as what's installed in freighters that might need to take out a pirate ship."

"You mean like in vids, with starships fighting each other?" Carla asked curiously. "Does that really happen?"

He hesitated. They all knew Fleet dealt with pirates, but he had never described just how. If it upset anyone that was too bad; the Council needed to know he'd had practice with the beam. "It's never happened to me personally," he said, "but we have to be ready to defend ourselves. I was trained to use the fire control system as a cadet."

Kwame asked, "If this is feasible, why didn't you say so long ago when we first talked about having no way to dam the river?"

"Because we expected to reserve power for later on. This will use up most of what's left of the antimatter—fuel that would otherwise go to waste."

Arwen looked unhappy. "I don't like the idea of blasting the natural features of a world," she said. "But I've got to admit that a lake would be worth it."

They all nodded. The long-desired lake would transform the settlement. It would give life to more crops and even to trees. The fish might thrive there. The kids could learn to swim. Peter, too, could swim—he'd always enjoyed that, and it would give him back a taste of freedom. To live by a lake would be even better than if they'd settled by a sea.

Thus it was that once Kira pronounced him fit to fly, Jesse went aloft once more, and for the last time in his life, sat at the controls of a starship. So many memories—not only of this one, but of all the others in his past. Memories now reaching back to his cadet days, when space had been new and thrilling and he'd dreamed of the worlds he would visit, the new regions he would explore. When to be part of the effort to reach them had meant more than anything Earth could offer, and he would have angrily denied any suggestion that its meaning for him would fade. And then, as time progressed, the sad years, the years of doubting that there even was a meaning, when space had become dull routine and he'd come to know that there would be no new worlds for him, that ships and settled planets were all he was ever going to see. . . .

Then for a brief time there'd been hope again, excitement again, the promised captaincy of a colonizer—the position to which in Fleet, only the best of the best could aspire. But the joy of it had lasted only a few hours after boarding. After that, his failures had haunted him. The astrogation error that almost claimed his passengers' lives, the forced choice of a settlement site that offered them only hardship, and finally the near-betrayal of the vision that had led them to stake everything they cared about on a venture too audacious to have much chance of lasting success.

Now, with awareness of his inner beliefs, he'd regained the vision. Now for the first time since youth he did not question it, nor did he doubt his own role in bringing it to fruition. He had come full circle—and had gained so much more than he'd ever imagined in those youthful dreams.

The orbiting ship was approaching the target area. Jesse bent over the fire-control console, and it was as if the years slipped away and he was nineteen again, programming the laser live for the first time, under the eyes of an instructor to be sure, but knowing that what he did would have real results in the real world. He had blasted a small crater on the uninhabited back side of Earth's moon. He had known, as he activated the beam, that he would hit the target— known even before the image of the blast appeared on his screen. He knew now, too, as he pressed the fire key, and the thrill of accomplishment was no less. He suddenly wondered if remote viewing might be involved in this; it was like the final landing on Maclairn the night of their arrival, when in a sleepwalking state he'd sensed his alignment with the shuttle pad. . . .

He stared at the imaging screen. A dust cloud blossomed and when it settled, the cliffs of the narrows were cliffs no longer; the blue line of the river stopped at the mass of boulders that now dammed it. It was a crude dam, but it would serve its purpose. Behind it, after the next flood, would be a lake to take the place of the sea they'd been unable to settle near. Fresh water would be more useful than salt water; he'd made ample amends, and there need never be any more regrets.

Abruptly, Jesse realized that he mustn't sit here dreaming. While focused on setting up the laser blast, he'd given no thought to the condition of the ship, but it was less stable than the last time he'd come. The flickering lights had finally died when he routed power into the beam. Now except for the LEDs of the consoles themselves, he was in darkness.

He fumbled in the catchall drawer for a flashlight. He could see to enter commands from console LEDs alone, but he would need light to reach the shuttle, and there would be little time once he ordered the starship's departure. As he pushed the drawer closed the artificial gravity cut out and he was thrown backward. Quickly orienting himself to zero-g, he floated to the Captain's console and began programming the maneuver. He hadn't stopped to think that without the AI to balance the power load, the sudden draw might cause even low-voltage systems to fail.

God, Jesse thought, what if he'd miscalculated? What if he hadn't reserved enough fuel to take the starship out of orbit—at least not far enough out to escape Maclairn's gravity? That would be a terrible irony, certainly. But he knew he had made no error. He'd checked slowly, carefully, and was absolutely sure of the numbers. The ship was set to go. After taking a last look around the bridge, he put his helmet on, then pressed Execute and swam toward the dark corridor.

When planning his exit he hadn't figured on zero-g. Experienced though he was with it, there was no way to move fast. There were handholds along the wall, placed there for just such emergencies, but it was hard to see them ahead in the feeble beam of his flashlight. He was, to be sure, wearing a spacesuit, but to use its jetpack inside a ship would be to invite collision with something all too solid. It dawned on Jesse that the ship would begin to move before he could get to the shuttle. Well, it wouldn't move faster than the shuttle could, and it wasn't a high-g maneuver, so perhaps that wouldn't matter. Once it was under power there would be gravity again, although unfortunately what was now the wall would become the floor—starships were not designed to lack artificially-maintained gravity while in flight.

He groped his way forward, and then as the thrusters kicked in, fell to the new floor and began to run. The airlock, when he reached it, was beneath him rather than ahead. What if it wouldn't cycle? *Into the sun!* Jesse thought in sudden panic. The ship was headed into the sun. . . .

His heart was racing—as if, he realized with chagrin, he had never had any mind training at all. Grimly he brought his body under control and entered the lock. It did cycle. The shuttle, ahead in the dark bay, lay sideways relative to the ship's gravity and proved difficult to climb into. But it, of course, was meant to fly in zero-g; nothing in it depended on orientation. He strapped himself in and after a moment of conflicting g forces as it moved toward the wide-open bay doors, he was past them and floating free.

With a sigh of relief, Jesse gazed at the departing starship. It had been a good ship until senility set in. It was the last starship he'd ever command, and he could not help feeling some regret at the closure of a chapter in his life.

He saw the drive flare briefly again as *Mayflower XI* broke orbit. Then he leaned back in the pilot's seat and watched it speed away.

Part Five

47

THE LAKE, DULY christened Lake Hari, took four years to fill. In rainmaking for the crops, Peter stopped trying to avoid floods and deliberately brought them on, being careful only not to cause so much of a downpour as to wash out the terraces. The valley floor was soon permanently under water and the river was history, at least above the dam. Jesse made no flights to survey the situation below it, for the shuttles had to be saved for emergency use. They might someday be needed for exploration beyond the settlement, and each of the two had only enough charge remaining for one such trip. Eventually the colony might be able to generate enough power to recharge them, but that would not happen soon.

The installation of the computer system in the shelter prepared for it went smoothly, and once the work was done, most people went back to taking the knowledgebase for granted. Carla, however, hovered over it. For the first year she did little other work apart from training assistants and studying AI in the hope of someday becoming knowledgeable enough to maintain the robots. Eventually she became satisfied that it would stay maintenance-free with no more troubleshooting than it had needed while aboard the starship.

Most of the others went back to farm labor. Soon after

the dam was created they planted sugar beets as well as grain—welcome after the years the settlers had been deprived of any form of sweetening—and also a few vegetables. Later, once the food supply was assured, they began planting fiber crops, as the supply of cloth for children's clothes was running low.

There were a lot of children; the population was growing rapidly. Most of the women had babies every second year; because they were nursing—usually nursing more than one child—it was rare for them to get pregnant oftener than that, despite lack of contraception. A daughter was born to Carla and Jesse when Tarin was two years old and Kel was five. They named her Francesca from Carla's former surname, Francesco, and called her Fran. Carla was by this time in her mid-forties, and it was unlikely that she would have more children. The option of IVF had, of course, been closed long ago when the supply of hormones required for it had run out.

With the farm work less critical, it became possible to return to the long-neglected copper mine. Once the surface ore had been dug out tunneling began, a job that required blasting. Jesse felt that since he was responsible for the overall safety of the settlement, he ought to be knowledgeable about the use of explosives. He set out to learn under the direction of Dan, who'd been a mine foreman on Undine, and thereafter he did more mining than farming—although a good deal of his time had to be devoted to general overseeing. At times, he could not help recalling that without beamed power, without more expert knowledge than anyone in the Group possessed, the effective use of the mineral resources they'd planned on might never prove possible. But he tried not to lose faith in Ian's goal.

The year of Fran's birth marked a new era for the colony, not only because of the progress in mining and the hope symbolized by the rising lake, but because living conditions had normalized. For one thing, meals were better balanced than in the past with the addition of vegetables, fish—which had been released in the lake and were flourishing—eggs, and occasionally roast chicken. An indoor chicken house was, to be sure, a lot of work to maintain. There was nothing of which to construct cages, so the chickens had free run of the floor and collecting the manure was a messy process, valuable though it was for cultivation of more crops.

More burdensome than the cleaning of the chicken house was the dispatch of the chickens chosen to be cooked. This had been a mechanized procedure on Undine, one with which no one but the growers of poultry had been involved. Like city dwellers in recent centuries on Earth, people had rarely thought about where roast chicken came from. At first, no one was willing to take on the job of killing, cleaning and plucking creatures they had raised from chicks; killing anything at all was totally outside the settlers' experience, and most preferred that it remain that way. Only when it became evident that the shelter would not accommodate an ever-increasing number of noisy roosters and aging hens had it been agreed that some must be eaten.

Traditionally, said the knowledgebase, small farmers had chopped chickens' heads off with a hatchet. Wringing their necks was said to be more humane, but nobody wanted to experiment on live, squawking chickens despite the specific instructions provided. These warned that the hardest part, in the physical sense, would be catching a grown chicken in the first place—a fact soon borne out by experience, as chickens are not devoid of telepathic sensitivity and the pursuers were unconsciously broadcasting their intent to kill. After several teams had given up, Jesse's advice was sought, as it still was on all practical problems that arose. It occurred to him that with the laser gun set on very low power it would be possible to stun chickens from a distance. Suppressing the inerasable memory of the last time he'd fired it, he managed to do this repeatedly; but he drew the line at finishing them off, for he knew that if he took on that job, he would be stuck with it for the rest of his life.

Some of the Group members were opposed to the whole project. "It's wrong for people to eat animals," Arwen declared to the Council. "We should never have begun raising chickens."

"I thought you were the one who argued for reverting to a less technological way of life," Jesse said. "All primitive cultures on Earth ate meat."

"The arguments presented for vegetarianism later were inconsistent," Reiko agreed. "They were advanced mainly by people who maintained that humans are no different from animals, that we should harmonize with nature instead of controlling it—yet a basic law of nature is that animals eat other animals. All species except herbivores kill prey. Humans are not herbivores. We could not have survived here this long on grain alone if it weren't genetically engineered."

"If any of you choose not to eat chicken that's your privilege, of course," Peter said. "But be aware that you have that option only because our crops have been technologically improved over natural plant species. We don't have the variety of plants available on Earth, or a means of extracting protein from them."

"I don't think anyone who's unwilling to kill chickens should eat them," Arwen persisted, obviously convinced that such a policy would settle the argument in her favor.

"There's some justice in that," said Teresa, who was having trouble recruiting enough chicken-stranglers. And so it had been agreed that all the adults except dedicated vegetarians would rotate on chicken detail. It didn't take long before they were as inured to it as farm families had been in ancient times.

For the children old enough to have viewed chicks as pets, however, it was more complicated. Initially there was an attempt to hide it from them, but being even more telepathic than their parents, they weren't fooled for more than a few days. They were naturally curious about the new and different food that suddenly appeared at supper, and its origin couldn't be kept secret. The kids lacked the background to know that animals eat other animals and that humans have done so since prehistoric times. To them it seemed a horrifying innovation.

"In the future, we mustn't let them near young chickens," said Peter. "Watching baby chicks is okay, but emotional contact with them past that stage is a bad idea, not only for the kids' sake but for the chickens' own. Animals bond telepathically both with each other and, if given opportunity, with humans; that's why people have always been unwilling to eat pets except when driven by hunger. Animals given human companionship are different from those raised for food—their minds are literally more developed, and they are far more aware. Neither side in the animal rights debate has ever grasped this distinction, but since we know about telepathy, we shouldn't ignore it."

Ivana was particularly loathe to taste chicken, and sat silent, with a reproachful look, whenever it was served. Kira didn't urge it on her. It had been learned long ago that no one could urge Ivana to do anything she had chosen not to do, or vice versa. Yet though she was a strong-willed child, her kindhearted disposition endeared her to everyone, including the other children, who came to her for help and advice almost as if she were an adult. She and Kel were, to be sure, older than the others—but in many cases only a few weeks older. Her seeming maturity was less a matter of age than of personality.

It was therefore a surprise when all of a sudden, one evening in her sixth year, her agemates refused to play with her. Jesse and Carla noticed her sitting by quietly herself while the others played bull's-eye, a game in which concentric circles were marked on the ground and points were earned by tossing small stones toward the target. "Don't you want to play, dear?" Carla asked. Despite Ivana's private inner life, she usually enjoyed activities with friends.

"They won't let me anymore," Ivana said sadly. "Not that game."

"Whyever not?"

"I don't know." Her face had a vague look, and both Jesse and Carla got the impression that she was lying.

That night they asked Kel about it. "Ivana said you and the other kids won't let her play bull's-eye with you. Are you mad at her, or what?"

"We're not mad," Kel declared. "But the game's no fun if she plays. She always wins."

That seemed strange; they had not noticed that Ivana was better coordinated than others her age, nor had they ever seen her practice tossing stones. And they knew Kel had won only last week. "What do you mean, always?" Carla asked. "She couldn't have gotten better at it than you are without practicing, and even then, not in just a few days."

"She did, Mom," Kel said. "Yesterday she hit the bull's-eye ten times in a row, even though she never hit it before. This evening she hit it six more times and still hadn't missed, so we told her she had to drop out."

Kira was surprised when she heard this, and she didn't want her daughter sitting on the sidelines. "It's not fair to kick someone out for winning," she said firmly when the children gathered the following day after supper. "Nobody's going to win all the time."

"I won't win more than twice, I promise," Ivana said. "Please let me play!"

Curious, Jesse and Carla watched. Ivana won exactly twice. But she wasn't purposely tossing stones wide of the mark, either. They landed precisely within a sequence of the concentric rings, never touching a line.

The kids didn't notice; they were content that they still had a chance to beat her. Jesse and Carla were puzzled. Kira, however, seemed thoughtful, and soon after the game ended she disappeared into Peter's room. The next morning at breakfast she told Ivana, "Uncle Peter would like to watch you toss the stones. Not in the game, but just for him, to see if you can make them land where he tells you to."

Jesse was enlisted along with Kwame to carry Peter's chair outside. For half an hour Ivana tossed pebbles into the rings, at first instructed aloud by Peter but later simply grasping his thought. Because she started with a pile of them and never retrieved any, the symmetric placement of the stones soon became obvious. "Look, Mom!" she said happily. "I made a pattern like Uncle Peter wanted. Can I make up one of my own?"

"Right now you can," Kira told her. "But not when you're playing with the other kids. They can't control the throws by thinking, the way you do, and so they'd feel left out."

"But why can't they?" Ivana protested.

"For the same reason they can't heal their own hurts yet," Peter explained. "Sometimes people are born with skills that other people don't have."

"Will they ever learn?"

"They will learn to heal themselves. But not even the grownups can guide things with their minds, Ivana. Maybe some of the younger children will prove able to. We don't know. So far, you are the only person who can do it, and you must never do it just to show off."

"I won't," Ivana promised. "But it's fun, so I'll do it when I'm by myself."

Back in Peter's room, Kira said, "It's finally happened! Controlled psychokinesis, after all the years you and Hari and Ian tried to achieve it and failed."

"We've done it en masse in rainmaking," Peter reminded her. "And poltergeists do it unconsciously, so we knew the potential was there. It was only a matter of time until one of our children, who've never been exposed to the idea that such things are impossible, would develop psychokinetic talent. Ivana is the most psi-gifted of them, so it's not surprising that she's the one."

"Are you saying she moves the stones just by *thinking*?" Jesse asked, incredulous.

"She can't consciously lift objects that are at rest, at least not yet, but she can guide moving ones. The ability to influence objects by PK wasn't unknown on Earth. It's a lot rarer than telepathy, and Ian had higher priorities than the attempt to gain it. It was not really relevant to our aims on Undine, except insofar as it's related to healing. Here, though, it's likely to become a part of our new culture, for our descendants, anyway." He paused and added wistfully, "I think I envy Ivana."

48

AS TIME PASSED it became obvious that a few of the other kids did have PK ability in addition to ESP. They all used telepathy more than the adults, of course. They'd become accustomed to it in the womb and as infants; as they grew, they used it not only with their parents but with each other, usually on a wordless level. As a result, they were not as noisy as typical children; they laughed and shrieked while playing actively, but were obligingly silent in the schoolroom. An outsider would have thought it unnatural, even without observing the occasions when cups tipped over or letter-tiles skidded across tables without being touched.

"I don't quite understand why they can do things we couldn't during our own childhood," Jesse confessed to Kira. "Peter said there's always an unconscious prenatal bond between a baby and its mother, even on Earth. Yet the majority of us weren't telepathic until we were much older. It's not due just to inherited talent—most of Ian's IVF children aren't any better at it than Kel and Tarin. Is it just because we use it consciously with them? If that were the case, the kids of psychics in the past would all have used it, too."

"It's more than that," Kira said. "It's a matter of the collective unconscious that's developing here. The same kids, of the same parents, would not have been telepathic on either Earth or Undine, because the unconscious skepticism they'd have been exposed to would have overpowered whatever confidence in it they started out with. That's the fundamental reason why we believed we could establish a psi-based culture on a new world."

Despite all his years of supporting this goal, Jesse had never before grasped how it was to be reached. It was not so much what they *did* here, he realized suddenly. How they *thought*, when no longer a scattered minority, would determine not merely the outward aspects of their culture but the individual potential of its members' minds. God, he thought, could it really become a better, more peaceful world on that account? When everyone sensed everyone else's feelings, there wouldn't be any reason for discord. This had, of course, been the case among the hand-picked adults, who were all pledged to support each other. But was it possible that it would hold true in succeeding generations? The kids didn't quarrel. Maybe they never would. Maybe humankind's long-sought answer to the problem of evil had finally been found.

Formal schooling was begun when the oldest children were six, with Velma, who had worked as a teacher on Undine, in charge. Unfortunately there were not enough textreaders for the kids to have their own; adults had to give up theirs temporarily during school hours and sometimes at home. There were only a few stand-alone computers, and no personal datakeepers other than those belonging to parents. This was going to be a big problem as the population continued to grow. As adults, these kids would not have the equipment all civilized people were accustomed to. They would always have to share the limited number of electronic devices that must serve an ever-increasing number of users. As for keyboarding, not much progress was made until it was realized that the phones, which no longer worked for communication, could at least be used for writing messages on their own screens. These were therefore allocated permanently to the school, with relief that a good use for them had been found.

It was suggested, somewhat radically, that without working phones, datakeepers or personal computers, the future population would need to know how to write by hand. Few of the adults had ever done this, although they were familiar enough with the letters on the screen to form them on paper if necessary. However, there was no paper. The knowledgebase said that there had been a time when school-children wrote on slates, but there were no slates either. And so the idea was given up. For writing anything longer than would fit on a phone's screen, taking turns with the existing computers would have to suffice. In the classroom, small pottery tiles with painted letters were used to spell out words.

School was fun and exciting to the kids. They'd been bored, for there was little for them to do during the long days, considering how few vid screens were available and the dearth of toys. They could run around outside only during the early morning and at dusk, and had already tired of the indoor singing games the younger children played. Having never known any other life, most were adapted to it; but they welcomed the new activity. Only a few remained restless.

Velma's son Brian was one of the discontents. He had always been a unruly child, bad-tempered and often at odds with his playmates. Kel didn't like him. "He's mean," he'd said to Jesse more than once. "He hits little kids to make them cry." Velma herself was uneasy around him, and was at a loss to know why. He was an IVF child and she had not been told who his genetic father was. Some members of the Council knew, but had revealed only that it was not Ian or Peter. The father himself had not been informed, which was just as well, considering that Brian was hardly a son to be proud of. There was no genetic problem in his background—of that, Undine's policy of implanting only genetically-perfect embryos assured them. Nor was there any possibility of bad parenting; all Group members had been chosen for their empathy, and Velma was no less empathetic than any of the others. She didn't know what to make of the child that had been born to her.

"It happens," Peter had said, when Brian's personality disorder first became evident. "I've worked with maladjusted children as a psychiatrist, of course. In some cases no one knew how they got that way, except that it wasn't genetic and it wasn't always poor care either, because many had been raised in the crèches by professionals, just as I was. In the Hospital I was forced to drug them. Here, he'll be spared that, at least." But Peter had seemed troubled.

"I never felt any love in him," Velma had confessed to Carla. "Not even in the womb—I tried to give love, but he just didn't respond to me. Not the way the rest of you say your unborn babies responded. And ever since, he's been getting more and more contrary."

By the time Brian started school Peter had been counseling him regularly for several years without progress. He, too, was unable to get a positive emotional response from him. Outwardly, Brian showed more than enough emotion, tending toward outbursts of fury. Underneath, however, telepathic rapport couldn't be established, despite Peter's superior skill in eliciting it. Yet surprisingly—and disturbingly, he said—Brian was a stronger-than-average telepath. He projected his angry feelings clearly, upsetting everyone around him. He simply didn't interact.

When the problems at school began, it was assumed that because Velma was Brian's mom he was so familiar with her that he didn't respect her authority as a teacher. But it soon became apparent that he disrupted the class just for the fun of getting a reaction—not so much from Velma, whose reactions he'd learned to ignore, but from the kids. They didn't encourage him. Their telepathic sensitivity was too well developed for them not to get bad vibes from him, and it made them uncomfortable. After awhile, Peter realized that Brian sensed this discomfort and that it was the very thing he enjoyed.

Peter did not believe in punishment. "The idea that people 'deserve' to suffer in some artificial way because of their actions is an outworn superstition based on a belief in vengeful gods," he'd declared. "Actions have natural consequences, and people shouldn't be allowed to escape those consequences.

Actions that harm or endanger others should be prevented. But to punish in the hope of 'teaching a lesson' teaches nothing except resistance to authority."

Consequently, Brian was not punished for acting up at school; he was simply excluded from the class. "You can come back when you decide not to bother the other kids," he was told. Because he bothered the younger children even more, he was not allowed in the playroom, either. After a few days of being isolated in his hut—by the outdoor heat, not by decree— he went grudgingly back to school and broadcast no more bad feelings. He wasn't a stupid child.

The next year it was decided to let the oldest children work on the farm. This, too, they welcomed. "The tradition of prohibiting child labor arose from abuses during the industrial revolution and from a shortage of jobs for adults," Reiko said. "In earlier agricultural societies kids worked alongside their parents. And it's going to become essential here, because we simply don't have enough adults to tend the added terraces we'll need for an expanding population." So the kids helped with planting and cultivation—work they enjoyed, since no one had told them it was considered laborious.

In addition to work with the crops, the kids took turns gathering eggs and feeding the chickens. By this time they were long accustomed to the idea that chickens were raised for food and were not bothered by it, as they weren't allowed either to make pets of them or to observe the process of transforming live creatures into meat.

On days when chickens were to be killed, Jesse continued to stun them before the current team moved in to strangle them. Arriving a bit early one morning, he found several children still spreading chicken feed. He stood at the fence that divided the shelter's interior, waiting for them to leave. Suddenly he noticed that Brian was staring at him with intense interest. "Why do you use a laser to stun the chickens?" the boy asked curiously. "You could do it just with your mind, couldn't you?"

Jesse had not yet pulled out the laser and had not

thought that the kids knew about it. To be sure, his mind had been on the task ahead of him, and he had not been shielding it from probing—something that was rarely necessary around children other than his own. Could Brian possibly have picked up his thoughts? In any case, the question was foolish. "Of course I couldn't stun them with my mind," he said. "Where did you get that idea, Brian? Only lasers can stun things." He almost told him not to spread such a fantasy among the rest of the kids but realized just in time that if Brian were warned it might upset them, he'd be likely to do exactly that.

Brian clammed up, obviously aware that he had touched on a topic he'd be wise not to pursue. Without further comment he left with the others, who had not overheard the exchange, and while dealing with the chickens Jesse gave it little thought. But later in the day he mentioned it to Peter. "It was an odd notion," he said. "Does it mean he hates chickens, or what?"

To his surprise, Peter turned white. "Oh, God," he said. "Have you talked to anyone else about this, Jess?"

"No, not yet."

"Then don't. I don't want it discussed by the Group."

"Why not?" It didn't seem important enough to matter; they already knew that Brian hated nearly everything.

"Because Brian was right," Peter informed him. "You don't need the laser to stun chickens. I could do it with my mind easily, and some of the rest of you could learn to. But that's a path we don't want to follow."

Incredulous, Jesse said, "Stun a living thing, just by mind power?"

"Think, Jess! We can heal. Isn't it obvious that we can also do the reverse?"

Jesse drew breath. Slowly, he said, "Is it possible that *Brian* might be able to do this?"

"God, I hope not—not at the age of seven. But I'm afraid it's only a matter of time before he tries it. This is my worst nightmare, Jess, the thing I have dreaded all these years—

the possibility that someone in the new generation would misuse psi."

"Well, after all, we do stun chickens. Would it really be worse to use psi for it?"

Peter gazed intently at him. "Jess, it might be hard to control such a power—to know where to draw the line."

With growing comprehension, Jesse replied, "You're saying we don't need to strangle them, either. We do it merely because we want psi to be viewed as constructive."

"It's the only way we can contain it safely," Peter agreed. "In our generation, there's nothing to worry about. Ian and I carefully screened everyone we recruited into the Group. But we are building a culture that will include all kinds of people whose qualities we can't predict. We don't want negative aspects of psi to gain a foothold in the collective unconscious."

"Because it might lead others to be like Brian?"

"Possibly, in the future when we can't count on the good parenting we're assured of now."

"Velma did her best to give him love," Jesse protested.

"Yes. With Brian the problem is inborn, though that's rare. As I've often said, personality isn't wholly dependent on genes and upbringing. There are mysterious factors involved in what a person becomes. Abnormalities have been found in psychopaths' brains, but it's known that thought modifies brain pathways—to assume that they're the cause of personality rather than an effect is to endorse the Meds' concept of the body's primacy, the one we fought so hard against."

"But then if the cause of defective character isn't physical, what is it?"

"I don't claim to know. Some traditions attribute it to karma, others to corruption by Satan—those are metaphors, of course, but they point to some underlying reality. Evildoers have existed throughout history. And always, people's innate predilection for good or evil has determined how psi has been used—white magic pitted against black magic, if you will."

"I'm not sure I'd class killing chickens as black magic," Jesse said, thinking that Peter was blowing the whole incident out of proportion.

"Psychopathic killers start with animals," Peter said. "That's true even when they use purely physical means to kill. On Undine there were no accessible animals and we drugged psychopaths into vegetables in any case. Here, conditions are more as they were in traditional societies on Earth."

"Peter . . . is Brian a psychopath?"

"That's how I'd diagnosis him," Peter said grimly. "I couldn't do so on the basis of behavior alone in a seven-year-old child—but I've probed his mind telepathically, Jess, and I find no trace in him of what I find in normal children."

"And you can't cure him?" He had assumed Peter could cure anything, given time.

"Psychopaths, in the strict sense of the word, are incurable. They're not mentally ill; they're simply born deficient. You remember our talks about how guilt feelings are experienced by everyone? A psychopath is incapable of feeling guilt, just as he's incapable of empathy. He gets pleasure from aggressive impulses he can't learn to suppress."

"What are you going to do about him, then, when he gets older?" asked Jesse, appalled.

Peter shook his head. "I don't know, Jess. God help me, I don't know. But for right now, he's got to be kept away from the chickens."

49

FOR A WHILE Jesse thought a good deal about what Peter had said. It had for the first time brought home to him why guilt was a universal reaction even among people who hadn't done anything to warrant it. During the past few years he'd had many sessions during which Peter had taught him to deal with the physical effects of guilt. It had been an arduous process because there wasn't any way to recognize those effects without reexperiencing the emotion. Just as during his initial mind training he'd been made afraid in order to learn how to control the effects of fear, he was made to face all the things he'd ever felt guilty about—not just the recent ones that had tormented him, but everything, going back to his years in Fleet and even earlier, to his adolescence on Earth. Sometimes it had taken hypnosis to bring them fully into consciousness. He had become clearly aware of how his body had been reacting biochemically to these feelings, and had understood that controlling the physiological reactions would set him free from illness and the effects of aging. All physical symptoms, including his recurrent backaches, had disappeared once he'd learned to do that. But he'd still felt that he ought not to feel guilty about situations in which he was blameless, even though Peter kept assuring him that it was normal. Now, having glimpsed what it meant to be incapable of guilt, he finally grasped the point.

He mentioned what he had learned about Brian to no one, as Peter had asked. But he took care to keep Tarin and Fran well away from him. There was no need to warn Kel, who by this time was familiar enough with Brian's idiosyncrasies to avoid him like poison.

He wondered if Peter had told Velma. He must have, if only to make sure she'd keep Brian from visiting the chicken house. Velma wasn't a family-oriented person and she had no permanent partner. But she had done the best she could with her son and would suffer terribly if the boy ever did anything to harm someone. It was fortunate that she had chosen not to have more IVF children, for he would have made the lives of younger siblings miserable.

Jesse soon became too busy to worry about Brian, for that was the year the lake rose high enough for use. Leaving supervision of the copper mine in Dan's hands, Jesse worked on the new irrigation system that raised water onto the lowest terrace, where trees were then planted. The seedlings had been carefully nurtured indoors in preparation for this event. Everyone turned out to help, envisioning the thicket that would eventually shade the area. The trees were genetically engineered to be fast growers, so it should be possible to have both shade and lumber in only a few years. They'd be able to build things of wood. And ultimately they would have some to burn—they'd need charcoal for smelting iron. People grew wistful just thinking about campfires, although the gatherings around the Lodge fireplace on Undine were a long way behind them now, in what seemed like a different lifetime.

In addition to the grove of soon-to-be saplings, there was now a beach; the robots cleared a level space for it. Creating a shallow area of water was judged impractical because it would have attracted crawlies, so the children were held in the arms of parents as toddlers and taught to swim while still very young. The adults had been swimming for several years by climbing down to the rising shoreline, reveling in the water after their long deprivation. But there'd been no way to relax beside the lake until it filled. Moreover, it had not been possible for Peter to reach it. Now he could be carried to the beach. It was well worth the long trip down the terraces and up again, supported by relays of willing friends, for he had always loved swimming and in the water he could still move under his own power.

"I used to wish we could have settled by a sea," said Carla, drying herself off after a plunge. "Now, though, we've got all we'll ever need right here."

But it wasn't long before the subject of Maclairn's seas arose again.

Jesse no longer kept a close eye on supplies, as they were growing all their own food now and they had relied on few other consumables from the pods. But one evening Dorcas came to him and announced, "We're running low on salt."

Salt? It was essential to life, and too little of it while working outdoors on Maclairn would lead to heat exhaustion; they all knew that and were careful to salt their porridge well. The pods had provided an ample supply. He'd never stopped to think that it would eventually run out. The planet certainly had salt deposits—but there weren't any such deposits on the plateau, much less in the adjacent mountains.

Reiko, always aware of history, commented that the salt trade had been a major shaper of events on Earth and that in ancient times, salt had been prized and fought over. The process of extracting large quantities from seawater had been a relative late development. That was, of course, how it was done on Undine, which had little dry land. On Maclairn they would have to get it from the ground. Jesse studied the data on mineral deposits originally obtained from orbit and found that there was no promising source nearby. Mostly, the salt was deep below the surface where heavy equipment would be needed to access it. The only places where it appeared exposed were, unsurprisingly, on the shores of seas. And in fact, a photo of the nearest sea showed a large white patch that could well be an open salt flat.

This, then, was the emergency for which he'd been saving the shuttles. He would have to fly to the salt flat and load up with as much as could be carried, for the trip would deplete the ship's remaining charge, leaving just one shuttle for future use. He would take only three people with him, he decided, though there were many who wanted to go along. The weight must be kept as low as possible to conserve power.

Carla wanted to be among the three. "All these years I've wanted to visit one of this planet's seas," she said longingly. "I suppose you can't favor your own family, but I'm as qualified to load salt as anyone else, and it does seem that since you've got to choose somebody. . . ."

Jesse hesitated. The trip was only marginally dangerous; there would be some risk in any landing on unprepared ground, of course, but he had no reason to expect trouble. In any case, he had learned his lesson about trying to protect

Carla. It was not his place to prevent her from doing what she wanted to do; to put her safety above the opportunity for a pleasant break in dull routine would be a surrender to his own fear of the pain any harm to her would cause him. And it wouldn't be fair to disqualify her on grounds of their relationship. Why shouldn't he take his wife on a trip with him? No one would object to that.

He decided to let her come. In addition he chose Viktor as copilot and Greg as a healer as well as his close friend. They took off at dawn on a beautiful morning, cloudless as usual, after his preflight check showed the shuttle to be in good shape despite having sat unused on the pad for four years.

Jesse rejoiced in being in the air once more. He had missed it more terribly than he'd let himself realize. Since they stayed in the atmosphere, at low altitude, it reminded him more of the happy days on Undine than of the tension accompanying his last space flights. The settlement's array of green terraces was much larger now than it had been four years ago; it turned the place into a true oasis instead of a mere dot against the barren desert surrounding it. But the greatest transformation had been made by the blue lake. On the ground it rarely looked blue, as it was narrow and reflected the yellowish canyon walls. From the sky it was a brilliant strip of sapphire. He hovered low over it, letting everyone enjoy the sight, before turning the thrusters to fly horizontally away.

This was the first opportunity anyone had had to take a close look at Maclairn's terrain from above. He checked on the dam first, seeing that water now lapped against its rim and had begun to trickle down the other side. With the next rain, the dry riverbed below it would begin to flood again. He wondered where that river emptied. Not into the sea toward which they were headed, for if bounded by a salt flat that was an old, drying lake, as most of those on Maclairn were. Perhaps in the past the planet had been wetter. Without a trained geologist and a way to explore distant ground areas, they would never know.

After they left rocky highlands they were over an even more desolate area, its yellow ground contrasting sharply with the deep blue of the sky. Jesse had seen this land from space, of course, but a planet never shows much surface detail from orbit; he was surprised to find that even from low altitude the land looked monotonous. There was some of the sparse desert plant life to which they were accustomed, extending on and on forever, it seemed, without variation. "God, it must be even hotter down there than at home," Carla said. He agreed; it wouldn't have been a good place to settle.

It didn't take long to reach the sea. It proved to be a dry seabed except for a pale blue center; looking down, they could see that the remaining water was shallow. "Why did we call them seas instead of lakes?" Viktor wondered. "None of those in the images are big enough to be called seas on Earth, and they're certainly all landlocked."

"Because they're salty," suggested Carla.

"We don't know that they all are."

"It was pretty much arbitrary even on Earth," Greg said. "The Great Salt Lake is saltier than the ocean, and the Sea of Galilee is a freshwater lake. But on other worlds, anything large enough to see from high orbit is labeled a sea. I suppose it's a tradition begun with the seas of Earth's moon, which the ancients thought were water but are really plains."

Jesse slowed the shuttle as they passed over it, searching for a place to land. There was a salt flat on only one bank. He would have to land near the edge of it or they'd have to carry the buckets of salt too far, and yet the seabed sloped downward. Turning the ship to its VTOL position, he aimed for the one spot that looked level enough to set down on. Viktor, who had landed only on the smooth pads at the settlement, gasped in dismay at the uneven ground rushing up to meet them. Jesse grinned at him as they settled, relieved to find it firm. "You never can be sure," he said. "Sometimes you have to rev up the engine and lift again, if the sensors detect any wobble."

The white surface of the salt flat glared fiercely in the sunlight as they disembarked. "We'll need to work fast," Jesse cautioned, "so as to finish before noon. The heat's going to be worse than what we're used to, even in flight suits."

Keeping their hats low to shade their eyes as much as possible, they walked a little way onto the flat, carrying the tools they'd brought to break off slabs of salt. The small ones would go into buckets, while the stretcher had been brought for moving larger slabs. It was hard, heavy work; only the stamina gained through years of stonesetting made it possible for them to fill the ship's hold in one morning. They paused frequently to drink, but postponed eating until the last bucketful of salt pieces had been stowed aboard.

"The sea's not what I'd call inviting," Carla said, glancing out through the ship's viewport as they pulled off their salt-encrusted gloves and flight suits. "I'm glad to have seen it, but it's put an end to my regret over not settling near one."

Jesse had been thinking along the same lines. It had worked out for the best after all, and his long regret over his choice of site had been unnecessary. Perhaps Peter was right; perhaps fate had indeed been watching out for them. "It's time we headed home," he said, "before we use up any more engine power on cooling." They strapped themselves into their seats and he began the liftoff sequence.

His first thought after completing it was that the cabin was too quiet—unexpectedly, the low hum of the auxiliary engine was still audible. It was a few seconds before he perceived, in shock, that the main engine had not kicked in.

50

CARLA DID NOT realize at first that anything was wrong. Only when she sensed Jesse's desperation did she become aware that the failure of the ship to lift was serious.

"What the hell is happening?" asked Viktor, in the copilot's seat. "The board's green."

"The engine's not getting power," said Jesse tensely.

"Huh? We've got plenty of charge, unless the indicator's gone bad."

"We've still got charge—I know how much was left when we landed. And the auxiliary's running."

"It had better be. We wouldn't last long in this heat if it wasn't." The cabin cooling was dependent on the auxiliary engine, Carla knew. The ship would be literally an oven without it; the heat outside was barely within the range of survivability and would be intolerable in the afternoon, despite their ability to control body temperature.

"How long is it likely to take to get the main engine going?" Greg asked.

"I don't see any way to get it going," Jesse admitted grimly. "It's not like a combustion engine. Either it runs or it doesn't. Since we've got power and it's dead, we know some part has given out."

"Could it be—the AI?" Carla asked. After the trouble with the starship's AI, that seemed likely; she knew all too well that such systems were not immortal.

"No," said Jesse. "It's not the AI; everything on the instrument board checks out. If the AI were going bad there'd be multiple failures. This is a failure in the engine itself."

They were all beginning to grasp what that meant. They were stranded here. They had water aboard for only a few days, even if they rationed it; and the sea water, assuming they could reach the sea after the sun went down, would be too salty to drink. There was no shelter except the ship, and when the charge gave out, its cooling would cease.

And none of this would matter in any case, because there was no way they could ever get back to the settlement.

The facts didn't have to be stated aloud; they were shared telepathically, as was the terror they engendered. For long moments there was no sound but the hum of the cooling system, steadily depleting the ship's remaining power.

Finally Carla ventured, "Maybe they can find us. You told them where we were headed, didn't you, Jesse?"

"Yes," said Jesse painfully, "but they can't come for us, you know. Bernie doesn't know how to land on rough ground."

"Is it that hard?"

"Could you have done it, Viktor?"

"No," Viktor said. "It takes training and practice, Carla. It's not like landing on the pad."

"Bernie's not one to give up easily. I think he'd want to try."

"That's not the point," said Jesse. "They have only one shuttle left. It's got enough charge for just one trip. Peter would let Bernie risk his life—but they can't risk the ship, however much they want to. If the landing failed, they'd have no way to get salt. He'll have to go somewhere else for it, to some other sea where the adjacent land is flatter."

"Without salt they'd all die eventually," Greg agreed. "People died of salt deficiency even on Earth, and it would happen sooner here because of having to work in the heat. Peter knows that. He'll put survival of the colony first, regardless of his personal feelings."

"How did we plan to survive after all the salt collected by both shuttles was gone?" Viktor asked.

"Nobody gave it any thought," Jesse said, "but there are three possibilities. We could someday generate enough power to recharge the shuttles. Or we could develop mining equipment for getting salt from deep in the ground. Or we could build boats to reach the dam and go overland below it, once enough wood is available. All those are long-term prospects. The loss of this shuttle halves the time we can last without them. Peter won't risk reducing the time to zero."

Carla knew that was true, and yet . . . *I can't believe it's going to end this way for us!* she cried out to Jesse. *Not after all you've already come through!*

I can't really believe it myself, Jesse responded. *All the things we worried about that never happened, all the narrow escapes, and then to set off fearlessly one morning and be defeated by some little thing we couldn't have anticipated. . . .*

And yet there's no way out. Oh, God, Carla, there's nothing I can do to save you . . . I can face death for myself, but not for you. . . .

At least he wasn't blaming himself for the trouble, she thought. And he wasn't saying it was wrong to have let her come. He had matured in the years since unwarranted self-blame had tormented him.

"Just what do you think's gone wrong with the engine?" Greg asked, not so much in the hope of fixing it—for he was too sensitive a telepath not to know there was no hope—as from curiosity. From a feeling that people about to die had a right to know why.

"Who can say?" Jesse answered. "I'm no more an engineer than the rest of you; I'm just a pilot. I know, though, that it was bound to happen sometime. These shuttles have gone for years without any maintenance other than what the AI aboard the starship provided while it was functional. It was just bad luck that it happened on our one trip into wild country rather than back on the pad."

"Maybe not *just* bad luck," said Viktor. "The aux engine hasn't been run any length of time under hot conditions before—we used it mainly to overcome cold nights and the cold of space. Maybe overheating affected some interface with the main. It seems too much of a coincidence otherwise."

"That's possible," Jesse agreed. "It's designed to handle heat, but that certainly could have affected the life of the components. Some part that was due to go may have been pushed past its tolerance. It may be a very small part—trivial, if we had a replacement with us and knew how to install it."

Carla lay back in her seat, ignoring further conversation. The full significance of what was happened to them was sinking in. *The kids*, she thought in despair. *God, Jesse, what about the kids? Fran's only two years old . . . Tarin just five . . . and Kel, what will Kel do without his dad? Someone will mother them and love them, but Kel's old enough to need the dad he looks up to. . . .*

They were all thinking of their families. "I'm thankful Ursula isn't here," Viktor said, "yet I can't bear the thought of how she'll grieve. Robyn, our youngest, is five now, and we're still hoping for another—" His voice broke. This was different from the other times they'd expected to die, Carla thought. Then death had been likely, not certain, and they had been in danger together, the whole Group. It was much harder when separated from loved ones.

Time passed. If what Viktor had said about the aux engine was true, then it could give out even before the ship's charge ran down. She knew she wasn't the only one who felt death might be imminent. They were not hiding their inner thoughts from each other; telepathic sensitivity was always enhanced by emotion, and their impulse in crisis was to seek comfort from the touch of other minds. Her bond with Jesse was wordless, but it anchored both of them.

Would they, in the end, meet out of their bodies as they had when going into stasis? Would they stay together after they died? For the first time in years, she thought of Ramón. Would she meet Ramón again, too? And someday, perhaps, Peter . . . she knew suddenly that she could not endure permanent separation from Peter, any more than from Jesse. And Peter would grieve for her now—for all of them; Jesse and Greg were his closest friends. Her heart ached at the thought of Peter, bound to his chair, waiting for word from them that never came. . . .

Out of the silence, Greg said, "Jesse, on Earth there were once salt flats so hard that they raced automobiles on them. I think planes sometimes landed on them, too. Could this one be as hard as that, do you think? It's level, and just as smooth as a pad."

"I don't know," Jesse said. "I never heard that when I was on Earth, but then I didn't pay much attention to history as a kid. The salt we walked on here wasn't thick enough for a shuttle to set down on, certainly."

"But we were just at the edge of it. It could be thicker near the center."

"It might be, but we don't know. And even if we did, it would make no difference, because the people back at the settlement don't know. This shuttle wasn't designed for point-to-point use on a planet, so they're not equipped to receive signals from us directly—all our comm depended either on the starship or on the satellite we lost."

Greg sighed. "That's true. For a moment there I thought I had an idea."

Carla, suddenly roused, burst out, "Peter would hear me if I called him! I know he would, especially if we all did it together—wouldn't he Jesse?"

Jesse turned in his seat, staring at her. "Yes—yes, there's a good chance that he would."

"Are you crazy?" Greg said. "It's much too far, Jesse. Nobody can pick up thoughts over such a distance as this."

"Urgency makes a difference. Carla and Peter reached me from the Island on Undine when I wasn't far from the city. The distance from here to our base isn't quite as great."

"I don't think you understand how telepathy works," Greg protested. "Carla may have been able to reach you—but the two of you are bonded. You're in love with each other. Love makes more difference than urgency—and even so, I know I can't reach Oksana, though I'm a much stronger telepath than Carla is."

"Neither you nor Oksana is as gifted as Peter," Carla pointed out.

"That's true. But I can't reach Peter from this far, either. I'm a trained psi instructor and if it were possible I'd already be trying it! What makes you think you could reach him when I can't?

Carla hesitated. Peter's love for her, and hers for him, was known only to Jesse and Kira. Yet they would need all their combined psi power to accomplish this, and a telepath as skilled as Greg would sense the nature of the link, perhaps with shock. *Jesse*, she queried, *should I tell him?*

Yes, but not aloud. I don't think we should tell Viktor; it's not something to spread around. Just let me handle it.

PROMISE OF THE FLAME

Watching Greg's face, she realized that the truth was being conveyed to him, and that he understood—that despite long, close association with Peter, he had never suspected what lay beneath his evident loneliness.

"Perhaps it's worth a try," he conceded. "There's nothing to lose."

"But there is," said Jesse. "We can't do it without being absolutely sure that the salt flat is thick enough to land on. Unless we can tell him it is, he won't be able to take the risk of sending Bernie—or at least he shouldn't take it. And contact with us would make it more painful for him to refrain."

"We can't know the thickness," said Viktor. "So you're saying we've got to put the colony's future survival before a chance of rescue."

"Does anybody have a problem with that?

They looked at each other. It had seemed such a promising idea . . . and, Carla realized, she *wanted* to contact Peter, apart from any hope of her life being saved. She longed to feel him close, draw courage from him. . . . But it wouldn't be right. He would stay in contact and would suffer when he felt her die.

"Think of Bernie," she said. "If he tried to land and failed we'd still die, and he'd die too. And our families would eventually die from lack of salt."

"So we're back where we started," Greg said. "The hours we're stuck in here are going to be pretty rough, folks. Do you want me to try telepathic sedation? Peter's taught me the technique, though I haven't done it with a patient yet."

"No," said Jesse. "I'd rather keep my mind clear as long as possible."

"So would I," Carla said, "and I want to be with Jesse till the end."

"Look, we don't need to stay in the seats," Jesse said. The back ones were still folded down; their salty flight suits were piled in a corner, but there was plenty of room to sprawl in. He and Carla moved there, clinging to each other. His arms steadied her. Hours or days? she wondered. Would their mind training keep them from going to pieces if the ordeal was prolonged?

"We're giving up too soon," Jesse reflected. "We can't just wait to die. At least we should be *doing* something."

"Maybe we can test the thickness of the salt," Viktor suggested.

"How?" demanded Jesse.

"Try to cut through it. If we can't, would that mean it's solid?"

Jesse paused, considering it. "I guess it would, if we go deep enough and put our strength into it. It's too hot now, but maybe when the sun goes down—"

Sundown was still some hours away. Would the aux engine hold out that long?

"We've got a big rock drill," Jesse recalled, "only it isn't charged. I didn't think to charge it before we left and I didn't want to use ship's power if it wasn't needed—it will add to the load of the aux engine. But that would be the best way to test. Probably the only safe way."

"In other words," said Greg, "we've got to risk shortening the life of the aux engine on the chance we may learn we can call for rescue, when it may mean we won't live long enough for rescuers to reach us."

"Well," said Carla, "we won't really be risking anything, because if we don't do it, we're going to die anyway."

This being true, Jesse put the drill on the charger. The hum of the aux engine turned to a whine that assaulted everyone's nerves. *If we can just make it till sundown*, Carla thought, *we could stay outside all night*. It wouldn't get as cold here as it did at the settlement's higher elevation. *They'll come by early morning if we call*. . . .

The hours crawled by. At last the sun dropped over the rim of the salt flat and they suited up again, wearily readying themselves for the long hike to its center. "We don't all have to go," Jesse said at first, but then realized this wasn't true; they needed to be together if they learned the salt was thick enough, because it would take a combined effort to reach

Peter, and if they did reach him, they would have to stay put to guide Bernie. They had nothing to mark the spot that would be visible from the air.

When they reached a place where the salt extended equally on all sides of them, Jesse began to drill. The salt was as hard as rock, certainly. Carla, exhausted, sank down on it a little way from the drilling site. It was warm, having retained the heat of the day, and she could feel the slight vibration as the drill bit in. Oh, please, she thought, please let it not break through. . . .

It didn't. They tried several more spots, taking turns with the drill, until finally Jesse declared that the flat was solid enough to trust. By this time it was dark, though the glaring white surface reflected more light than seemed natural from their small flashlights. *Now*? asked Carla, as Jesse sat down beside her.

Now, he agreed, beckoning to Greg and Viktor. "Let Carla lead off, he told them. "But put as much mind power as you can into joining with her—just as we do in the Ritual."

Carla closed her eyes and called desperately, *Peter! Peter, we need you, I need you . . . answer me, please . . . we'll die soon unless you hear us, Peter. . . .*

She felt Jesse's mind join hers and then Greg's, wordlessly amplifying the plea. Peter would be in his room now, even if he'd been carried into the Commons for supper. He'd be worried because they hadn't returned yet, sensitive to any message. . . . She visualized him, reaching out, wanting to touch his hand. *Peter . . . I love you, if I die, know that I always loved you. . . .*

Carla? Relief flooded into her as his response came through. *Where are you, Carla?*

The salt flat . . . we're stranded. The ship can't take off.

Stranded . . . oh God, Carla! She sensed that he believed there was no way to rescue them.

The main engine's dead. Bernie can pick us up—

Carla . . . he doesn't know how to land.

Jesse's thought broke in, strong, steady. *He can land.*

The salt flat's level like a pad, and solid. It's okay to send Bernie.

Thank God! Don't worry . . . Bernie will come.

Wait till dawn—he can't land in the dark. But we have to be out of here before noon.

I understand. Carla, oh Carla . . . you're going to be all right. . . .

Through the night, he kept reassuring her at intervals. She knew he would not sleep until she was safe.

When Bernie arrived, soon after dawn, they got to their feet and waved him in. Then, mustering strength they hadn't known they had, they transferred the salt load from the first shuttle to the second, which Jesse piloted to another landing close to it—they could not leave without the salt, since no more shuttle trips could be made.

At long last, the moment came when they were back over the settlement, dropping toward a routine touchdown on the pad. This was the last time Jesse would ever fly, Carla realized, sensing that his joy over their safe return was bittersweet. For herself, she was glad to be done with journeying. As she looked out at the familiar landscape, she felt for the first time that it was no longer a new and inhospitable world, but home.

51

AS THE CHILDREN grew older, decisions had to be made about their education. In Peter's view, it was crucial for the kids to know about all that humankind had achieved—all the things their own world couldn't offer them—so they would be able to pass that heritage on to new generations and keep striving to regain what other worlds possessed. "That's what it means to be stewards," he said. "On Undine we were stewards of mind powers. Here we're nurturing those powers, preparing to offer them to people of the future. But now we are also stewards of human knowledge. Both are needed for civilization to advance. To gain one would be of small benefit if we lost the other."

This was, of course, the same issue that had arisen over preservation of the knowledgebase, and Jesse had made his commitment at that time. It saddened him to think of Kel, Tarin and Fran learning to want what they could never personally have, yet that would be better than *not* wanting, not caring if the colony stagnated. Moreover, study was not enough. Every generation must have hands-on experience with technology so that the desire and ability to develop it would be retained until resources became available.

Most people now agreed with this policy, but as before, there were opponents. Arwen and her faction in particular wanted their kids to focus entirely on psi development and grow up content with the physical world that surrounded them. Since these people were in the minority, their preference made no real difference to the colony's well-being, and so it was declared that school beyond basic literacy would not be compulsory. Parents would make their own decisions about what their offspring would be formally taught.

It was quite likely, Jesse realized, that the kids would learn whatever they wanted to learn, no more and no less. Classes were held each afternoon—there were of course many teachers now, Michelle and Edris among them—but the older students weren't required to attend. It wouldn't have been practical without paper, books, or enough computers to go around; they'd have needed to study at different hours anyway. Free access to the knowledgebase was the right of everyone on Maclairn, and though textreaders were in short supply, all children old enough to read were entitled to regular turns with them. It became apparent that some kids were trading their textreader turns for toys, extra turns at video games, and even credits—but the trades went both ways and it was good that the young people most interested in reading got the most chances to do it.

Much of the kids' time was devoted not to study but to work; at eleven, the oldest were in charge of the planting and hand cultivation, leaving the adults free to build more retaining walls. As many kids as possible spent a few hours per week as apprentices, maintaining such technology as the colony had, so as to equip them to become successors to the founding generation. Many also were skilled in making pottery or weaving grass mats, baskets, and sandals. Without these occupations they would have faced intolerable boredom, considering the lack of adequate video facilities. They were paid the same as the adults—one credit per hour of useful work for the colony, plus the proceeds from selling their handcrafts—and, like the adults, were free to choose how many hours to devote to it.

This left plenty of time for recreation. Swimming was enjoyed by everyone. At dusk when it was cool enough, there were sports; new ones had been developed to fit the crude balls available and to take advantage of telepathy in teamwork. Later in the evening, besides vids on the few screens available, there was recorded music to listen to and sometimes dancing.

Kel was among those who loved to read, and unlike his friends, who preferred fantasy fiction, he was especially fascinated by anything having to do with Earth. This was natural, since he knew that his dad had grown up on Earth and he'd been hearing about it since early childhood. By the time he was eleven he knew far more about Earth's wonders than most of the adults. Jesse had, however, edited his recollections of Earth somewhat in talking about it to Kel. His memories of it weren't happy; he'd left for the space academy as soon as he'd finished school and had not been back. Conditions in Earth's crowded cities, the squalor and violence, the regimentation, were not, in his opinion, appropriate topics for discussion with his young son. So he'd told Kel about the bright spots in his boyhood and had described only such features of the mother world as he thought would appeal to him, leaving the boy to read more on his own. Naturally, Kel hadn't sought out scholarly texts, and those in the knowledgebase intended for students had been sanitized. Furthermore, it had been decided not to make vids dealing with crime and modern warfare available to the kids, as admiration of humankind's positive achievements was what the Group wanted to foster. As a result, his conception of Earth was considerably rosier than the reality.

Little was said to the kids about life on Undine, beyond the fact that their parents had come to Maclairn in order to escape it. Since it was a small, obscure colony among the many Earth had established, the knowledgebase gave no more than the bare facts about it, and nobody wanted to revive the dark memories. Nor did anyone want to tantalize the children with descriptions of the beautiful sea and the tree-clad Island. Those were not among the longings that must be aroused to serve the future.

All in all, Maclairn had become a happy place. Such conflicts as existed were minor and, because of telepathic empathy, were quickly resolved. New babies continued to be born. The crops were thriving, mining was underway, and the trees would soon be large enough to provide lumber. Already they offered shade; some had even been planted around one of the cisterns on the plateau, softening the barren look of the living area. There was always enough to eat now, and no worry about survival in the years ahead.

Yet Peter seemed troubled. Not everyone noticed it, but it was evident to Jesse and Carla. It wasn't just that he was personally lonely; friendships and his love for Ivana had largely filled that gap. It certainly wasn't due to his physical handicap, to which neither he nor anyone else paid any attention beyond the necessary aid that had become routine. The psychiatric problems of his former patients had long ago been resolved, and he was now introducing the older kids to neurofeedback training—both through games and in simple forms of control such as changing body temperature—in preparation for the more difficult mind training that would come later. This took up most of his time, and it was work that he enjoyed. Jesse was puzzled as to what could be wrong.

And then one morning when the kids went to feed the chickens, they found three dead hens. Teresa was puzzled; the birds had never been sick and hadn't been pecked by the others as chickens often are. That meant that they'd died suddenly, mere minutes before, because chickens are cannibals and generally attack once a cagemate is down. "I just don't understand it," she said to Jesse, who had been called in his role as the settlement's troubleshooter.

Jesse, chilled, understood all too well. Brian had not been given chicken-feeding or egg-gathering duties, but the door of the shelter that contained the chicken house was not locked. There really wasn't any way it could be, nor could he be constantly watched.

The dead chickens were first examined by Kira, whose healer's sense told her that their hearts had stopped abruptly and that there were unusual signs of internal damage. They were then dissected by the biologist, Corrine, whose assessment agreed—there was no way the deaths could be considered natural.

When Peter confronted him, Brian showed no remorse— he reacted with only a self-satisfied smirk, proud of his newfound power over life and death. Peter, at a loss for a real solution to the problem, resorted to hypnotizing him and implanting a suggestion not to go near the chicken house again. "Why not just inhibit him from killing chickens?" Jesse asked.

"If hypnosis could prevent killing, or any other crime for that matter, human history would have taken a different course," Peter pointed out. "People can't be hypnotized into doing anything contrary to their inner nature. I could no more wipe out Brian's destructive tendencies than I could create such tendencies in Ivana or Kel."

Punishment would not work, Peter said, even if he set aside his disagreement with the principle of it. "There isn't anything more we can do," he told the Council, "because Brian doesn't respond to disapproval in the way a normal child would. The less fuss we make about the chickens, the better, because he's excited by our revulsion. Emotion from us is what he wants. Our best hope of this not happening again lies in showing no reaction."

The question of corporal punishment did not arise, as that was unknown on Undine. Privately, Jesse felt that it might do some good, but Peter, sensing this thought, quickly squelched it. "Psychopaths don't learn from it," he said. "If they did, there would be no psychopathic serial killers on Earth. What's more, it puts the seal of approval on violence against humans, which is the last thing we want Brian to start thinking about." He seemed deeply disturbed as he said this, and Jesse realized that Brian, at eleven, was getting big enough for his strength to be a potential problem. Fist fights didn't occur among his agemates, who had too much telepathic empathy to want to hurt each other. But Brian had always been prone to hit younger kids.

The other children were not told how the chickens had died. Brian bragged to them about it, but they didn't believe him. Since they knew he was an inveterate liar, they chalked it up to that, although the strongest telepaths among them sensed that he believed what he said at least while saying it. Adults in the Group weren't aware that psi could kill, and Peter felt it was best not to tell anyone outside the Council except Velma. There was bound to be a telepathic undercurrent of dismay if it got around, which would merely feed Brian's sick impulses. It was fortunate, Jesse thought, that there were no pets on Maclairn. No dog or cat would be safe around him. But as it was, there was little actual harm he could do, considering that the chickens were destined to be killed anyway.

52

PETER REMAINED DEEPLY disturbed about Brian. "We can't hope that the peace we've enjoyed will last forever," he said to Jesse. "There's been a unique situation here. We were all judged trustworthy when recruited and most of our kids have proved equally so—they've all had caring parents. But that's not enough in cases like his, and sooner or later, there will be more trouble."

It wasn't long in coming. Some of the younger children—Fran, Viktor's daughter Robyn, and a few others—were playing outside at dusk one evening while Ivana supervised them. Peter, with Jesse and Carla at his side, was watching from his window. Suddenly they heard angry voices. Ivana was saying, "Go away! Go away and let the little kids alone, Brian."

"Oh, dear," said Carla. Brian was all too apt to pester the children, although he did not hit them in Ivana's presence because she, like the adults, healed their pain instantly and telepathically warned them to show no reaction. Everyone now knew that this was the only way to deal with Brian; Jesse wondered what he'd done to goad her into ordering him off.

"I'll show you, Ivana," Brian said. "Just you watch—you're not going to like it but you can't stop me!"

In the next moment Ivana began to scream.

Through the window Jesse saw that Fran's straw-filled doll, which lay on the ground near where they'd been playing, was blazing. Somehow, inexplicably, it had been set on fire.

Peter's face froze and his eyes focused intently. Within seconds, equally inexplicably, the fire died, leaving the doll a blackened heap. Carla rushed outside to comfort Fran. The other children had run away, frightened by Ivana's hysterical screams. Her mind was broadcasting, *Uncle Peter! Uncle Peter! Don't let it happen anymore....*

Ivana, oh Ivana, it's okay now. The fire's out, Peter responded. *Don't cry, you know Brian wants to hear you cry....* Her terror had subsided to sobs, but she was still uncontrolled, which wasn't at all like her. Jesse could not fathom what had happened. There were no matches on Maclairn. Flint firelighters required direct contact with something combustible. How could a fire have been started from a distance?

Carla, bring her to me, Peter called. *She's too upset to respond to me.* His emotion was so strong that he too was broadcasting powerfully enough for Jesse to overhear.

While they waited, Jesse ventured, "What set it on fire, Peter?"

"Brian did. With his mind. It's one of the powers long known to exist. If I hadn't been watching—"

"You mean Brian is going to be able to *burn* things?" Jesse asked in horror.

"It takes a good deal of emotional energy. I don't think he'll bother if he doesn't get a strong reaction—the kids have never seen fire and might not have been scared if Ivana hadn't screamed. Now I'll have to desensitize them, and I'll have to warn the adults to remain calm. It's the only defense we have."

He didn't sound convinced; they both knew that it wasn't just a question of being scared. The telepathic perception of Fran's sorrow over her doll would be satisfying to Brian.

"Did you know this could happen, Peter?"

"Not this specifically. Firesetting with matches is characteristic of psychopathic children, though, and Brian is psi-gifted—his killing of the chickens proved that. I can't predict what powers he'll develop. There are some the rest of us wouldn't choose to pursue."

"You—you have them, yourself." Jesse realized. "You put that fire out . . . can you start them, too?"

"Ian taught me what I may need to know in order to protect my people."

Still perplexed, Jesse said, "Ivana hadn't seen fire before either, and has no reason to fear it. Why did she scream? And why did she tell Brian to leave beforehand when she knows better than to provoke him?"

"That's what I want to find out," Peter said. "It's not what I'd have expected from her. But he may have threatened her telepathically."

Once Ivana had been brought to Peter and had taken refuge in his arms, Jesse and Carla quietly departed, leaving them alone. The next day Peter gathered all the children in the Commons and explained about fire, lighting several of the precious candles—it was possible to make candles now that chicken fat was available—and emphasizing that they were dangerous if touched but otherwise not to be feared. There wasn't any chance of a large fire in the settlement, since the prefab shelters were fireproof and everything else was built of stone.

Ivana stood in the back during this session, cringing. Peter, with the assistance of several adults, passed candles from child to child, hoping to nip phobias in the bud. When he offered one to Ivana she refused to hold it, despite the fact that she loved and trusted him. For her to develop a true aversion to fire would be disastrous, Jesse thought. It was only a few years until she'd be old enough for the Ritual, and Ivana, among all the children, was the one they'd assumed would be best prepared.

"Uncle Peter," she demanded when the other kids had gone, "why is Brian bad?"

"Nobody knows. There are many reasons why people do bad things, but Brian *enjoys* doing them. Sometimes a person is just born that way, and we don't know why."

Anxiously she asked, "Are there any other people like him?"

"Not here, at least not now. On other worlds there are."

Yes, and on other worlds they were locked up, Jesse thought. There was no way to put a lock on a stone hut, short of iron bars that couldn't be manufactured on Maclairn. What would they do with Brian when he became a grown man?

Nothing more was said about the incident. But the next night pottery began falling off tables and the wicker stool in Kira's room tipped over by itself. Evidently a poltergeist was at work again.

"It's to be expected," Peter said. "It's common among

troubled adolescents with psi talent, and our oldest kids are entering puberty."

"Is Brian responsible?" Jesse asked.

"I doubt it. It's usually brought on by conflicting emotions, which after all are normal in kids this age. Brian isn't conflicted—he does what he feels like doing and never doubts his own impulses."

"Besides," said Kira, "there was the stool in my room, which no one was anywhere near except Ivana. She reached menarche a few weeks ago; that probably explains it."

"Ivana is so mature and well-adjusted, though," Carla protested.

"Right now she isn't," Kira admitted unhappily. "Ever since the day the doll was burned she's been withdrawn. She's hiding something from me, even telepathically, and I can't get her to open up."

"I can't, either," Peter agreed. "She's closing her mind just as an adult might, which is another example of her advanced psi skills. For her to do that with the people she loves is unnatural, and it worries me."

"I wonder if she might drop her guard with someone not quite so close," Kira suggested. "With Carla, maybe."

"That's possible. It's worth a try," Peter said. And so the next day Jesse and Carla took Ivana aside while the other kids swam, and cautiously broached the subject.

"Ivana, dear, you don't seem happy," Carla said. "You're not afraid Brian will harm you, are you? He can't, you know. Your mind's better balanced than his, and you don't have to let him get to you."

"I know," Ivana whispered, her eyes filling with tears. "I'm not afraid of *him*."

"Then what is there to be afraid of? Your mom and your Uncle Peter feel hurt because you haven't confided in them. They love you and want to help—"

"Oh, I can't tell Mom! I can't tell Uncle Peter! Not ever— I don't want them ever to know I'm bad like Brian!"

"Darling," Carla protested, shocked. "You're not bad and

there's nothing you could do that could make them think so! They love you more than anything else in the world, you know that. Whatever gave you the idea that you're like Brian?"

Ivana, obviously tempted to share the agony of her secret, raised her eyes to Carla. "Do you promise not to tell?"

"I promise not to tell anyone but Jesse if you don't want me to. But it might be a good thing for you to let me, if it's hard to do it yourself."

Ivana turned to Jesse, querying miserably, "Do you promise not to tell, too?"

"Not without your permission," he replied reluctantly, thinking that if this was something Peter should know, it would be essential to persuade her somehow.

Ivana bowed her head again, shrinking from the touch of Carla's hand. It was apparent that they were communicating silently. After a brief pause Carla's thought came through to Jesse: *Oh, my God! She's afraid that she'll start setting fires, too! She thinks she's got the same evil power Brian has!*

Jesse didn't hesitate. He'd agreed not to reveal Peter's confidences, but Peter must be told of this and there was only one way to get Ivana's consent. "Lighting fires isn't always bad, Ivana," he said. "Of course it's bad to destroy someone's doll—we all know you wouldn't do that. But the power to control fire with your mind isn't bad in itself. Uncle Peter has it, too."

"He *does*?" Both Ivana and Carla looked at him in astonishment.

"Of course. Who do you think put the fire out?"

I thought it just burned out, because the doll was mainly straw, Carla told him.

No. Control over fire is a psi gift like others; Ian taught it to him. Ivana probably does have it, and seeing Brian use it jarred her into sensing that she does. She may have picked up the skill from his mind. To Ivana, he said, "Peter won't think you're bad. You must let us tell him, so he can teach you to use your power safely without hurting anybody."

Slowly, Ivana nodded.

Later, the four adults met in Peter's room to talk about what had happened. "Why didn't we know about this power before?" Kira asked.

Peter pondered it. "On Undine, we isolated ourselves on an island in the metaphorical sense as well as the literal one," he said slowly. "In our limited time away from outsiders, we focused on the aspects of psi that were of benefit to us. Ian carefully kept people who might misuse it out of the Group, and he discouraged awareness of its negative aspects. There is an innate fear of fire in the collective unconscious of the settled worlds, passed from generation to generation since prehistoric times on Earth. In the Group we had channeled the power of that fear into the Ritual, the symbol of all that is best in us. He felt that to avoid inner ambivalence about our own mind skills we must remain unaware of their destructive potential."

"Ignorance didn't protect Ivana," Carla pointed out.

"No, yet I don't want to make the existence of pyrokinesis generally known to the kids—some of them aren't mature enough not to strike out with it in the heat of anger. For adults of proven reliability it's another matter. I now see I've made a mistake in continuing Ian's policy this long. All psi powers can be used either constructively or destructively. We have to live with the knowledge that we can unleash them, and be prepared to do it wisely."

"If so, then there must be some positive way to present this one," Kira said.

"There is, but not for the children's eyes. From now on it will become a part of our most fundamental symbol—I will use it to light the torch in the Ritual."

During the next few days Peter called in the most psi-gifted people—Arwen, the neurofeedback instructors, and Brian's mother Velma, among others—and taught those capable of it to ignite and extinguish small fires. There was nothing magical about it, he said. It was simply an extension of the ability to control temperature; if something combustible was made hot enough, it would burst into flame, but they could not create fire out of thin air.

"You need to be able to put out any fires that Brian starts," he told them. "Don't make a big deal of it, because that's the response he's aiming for."

Ivana, too, was taught to handle pyrokinesis, although under normal circumstances she'd have been considered too young. She proved to have more innate ability than anyone else—but it still frightened her, as if she did not quite trust herself with such power.

53

WHEN THE KIDS were thirteen, a major milestone in their lives arrived. They were old enough to become adults by the standard the colony had adopted.

This had been discussed off and on for many years and had been formally decided when the first of them, at eleven, had reached puberty. Jesse had been surprised and a bit shocked to find that the consensus of opinion on the appropriate age of consent for sex was different from what he, having grown up on Earth, had taken for granted. But conditions on Maclairn *were* different, after all. In fact they had been different even on Undine—the frenetic teen subculture of Earth, in which sex was simultaneously glamorized and cheapened, was a phenomenon unique to that planet. No colony world set its adolescents at loose ends with neither the innocence expected in traditional societies nor the privileges and responsibilities of adulthood. On Undine, regimentation and drugging had squelched the normal impulses of the young; it went without saying that the Group had found such a system unacceptable.

The kids of Maclairn had been doing the same kinds of work as adults since they were ten, and most had shown no signs of irresponsibility. Even more significantly, a generation of telepaths, young people who'd been close to each other emotionally all their lives, couldn't be expected to deny the natural desire to intensify that closeness that would come with physical maturity. The enhancement of telepathic sensitivity that could be acquired only through sex was in any case a necessary step in preparation for the Ritual. For the adults whose ESP was merely latent, this had required intimacy with an experienced partner; but having used telepathy since infancy, members of the new generation would need no teaching.

In the society of Undine, sex among adults had been viewed more liberally than on Earth, so the colonists weren't used to arbitrary rules. Within the Group, however, there had been a natural and inevitable restriction—because sex did enhance telepathic communication, mind-to-mind contact was felt to be an essential component of it. Sex involving union of bodies without any merging of minds had been unthinkable, not because of any rule but because having once experienced a full union, no one could find a lesser one satisfying. For this reason there had been no sexual involvement between Group members and outsiders. Also for this reason, sex within the Group had never been in any sense casual. Love often developed quickly, without the period of getting to know each other needed by couples incapable of telepathic sharing; it had been so with Jesse and Carla. Relationships sometimes were temporary. But they were not based on mere physical attraction, and there was no reason to fear that they would be among telepathic adolescents.

So only one further rule needed to be established, other than the existing one against sex between kids raised in the same household. And this was already instilled; they had all known since early childhood that at no time, for any reason, was it permissible for one person to hurt another. The reason such a caveat would be sufficient when it couldn't possibly work on any other world, Jesse saw, was that it would be impossible for young telepaths not to be aware of the feelings—both physical and emotional—of their partners. They could not hurt each other unknowingly.

There were, of course, no contraceptives on Maclairn—they were not only unavailable, but unwanted, since maximum population growth was desired. Maturity in girls was therefore to be defined not as mere menarche but as readiness to bear a child, something safer here than on other worlds, since pregnancies were continuously monitored by healers. No other policy would be feasible, for any attempt to enforce a waiting period would fail sometimes, and why embark on the long road of misery to which births deemed illegitimate had led throughout history? To be sure, girls of thirteen or fourteen might not be emotionally mature enough to assume full responsibility for babies, although most had been helping with the care of infant brothers and sisters for years. Their mothers would have to assist, as had been the case in many traditional cultures. The dominant society of Earth and its authorized colonies was not the only one humans had ever found successful.

One final consideration was the matter of living space. The huts, occupied by large families, were becoming unbearably crowded despite the rooms that had been added to most after brick and wood for roofing became available. The sooner the oldest kids moved out, the better; but there wasn't room for all of them in the single prefab shelter that had been retained as sleeping quarters. And so parents welcomed the idea of letting couples in their early teens start families of their own.

Though there was no disagreement within the Group about these issues, other questions had been harder to resolve. How was sexual eligibility to be made known socially, and when were young people to be considered adults for purposes other than sex?

Some societies, Reiko said, had had formal puberty rites. The passage from childhood to adulthood had been an occasion for an ordeal of some sort, followed by celebration. This seemed like a good idea. It would fit perfectly with the

Group's existing system of initiation into full membership through the Ritual. Unfortunately, there were two problems with it. In the first place, over a hundred babies had been born the first year and over fifty each succeeding year; it would be impossible to hold the Ritual as many times as that. In the second place, and more basically, not every young person was going to be capable of thrusting a hand into fire at the age of thirteen. Some might never become capable of it at all.

Membership in the Group had always required commitment in the Ritual. It had been vaguely assumed that adulthood in succeeding generations would, too. To the dismay of most members, that just wasn't going to be practical. Yet people who had not participated in the Ritual could not be allowed to attend it, for seeing what it involved would preclude their own initiation, if and when their turn came. No one could touch fire for the first time knowing beforehand that it would be demanded; the courage to do it depended not only on telepathic support, but on being given no time to think it through. And how could some young people, even some with babies of their own, be excluded from Group gatherings?

Regretfully, it was decided that people who had experienced the Ritual must be distinguished from those who had not. Many past societies had conferred special status on adults through religious rites, and after some thought it became apparent that for this purpose the Ritual was comparable. Moreover, people began to realize that kids unready to thrust their hands into fire were not ready to make the commitment to stewardship, either. In fact some might not be ready or willing to make any of the pledges—they were, after all, meaningful only insofar as they were voluntary, and must never be allowed to become mere rote.

There remained the matter of how to designate which kids had reached adulthood. Someone then pointed out that the Group had always had two stages of initiation. The first, the acquisition of immunity to physical pain, had involved an ordeal with a specific protocol, and there had been an inherent dividing line between people who had been through it and outsiders. The children—except for Ivana, who had learned spontaneously at the age of three—must in any case be taught how to feel pain without suffering, a skill prerequisite to the other steps in learning volitional control of their bodies. This, then, would be the occasion on which a child attained adult status. It would occur when he or she turned thirteen or became sexually mature, whichever was later.

Jesse had been dreading the time when his son must undergo this ordeal. "It won't be as bad for Kel as it was for you," Peter pointed out. "You tried to be stoic, remember, and had to be shown that that doesn't work. Our kids aren't under the impression that they should be heroes to uphold the honor of Fleet. And they've experienced the state of not suffering as children, when adults relieved pain for them, so they won't view it as impossible. Since they're already accustomed to neurofeedback training, they should be able to reach it without the multiple follow-up sessions most adults require."

"God, Peter, what if he fails?" Failure in the test was a real possibility; it had to be, for no one could stick it out unless the stakes were high. On Undine, failure had meant permanent ineligibility for the Group. For the kids, it would mean a year's delay before another attempt was allowed.

"He won't fail. He's much too strong-minded," Peter assured him. "It's going to be different with the kids than it was when I chose only people I was sure of, because they'll all want to become adults and I'll have to let everyone try. But I haven't any doubts about Kel. And don't forget that he'll have my wordless telepathic encouragement, as candidates always did."

"I know," Jesse responded, with a rush of sympathy. The telepathy would work both ways; Peter would literally share the pain of every one of these children, over a hundred of them in the first year alone. The rest of the mind training could be delegated, but not this. He was the only one with the strength to stress them enough to alter consciousness and the skill to support them subtly. But the emotional impact of subjecting them to it would drain him, even though he knew it would free them from physical suffering for rest of their lives.

The young candidates were required to swear solemnly never to give away the secrets of the ordeal to those who hadn't yet been through it; foreknowledge would make its carefully-designed teaching strategy ineffective. As time passed, rumors would no doubt spread—probably exaggerated ones intended to scare younger kids. Since Kel was the oldest boy in the colony, he'd heard no such rumors. Thus he was more than eager for the experience and wasn't expecting it to be in any way unpleasant. Jesse felt he was entitled to some warning.

"It will be very frightening, Kel," he told him. "It's okay to be afraid—that's part of it. But after it's over, pain will never hurt you again. So just do what Peter tells you and remember that he won't let you come to harm."

"Dad," Kel protested scornfully, "what do you think I am, a baby? I'm not scared and I'm not going to be." *Parents*, Kel was thinking. *Why can't they see I'm grown up?*

There had already been some conflict between them. Kel, who'd been so close to Jesse as a child, was now feeling the rebelliousness of adolescence. There wasn't much to rebel against in the happy society of Maclairn, but Kel had found his own area of discontent. Currently he cared about only two things, and one of them was Earth.

To Jesse's dismay, Kel's interest in Earth had developed into an almost obsessive desire to go there. That this would always be impossible was something he understood in theory, but did not emotionally accept. "Maybe someday a starship will come here," he'd said more than once. "Maybe they'll land and take me back with them."

God, I hope not, Jesse thought, but he knew, of course, that there was no real danger of Fleet looking for them. *Mayflower XI* had been too old a ship to be worth a search.

The kids had been told that their parents had seized the ship in order to get here, but they had no comprehension of what that meant. Certainly Kel didn't know that his dad would be executed as a mutineer if they were ever found. Like kids anywhere, he was interested in space, had read about starships, and had seen vids of them; but he didn't grasp the vastness of the gulf between the stars.

Jesse, for his part, tended to forget that he himself had wanted nothing more than to get into space when he was Kel's age. He had, after all, longed to get *away* from Earth. Surely Kel, whose wish was to see Earth rather than to stay in space, had no comparable justification for the frustration he evidently felt. After the long struggle to survive on a new world for their kids' sake, it was galling to be constantly told that Kel thought an old one might be better. And so they'd argued—but Jesse had refrained from pointing out Earth's deficiencies. It had been agreed that the kids should be encouraged to restore as many as possible of the good things that existed there. So he hoped to direct Kel's admiration of Earth toward determination to strive for the improvement of Maclairn. The boy had the makings of a fine engineer; he was the most apt of Kwame's apprentices and it seemed to Jesse that it would be well for him to spend more time on math and less time poring over pictures of a planet he could never visit.

The only other thing Kel cared about at present was Ivana.

The two had been close friends throughout their childhood; Jesse could not define the moment when the friendship had changed into something more. Now Kel and Ivana were inseparable. And of course, the match between them had long been desired by both families, so there was no reason to oppose what was likely to happen as soon as they were both officially adults.

Ivana was nearly two years past menarche and Kira had said pregnancy, if it should occur, would not be dangerous for her. She was thus eligible for adulthood on her thirteenth birthday, the first of the new generation to reach that milestone. Since she had already mastered the state of consciousness needed for immunity from pain, the normal test would have been meaningless in her case. Had other kids been through it, they might have resented her being spared; but as it was, nobody questioned her new status. Ivana herself, however, didn't want a status different from Kel's. "We were born on the same day," she said. "It wouldn't be fair."

So the celebration was delayed, and Kel's ordeal was begun on their mutual birthday. Ivana was ordered to stay far away from the neurofeedback lab while it was going on, for she would have shared his pain telepathically and could not have resisted the temptation to relieve it, as she'd been accustomed to doing when playmates were hurt. In fact, for some years yet she would have to avoid being nearby when any of the kids were undergoing it. But once she was older she could become a skilled neurofeedback instructor herself, Peter said, for he believed she would develop all the qualities that role required. "Exceptional empathy is a burden sometimes," he told her, "but it's an awesome thing to be able to help someone gain mind powers."

The next day, after Kel's triumphant success, the Group held a picnic by the lake in honor of them both, complete with some of the ale there was now spare grain enough to brew. It was a key event in Maclairn's history, after all. Never again would the founding generation be sharply divided from the children.

Peter was carried down to the beach for the occasion. He and Kel were both high—not from the ale, but from volitional entry into a new state of consciousness, mutually experienced while on dual neurofeedback. Jesse remembered the day it had happened to him, the moment when he first discovered how it felt to be in control of his own sensations. It had been the most joyous day of his life until then, though later he'd known even greater joy with Carla. He, too, had been in telepathic contact with Peter; that was when the bond between them had been forged. Afterward they'd joined hands with other Group members and had run to the shore, plunging exuberantly into the bay. . . .

What a contrast to now, when Peter had to be helped into the water. And yet today Peter seemed truly happy. He still had the ability to enjoy life moment by moment, disregarding worry about the future, even though the hope of regaining the high technology he considered vital was fading year by year.

"Do you realize," Carla said as they sat watching him swim, "that in just a few years we'll be outnumbered? That there'll be more teenagers than original Group members? They could vote us down if a controversy arose."

"The Council will still be in charge," Reiko pointed out. "That's why we set it up as a permanent advisory body instead of scheduling ongoing elections. It's true enough that we'd all be replaced by teens if a vote were held every few years. And when the population's large enough to need representative government, there will have to be a minimum age for holding office. The kids may be ready for sex, but they're not ready to govern."

"In that case, we'd better adopt a constitution soon," said Kira. "Otherwise a provision for a minimum age will never get into it."

Jesse frowned at the thought that had just come to him. "We want the kids to start families young because we now need population increase," he said. "But in comparatively few generations, exponential increase would overrun the world, considering our increased lifespan. Besides, a woman would be worn out if she bore a child every two years from her early teens into her late forties—and yet we have no way to produce contraceptive implants."

"We won't need them," said Kira. "A healer can seal a woman's tubes—or a man's, for that matter—easily, without any surgery required, once she wants no more babies."

Kel and Ivana sat apart from them under the shade trees, their arms entwined. His son, a man, thought Jesse. God, how he loved him! If only there weren't the discord between them, if only Kel would get over his boyish preoccupation with Earth and settle down to learning something useful to the colony. . . .

But Ivana would see to that, no doubt. She was a sensible girl, advanced for her age in more ways than psi-giftedness. He knew that Peter intended her to become his eventual successor, and in the years ahead would train her just as Ian had trained him. He and Carla would feel honored to have her as the mother of their grandchildren, quite apart from the genetic tie to Ian it would give them.

Reaching for Carla, Jesse pulled her close to him. "They're grown up," he said. "The firstborn of Maclairn, and the hope of its future. This is the start of a new era, Carla— we got through the hard part, and now, whether or not we can become what Ian envisioned, our own lives will be good."

54

FROM THE BEGINNING, Jesse knew that the biggest problem that would come with the kids' new status would be what to do about Brian.

Unfortunately, Brian was larger than his peers and was among the first to reach sexual maturity. He was a handsome boy, physically attractive by the usual standards— but of course none of the girls were attracted to him. They all knew him too well. They had been taught that sex meant blending minds as well as joining bodies, and the last thing anyone wanted was to have her mind invaded by Brian's. So the question of how to deal with his normal sex drive would have been a serious one, even apart from his less normal tendency toward violence. The latter, however, was an issue of urgent concern.

Nothing the colony's kids had heard about sex suggested that it could be anything but good, a bond between two people who cared about each other and took joy in sharing more than physical pleasure. That was how it was for all the adults they knew. In their eyes, that it was inherently consensual went without saying. Nobody had felt it necessary to tell them that on other worlds, among non-telepaths, this was not always the case. They'd read history, to be sure, but any mention of rape they took to be an aspect of the violence accompanying Earth's ancient wars. They had not been exposed to crime fiction. That a modern man might force himself on a woman was beyond their comprehension. They couldn't have imagined why he would even want to.

Thus the girls weren't well enough informed to be physically afraid of Brian, and the adults hesitated to disillusion them. Maclairn was a world where everyone trusted everyone else. Group members were bound by a pledge to support each other. Was this carefree atmosphere to be spoiled by saying that young women must now avoid being alone anywhere, that they must always be accompanied on the terraces or the swimming beach or when walking between the huts? Such advice, familiar enough to Jesse from his youth on Earth, seemed unnatural and outrageous to most of the colonists. On Undine there had been no necessity for it—there, the police could be summoned with a single touch of a phone, and potential sex criminals were already in the Hospital in any case. They didn't see how they could explain a need for caution without distorting the kids' conception of sex itself.

Peter was torn. "I agree there's some danger," he said. "Brian would have no compunctions about rape, and it doesn't seem right not to warn the mature girls—and even older women—to be on guard. Yet the culture we've created here, a culture in which telepathy makes all ordinary concern about crime superfluous, is too important to be destroyed by the existence of one depraved individual."

"What have you and Kira said to Ivana?" Jesse inquired.

"Ivana doesn't need to be warned. She steers clear of Brian and senses his mind; if he ever intended to harm her she'd know from a mile away. It's the people with less telepathic ability that I'm worried about." Jesse knew that Peter was deeply troubled. So far, ignoring Brian's destructive acts, thus depriving him of the satisfaction of an emotional response, had worked; but rape could not be ignored. If it were to happen, what could Peter possibly do?

"Rape isn't what most concerns me," he said to Jesse. "Every society has to deal with the problem of rape. Here, there are greater potential dangers. We knew in the beginning that we'd be taking a risk by loosing psi powers into the collective unconscious of a world. So far it has done no harm. All the adults are known to be trustworthy and they've all raised their kids well. And yet we have Brian, whose powers we know to be dangerous. How many more in future generations, further removed from our hand-picked founders, will be a threat to us? They won't have to be psychopaths to misuse psi—mere irresponsibility could lead to disaster."

"You and Ian must have known this all along," Jesse said, frowning.

"Yes, and it's always haunted me. I've dreaded the time when it would have to be faced. And that time is coming, Jess. Just as new technologies have always carried risks, so do new mind powers. To reject the good consequences in the hope of escaping the bad ones would mean no advance could ever be achieved—and fortunately, humankind has never done that, despite the urging of those who valued safety over progress. But that doesn't mean the bad ones don't cause trouble, or that we're not responsible for the suffering it causes."

With a flash of insight Jesse said, "That's the universal guilt complex talking, Peter. You don't really believe we're to blame for whatever harm misuse of psi causes here, any more than you believe humans are collectively culpable for misuses of technology on Earth."

"You're right, of course," Peter agreed. "Still, if I personally fail in handling whatever situations arise—"

"If you do it won't be from lack of trying. And as you've been telling me since Day One, that's all that counts."

Brian had passed the test of adulthood with no difficulty. This had been more of an ordeal for Peter than for the boy, as he'd needed to establish telepathic rapport with him, enhanced while they were both stressed by pain. Close contact with Brian's mind had been, to say the least, distasteful. "Thank God it was brief," Peter had said. "It didn't take long to teach him the fundamentals of pain control, since psychopaths are not as sensitive to pain as other people in the first place. I'm not sure he's acquired total immunity to it, but that's not going to matter—it goes without saying that he will never be eligible for the Ritual, and so he won't have to touch fire."

Too bad, thought Jesse grimly, considering how he liked to start it. Small straw fires had appeared from time to time but had done no damage; there wasn't anything combustible in the settlement except for small toys and the woven mats, baskets and furniture in people's huts. His mom never spoke of what happened in his own.

It had been over two years since the killing of the chickens. As the incident hadn't been repeated, the hypnotic suggestion to stay away from the chicken house had apparently stuck. Brian's desire to kill seemed to have been satisfied by his discovery of the full-grown crawlies, a few of which occasionally appeared on the lowest terrace near the lake. Since Jesse would have had to shoot them with the laser if they'd ventured any higher, he told himself that Brian was doing the colony a service by practicing his deadly heart-stopping skill on them. But inwardly he was appalled. It was not a skill that ought to be practiced.

"I'm uneasy about Brian," he confessed to Carla. "There's no way we could confine him even if he'd committed a crime that warranted it. I'm afraid there's trouble ahead."

"That's what Arwen says," Carla said. "Not about Brian specifically, just that she's got a feeling that something bad's about to happen."

"Oh? She hasn't told me that," said Jesse, surprised. In all the years since her visions of the flood and of the wind pumps, Arwen had not foreseen anything else. There hadn't been any calamity to foresee, of course. If she was again sensing one, the warning might be all too real.

"I can't bear the idea of anything going wrong now that our son's grown up and we're so well established here," Carla murmured. "Yet I suppose we can't stay peaceful forever."

"We never thought Maclairn would be paradise," Jesse agreed.

"Not in the physical sense. But in the social sense we've very nearly achieved it," Carla said. "Sure, we've had hardship and danger and several times we've almost died, and it's hardly a garden spot as far as scenery goes. But there's no illness, no crime, no violence except Brian's minor transgressions—and with that one exception, we all *like* each other. There's no poverty other than the deprivations we all share. And above all, there's no regimentation, no government breathing down our necks. We're free! It's like the ideal so many people sought on Earth where it just wasn't attainable. Through the use of psi, we've finally found the perfection all those earlier societies gave up on."

Jesse frowned. "I'm not sure it's possible even in principle to have an ideal society. It's contrary to human nature, Carla. As new generations come along, there will always be a few people who stir up trouble. Besides, if it were too perfect, nobody would care about striving toward something better."

"Wouldn't they? Aren't we preserving the knowledge-base so that they will?"

"They haven't done it yet, and if they were totally happy with things as they are, they never would. That's the argument we used to counter Arwen's, isn't it?"

"Yes, but we were thinking about technology," Carla said. "Of course we want to gain advanced technology. But we don't have any reason to want more social change."

"We're likely to get it whether we want it or not," Jesse declared. "We have what we have because we've worked for it. The kids take it for granted and get restless. Look at Kel, who thinks he'd be happier on Earth."

"He wouldn't be, really."

"Of course not, but if he had any way to get there he'd jump at the chance. And so by definition our society isn't perfect, because Kel doesn't believe it is, and in a perfect society there would be no discontent. But if there were no discontent, there would be stagnation, and there'd be people who didn't like stagnation . . . don't you see? It goes around in circles. Social perfection can't exist."

"I suppose not. But for awhile, I want to think it can."

It was only a few nights later that the crisis came. The older kids were in the Commons, having pushed the tables back so that they could dance; there was loud music playing as Jesse approached on his way in to see Peter. Several of them stood in the shelter's open doorway, arguing, and he heard Kel say, "Take off, Brian. The girls all said they don't want to dance with you, are you deaf or something?"

"You think you're such a big shot," retorted Brian angrily. "You've got Ivana and your dad is Peter's deputy and you think you've got a right to run everything. Well, you don't. If I want a girl I'll have one, I don't care what anybody says. There are plenty of girls besides the ones in here."

Jesse's heart chilled as Brian stormed angrily outside and headed toward the huts. There was no immediate danger, he knew, for the girls were all inside; he would have seen if any of them had left before Brian. What had he meant, plenty of girls besides those? There could be at most one or two who hadn't attended the dance, and they would be in their huts with their parents. Nevertheless, he turned and followed the boy, fear rising in him from some inner sense of impending disaster.

Almost immediately, as he neared the central well, he heard screams. Jesse moved fast. In the dark he couldn't see just what was happening by the well, but it didn't take sight to know what Brian was doing.

The girl had been thrown down by the time he reached them; he could not make out who it was. He pulled Brian off her, seizing him by the shoulders and knocking him roughly to the ground. Brian was no match for him, as Jesse was taller and heavier, but he was by no means subdued. He glared at him, hatred pouring from his mind in a torrent; every telepath within range rushed to them.

"I'll—kill—her!" Brian raged.

"No, you won't," declared Jesse. "You're not going to kill anything, ever again, no matter what we have to do to you."

"You can't stop me! I was going to kill her anyway, and I still can. Just you see!"

Behind him, a crowd had gathered. "Oh, my God!" someone cried out, "Oh, my God, it's Robyn."

Robyn? But Robyn wasn't one of the mature girls. She was only ten years old.

A upturned bucket lay on the ground beside her; Ursula, her mom, must have sent her out to the well for water. The children had always been safe outside. Even when he and Peter had discussed the danger of rape, it hadn't occurred to Jesse to worry about the younger ones.

By this time Bernie and several other men were helping him to hold Brian down. The kids at the dance had streamed out of the Commons; Reiko and Dorcas were on hand, keeping them back. Out of the corner of his eye he saw Kel and Ivana clinging together in distress.

Robyn still lay flat, crying hysterically. God, thought Jesse, did he finish it? Is she injured? He could not turn to see, but Carla was with her, drawn by the shock of the feelings he'd unconsciously broadcast. He couldn't shake off his fear. It was more than horror at the age of the girl. Something was wrong, something beyond what had already happened. Yet Brian, with a glassy stare on his face, was pinned to the ground.

Suddenly Robyn's cries stopped. "She's fainted," Carla said. "I can't revive her, we need a healer—"

Brian's expression morphed from rage to intense satisfaction. "*I* did it!" he said. "It worked just like I knew it would. I killed her—I told her I would but she kept on screaming anyway and so I killed her."

"Shut him up, somebody," said Dan. "We don't want to listen to this garbage. Let's move the girl to the infirmary."

Viktor and Ursula, Robyn's parents, arrived on the run; they'd been in the farthest hut from the well when she began to scream. "Oh, God, is she okay?" Ursula cried, seeing that Robyn lay limp and still. "She's so pale, Carla! What happened?"

Jesse wondered who would have to tell them what had happened. He hoped it wasn't going to be him. Best to wait until a healer could say whether any physical damage had been done. . . .

With relief, he saw Kira approaching. "Stand back, everyone," she said, and knelt beside Robin. "She's—bleeding," Carla said in a small voice. Then there was silence, and Jesse realized that she was giving the details to Kira telepathically.

A sense of dread permeated the gathering; Jesse could tell that they all felt it. Brian was less agitated, now; his face had gone slack. "I did it," he mumbled, "I can do it over and over now, I found how to do it with people."

"My God," said Bernie. "Is he talking about sex? He discovered sex and he thinks rape is the way to do it?"

Kira rose, her face white. "He doesn't mean the rape. He means what he did with the chickens. Robyn is dead."

55

IT WASN'T FROM loss of blood, Kira said—there hadn't been that much bleeding. Robyn's heart had simply stopped, as the chickens' hearts had. Brian had killed her with psi. And now that he'd found he *could* kill, he was likely to do it again.

Peter must be told at once, of course. Carla, with Viktor and the weeping Ursula, headed for his room as soon as Ingrid came to take charge of Robyn's body. Kira, after examining it very thoroughly, turned her attention to Brian. Once he'd quieted down she placed a firm hand on his head, telepathically sending him into sleep. "Take him to the infirmary," she told Jesse. "It's the only place we can keep an eye on him until Peter decides what to do."

Word spread fast, and the Council, numb with shock, gathered by Peter's door without being summoned; there was nowhere else they could turn for answers. Jesse sensed that few of them had ever conceived of anything like this. The murder horrified them, but the rape of a prepubescent girl was simply beyond imagination. Sexual perversion was not discussed on Undine; psychological checkups being mandatory, anyone prone to it was imprisoned in the Hospital long before taking any action. All crime there was considered illness, and the details of potential sex crimes were no more made public than were technical descriptions of heart disease. Nor were such crimes featured in entertainment. Unlike people who'd grown up on Earth as he had, the colonists had not been exposed to fiction that dealt with them.

Peter, as a former Hospital staff doctor, was of course well-informed. When the Council entered his room pain was evident in him, but not surprise. He'd known all along, Jesse realized. He'd examined Brian repeatedly since childhood and must have been aware that more was wrong with him than cruelty and a desire to kill chickens. Yet he'd been helpless. There was no way he could have placed a guard on him around the clock.

Viktor and Ursula had been led away by Ingrid after a private talk with Peter. Carla, now sitting beside him, was pale. "It might have been Fran," she moaned as Jesse came to her. "Oh, God, Jesse—it could have been Fran just as easily as Robyn." He sank down on the floor mattress and put his arm around her, pressing her tight against him. He couldn't think of anything to say.

"Where is Brian now?" Peter asked.

"He's sleeping," Kira said. "I've sedated him telepathically, but that can't be maintained for more than a few days."

"Are we absolutely sure he killed Robyn?" Reiko asked.

"He claimed to have done it, but he's prone to boasting, after all. Couldn't she have died from fright during the rape?"

"No, if she'd died naturally there wouldn't have been the internal trauma I saw. I checked thoroughly with my healer's sense and it was different from anything I ever observed in my years as a physician. But it was comparable to what we found in the hens he killed."

Peter said, "I knew he was capable of killing, but I couldn't act when he wasn't guilty of any crime. Now I must. We have no professional police to deal with this situation."

"Thank God, we do have a professional psychiatrist," Kwame said. "What's your plan, Peter?" They all evidently expected Peter to step in and cure Brian; much as they'd hated the Hospital's tactics, they had assumed psychiatrists could help anybody who was really sick. Aghast, they listened as he told them what he'd told Jesse long before: Brian was a psychopath, and was therefore incurable. He would have cured him long ago if it were possible.

"But then what *can* we do?" asked Teresa in despair. "There's no way to lock him up; we haven't any building that can be barred, even if we had bars and a way to secure them—"

"Stone's the only material strong enough," said Dan. "He's got to be confined to his hut, even if Velma has to move out."

"But it has only woven matting for a door."

"Chain him, then."

"Like an animal?" protested Arwen. "And anyway, we have no chains."

"Locking him up isn't feasible," Reiko declared. "Think how many years we're talking about here. He's thirteen and may live more than a century more. We're not equipped to run a prison; we can't spare anyone to guard it. And solitary confinement for so long a period would hardly be humane in any case."

"It would drive him more insane than he already is," Kira agreed.

"But we can't *not* lock him up," said Carla. "He's a danger now to all our kids, maybe even to adults if he gets mad enough at someone."

Peter said, "You're all forgetting something. Locking Brian up wouldn't protect us. He's killed with psi in the presence of witnesses and has vowed to do it again. Physical barriers make no difference to psi. Even if we walled up the hut and fed him through a hole, he'd still be a danger to anyone nearby."

"Oh, God," whispered Teresa. "Are we powerless, then?"

"We *can't* be," said Jesse. "A colony can't be at the mercy of one deranged person. That's just not how things work. There has to be a solution."

"The solution on Undine was drugging," Kira pointed out. "Even on Earth they've drugged dangerous mental patients for centuries. I hate to say it, but perhaps we were a bit too extreme in our condemnation of that."

"Drugs would be justifiable in this case," Peter agreed. "Even I would have no qualms about giving them to a psychopathic killer who posed a danger to others. But we don't have any drugs here. We didn't retrieve those in the starship's sick bay, and they'd have run out quickly even if we had."

"There was a time on Earth before those drugs were developed," Teresa said. "What did earlier societies do, Reiko? Would the knowledgebase tell?"

"Earlier societies, and even some later ones, simply killed dangerous criminals," Reiko said. "Small communities like ours hanged them from the nearest tree. Larger societies went through a lot of judicial rigamarole and used various methods of execution, mainly to isolate the average citizen from personal contact with the process."

Kwame said, "We all know execution existed. There were virtual executions on Undine—Ian's, for one, and before that Ramón's. That's hardly something a less oppressive society would consider."

"Execution is generally viewed as punishment," said

Peter, "and I believe capital punishment is wrong. But executing a murderer who's likely to repeat the crime, not to punish but to protect the public from harm, is another matter." He glanced around the circle, meeting their eyes, and added, "It can't be denied that killing in self defense, or in defense of others, is sometimes necessary."

Arwen was the first to pick up the telepathic undercurrent. "You can't be saying what I think you are," she gasped.

Painfully, Peter replied, "You all know what I'm saying, because we've agreed there is no other answer."

Kwame stared at him in horror. "Oh, my God. You're not serious!"

"Execute a thirteen-year-old boy?" Kira exclaimed in dismay. "I agree, that can't be seriously considered, even though he's an adult by our criteria."

"Do you have an alternative to offer?" Peter asked. "Does anyone?" In the silence, he went on, "Brian's violent nature cannot be changed by any sort of therapy. Sooner or later he will kill again if we do nothing. It's up to us to defend ourselves from that threat. There's no one to take the burden off our hands—that's the price we have paid for choosing to become an independent society rather than a mere group of discontents within a larger one."

Soberly he went on, "In a larger society everything would be done for us, as it was in the one we left. We're willing to grow our own food rather than have it delivered to us by a complex distribution system. We're willing to make our own arrangements for clothing, power and even water, knowing that what we don't provide for ourselves will not be given to us by any protective agency. If there were dangerous animals here we would accept the responsibility of dealing with them, as pioneers have done in countless other cultures. Don't you see that we must also take full responsibility for dealing with human predators? There are psychopathic killers in every society. Either they are locked up, which we haven't the means to do; or they're drugged, which we can't do either; or they are executed. There is no fourth way."

No one dared to respond aloud, but the truth of this was gradually grasped through telepathy. Finally Kira said, "I can't contest your logic, Peter. We'll think about it."

"We don't have time to think about it. The threat is immediate."

"But surely you wouldn't suggest acting without long consideration—"

"Kira," said Peter sadly, "I have been considering this ever since Ian and I first talked about emigration. He said to me, 'Do you know what you're taking on, Peter? Do you understand that a small independent colony will have no protection against the destructive use of psi in new generations unless you provide it?' I swore to him that I did, and I have agonized over it from that time on. When I probed Brian as a child and found him potentially dangerous, I knew what might eventually have to happen; the only question was when."

"God, Peter," said Jesse. "As far back as the day I first told you what he said about stunning chickens?"

"Long before that, though I tried to pretend we might be spared."

"So you think this must be done . . . soon?" Reiko asked.

"How many more kids do we want to see raped or killed while we're waiting?"

"But—*how*? You wouldn't hang him!"

"No, of course not. It can be done the same way he did it, via psi."

"But who would be capable of that?" Kira protested. And then, absorbing Peter's silent communication to her, she said, "Oh . . . it's simply the reverse of healing, isn't it. . . . How could I have worked as a healer all these years, and not know?"

"There's a lot besides fire that Ian didn't discuss with everyone," Peter said gently. "Not even with you, though he loved you—perhaps because he did love you, he wished to spare you certain kinds of knowledge."

"I knew something about it," Reiko admitted, "and Hari

knew more. About the historical use of black magic in various cultures, that is. You mean he taught you the actual psi technique behind the metaphors?"

"Yes. It's not confined to black magic; like all other techniques it can be used either for good or for evil. If Brian were older and a trained adept, there would be danger in it; there might be a psychic battle between us. As it is, my power far surpasses his."

"Will he—suffer?"

"No. It will be quick and painless, in fact it can even be done while he sleeps. He's in the infirmary now, isn't he, Kira?"

Kira nodded. "This technique's just an—extension of the sedation?"

"That's right. No one but me needs to be involved. I suggest that you all leave now, and don't talk about him except among yourselves. If anyone asks, say the Council is handling the situation."

Silently they rose and left the room, keeping their thoughts tightly shielded against probing. Carla, her eyes wet, approached Peter, her anguish for him overflowing, but Jesse motioned her to go. *Don't try to comfort him*, he cautioned. *He's keeping a grip on himself and your love for him would only make that harder.*

She went with the others, but Jesse stayed behind. He had no intention of allowing Peter to bear this burden on top of everything else he'd suffered.

"Peter . . . let me do this for you," he said when they were alone. "With the laser gun, I mean. I've—been inured to it, you know. Killing's accepted in Fleet, something that from the time we're cadets we know may become necessary, whereas for you—"

Peter shook his head. "In Fleet, does a captain let his second in command do his dirty jobs for him? Would you respect a captain who did?"

"Yes, if the subordinate was better trained and more experienced."

"You're trained to use a gun. But you're not an executioner, Jess, any more than I am."

"No, but I've killed before, and you haven't. Why should we both have to live with the memory of it?"

"There's no existing load on your conscience. You killed two pirates in the heat of an engagement, purely in self defense."

"And isn't this a matter of defense? Isn't that what you emphasized to the Council?"

"It is, but it's nevertheless execution, planned in advance. It's not the same thing as a fight, and you know it—you are merely offering to bear what's mine to bear."

"If I can do that, I'll be glad of it," Jesse declared. "It will be better than having to watch what it would do to you." Merely being forced by the Hospital to give brain-damaging drugs had been agony for Peter; Kira had believed it would eventually have destroyed him. . . .

Peter took his hand, gripped it. "Jess, I know you want to help, and I'm grateful to you. But it *wouldn't* help—it would actually make it worse for me in the long run. Oh, it would be easy to let you shoot Brian while I merely authorized it, as countless leaders have authorized executions in the past without even observing them. I take back the question I just posed about Fleet because I know they execute mutineers and I'm sure the admirals don't do that personally. I could tell you to go ahead. But then I'd never know, you see, if I believed underneath that it was right."

"You'd still have the responsibility. You simply wouldn't have to do it with psi."

"That's just it, Jesse. In order to use my healing gift in reverse, I will *have* to believe I'm doing the right thing—not just on the surface of consciousness, but deep inside where psi originates. Otherwise it won't work. It's one of the things that can't be done by mere will power. And so I can never fear in the future that I've violated my integrity, because by definition, anything done by psi is in accord with the inner convictions of the person who does it."

"If that's true, how can psi be misused?" Jesse protested.

"It's misused in terms of harm done to others. When Brian used it to kill he didn't go against his conscience—a psychopath simply doesn't have one. There are also situations where psi is used destructively by people with warped consciences, but I think we can assume mine is intact."

"Then you're saying only evildoers can kill wrongly with psi?"

"Exactly. I could teach you to kill chickens with it, but not to commit murder. That's a built-in safeguard—if normal people could kill their enemies with psi, the death toll would be high enough to threaten human survival. There'd have been no need for physical weapons in Earth's wars."

"I guess I see," Jesse admitted slowly. "If you can do this, you don't ever have to be afraid of not having been sure that it's the lesser of evils."

"No. I only have to face the pain of knowing that it *is* evil, even though not to do it would result in a worse one."

"Peter, it's not fair!" Jesse burst out. "You've had too much pain in your life already. Fate, or whatever it's called, can't have laid this on you."

Peter said slowly, "Ian dreamed that I would someday face a terrible test. When I lost my legs, we all assumed that was what the dream meant. But maybe it wasn't, Jesse. Maybe *this* is what his prescience revealed to him. Because as to living without legs, I had no real choice—they were gone, and I had to adapt. It wasn't a test at all. Now, to protect the colony, I must choose."

They both knew that under the circumstances no other choice was possible. If anything could help Peter now, Jesse realized, it was the belief that Ian had foreseen it, whether he actually had or not. "As you once told me," he conceded, "he warned you so that when it happened you wouldn't lose courage."

They said no more aloud. *Go now, Jesse,* Peter commanded. *Tell Kira to take Ivana away and to come back at dawn, alone. And see to it that no one enters the Commons before then.*

The infirmary was near Peter's room, in the corner of the Commons on the far side of Kira's. If psi could kill through walls, it wouldn't be necessary for Peter to be moved any closer to it.

Brian was asleep in the infirmary, and Jesse knew he would never wake.

56

A BRIEF MEMORIAL was held for Brian the following afternoon at the burial site, to which Peter had been carried. The full Council attended, as was proper. Apart from Velma, whom he had seen privately earlier in the day, few others came. People had been told merely that Brian had died in his sleep, and if anyone suspected there was more to it, they did not say so. There was a general feeling of relief in the Group, although out of common decency all but the children refrained from speaking ill of the dead.

Peter spoke at the service, expressing sorrow not over the loss of the boy's life—for though he guarded his mind from intrusion he could not have lied to telepaths—but over the harm Brian had done to himself and others. His voice did not waver. Jesse thought he'd seen courage before, but this surpassed all previous displays of it. Afterward, he said to Carla, "Now is the time he needs someone, just to sit with him and share tears. He won't admit it, of course, but he shouldn't be alone tonight, and you're the only one he'd be glad to see. So go, and don't worry about me or the kids." She didn't return to the hut until morning, and he did not ask what had passed between them.

Kel was devastated by the murder. "Dad, I drove him to it," he said miserably. "I made him mad and then ordered him to leave the Commons just when Robyn reached the well—"

"You couldn't have known, Kel," Jesse said. "Don't blame yourself for something that can't be undone. It was not your fault, and you'll only make yourself sick if you go on telling yourself it was." He knew from personal experience, of course, that this advice was unlikely to be followed.

"Dad . . . why are there people like Brian? I don't mean what makes them that way, I know Peter says it's just how they're born . . . but *why*?"

Jesse paused, trying to frame a response. Finally he said, "That's a very old question that's been asked since the beginning of time. And nobody really knows the answer, but you see, Kel, it can't be just a matter of brain defects, the way the Meds on Undine thought, because if it were, that would mean all of us are totally controlled by our bodies—that we don't have any choice about being good or evil. And we do have a choice. We have what's called free will, yet it wouldn't be free if there were no alternative to choosing good. At least that's what many wise thinkers have said in the past."

"Did Brian choose?"

"Well, he was a human being, so he must have had free will. But how or when he chose is beyond our understanding. It's a paradox, because as far as we can tell, there was never a time when he didn't want to hurt people."

Robyn's memorial was held two days later, in the assembly ring with candles and music. There, Peter said more, not mentioning Brian, but eulogizing the girl and expressing grief not only over the tragedy of her death, but over the colonists' loss of innocence. "We've been a group distinct from society, pledged to each other and to our goal without need to concern ourselves with outsiders," he said, "and we can never be that again. From now on we will live as people do elsewhere, subject to all the threats and sorrows of contact with human evil. We—at least most of us—did not think such things could touch us here. We thought that because we were all personally selected for trustworthiness, no evil would come into our midst. But Maclairn is not a utopia, and it's not only physical hardship with which we're destined to deal. There are evil individuals born into every world, no matter how well its culture nurtures the majority. Ian knew this, and he made sure that I knew it, though I kept the dangers of which he warned me hidden in my heart.

"For a short time, fate allowed us to live free of the worries and responsibilities that come with citizenship in a normal society. Now we've been expelled from the garden, so to speak. Yet we still have our dream; we are still stewards of something precious, something that even if misused by a few, will be a force for good that can transform the future of humankind.

"Many times we've gathered here now, a select company of founders. Now for the first time there are young people among us, the firstborn of this new and promising world. When next we gather it will be to bring new members into our Ritual fellowship. Let's rejoice in that! Let's rejoice in the widening of our circle, and put behind us all regret over what can never be regained. We'll always mourn the death of Robyn, but it would be of no help to the new generation to mourn for ourselves."

As always, the assembled people responded to Peter's words and to the telepathic feeling with which he backed them. Jesse was again awed by his courage. He'd conducted so many funerals . . . for Ian . . . for the deaths in stasis . . . for Hari and Claire . . . for Anne . . . but surely this one must be the hardest. Yet every time he had used the occasion to inspire hope beyond mourning, reconciliation to more than the fact of an individual death.

And so though people wept, they left the assembly ring in higher spirits than on entering it; and in the weeks that followed, life went on. Kel and Ivana underwent their mind training, learning to control their heart rates, biochemistry and other physiological responses, and to self-heal. They took to it easily. They were not hindered by fear of their own power over their bodies, as Jesse had been when first discovering it in middle life. They'd always known their parents had

such power, and they didn't have false assumptions to un-
learn. They could have progressed still faster if the
neurofeedback equipment had been available more often
for practice, but there were many trainees sharing lab time
now.

Once their training had been completed, they were both
judged ready for the Ritual. In an unprecedented move, Peter agreed to hold a single rite for them. It had always been
thought too difficult to support two novices simultaneously
in the handling of fire. But Ivana and Kel, having been born
on the same day, wanted to share the honor of being first; and
they were so closely attuned to each other—and to him—that
he decided it would be safe. Jesse and Carla were to participate as Kel's sponsors; Kira would be Ivana's, doing double
duty as Peter's backup. Greg, who'd been one of their
neurofeedback instructors, was to be torchbearer.

On Undine, participants in the Ritual for a novice had
worn white, a color never worn at the Lodge at other times.
Here, no one had any clothes except their old ones, the same
durable synthetic garments the adults had been wearing
for nearly fifteen years. Some of the older kids wore clothes
that had once belonged to the banished crew of *Mayflower
XI*. Such fabric as had been provided by the pods, or had so
far been produced from the fiber crop, had gone for children's
clothes and was being handed down from one member of a
family to the next.

So when on the appointed evening Teresa brought out
seven sleeveless white tunics, loosely made to fit wearers of
any size, everyone was astonished. "I saved out part of the
fiber harvest," she said, "and we've been working on them
secretly for a long time. They are not for you to keep, of
course, except Peter's—they will be saved for the Ritual, for
every time it's held for someone new."

The participants arranged themselves in a semicircle in
front of Peter, kneeling as they always had since the loss of
his legs, while Kwame and Dan held him upright. Kel and
Ivana knew nothing of what was coming, of course, except

that they would make solemn promises and would be asked to confirm their sincerity in some mysterious way. They were both glowing. *They're so young*, Jesse thought. *How can they grasp what commitment means?* The white garments of the figures around him reminded him of his own commitment, long ago on another world. He had never for an instant regretted it. He'd by now almost forgotten his years in Fleet, and the thought of them did not evoke any nostalgia.

As Greg came forward with the torch it burst into flame, lit not by a candle as they once used to do, but by Peter's mind. The young people, who had never seen so much fire, gasped—and to Jesse's dismay Ivana shrank back, obviously terrified. What had gone wrong? There had been no suggestion yet that she would have to touch it; surely Peter had withheld any telepathic projection of that thought, just as the rest of them were doing.

Oh, God, Jesse thought. If she panicked they'd all be in danger of getting burned. The mutual support that made fire immunity possible depended on the focused participation of everyone, including the onlookers. There had never been a failed Ritual. Yet at this stage, Peter could not halt the ceremony without causing psychological scars worse than the potential physical ones—which could, of course, be healed. Calmly, he proceeded with the opening summarization of the Group's ideals.

The pause for private meditation was longer than usual; Jesse realized that Peter was communicating silently with Ivana, offering her courage. His voice was steady when he began the words of the rite: "Jesse and Carla, do you wish to sponsor Kelstrom in his commitment to the Group, sharing the peril of his pledging, and do you believe him qualified to undertake this commitment safely?" They answered in unison, "Yes, we do."

"Kira, do you wish to sponsor Ivana.... Kelstrom, do you by your own free choice commit yourself to live by the precepts of the Group.... Ivana, do you too wish.... Will you support fellow-members of the Group in all ways....

Do you believe that your mind has power over the well-being of your body, and that it can protect or heal you from sickness, injury and pain?"

Greg lowered the torch to waist height, its shaft now horizontal between the two novices. Without hesitation Peter went on, "Unfaced fear is the destroyer. We will acknowledge fear and accept it, we will go past it and live free...." He'd done this so often over the years and yet, Jesse thought suddenly, this time would have been different even if Ivana weren't afraid—it had never been done with anyone so young before, and he could hardly help being apprehensive for her when she meant so much to him....

"...We believe that we are stewards of a flame that will illuminate future generations. And we now seal our commitment with the symbol of the mind's power, which is fire." There was a surge of tension as he thrust his hand into the flame. "Kel, Ivana, put your hands on mine," he commanded. He was smiling, and his psychic projection to her was so strong that they all sensed it: *Ivana, you must! I know it's hard, but you must do this or you'll never be at peace with yourself....*

Kel was stunned but did not falter; he touched Peter's hand confidently, as did Jesse and the rest. To them, as always, it was a high beyond all other highs; nothing could match it. The rapport between them was a solid bulwark against any possibility of harm.

Ivana was trembling; she seemed to fear the mere presence of the torch as much as what was being asked of her. By this time their hands had been in the flame too long. *Carla, pull Kel back!* Peter commanded. *Kira and Jesse, wait. Burns will heal quickly; Ivana won't, if she backs off from her destiny now.*

Kel, grasping this, shook off Carla's arm and cried out, "Ivana, you've got to! Don't you see that we're all getting burned while we're waiting for you? Come on, take *my* hand!"

In horror, Ivana saw that Kel's hand, still bathed by flame, was turning red. That anyone might be endangered had not occurred to her, for none of them were in pain and she knew the adults did not share her fear of fire. But Kel! Instantly Ivana reached for his hand, shaken out of her paralysis by the realization that a person she loved was placing himself at risk.

It had all taken place within seconds, of course; but time had stood still; and once Ivana was one with them, it was as if there had never been any break in the magic of it. As the six participants withdrew their hands and rose from their knees, Kel's face and Ivana's shone with the exultation a first Ritual experience always produced. Her hand still touching his, she swiftly healed his burns, not waiting for Peter or Kira to do so. The terror she'd felt had evaporated.

There will never be a night like this, Jesse thought. *I believed mine was the high point of my life, but to share it with my son—my son and soon-to-be daughter—surpasses all that's gone before.* . . . And he knew Peter was thinking the same, in spite of all the many times he'd experienced it, for though Ivana was not his daughter, he loved her as much as if she were. Perhaps in this he would receive some measure of the happiness he deserved, to balance all the tragedy and grief behind him.

Greg moved to extinguish the torch, but Ivana, with renewed confidence, said, "Wait."

They all looked at her in surprise. "Uncle Peter," she said, "you've given me so much, I want to give you something—something I know you've wished for."

If she could, it would top everything, Jesse thought. Gifts were virtually known in this world where so few material possessions existed, but he knew Peter would cherish any token she might offer.

They all watched, mystified, as Ivana drew out a small golden stone from beneath her tunic and held it in front of her—not with her hand, but with her mind, letting it float in the torchlight. They'd long known that she could direct moving stones, but she had not kept one still before, at least not where anyone could see. Probably she couldn't have sustained it so long if it hadn't been for the extreme high, the unprecedented psi power, engendered by the placing of her hand in fire.

"Take it, Uncle Peter," she said quietly. He reached for it, but she shook her head. "No, not that way. Take it with your mind, drawing the skill from mine, just as I drew on you when I touched the flame."

Peter froze, his eyes wide with awe, and then slowly, steadily, the stone began to move toward him. He had tried for years to gain the psychokinetic ability Ivana and some of the other children possessed, and had failed. Even the attempt to match mind-patterns in the neurofeedback lab had proved fruitless. He'd come to the conclusion that one must be born with it. In spite of all his knowledge of psi, all his skill in imparting skills to others, it had not occurred to him that he might receive this power from Ian's daughter in the way he'd received so many from Ian himself.

Jesse held his breath, as they all did. If it did not work, Peter would be crushed. And then he realized that there was no risk, for Ivana still controlled the stone; she would not let it fall. Instruction was often done that way, as Peter knew better than anyone. The novice was never sure exactly when the balance shifted. Perhaps that had always been true even with the fire.

The stone moved closer to him . . . then Ivana stepped back, relaxed, and they knew that the shift had occurred. Peter let it hover for a few moments before taking it into his hand. *My dearest girl*, he told her, with enough intensity for them all to hear, *I'll treasure it always, all the rest of my life. No gift could ever mean more to me than this.*

Later that night, when they talked it over, it was agreed that other adults probably could not have done what Peter had done—and could still do, for having once grasped the mind-pattern, he found himself able to produce it at will. He was exceptionally psi-gifted; he was high from the Ritual and stirred by his close rapport with Ivana—and there might also have been another factor, Jesse suspected. Could Peter, despite his awareness of how often people feared latent powers, have had a deep-down terror of releasing his own? For years, he had suffered privately from anticipation of the ordeal that had recently fallen to him. To have gotten past it might have freed him to loose all the psi force he could muster.

Most significant of all, perhaps, was the fact that Peter's physical limitation made psychokinesis especially urgent for him. Just as a blind person develops acute hearing, he had gained extra psi power to compensate for the mobility he had lost. He had previously been unable to get anything from across the room without calling someone. Now he could bring small items within reach. He still had a long life ahead of him, bound to a chair; who could say what he might be able to do with his mind in the future?

"What happened to Ivana at the beginning, when she shrank from the torch?" Carla asked. "I never knew you to undertake the Ritual with someone not quite ready, Peter."

Kira said, "For some reason she still has a phobia about fire. I was reluctant to let her try the Ritual so soon, but Peter said it would be best for her to share her first one with Kel."

"She needed to face her fear before it got any more deeply entrenched," Peter said, "and young love is a powerful motivator, as you saw."

Ivana had always been exceptional, and it was not surprising that she had risen to the occasion. What Kel had done out of love, heedless of his own peril, was another matter. He was prone to act impulsively, to be sure; but Jesse had not realized quite how much initiative his young son had developed.

For a few days after that, things went back to normal. Then one afternoon as they were leaving a Council meeting Arwen said, "Jesse . . . be careful today. I—I've got a strange feeling that you're in some sort of danger. Maybe you should stay indoors—"

"Indoors? That's crazy," he protested. "There's nothing

dangerous around here, but if there were I'd need to be out doing something about it."

"I've sensed for weeks and weeks that trouble's coming, though I can't see what kind," she told him, obviously quite upset. "After what happened with Brian, I assumed that was it . . . but the feeling didn't go away. And today it's stronger than ever. I've been afraid for Peter—but now I'm just as worried about *you*."

Jesse frowned. Arwen's precognition had proved accurate before, yet if there was danger it could hardly affect both Peter and himself without imperiling everyone else. In any case he could not sit around in the Commons waiting for some unnamed threat to appear.

He and Carla had barely reached the door when the plateau reverberated with an unmistakable sound—and Jesse, unbelieving, stared up in dismay to see a ship hovering over the settlement.

Part Six

57

THE SHIP CAME down out of a clear sky, hovered, and then landed on the unoccupied second shuttle pad. It was lighter than the Group's own shuttles, and skillfully handled. "That's an explorer's shuttle," Jesse said. "The starship it came from will be a small one, probably no more than four in the crew. And they'll be armed."

He did not need to put what he was thinking into words; Carla sensed it immediately. The size of the ship didn't matter. Whatever threat was posed by the crew didn't matter. Armed or not, with or without prisoners, the starship would eventually leave Maclairn and report its location to Fleet. And that would be the end of the Group's independence. Even if they weren't transported to a penal colony, their new culture would cease to exist.

"Jesse," she said, "you shouldn't be seen! There's probably no statute of limitations on mutiny, much less on hijacking."

"I'm not important enough to warrant a search," he assured her. "It's been nearly fifteen years, and explorer crews are young—they'll never have heard of me."

"There could be a bounty, or something."

"For me? Not likely. After all, we didn't really steal from Fleet—our starship was scheduled to be decommissioned and its scrap value was covered by the property we left be-

hind on Undine to be transferred to them. It's just bad luck
that they stumbled on this planet."

Nevertheless, *Mayflower XI* was on the missing list and
the explorer ship might have records stating that it been hijacked, so he gave in to her insistence that he go back into the
Commons. It was quickly agreed, and telepathically passed
on, that people should stay where they were while Carla and
Kwame, as representatives of the Council, walked out to the
landing site to greet the visitors.

They came forward, two men and a woman. "I'm Captain Alan Renard, and these are my officers, lieutenants
Nadia Farman and Jiri Doubek," said the leader. "We're
from the explorer ship *Picard*, and we're searching for Edris
Monroe."

It was Edris for whom the bounty had originally been
offered, Renard explained. Her wealthy parents on Undine
had been devastated by their daughter's departure, and they
were prepared to pay handsomely to get her back. Not even
their vast resources were sufficient to charter a starship,
but they had been advised by Fleet that explorer ships on
routine missions were more likely in any case to come across
the world to which the Group had fled. Their crews would
certainly be on the lookout for an unauthorized settlement
if there was money to be had by finding it.

But it must be a larger sum of money than might be
gained by keeping the find secret if the planet happened to
be rich in some easily-transported commodity. Smuggling
was generally a more profitable trade than bounty hunting.
The Monroes, not wanting to take any chances, had pulled
strings. They'd offered to throw their rather considerable
political power behind Peter's old nemesis Warick, who was
running for Hospital Administrator, on condition that his
platform include a promise to bring to justice the criminals
who had enticed innocent citizens to join the cult registered
with Fleet as the Stewards of the Flame. The criminals
named by him were Peter Kelstrom, the traitorous ring-
leader and Jesse Sanders, the renegade Fleet captain who,

with Kelstrom's connivance, had escaped treatment for mental illness and had conspired with him to steal not merely a starship, but a substantial portion of the capital that should have stayed on Undine's tax rolls to be used for the common good.

Warick must have had mixed feelings, Carla thought, since he knew Peter was aware of his implication in a disastrous series of arsons and he had tried to silence him. Surely he wouldn't have wanted the investigation that was bound to ensue if he was brought back. Peter would be judged criminally insane, but he would be entitled to a hearing and could hardly be expected not to reveal what he knew. His examination under truth serum alone would bring it to light. On the other hand, Warick might have thought the chances of finding the Group to be smaller than the Monroes hoped. Besides, it was likely to take years, and in the meantime he'd have enjoyed at least one term as Administrator, the top governmental office on Undine. That might well give him the power to suppress Peter's testimony.

No doubt the platform itself had been an effective campaign strategy. Many families must have been dismayed by the defection of relatives. Many, too, must have been outraged if it had been found that the bodies of their deceased loved ones were not in the Vaults, where according to the prevailing belief they would have remained "alive" indefinitely. These people had undoubtedly been delighted by Warick's addition of Hospital funds to the bounty, on which interest had been compounded for years by now. In any case, Renard said, the price on the heads of Peter and Jesse had eventually surpassed the reward for Edris, and there would be room for all three aboard *Picard*. Aid to the rest of the Group would have to wait for larger ships, but in the meantime they could take comfort in the knowledge that the men who'd led them to this desolate world were being punished.

Did they expect Edris to leave her husband and six children, one of them a newborn infant? Carla thought bitterly. For a moment, to her shame, she found herself wondering if she could persuade the bounty hunters that grandchildren might be worth more to the Monroes than Warick would pay for Peter and Jesse. But of course, Edris was equally entitled to the Group's protection; and in any case, once Maclairn's location was revealed, Peter and Jesse would not stay free for long.

Nor would any of them.

After all the struggle, all the heartache, were they now to lose everything they'd achieved over the years? It would be useless, she knew, to insist that they didn't want any aid. It would be incomprehensible to outsiders that they might prefer this small, relatively primitive settlement on a barren planet, with no comforts and no resources worth exporting, to the benefits of civilized society. The one hope, that these officers might agree to shield the innocent passengers from prosecution for crimes that would land them in a penal colony, was quickly dashed. "Don't worry," Renard assured her. "All charges against your party have been dropped. Fleet recognizes that the blame lies entirely with Kelstrom and Sanders."

Noticing her hesitation, he made a wrong guess as to its cause. "I suppose they hid when they saw us land, and you may fear that they'll retaliate in some way if you help us find them. Guilty men do desperate things. I promise you they won't have a chance. We'll have them in custody before they know what's happening, and be on our way as soon as Edris Monroe is aboard."

Carla said the only thing she could think of to say. "I hate to disappoint you, but Peter Kelstrom and Jesse Sanders are dead."

Stunned, Renard and his crew stared at her. "Both dead? Are you sure?"

"Of course I'm sure. Jesse was my husband." She hoped none of the officers were latent telepaths.

"How did they die?"

"In a flash flood, many years ago. Another man was killed, and one lost his legs."

"We'll need proof," said the woman officer, Nadia Farman. "DNA samples. I'm afraid we'll have to disturb the graves—"

"There are no graves now; they are under the lake." At their obvious dismay Carla added with asperity, "What, do the bounty notices say, wanted dead or alive?"

Farman replied hastily, "I'm sorry if I seemed unfeeling. I know women often care deeply for men who involve them in crime. You must have had a hard life in this hellhole; the heat alone is barely survivable. You'll be in safe hands soon, and Fleet will try to make it up to you."

"As the victim of a felony perpetrated aboard a ship of ours, you're entitled to compensation, Jiri Doubek added. "All of you are—modern conveniences will be brought in at no expense to you and you'll be given free health care and schooling for your children."

The children! The older ones, and Kel in particular, would be eager to see this shuttle and talk with its crew. They must be warned not to reveal her lie. *Jesse . . . Jesse!* she called silently. *Keep the kids away . . . and make sure everyone understands not to let on that you and Peter are alive.*

They're looking for us specifically, then?

Yes, for both of you. I told them you died in the flood. But Jesse, they want Edris even more. Make sure that she and her kids are hidden.

Edris? She never committed any crimes.

Her parents want her back, and they enlisted Warick's help to raise the bounty. If Peter's caught he'll be turned over to him.

Warick—oh, God.

Tell Peter. And find some way to stay out of sight. I can't stall them for long—we'll have to offer them a meal and shelter for the night.

The officers were looking at her strangely, wondering why all of a sudden her mind seemed far away. Kwame covered for her. "Edris is married and has a family," he said. "She won't want to leave, and we're certainly not going to force her."

"It's not up to you," said Renard, "and we'll use force if necessary."

"That will be hard to do if you can't find her," Carla said. "I assume you don't mean to shoot us if we don't turn her over to you." Fleet was ruthless at times, she knew, but not brutal. They would not kill innocent hostages. But they clearly weren't expecting refugees to stand up to them.

"Cooperation will expedite the supply ships of which you're evidently in desperate need," Nadia Farman said, looking around at the crude stone huts of the settlement. "We saw your terraces as we came in, and it didn't look as if your harvests are large. And surely you must be short of medical supplies—"

"Our leader, Kira Tarinov, is a physician," Carla assured them, reminding herself to inform Kira of her promotion before they were introduced to her. "She seems to be managing."

"Nevertheless, if you have children to feed, you'll want quick assistance."

"We're doing fine, thank you," said Kwame. "But you'll want to see for yourselves. Come along, I'll give you a tour." This was necessary, Carla realized, for they would inspect the colony thoroughly in any case, and it should be with a guide who could steer them away from things best not noticed. Meanwhile, she could make arrangements for hiding the fugitives.

Peter was in the main area of the Commons, where the ship's officers would have to come to eat, and Carla's first concern was for getting him carried back to his room in case they barged in unannounced. But Peter had other ideas. "I'll talk to them," he said decisively. "They won't recognize me, and if I'm introduced as someone else, they'll never give it a second thought."

Kira frowned. "Peter, they'll have pictures, and you don't look much older than you did on Undine. You've scarcely aged at all."

"That's just it—they will be looking for an older man. But more than that, they won't notice my face after they see that I have no legs. They will be so shocked that they'll move on, and try to forget that I even exist."

Carla had to agree that he was probably right. No one from a civilized world, other than medical personnel, had ever seen a person with missing limbs. For Peter, the bold way would be the safest way. But Jesse and Edris must stay hidden. That would be relatively easy to accomplish. The hardest part would be keeping the children from giving anything away—and of course they must conceal the colony's possession of psi powers, too, which would be hard to make the kids understand.

Quickly, she assigned some of the thirteen-year-olds to round up the younger ones and see that they stayed in the schoolhouse. Gradually the people in the Commons dispersed, having been delegated to make the rest of the colony's residents aware of the situation. Carla, knowing that she would be watched, did not dare contact Edris herself; she left it Jesse, who was no more likely to be seen in Edris's hut than in their own.

Edris was devastated at having been the unwitting cause of the colony's discovery. *She offered to give herself up if it would make them leave*, Jesse reported, *but I told her there'd be nothing to gain by that. They will send more ships back here anyway. She'll be identified then and taken, but on a larger ship they may let her family go with her. There's no point in her being separated from them if it can be avoided. And I'll be damned if I'll give these bounty hunters the satisfaction of bringing her in personally.*

He seemed all too sure that they would find her. When Fleet returned, would Jesse and Peter too be unable to escape identification? Unable to face that thought, Carla pushed it from her mind. But her heart went out to Edris, who still had feelings for Peter and must feel anguish at knowing that in leaving home to join the Group, she'd triggered a chain of events that might lead to his capture. She would never forgive her parents. Moreover, she and her husband were not closely bonded and whether he'd choose to go back to Undine was questionable. Her children, one of whom was Peter's son, would be placed in crèches there. All in all, her future was not bright—but then, was anyone's?

As Kwame entered the Commons with the explorer crew, having shown them around the settlement with as much courtesy as he could muster, Peter projected a telepathic warning not to panic at his presence. *Don't ignore me,* he instructed. *Be casual about it, but bring them over. I know how to handle them.*

Reluctantly, Kwame escorted them to the table where Peter's chair had been placed. "You asked about the children's schooling," he said. "This is one of our teachers."

"I'd get up," Peter said, "but as you see I'm confined to this chair." He had thrown the blanket off his lap so they would be sure to see why. "I'm not good for much else anymore, but teaching suits me, and the kids respect my limitations."

The bounty hunters were speechless, staring at him in sheer horror. "I wish I could say that you're welcome here," Peter went on, "but I'm afraid I can't. We like the life we've made for ourselves, you see. We don't want to see it change."

"You feel no resentment at the position Kelstrom and Sanders placed you in?" Renard asked incredulously. "Stranding you without access to the medical facilities that could make you whole?"

"No, I can't say that I do," Peter replied with a straight face. "Wholeness in the medical sense isn't everything. I'm happier here than I was on Undine, and I have Kelstrom and Sanders to thank for that. Frankly, I'm glad that they're now beyond Fleet's power to punish."

As he had predicted, the officers quickly moved away from him, eager to be introduced to the presumed leader, Kira. But Nadia Farman turned back, and in her face Carla saw more pity than indignation. "We want to be of help," she said. "Since we'll have only one prisoner to take to Headquarters, we'll have room for one or two passengers. We'd be happy to take you to the hospital there, to get you walking just as soon as possible."

"No, thanks," said Peter. "I believe I'd rather stick with my friends."

58

THE COUNCIL, CONVENED by telepathy, met in Peter's room late that evening—but not so late that the bounty hunters, if they decided to spy after dark, would wonder what was going on. Small groups were getting together in the huts, too, after being warned to keep a close eye on the children. It would be thought normal for people to gather and discuss as momentous an event as their deliverance from abandonment on a desolate, unopened world.

Everyone was stunned, frozen. At first there seemed to be no words for their dismay. It simply hadn't occurred to them that after so many years they might be discovered. It had occurred to Jesse, to be sure, but he'd kept such speculations strictly private, not only to avoid worrying the others, but because he'd managed to convince himself that the chance of its happening was too remote to worry about.

Finally it was Kira who asked the question to which they all knew there could be no answer: "What are we going to do?"

Peter didn't try to pretend that he might come up with a solution. "Fate has always favored us," he said quietly. "If our luck has run out—if it's just not in the cards for what we've built here to endure—then that's what we have to accept. The Group has always believed in facing hard facts squarely. We'll gain nothing by denying them."

They couldn't argue. Peter was facing death. They were all aware that he would be put into permanent stasis if he was returned to Undine, as was no doubt a condition for collection of the bounty. Warick would make sure of that even if the relatives of other Group members didn't rise to demand it. He had made a fool of Warick. He had deceived him for years about the Group's existence and his own double role at the Hospital, as well as about the people he'd smuggled out to die in peace. If it hadn't been discovered by now that those bodies were not in the stasis vaults, it would be as soon as he was given truth serum. He might then be charged with the murder of all the people who allegedly could have been kept "alive" indefinitely, in addition to manipulation of financial accounts and complicity in the hijacking. And Warick, who was well aware of how Peter felt about the Vaults—of the agony he'd not tried to hide when Ian was consigned to them—would take great satisfaction in condemning him to the same fate.

But the sentence wouldn't be carried out immediately. Undine claimed the "finest hospital in the galaxy" and that hospital was dedicated to cutting-edge research. Peter's file there would show that he was nearly sixty years old by Earth reckoning, yet because of Group members' slow aging, he looked little more than thirty-five. The Hospital would want to know why. The secret of the Fountain of Youth, if marketed to other colonies, would be worth a good deal to Undine's treasury—far more than enough to compensate for the bounty. Whatever measures were necessary to extract that secret from Peter's body would be undertaken. Autopsy being precluded by the belief that the corpses in the Vaults still lived, this would be done prior to his consignment to stasis. Jesse, recalling the extent of the invasive three-day physical exam he himself had undergone merely for producing a standard baseline record, blanched at the thought of what Peter would undoubtedly be subjected to.

Beside their anguish for Peter—and for Jesse, whose doom as a hijacker and mutineer was sealed beyond any possible doubt—the others' own future seemed of minor concern to them. But it, too, had to be faced. "Will they take us all back to Undine?" Teresa questioned.

"No," Peter said. "There are too many of us now to be

self-supporting on Undine, what with all the children—and the crèches aren't set up for so many. Possibly a few people like Edris will be sent there, if their relatives pay enough."

"Earth, then. If we've been cleared of all charges as Renard said, they can't send us to a penal colony."

"Earth is overpopulated," Reiko pointed out. "It will have to be some other world, maybe Liberty, the one we were officially headed for."

They had not grasped what was in store for them, Jesse realized. Better for them to hear it from him than to find out later, as a shock. "We haven't the funds to pay for passage to another world," he said, "and we've already demonstrated that this one's habitable. So they will keep us here—"

"But that's great!" exclaimed Kwame.

"No. They'll come in force and impose a government run by the League. When they've got this world sufficiently terraformed and some air-conditioned barracks built to replace our primitive unsanitary huts, they'll open it up to other settlers. Those with capital to invest will be in control; our credits will be worthless and officially-qualified personnel will take over the professional work we've been doing. Probably you'll end up as full-time mine workers."

"And the children?" Carla asked in a small voice.

"They'll be placed in government-run schools—that is, if they're able to hide their psi powers well enough to avoid being diagnosed as mentally ill. They'll be considered maladjusted at best if they're forced to conform. And of course our newly-initiated adults will find themselves minors again, with more restrictions on conduct than they've ever imagined."

"Dear God," said Kira. "It will be worse than what we escaped from on Undine."

"Will all we've gained go for nothing, then, Peter?" asked Arwen.

"Not for nothing. We *had* it. We proved that a society like ours could thrive. We became what humans can be, which is all we ever hoped to do on Undine. That's more than most people accomplish in life."

After a painful pause, Dan declared, "I'd never have thought I could say what I'm about to say. We've never condoned violence. But defense is a legitimate reason for it, as you've argued before, Peter. We'd be defending your life and Jesse's as well as our own interests if that crew never got back into space."

"It wouldn't help," Jesse told him. "An explorer is never left unmanned, so there's at least one officer still aboard the starship. If anything happened to those on the ground, or if they were simply imprisoned here, she'd jump immediately and send a Fleet force back."

For some time no one spoke. Then Kira said, "All these years, in one crisis after another we've asked ourselves what Ian would say. What would he say now?"

"That we mustn't lose courage," Peter declared. "That however sure the future may seem, it may be changed by unforeseeable events. And above all, that we must have faith in the power of our own minds. Because that's what it's all been for—building the colony was only a means by which to achieve it."

"The power of our minds can't be taken from us," Kira said with assurance.

We win simply by being what we are. Jesse thought back across time and space to the moment Peter had said this to him. He had not understood it then; he'd been impatient for political activism. Later, after his seemingly-miraculous release from the Hospital, he had begun to grasp its meaning.

"It's all still true," Carla reflected. "Everything in the pledge, all the ideas we've lived by. If it weren't—if our minds weren't all that really count—it wouldn't have been valid in the first place. What we've suffered in the past would have been pointless."

"Yes," Peter agreed. "If it was ever true, it always will be. So let's say it now, together, even without physical fire as a symbol. What we're about to go through will be fire enough."

They joined hands, slipping through Peter's psychic guidance into the altered consciousness needed for the Ritual. "... We will trust the power of the mind over all restrictions, whether imposed from within or by the world outside.... We believe that we are stewards of a flame that will illuminate future generations...."

"We are stewards more than ever, if we must keep our achievement secret," Arwen acknowledged.

Through tears, Reiko said, "We *will* pass it on! The children's psi powers are well enough established for us to keep on communicating, whatever the conditions we're forced to live under. They'll transmit them to our grandchildren. And if this planet is opened up, then someday, somehow, our descendants will keep the flame alive."

Later, as Jesse and Carla walked back toward their hut, Jesse said, "They'll find me here sooner or later. Maybe this crew will give up, but when the bigger ships come—"

"I suppose so. Is there no way at all of disguising you?"

"No. They'll bring DNA records and check everyone."

"Where will they take you?"

"To Fleet headquarters on Earth's moon."

She paused, then asked in a low voice, "And how ... do they do it in Fleet? Execute mutineers, I mean."

"You don't want to know, Carla," he said. But he could not keep it from his thoughts, and was too slow in closing his mind to her. She turned pale, picturing it—the air seeping away as they cycled the airlock, the condemned man gasping for breath.... Having faced the possibility of air shortage on *Mayflower XI*, she had all too vivid an understanding of what it would be like to die from the lack of it.

"I—I used to think being put into stasis to die, as Ramón and Ian were, was the worst thing that could happen to anybody," she whispered. "Oh, Jesse—"

"Well, at least there's no hypocrisy about it," he said. "No medical trappings, which is more than can be said of the methods used in most places." He couldn't claim that the prospect didn't frighten him; telepathy precluded lying. But he was more worried about her feelings than about his own.

Before they reached the hut he stopped and took her into his arms. "Carla . . . we don't know how much time we've got, so I'll say this now. Don't grieve for my sake. I've had a good life these past fifteen years, better than anything I ever imagined before I met you. Our love overshadows all the trouble and danger we've been through—it's been worth whatever price I have to pay, and the only thing I really mind about what's ahead for me is the thought of leaving you."

She clung to him, her face wet with silent tears. "Then let's make the most of what's left to us, starting tonight—"

His mind now shut tight against sensing, he shook his head. "They'll find me, but I'd like to put that off as long as I can. And so while the crew's here I think I'd better hide in the mine tunnel, in case they search the huts."

"Oh—yes! I'll see that the kids are in bed, and then come to you."

"No," he said with pain. "The bounty hunters might miss you and start looking for you."

"But just for an hour or two—"

"Carla, I don't think that would be wise. Maybe tomorrow night, if I have to stay that long."

"Okay," she said, puzzled and obviously hurt. It was heartbreaking to reject her, but at all costs they must refrain from making love. During sex he could not close his mind; hers would merge with it, and she would perceive a thought that he could not let her share.

59

THE NEXT DAY dragged by slowly for Jesse. No one came to the copper mine; he'd warned Dan that activity there might draw attention to it. Though probably it had been noticed from the air, nothing had been said to suggest that it was currently being worked. He sat alone near the mouth of the sloping tunnel after bringing the robots inside to hide them.

Carla contacted him telepathically from time to time. Aware that thinking of the future must be painful for him, she didn't refer to what was to come; she merely kept him informed of the situation outside. It was difficult, she admitted, to keep the kids away from the Fleet officers, who were friendly to them in the hope that they might reveal where Edris was. The main worry was that one of them might let slip some indication that he and Peter were still alive. Those now officially adults could be trusted not to do so; still despite their protests, contact was being discouraged. They were fascinated by the strangers, having no true grasp of the danger discovery posed. And Kel, Jesse knew, must be dying for a chance to ask them questions about Earth.

The bounty hunters, Carla told him, had not taken long to conclude that they would get no cooperation from the exiles, who—inexplicably in their eyes—did not want to be rescued. They had little hope of recognizing Edris, whom they erroneously assumed would look much older than she did in her file picture. And so they'd resorted to what seemed to them a likely means of finding her: bribery. Ten percent of the bounty, they'd announced, would be paid to whoever turned her over to them. As this was a great deal of money and the colonists would be penniless once the League took over, they fully expected a response. When by evening they hadn't received one, they were stunned and discouraged.

They're not likely to stay on Maclairn long, Jesse assured Carla, his spirits rising for reasons he did not mention. *They'll collect part of the bounty just for reporting her location, so they'll waste no time getting to Fleet Headquarters.*

Thank God you'll be able to stop hiding! I want you with me for as much time as we have left.

Then come to the mine tonight—late, after they've gone

to bed. It's safe. They won't be watching you so carefully anymore.

I will! Oh, Jesse, I will!

Get Kira to stay with Fran and Tarin, he told her. *And Carla—don't contact me from a distance again. If we're going to be awake half the night, I should get some sleep. God, I love you, Carla. . . .*

He had no intention of sleeping. At sunset, venturing to the mine's entrance for a breath of fresh air, Jesse steeled himself to the knowledge that it was now time to act.

There was only one way to save the colony; he had known that from the moment the ship had first appeared in their sky. It would have reported their whereabouts even if there had been no bounty. They had built an unauthorized settlement on an unopened world, which was in itself a serious violation of League law. They were living outside the law. Their children weren't receiving medical care or an approved education. This would not be allowed to continue; they'd be placed under the authority of a caretaker government that would leave them no vestige of freedom.

Jesse clenched his fingers. He alone could prevent this from happening. No one had guessed that he could, and he could not bear to tell Carla face to face. So he must part from her without even a farewell, to spare her pain for a little while, at least—anyway, long enough so that he would not have to see it. Was he truly being kind, he wondered, or was it selfish to deprive her of the last few hours they could ever have together? He wasn't sure, but he knew that his strength was limited and that he must save it for the action demanded of him.

With a sigh of resignation, he looked his last on the setting sun of Maclairn and the familiar landscape that he'd come to think of as home. Then he retreated into the tunnel, where he sat down to record a message to Carla.

She would keep watch on the Fleet officers' movements, and once they'd gone to bed in the sleeping shelter, she would come looking for him. But he wouldn't be here waiting for her.

As soon as it was dark enough to move he must see Peter, painful though that conversation was going to be.

Peter would be alone in the Commons building once supper was cleared away and everyone had retreated to the huts. Kira would be putting Fran to bed, and Ivana, who still shared Kira's room, would be with Kel somewhere— probably somewhere private. He was not sure where the kids went for lovemaking, since it was too cold after dark outdoors; he suspected they had some arrangement with regard to buildings known to be unoccupied at specific hours. In any case, they seized any chance to be alone together.

He wished he could see Kel one more time—all the kids, of course, but especially Kel, his firstborn son. It was hard to acknowledge that he was grown up when by most worlds' standards he was still a boy and in many ways he behaved like one. His desire to go to Earth, to be sure, was more than mere adolescent defiance; it was based on ignorance and inexperience. Of course Earth seemed attractive to him! He'd idealized it, as if it were the setting of a story. Jesse hoped he'd never have to learn the reality.

Reluctantly he set his datakeeper, with the message light flashing, where Carla would see it. Then he gathered up the things he would need and under cover of darkness, made his way to Peter's room. From Carla he could withhold the full truth, but Peter had to be told.

Peter sat by a dim lamp, a textreader in his lap. "Jesse!" he exclaimed. "You shouldn't be here. If they see me again they won't be suspicious, but you—"

"It won't matter now, and in any case they won't search anymore tonight."

"How much longer do you think they'll wait around?" Peter asked.

"Not long. They'll be leaving as soon as it gets light."

Peter sighed. "And then how much time will we have before Fleet arrives to take us over?"

"Fleet's not going to take us over, Peter."

"Why wouldn't they?"

"Because I'm not going to let them. I may be able to disable *Picard*'s hyperdrive controls so that it can't jump—can't leave this solar system."

"That's great, except that the shuttle hasn't enough charge to lift, and in any case the crew here would see if you tried to take off in it. There's no way you can get to *Picard*, let alone board it."

"Of course there is. They'll be delighted to provide transportation."

"Oh, Jesse. Things are bad enough without you giving yourself up for the sake of a long shot."

"Have you got a better idea?"

"No, but this one seems a bit too dicey. Does Carla know?"

"In a little while she will; I left a message. She'll see that I have no real choice."

"Wrecking a starship's hyperdrive under the eyes of its crew while you're their prisoner sounds damn near impossible to me," Peter said. "If you can't manage it, we'll be taken over anyway—and you'll be executed sooner than if you let things ride."

"I guarantee that won't happen," declared Jesse grimly.

Peter eyed him thoughtfully. "What don't I know that's given you so much confidence all of a sudden?

"Well, there's Plan B, the part I didn't mention in my message to Carla," Jesse confessed. "Before I left the mine I raided the explosives supply and stashed the makings of a bomb under my shirt. I doubt that it will occur to the crew to search me."

He sensed Peter's surge of emotion—first shock, then awe at the realization that the colony could, in fact, be saved. Painfully Jesse added, "The only reason I'm telling you is so that you won't have to wait forever, expecting Fleet to arrive. If they don't show up in the next hundred days, you can assume the ship didn't get to them."

After a pause Peter said, "Jesse . . . is there a real chance that you can disable just the hyperdrive? If not, if the starship's got to be blown up, then it would be better for me to do it. That's something that wouldn't require legs, and you're needed here."

"There's a chance," Jesse assured him, closing his mind tight against telepathic probing so that Peter would not perceive how slim that chance was. "And you're less expendable than I am. Others can do everything I do, since we won't have to go into space again. But the mind training of the kids depends on you—not to mention the inspiration that holds this colony together."

"But Carla needs you. To lose a second husband, after Ramón—"

Yes. There was that, and he didn't doubt that Peter cared enough for Carla to give his life to save her from sorrow. Yet she'd suffer whichever of them died, and there *was* a small chance that they both could live.

"Promise me that you'll take care of her," Jesse said. "I know there can't be a full consummation for you, but there could be . . . physical contact. Enough for the merging of your minds. She loves you, Peter—she always has, and I've never felt threatened by it. If I'd never come along, the two of you would eventually have married on Undine. I don't mind doing what I've got to do, if it comes to that, but I can't face the thought of her being left to grieve alone."

"You don't need to worry on that score," Peter promised. "Or about your kids, either. I'll be like family to Kel from now on anyway—I know Ivana's feeling for him is more than mere infatuation."

"They're just thirteen," Jesse reflected. "Too young for lifemating, though Carla and I have always hoped they might someday give us grandchildren."

"That's your Earth background speaking," Peter said. "Even on Undine thirteen is not too young to fall permanently in love—and here, after all, they're legally adults."

"Yes, but it's hard for me not to think of Kel as a boy," Jesse said. "In a lot of ways he's a typical kid with no regard for what the future will demand of him. He's backed off from his focus on Earth just for Ivana's sake; he doesn't listen to me anymore. Sadly, we're no longer as close as we once were."

"Never think that Kel doesn't love you! As you say, he's adolescent and impetuous. He's shy about showing affection for his dad. But that's a façade. He'll be devastated if—" Peter broke off, realizing that this line of thought would merely add to Jesse's suffering.

"I've got to go," Jesse said. He knew that if he did not, he would soon be in tears.

"This won't be the first time you've saved my life," Peter said, "and I've never found words enough to thank you. But if it turns out to be at the cost of your own—"

"Hardly that. I'd live half a year longer, maybe less, if I let them take me to Headquarters, and that time would be spent in prison. I'd be paying an impossibly high price for it, don't you think?"

I suppose you would, Peter admitted silently, with conflicting feelings that he couldn't express aloud.

He leaned forward and Jesse stooped to embrace him. In his mind he saw Peter as he'd first known him on the Island, tall, strong, with the sparkle of youthful enthusiasm in his eyes despite the maturity obscured by slow aging. *How did we come to this?* he wondered. *You facing God knows how many more decades confined to a chair, me about to blow up a starship and myself along with it—after all the ordeals we got through together, is it really going to end this way?*

No. What we achieved will last forever, Peter assured him. "We were naïve," he went on, as Jesse started to go. "We had no real notion of what settling an untamed world would mean—yet you pulled us through. And now we owe our future existence to you, too. You'll be enshrined in this colony's history as our founding hero for generations to come."

"Hero?" Jesse protested. "All I've ever done is try to overcome the consequences of my past mistakes."

"Then thank God for those mistakes," Peter declared,

"if you're saying that without them you wouldn't have taken on so much."

"Be that as it may, it's not what I've done that will be remembered. This is the only colony where something really new—new power of the mind—has been fostered. Someday that will be important. Someday our history will be viewed as the dawn of a new era for humankind. And for that, you are responsible. Your name, not mine, will be known throughout the galaxy."

"Not likely," Peter said, forcing a smile. "I'm not Peter Kelstrom anymore, and 'Peter the Great' has been bestowed elsewhere by historians."

"Peter of Maclairn. That's how they'll know you when history is written."

"I never thought of that—I've inherited Ian's name after all, as if I'd been his true son on a world where family names meant something."

"It's fitting." Peter had proven more than worthy of the trust placed in him by Ian. Ian, who'd foreseen so much . . . had he, perhaps, seen the shadow of this ultimate crisis? Vividly, across more than fifteen years, Jesse again recalled the dream in which Ian had come to him, and the overpowering conviction he'd felt in it that Ian depended on him as well as on Peter, the Group depended on him, if he lost courage the Group could not survive. . . .

"Fitting for you, too," Peter said, gripping his hand. "Godspeed, Jesse of Maclairn." *And if we don't meet again on this world, perhaps somehow, in some other time, wherever Ian is* . . . It was not a thought that could be expressed aloud, but Jesse knew suddenly that Peter believed in more than fate—he would have to, to keep on as he had despite the cruel blow fate had dealt him. Jesse was not sure that he himself did; but it would be unthinkable to question Peter's faith in the unseen.

I won't say goodbye, he replied silently. *One way or another, we'll be in touch.*

60

WHEN CARLA HEARD Jesse's message her first impulse was
to find him, stop him somehow from giving himself up—but
of course, he was right. There was no other way the colony
could be saved, no other way *he* could be saved from execution. If there was any possibility of disabling the starship's
hyperdrive, he had no choice but to attempt it. She wondered why he'd been unwilling to mention it to her earlier.
He knew she wasn't prone to balk at danger.

Once the explorer crew had him in custody they would
stop searching for Edris. They would be entitled to the bounty
for her even if she wasn't found until a force was sent back
to subdue the colony—and they'd expect to be paid right away
for Jesse. That would make them rich enough to wait for
the rest, she thought bitterly. But they would not get it unless
Jesse failed, and he wasn't the sort of man who failed. She
had believed underneath that he would find some way to
deal with the situation. And now he had.

Reluctantly, Carla obeyed Jesse's request not to contact
him telepathically while he waited for the shuttle to take
off. After a sleepless night she went instead to Peter, and
together they watched from his window as it rose into the
pale sky of dawn. She smiled and said, "It shouldn't take
long after he reaches the starship. They'll come back as soon
as they realize they can't jump, I suppose. They're not going to be happy, but they're smart people with skills we can
use. Probably in time they'll accept mind training. What a
shock they'll get when they learn who they're going to receive it from."

Peter was silent. His mind was closed to her . . . when he
should be elated by knowing the colony could be saved. That
his own life would be spared. In dismay Carla recalled the day
on Undine when he'd told her Jesse was to be released from
the Hospital. He'd looked then much as he did now, too
troubled to meet her eyes. Aren't you glad? she'd asked in

confusion, and he'd assured her that his joy was immeasurable. But there'd been underlying anguish he wouldn't reveal, for he'd known the price would be Ian's death. . . .

Suddenly cold, she burst out, "Peter? Will disabling the hyperdrive be harder than Jesse told me? Is there a chance he really might fail and be taken to prison after all?"

"No," Peter said. "I don't think there's any chance he'll be taken to prison."

It had been hard to convince Kel that Jesse would be imprisoned if he was found. Predictably, he'd put up an argument when Carla first warned him about staying away from the bounty hunters. "Mom," he'd said, "they're from *Earth*! I can't see why it would be so bad to talk to people from Earth."

"You might accidentally let something slip, Kel—some little thing that might suggest that Peter and your dad aren't dead. We can't risk that."

"Well, what would happen if they knew? Why is Dad hiding from them, anyway? I know Edris's family would pay them to take her back to Undine, but what would they want with Dad?"

"He broke laws, Kel," she said. "Fleet wants to punish him."

"What good would that do them? They must know he'd never hurt anybody." Kel was genuinely puzzled; laws and punishment were unknown concepts on Maclairn. He'd heard of prisons but had assumed that in modern times they were only for dangerous people like Brian.

She had not wanted to tell him, but it was evident that she would have to. "They haven't forgiven him for taking the starship," she said. "They would put him in prison, and then later, they would execute him."

"Execute him? *Kill* him? I don't believe you!"

"It's true," Carla said sadly. "The reasons why are complicated, but they don't really matter, do they? We just can't take any chances."

Kel still didn't believe it, she felt; but he agreed that

Jesse must be hidden. Shaken by the discussion, she let it drop and did not notice that he hadn't actually promised not to speak to the officers.

Now, after getting breakfast for Fran and Tarin and sending them to school, Carla went to the computer building, determined to put her mind on work while waiting. But the shuttle returned before she'd gotten started; Jesse must have worked fast. Joyously she ran to meet it. A group of people gathered, puzzled. No one had known that he was aboard when it took off earlier—she and Peter had honored Jesse's wish that they not tell anyone—so the others were surprised and not at all pleased to see it return. The kids, too, crowded around the landing site, and this time she didn't stop them. There was no longer any need for concealment.

Renard and another officer, a woman they had not met, emerged from the ship and approached her. "This is the fourth member of our crew, Lt. Mei Luong," he said.

As he spoke, Kel and Ivana rushed up to them, obviously finding it hard to contain their excitement. Both seemed brimming with enthusiasm at the mere sight of the shuttle. They had no comprehension of what would happen to the colony if Fleet returned, and hadn't been told that Peter would lose his life.

"Mom," Kel said. "You're not going to like this. But it's what we've got to do. We've thought about it a long time, and well, it's *our* lives—"

"I don't know what you're talking about," Carla said in confusion. Not that she ever knew what was on Kel's mind these days, but usually he spoke intelligibly.

"We talked to Captain Renard last night. He said since they've given up hope of finding the people they're looking for, they've got room for us. We're going to Earth!"

"Earth? He must have been joking, Kel."

"We were afraid maybe he was. He couldn't take us to *Picard* with the other two crew members, the shuttle only holds four. But they've come back for us! He kept his promise!"

"That's not why they returned." *Your dad will explain it to you—to everyone—in a few minutes.*

Dad? But he's still hiding, isn't he?

No, he— Carla broke off. There was no sign of Jesse, and the officers didn't appear to be downcast, as they surely would be if they knew they couldn't leave.

Renard said, "Your husband is a brave man, Ms. Sanders. He surrendered to us for your sake rather than hold out until the force arrives, when you'd be left with nothing. I can assure you that his share of the bounty money will be transferred to you as soon as the League gets a workable government established here."

With difficulty Carla controlled her reaction. That was the story he'd used to explain giving himself up, of course. Evidently he had not had a chance to disable the starship yet; probably he had waited until half the officers had left it. It was a stroke of luck that they'd done so, but why had they?

Mom, what does he mean about Dad? Kel questioned in confusion.

It's a secret, Kel. He needed to get aboard the starship, so he pretended to want the money they offered.

But the starship's going to Earth! You said it would be dangerous for him to go. . . .

On the verge of explaining to him, Carla held back. Kel was inexperienced in shielding his thoughts. He would tell Ivana, surely, and one of them might inadvertently give it away. Since he had not really believed her when she'd told him that Fleet would execute Jesse if he was caught, he wouldn't be unduly worried by his apparent capture. He was, after all, under the impression that Earth was a wonderful place. *Your dad will be okay,* she assured him. *He has a plan.*

"You have children, Ms. Sanders?" asked Mei Luong.

"Yes, two besides Kel here."

"Kel is your son?" Renard was obviously startled. "We didn't know that when we agreed to take him with us, and

I must say I'd have hesitated to choose the child of a wanted criminal. But having met your husband, I'm inclined to think it was a good thing. In view of his sacrifice for his family, he deserves to know his son will receive a fine education."

In shock, Carla burst out, "You were serious? You really meant to take Kel to Earth?"

"Why, yes. He'll receive much better schooling on Earth than can be managed here—I'm sure a scholarship can be arranged. We want to make a start on rectifying what the children have lacked on this world."

Yes, she thought, and before they had Jesse, they'd no doubt felt that living proof of the colony's existence might expedite the paying of the bounty. She wondered if taking the kids along had been their idea or Kel's.

"We have room for only two so we picked those who said they were the oldest," Renard went on. "Your son and this girl, assuming that you and her family allow it."

"Certainly not!" Carla exclaimed.

"Mom!" Kel protested. "We're adults now."

"Hardly that," Renard said, smiling.

"Actually," Carla admitted, swallowing her dismay, "at thirteen they are adults under our law." She made a quick decision to give in gracefully. It would do no harm for them to take a brief trip into space, and perhaps it would get the desire to leave Maclairn out of Kel's system. They'd be back within a few hours. "I can't stop him if he wants to go," she continued, "and I do want him to get a good education, of course."

Kira had joined them, naturally appalled by the telepathic communication she was getting from Ivana. Carla longed to reassure her, but Jesse had told her not to reveal his plan and Peter surely would explain, once he learned that the kids were aboard. *Let Ivana go*, she advised Kira. *Peter will tell you it's all right.* Aloud, for the benefit of the officers, she said, "It's not as if we wouldn't have contact with them once interstellar comm capability's installed here."

Embracing Ivana, Kira said, "I want you to be happy,

darling. I know being with Kel means more to you than anything else now, so I can't hold you back—you'll find things different on Earth and you'll have to wait a few years to be married, but in time you'll have a better life than we could give you here."

"I love you and I'd rather stay with you," Ivana said tearfully, "but I can't let Kel leave without me." And then silently, *Tell Uncle Peter I love him more than I can ever say. I wish I could go tell him myself, but there isn't time. . . .*

Carla hugged Kel, wondering what it would feel like to do so if she were really going to be separated from him. Historically, mothers had often had to say goodbye to their sons, she reflected, though it hadn't happened in a small colony like Undine. She was thankful to be spared that sorrow. As she and Kira stood back from the shuttle and watched it lift, though, she felt sudden apprehension. What if Jesse should fail? That couldn't happen, Peter had said there was no chance of his being taken to prison. . . .

But if something went terribly wrong—if Jesse was caught and the ship did get away, then what Renard had said was true, Carla realized. It would be better for Kel and Ivana to be educated on Earth and become eligible for careers than to live in poverty on the kind of world Maclairn would become if taken over. So whatever happened, she had made the right choice. She would rather lose contact with her son than see him doomed to perpetual mine labor. And Peter, much as he'd suffer from the loss of the short time he'd have with Ivana if the plan failed, would be glad she was assured of a brighter future.

61

PETER'S REACTION, WHEN she and Kira went to tell him about the kids, stunned Carla. To her astonishment she sensed shock and horror in him before, almost instantly, he closed his mind against telepathic probing.

"Kira, things wouldn't be good for Ivana and Kel under an imposed government here," he said slowly, suppressing all sign of feeling. "Be thankful that they've escaped that." Incredibly, he said nothing about Jesse's plan.

Bewildered and hurt by his strange indifference to Ivana's departure, Kira left the room. "I suppose you're right that we shouldn't reveal what's happening until Jesse's back," Carla said, "but in Kira's case it seems cruel. She thinks she's lost her daughter—and we could trust her not to spread it any further, after all."

"Carla." Peter beckoned and she went to him, stood close enough for him to reach her hand. "Oh, God, Carla—Jesse wasn't expecting them to take passengers along! It's made things far worse than you know."

"But they'll be gone only a little while. You said you don't think the ship will go to Earth—"

"Jesse didn't tell you his whole plan," Peter said painfully, "and now I've got to. There was never any chance that he could disable the hyperdrive."

"There wasn't?" Confused, terrified by his surge of emotion, she clutched his fingers.

"Of course not. Just think—he'd have to do it under the eyes of four armed officers who know he doesn't want the ship to jump! And it wouldn't be a quick process. He'd have to dismantle a control panel to get to the wiring underneath. It was a fantasy he concocted for our sake, though he was trying to believe it might be possible."

"Then *why*, Peter—why did he surrender to them if he can't save us by it?"

"He believes he *can* save us. He's planning to destroy the ship."

"Destroy it? Shoot it down, you mean? How can he—he'd need to be in our own shuttle, which can't fly now and isn't even armed."

"I don't mean shoot it down. He took explosives from the mine with him, Carla."

Her knees weakened and she sank onto the mattress

beside his chair. "Oh, my God. He knew he's not coming back. That's why he wouldn't let me near him—I'd have sensed it."

"He didn't want you to find out until afterward," Peter went on. "I offered to go in his place, but he wouldn't hear of it. If I weren't stuck in this chair, if I could have gotten hold of the bomb makings and turned myself in before he did, I'd have forestalled him. Why should I live a long life handicapped, when Jesse, who's whole and strong, could serve the colony better?"

You're our focus, Carla responded, *and the Group couldn't do without you. Jesse knew that, and besides, he cares too much about you to let you die in his place. But to have lost him without even a chance to say goodbye . . .*

"You'll lose us both if that ship gets away from here," Peter reminded her. "Jesse said that if he didn't act, he'd be paying too high a price for less than half a year of life in prison. And that's true. He had nothing to gain by waiting to be executed; he'd be happier dying quickly in the belief that he'd bought our freedom. But now, of course, the situation's changed."

Carla's heart lurched; the blood drained from her face as she was jerked back to the immediate crisis. "Oh God, Peter! Kel and Ivana—"

"He may have acted while part of the crew was away; I hope to God he has."

"I would have sensed it if—if he'd died . . . when it happened, I mean."

"Yes, with the starship no farther away than low orbit, I think you would. And the shuttle crew would have known as soon as they were in space that it was gone; they'd be back here by now. So it hasn't happened yet."

"He *wouldn't* do it if the kids are on board!'

"Of course not. Not if he's aware that they are."

"You mean he might not be?" She was faint, stricken by a stronger surge of fear than she had ever felt.

"He'll be locked into a cabin. It's unlikely that their presence would be concealed from him on a ship as small as that . . . but we can't be sure."

Peter . . . my God, Peter, we won't know whether or not they're safe, not until a lot of time has passed.

If Fleet comes to take over here, we'll be told that they are. Otherwise . . .

Otherwise Peter would survive with the knowledge that his life had been bought with Ivana's; she thought he would rather die. And she would know that it had been bought with Kel's. . . .

"Either way, there'll be tragedy that shouldn't have happened," Peter declared. "If Jesse does find out about the kids, then they've brought about the colony's destruction—there was an absolutely sure way of preventing that, you see, and now he won't be able to use it."

"I let them go," Carla moaned. "I'm to blame! None of this was their fault, they couldn't have guessed."

"You couldn't have guessed either. Like everything else that's confronted us, it was no one's fault. And in any case, if you'd held Kel and Ivana back, Renard would have taken someone else."

She knelt beside his chair and rested her head in his lap, aching at the knowledge that if the bomb wasn't used, within a few weeks he too would be taken from her.

"There's no solution," Peter said. "Unless . . . unless Jesse acts now, before the shuttle gets there."

"He—he still may," Carla reflected. "He wouldn't want more crew members than necessary to die."

"But since he hasn't done it yet, he may be waiting until shortly before the jump, just in case a chance to damage the hyperdrive does turn up. He may even intend to wait till after the jump when there's no longer anything to hope for."

Carla buried her face in her hands, not wanting Peter to see her tears. She couldn't regret Jesse's decision. He would not be Jesse if he'd backed away from it. And it was true enough that he was going to die anyway, one way or the other. If he couldn't disable the ship there was no conceivable escape from that.

"Carla," Peter said. "I was thinking, sitting here after he left me, that perhaps it was fated from the beginning. He came to us on Undine from space, suddenly in our time of need, by such an unlikely chance—"

"Synchronicity, you called it."

"Yes. He arrived when we needed him, and pulled us through . . . made possible something that could never have been achieved without him. Because of him, we made a leap in human evolution that could only have been made on a new world. And now that we're established, when except for the bounty hunters, there'd be no danger of the colony folding . . . for him to go back into space, to die there, could be part of the pattern. As if he were only lent to us, to enable us to fulfill our destiny."

"You're suggesting something beyond mere fate, Peter."

"I suppose I am. Jesse has human failings. He's always undervalued himself, even while he was fulfilling every expectation we ever had of him. But Ian, the wisest man who's been seen in a very long time, trusted him. He emphasized that he trusted him *in all things*. And perhaps this was what he meant; perhaps he had still another premonition besides those we know about. His last act before he gave his life for us was to make telepathic contact with Jesse. It may be that he knew even then that Jesse would someday follow in his footsteps."

"But as you've always told us, precognition isn't predestination," Carla protested. "Now if Jesse doesn't act in the next few minutes he'll die horribly on Earth's moon, while you're put to death on Undine and the rest of us become little better than slaves. Even Kel and Ivana will suffer, compared to what he thought he could gain for them! They'll be miserable on Earth—the authorities won't let them live together at thirteen, they'll forbid them to even see each other if they suspect they've been having sex, and the kids are too naive to conceal it. . . ."

For a long time Peter said nothing, seeming detached and far away. Then he said, "Carla, I wouldn't have burdened you with this knowledge without a reason. If Fleet does return here, you would never have had to learn that we might have been saved, and if it doesn't, I could have let you assume the ship was lost in a miscalculated jump. But there is a chance—a small chance—that you and I can undo the damage."

She looked up at his face through a blur of tears. "Undo it? How?"

"The last night on Undine, you and I together reached Jesse telepathically over a very long distance. A longer distance than was theoretically possible, longer even than the distance between here and the salt flat from which you contacted me a few years ago. It happened only because of our extremity. Conceivably, in urgent circumstances, it might be done again."

"You were drugged at the time, Peter."

"You weren't. And I was in a state that I've since learned to reach through volition."

"Aren't distances in space much greater?"

"Yes, but the explorer ship is still in low orbit. When it's over us, that's no further than the distance from the Island to the city; it's merely straight up."

"But how would we know when it's over us?"

"I've just seen it by remote viewing," he told her. "It will be overhead a few minutes from now, before the shuttle has had time to reach it, which almost seems like another case of synchronicity."

"Then . . . we could contact Jesse. Let him know Kel and Ivana are coming."

"Possibly. But have you the courage for this, Carla? The courage to project thoughts that will cause him to blow himself up right away? You can't fake it, you know—even more than ordinary telepathy, such a long-range communication will have to be emotionally genuine."

She bowed her head. Finally, when she knew it could be

put off no longer, she whispered, "We can't take the chance that he won't be told that the kids are aboard. Besides, I don't want you to die, Peter . . . and I don't want Jesse to die by execution. It will be better, even for him, if it happens now."

62

ABOARD *PICARD*, JESSE pressed his face close to the small viewport of the cabin in which he was confined, peering out at the golden surface of Maclairn. It had been a good world, in the end. He'd have liked to be buried there. But he knew he was never going back to it.

He had not really thought there'd be a chance to disable the starship's hyperdrive. He had pretended to himself that there was, mainly for Carla's sake and Peter's—but underneath, he knew better. The crew was well aware that he would have everything to gain by preventing the ship from jumping; they'd be fools to allow him near the bridge. Even if they did, he would have to be there when only one of them was present and would have to knock that officer out before he, or she, had a chance to yell for help. Vid heroes did such things. Men like himself, long past youth and unaccustomed to fighting, did not. And it would take time to damage the hyperdrive controls past the possibility of repair. Supposing that he managed to land a blow that silenced the officer, the others would appear anyway before he finished the job.

No, it wasn't going to happen. So he had no choice but to blow up the ship. If he failed, he'd be taken to Fleet Headquarters and in due course executed. Either way, he had seen the last of Maclairn and the people he loved.

The crew's offer to split the bounty had been a break. The one problem in the plan had been that if he simply turned himself in after having been declared dead, they would suspect a trick—might even suspect that Peter was not dead either, and stay on the surface until both of them were in custody. Unsure that his scheme would prove workable, he'd been unable to try it the first night. Today, before dawn, he had simply wakened Renard and claimed the money for his wife. Since it was reasonable to suppose that a man who expected to be caught eventually might give himself up to spare his family from lifelong poverty, the officers had not questioned his motive. He didn't know whether they'd ever intended to keep the bargain; there was no way they could be held to it. But that question was now moot.

The necessity of killing the explorer crew had bothered him. They believed him to be a criminal and could hardly be blamed for their desire to collect the bounty money. They didn't deserve to die, and it wasn't in his nature to view murder as justifiable. But when he balanced their lives against Peter's, there was no question in his mind about what course he'd take. He would gladly kill to save him, Jesse thought grimly, even if it were not for the larger issue of preserving Maclairn's freedom.

And then he'd thought, would he really have to kill the crew? He was locked in a small cabin. Either they had it under video surveillance, or they didn't; if they did, it would be impossible to fashion a bomb. But if they weren't watching, he could rig it so that it would go off if the compartment's hatch was opened. He could then warn them, give them a chance to board the shuttle and get away. Surely they'd choose to save their lives when nothing could be gained by sacrificing them—but if they refused, their deaths would be on their own heads.

Right now, though, the shuttle wasn't available. He had seen it leave shortly after he boarded—evidently two of them had gone back to make one last attempt to find Edris. He would have used the explosives then, killing only the remaining two, if the way to spare them all hadn't occurred to him. Would they stay for days, leaving him here wondering how many hours of life were left to him? If they didn't come back soon he would have to act; he couldn't risk having someone enter to bring him a meal. So he would build the bomb now, and arm it. But before detonating it he would wait as long as he could for the shuttle's return.

Jesse took a deep breath, committing himself to the danger of revealing, to any spy camera there might be, what he carried beneath his shirt. Unbuttoning it, he detached wire and explosives from his body. The use of them was familiar to him from past work in the mine with Dan; he set to work wiring a charge to be detonated either manually or, if the hatch seal was broken, instantly. On second thought he decided to include a dead-man mechanism that would set off the explosion if he lost consciousness. Conceivably, if the crew was warned, they could evacuate the air from this compartment and jump without attempting to open it.

His hands did not shake. Yet felt himself grow dizzy; the walls of the compartment seemed suddenly flat, unreal, like a mere projected image. In his mind he heard voices calling, *Jesse . . . Jesse . . .* There was a hum in his ears like the motor of a seaplane, and he was swept back across the years to that night on Undine when Carla and Peter had been stranded . . . he was there again, alone in the plane above the dark sea, knowing he must not turn toward the Island, yet unable to ignore their call. *Jesse . . . oh, please, Jesse . . .*

Carla? Her voice was more than memory! *Carla, don't! I love you so much . . . but I have to do this. Don't make it harder than it already is. . . .* Peter must have told her the truth. How had she forced him to? Had she guessed it all along?

You don't understand! I know what you have to do. That's what I'm telling you . . . I love you, I'll always love you, but we don't have any more time . . . Kel and Ivana. . . .

She was saying goodbye, then. She was forgiving him for avoiding her the past two days, for leaving her without so much as a kiss, and reminding him that Kel loved him, too.

No more time? The ship would not be over the settlement long; only for moments would the distance to the surface be short enough for communication. Already the contact was fading, yet he sensed Peter, too, calling *Jesse! Jesse! Do it now, you won't have another chance. . . .*

Did they believe his nerve would fail if he waited? *Don't worry, I'll do it when the shuttle gets here . . . the crew can escape in the shuttle—*

No! No! Don't wait for the shuttle! Don't . . . Their voices receded. They were now too far away for him to grasp the concept they were trying to convey to him.

Carla . . . I love you . . . in my last instant of life I'll see your face. . . . Deeply shaken, he completed the wiring by force of will and then lay back on the bunk. Time passed. Perhaps, Jesse thought, his nerve *would* fail. It might have been better not to wait for the shuttle—for some reason he now felt this quite strongly. No matter, because the ship shuddered and he realized that the shuttle had docked.

This was the end, then. You lived year after year—fifty-six for him now—and faced all sorts of dangers, still the thought of the end was a mere abstraction . . . and then, all at once, it became real. Resignedly, Jesse rose and got a firm grip on the detonator, activating the dead-man contacts as he did so. Then with his other hand he banged on the wall, calling out, "Renard! Come where you can hear me. We need to talk."

Footsteps approached, loud on the metal decking of the ship. "Don't touch the hatch," Jesse added quickly. "I've got a bomb in here that will detonate if you do."

"A bomb? What are you talking about?" Renard was clearly unconvinced.

"I'm saying this ship isn't going to leave the solar system. We're not going to let Fleet take over our world. We've achieved too much there to give it up."

"Don't be ridiculous, Sanders. You can't keep us here by threatening us with an imaginary bomb."

"Of course not. The only way I can keep you from jumping

is by setting it off. If you want to survive, get your crew into the shuttle and move out of range."

There was a pause, more footsteps, and faint voices Jesse could not make out. Then Renard said, "Stand back. We don't buy your talk about a bomb, and we're coming in."

"That's your privilege," Jesse replied. "It won't matter to me whether you do or not, except that I'd prefer not to kill you along with myself."

"God," said one of the female officers, "a suicide bomber! It's possible. They've got mining explosives down there."

"Your file says you were a mental case," Renard said, "and maybe you still are. But you're not going to blow up the ship, Sanders."

"Yes, I am. If you don't think so, come on in—you won't live long enough to be surprised."

"I don't think he's insane, Alan," the other woman said softly. "Not if they're serious about not wanting their world taken over by the League. And I don't think it's a bluff, either—you've said yourself that he's a brave man."

"That's true. So we were damned lucky when we chose our passengers." Renard raised his voice. "You won't blow up the ship," he repeated. "Not while your son Kel is aboard."

Startled, Jesse hesitated. Kel? That was a creative ploy, quite a smart one. He'd hadn't known they were aware that he had a son named Kel. But someone might have mentioned that Carla did, and this morning he'd convinced them that his family was important to him. "You can't fool me with a story like that," he declared. "What would my son be doing here, when you aim to jump?"

"Speak to your dad, boy," said the first woman. And then the bottom dropped out for Jesse, as he heard Kel say, "Dad! Dad, what do you mean, a bomb?"

"Oh, my God. Kel." Weak-kneed, Jesse clutched the detonator in his hand, staring at it in horror. If his fingers had loosened on it, the bomb would have gone off. He would have killed Kel. Carla knew; that was how she'd been able to reach him across such a vast distance, why she and Peter had wanted him to act before the shuttle docked. She'd tried to convey something about Kel, but he'd misinterpreted the message.

"Why, Renard, why? Are you taking hostages now, or what?" Surely Renard couldn't have guessed that he'd need one to protect his ship. "Did you think you could get me to tell you where Edris is by kidnapping him? I'm not gullible enough to think you'd harm an innocent boy."

"It's nothing like that, Dad," Kel said. "We're going to Earth! They had room for us so they let us come. You know how much we want to see Earth."

"We?" Even as he questioned, he knew the answer. Kel would not have agreed to be separated from Ivana for long, certainly not for a lifetime.

"You don't know what you've done," he said despairingly. Of course they didn't. They had been shielded from the reality of what would happen on Maclairn—and naturally they'd had no idea how he'd planned to prevent it. Now it could not be prevented. Peter's death could not be prevented. How could Ivana live with herself when she found out about Peter?

Numbly, Jesse disarmed the detonator and dismantled the wiring. Without it the explosives were harmless; he didn't bother to move them. "Okay, Renard," he conceded. "You can come in now and take the stuff away."

63

THEY TOOK THE explosives from him and gave him food, but did not let him out of the cabin. Kel and Ivana were quartered elsewhere, presumably in a similar one—Jesse realized that because explorer ships had only four cabins, the officers must have doubled up. No doubt it had been planned for him to share one with Peter, while Edris was given privacy; now they'd evidently put the kids in together. Probably they saw no harm in it. They would be appalled if they knew the elders of Maclairn encouraged sex between thir-teen-year-olds.

How long before the ship jumped? Jesse wondered. Not that it mattered. Locked up as he was, he could not even think about disabling it.

Dad? Kel called to him. The cabins were separated only by thin walls; it would be easy to converse. *Dad, were you really going to blow up this ship?*

Yes, Kel. It would have been best. They will kill me any-way soon after we get where we're going.

No! I can't believe they would! Mom said so, but she was just trying to keep me from wanting to talk to Captain Renard.

That's not true. I'm guilty of the crime I'm charged with. They have a right to execute me, and they'll do it. He de-cided not to mention that it would also be done to Peter. There was still a chance the kids might inadvertently men-tion Peter to the crew—and in any case, knowing the truth would hurt Ivana too much.

But you can escape! Mom told me you had a plan. . . .

She didn't know that my real plan was to destroy the ship, which I can't do now that you've defied her and snuck aboard.

I didn't sneak. She let me go.

Your mom let you board the shuttle? Carla wouldn't have . . . unless at the time, she'd been sure he could disable *Picard*'s hyperdrive and bring them back. She must have told Kira that he could, if Ivana too had departed openly. Obviously, they had not consulted Peter.

We told her we're adults and we were going to make up our own minds. But she didn't argue long. The Captain said the school they'll send us to on Earth will be better than the one at home.

There was some truth in that. There would indeed be more opportunities open to the kids on Earth than on Maclairn as it would be in the future. But they'd come at a price, and he doubted that even Kel's fascination with Earth would make him willing to pay it. His attachment to Ivana had shown every sign of being a lasting one.

What was the plan Mom thought you had? Kel asked.

She thought I could just damage this ship, fix it so it couldn't leave our solar system and would have to go back to Maclairn. But I won't be able to do that.

Then why did Mom believe you can?

Because I lied to her. I didn't want her to know I was planning to die.

Dad . . . if you could keep the ship from jumping, would it save your life?

Yes. It would save a lot more than my life, much more than you understand. How could he explain to Kel what it would mean for Maclairn to lose its independence? The boy had no comprehension of what societies elsewhere were like. Moreover, though the kids had been told that people on other worlds didn't use telepathy, the fact that psi talent was viewed as mental instability there had not been emphasized. We wanted them to view it as totally natural, he thought ruefully. We assumed the detailed study of history could come later, after psi capability had become an integral part of their thinking.

Now, he realized, he had to prepare them, especially with regard to Ivana's emerging psychokinetic powers. He must make sure they knew how vital it was to conceal their true abilities. Otherwise, on Earth they'd be likely to end up in a mental institution, or at best, be drugged—not as drastically as he had been on Undine, but nevertheless in a way that would ultimately destroy them.

Kel, he began, *we've got to talk about something important. I know you don't always listen to what I tell you, but in this case you need to, so you can pass it on to Ivana. She will be in danger on Earth, even more than you will, if she doesn't know how to protect herself.* This would get Kel's attention better than anything else would, he felt.

Okay, Dad. But why don't you just tell both of us?

Directly? It's too complicated for that—you could both

pick up vague ideas from my mind at the same time, but this has to be focused like conversation.

Ivana can converse with me and her mom and Uncle Peter together.

Well, Peter has a lot more psi talent than I do.

But she has just as much. He said so, he taught her. He said she could teach the little kids to do it.

This was news to Jesse. *Ivana?* he queried. *Are you there? Can you hear me in your mind when I communicate with Kel?*

Yes, Uncle Jesse. I heard everything you told him.

Thank God. If she could get the details along with his emotions about them, both she and Kel would be far more likely to take them seriously. *You'll be in danger on Earth,* he repeated. *It's not the kind of world you think it is. I know. After all, when I was your age I lived there. . . .*

Half an hour later, he felt that they had absorbed it. They were, of course, stunned. The idea of hiding their mind powers was foreign to them. That they could not even heal their own cuts and bruises was beyond their comprehension. That they must pretend to suffer pain when appropriate struck them as crazy. But most of all, they were dismayed at the prospect of concealing their love for each other.

On Earth, thirteen is too young, Jesse told them sadly. *It's against the law there for you to be lovers.*

Mom said we'd have to wait to be married, Ivana recalled. *She didn't say we couldn't be together at all.*

She didn't explain that? Kira, Jesse realized, had not been to Earth and might never have studied the details of its restrictions on minors; on Undine, where contagious disease didn't exist and permanent contraceptives were required for everyone, surreptitious sex was viewed more liberally. And anyway, she'd undoubtedly believed the kids weren't really going to be taken away.

She didn't have time to say much, the ship had to leave, Kel pointed out.

Well, on Earth you can't make love. They'll not only sepa-

rate you if they find out—they will punish you, send you to a school for delinquents. So you can't risk it. I know it's hard, but you must wait until you're older.

We can pretend to be older, declared Kel.

No, you can't. The date we left Undine is known to the authorities, and you couldn't have been conceived any earlier than that.

There was a painful pause. And then, innocently, Ivana asked, *But Uncle Jesse, they'll know we've had sex when the baby comes, won't they?*

Oh, my God! Oh God, Ivana, you're not already pregnant, are you?

She is, Kel responded. *We just found out a couple of days ago, we haven't told anybody else yet. We thought you and Mom would be happy for us. We've named him Sanders, after you. We're going to call him Sandy.*

But Ivana, Jesse protested, *if you haven't told your mom or some other healer, how can you be sure?* Kira wouldn't have let her go for even a short space trip, if she'd known. . . .

Ivana's a healer herself, Kel pointed out. *She knows.*

It would be pointless to ask how they'd thought they could care for a baby while in school on Earth. At home, women worked and studied with infants on cradleboards, pausing to nurse them with bare breasts, and no one gave it a second thought. The kids knew nothing of organized schools. But far, far more serious was what they did not know of Earth's laws.

Only a few minutes ago Jesse had thought things could not get any worse. He'd been resigned to the grim future ahead of him. Now he did not see how he could face the pain of telling his son and new daughter the truth . . . and yet he had to. He had to warn them.

Kel, Ivana, he began, *as I told you, it's illegal on Earth for you to be lovers at your age. It's illegal for you to have a baby, too. In fact it's illegal even for adults to have a baby if they don't have a permit from the government. Earth is overpopulated, you see—*

They did not see. *They can't stop us, now that I already have one,* Ivana said.

But they can. Oh, Ivana, they can. They won't let you keep the baby.

You mean they'll send it to a crèche, the way Mom said happened on Undine? Kel asked. *She said kids couldn't live with their parents except during offshifts—*

That's not what I mean, Jesse replied miserably. *I mean they won't let it be born.*

But it will be, whether they want it or not, protested Ivana. Having been raised in a colony where babies were needed, where contraception didn't exist and all the young women she knew were perpetually pregnant or nursing, how could she conceive of any alternative? How could he possibly explain abortion to a girl who been taught that the telepathic bond between mother and child was formed in the womb?

There was no way except the direct way. *They will kill the baby before it's born, Ivana,* he admitted, bracing himself for her shock and Kel's.

The emotional force of their reaction nearly swamped him. *They couldn't!* Kel burst out. *They're different from us, but they're not murderers.*

It isn't murder in their eyes—not unless the baby is much older than yours. It is just a medical procedure. Unthinkable though abortion would be on Maclairn, the Group did not believe it was morally wrong when done early, before the fetus had developed a brain. But it would be past that stage before it was discovered, and in any case, forcible abortion would be a horror past contemplation. Forced medical treatment was what they'd left Undine to get away from. For Ivana, given her upbringing, it would be doubly devastating. It would scar her in a way from which she could never recover.

I can't let them do that! Ivana insisted.

No. You have to escape. Somehow you have to get away from the school. There was a chance, a slim chance, that she could evade arrest. Possibly she could find a church that would take her in. But she'd be required to give the baby up for adoption, and she'd be permanently separated from Kel. . . .

No, she won't, Kel declared. *I'll go with her. We'll stay together, always.*

Oh, Kel— Jesse could not argue. Kel would no more desert Ivana than he himself would desert Carla. He might seem like an irresponsible kid sometimes, but underneath, he was not a person to take his commitments lightly, even apart from the fact that he was in love.

But if they ran away together, they would have to hide. Forever. Without identification or formal education, they could never get work on Earth, even after they turned eighteen. They would become street people. Earth was teeming with the homeless, the destitute, surviving on what they could scrounge or steal, victims of crime lords who forced them into thievery or worse, too often into prostitution. . . .

It might have been better if he'd blown up the ship.

He didn't really believe that. But he had thought he could face execution bravely, knowing the son he loved would outlive him, knowing he and Ivana would be trained for good jobs and might someday find a way to use the mind powers they'd been given. How could he endure prison, aware that if not drugged or institutionalized, they were living in squalor on Earth's streets?

He wondered what Ian would say. He'd often been told that Ian believed in relying on courage. The memory of that had sustained Peter, would continue to sustain him through the grueling prelude to his own execution. But Peter would die without ever having to know how bad things were going to be for the foster daughter who'd shown such promise. . . .

Uncle Peter? Is he going to die, too?

Oh, God, thought Jesse. His telepathic control was slipping, and Ivana was extraordinarily sensitive; she was perceiving what he hadn't intended to let her know.

It was too late to shield his mind from her; they were

both in too emotional a state for that. He could not keep her from drawing on his knowledge of what awaited Peter. And Ivana was intelligent enough to realize that if she and Kel hadn't boarded the ship, neither Peter nor her baby would be in danger.

Silently, she began to weep; he could sense it even though he could not see. Ivana might be a psi prodigy, but she was still adolescent, with all the turbulent feelings of adolescence, and she hadn't yet had enough mind training to cope with them. Jesse sensed her agonized groping for some way to undo what could not be undone, and he knew she was on the verge of hysteria.

Dad, Kel cried silently, *I never meant to break my promise!*

What promise? Kel had never made any agreement not to try to get to Earth; his wish to go there had been viewed as mere fantasy.

In the Ritual. We pledged to support each other, all the members of the Group. And now they're going to lose everything because of me, and Uncle Peter's going to die, and Ivana's never going to forgive herself for that, or for what happens to the baby. . . .

It's not your fault, son, Jesse lied. *You couldn't have foreseen it, so you haven't broken the pledge.* We didn't educate our kids well enough, he thought miserably. We taught them to manage physical pain, to preserve their physical health—but we never imagined their having any contact with outside society. The isolation of Maclairn wasn't supposed to end in their lifetime. Yet it was wrong, perhaps, to shield them from knowledge of how life is in the rest of the universe.

I talked Ivana into coming, Kel persisted. *She didn't really want to leave home after she found out she's pregnant, and I told her we could have so much more on Earth—*

We all feel to blame for what's past, sometimes. You can't look back, only forward to what has to be done in the future. He himself had learned this the hard way, Jesse thought ruefully. He'd hoped Kel would not have to learn so young.

Now they could not look forward. He would die horribly on Earth's moon; Peter would die in stasis on Undine after medical procedures that did not bear thinking about; Carla and Kira would live out their lives grieving on a tightly-regimented Maclairn. The kids would struggle futilely to exist under the worst possible conditions on Earth. And his grandchild—his namesake, the first of a third generation—would be born into poverty far from Maclairn, undocumented, a fugitive from the law who would never be eligible for citizenship. There was no way out for any of them.

Feeling the ship vibrate, he turned again to the window. They had broken out of orbit. Maclairn was receding, shrinking into a small bright globe overshadowed by the vast black universe that surrounded it. He remembered how he had first seen it, not in reality—for he'd been in stasis as they approached—but in the dream through which Ian had shown it to him, and later in the online images from which he and Peter had chosen their destination. A golden world studded with sapphire seas. A world full of promise . . . a world where mind powers could flourish. That bright vision, too, would soon be enveloped by darkness. Perhaps it was just as well that neither of them would be around to watch.

64

AFTER A TIME Jesse became aware that Kel was urgently calling him. *Dad! Something's wrong with Ivana—she just sits here, staring! She's shut me out of her mind—*

Then take her in your arms, Kel. She needs your support, your love. Love was all that was left to them, Jesse thought despairingly. It was the only thing that could possibly sustain them.

I've tried. She pulls away from me. I can't wake her up.

Oh, God. Even as a small child she'd sometimes seemed

dreamy and far away. Did her exceptional psi talent mean she was prone to escape into some other place, as Claire had?

This could not be allowed to happen. Ivana must stay in touch with the real world if she was to have any chance of escaping when she arrived on Earth. Moreover, if she appeared to be abnormally withdrawn, they would send her to a mental hospital. If the crew reported seeing her in an unresponsive state, she might be sent for psychiatric evaluation anyway.

There would be days on the ship after it jumped, while it traversed Earth's solar system in normal space. Somehow they would have to get through those days. He would have to advise them, give them all the information he could about how to escape and how to find abortion opponents who would hide Ivana when her pregnancy began to show. How to survive on the street, when it came to that . . . though he himself had no street smarts.

He could not let her retreat from what they were facing. *Ivana?* he probed. *Ivana, we need to know you're okay.*

She did not answer. Yet perhaps she was simply rejecting contact on purpose; Kel might not be capable of judging. If only he could see her himself. . . .

He could see telepathically through Carla's eyes—always during sex, but occasionally at a distance if he went into altered consciousness. But it was possible only because they were closely attuned through long experience. He was not that close to Kel. And even if he were, when in full enough rapport with Kel to see through his eyes, he would have no hope of communicating with Ivana. He hadn't enough psi ability to do both at the same time.

If she's sick, we've got to make them take us back! Kel burst out.

Back? Back to Maclairn? They won't— Jesse cut off the thought. Of course the crew would not turn the ship around because two adolescent kids had changed their minds about wanting to go to Earth. But hope of persuading them might rouse Ivana from the frozen and perhaps dangerous state into which she had fallen.

Are you locked in, Kel? he asked.

No. They just told us to stay here while they're busy. They've been nice to us, they said we could visit the bridge after the ship jumps.

After it jumps it can't go back, Jesse pointed out.

Dad . . . you said the ship could be disabled so it couldn't jump—

No. I said it can't. Even if I could get out of here, I couldn't fight four officers and win.

Would it be hard to disable if the crew weren't watching you?

No, Jesse told him. *It would be simple, but it would take time.* Useless as it was to speculate on this topic, it might distract Kel long enough to steady him for another try at contacting Ivana.

How would you do it?

There's a control panel on the bridge. I'd have to dismantle it and rip out the wires and ICs underneath, destroy them so they couldn't be repaired.

Dad, Kel suggested, *maybe I can rip them out. I could hit one officer over the head if Ivana could distract the others to keep them out of the bridge—*

No, Kel! Jesse burst out in alarm. Kel had inherited his own propensity for acting fast, without worrying over the consequences ahead of time. And he had demonstrated his willingness to take risks for Ivana's sake. . . .

Would it do any harm to try?

It would do a lot of harm! You'd fail, and be treated as a criminal. You'd lose your chance to help Ivana escape.

Kel didn't reply. *Your first idea was better,* Jesse told him. This was true enough, even though neither idea would work. *If we can wake Ivana she might be able to talk the crew into taking you back to Maclairn. But we haven't much time.*

She's awfully pale— Kel's desperation was overwhelming; it was getting hard to maintain silent conversation. If the boy gave way to emotion, Jesse realized, there would be no way of knowing what was happening. He felt trapped, impotent, imprisoned in this cramped cabin with no way even to see the kids. . . .

No way? He shrank from the thought that was pushing up into his awareness. Peter and some of the others could see through walls without a telepathic link, not vaguely as they did in remote viewing, but because they somehow left their bodies. The mere thought of this had always frightened him. Yes, when going into stasis he and Carla and met briefly beyond the coffin-like units in which they were confined. And three more times after that he'd experienced such a state—while fasting, when in terror he'd looked down at himself; again while experiencing anoxia; and finally, while ill with the virus, in actual contact with Peter. Still the idea of separating from his body deliberately was repugnant to him. What if he couldn't return to it? For thousands of years, Peter had said, people on Earth—even people without psi talent—had been having out-of-body experiences, frequently by choice. It wasn't a thing he wanted to choose.

Yet he could do nothing for Ivana without knowing more than he could learn from behind a wall. And what the hell, he thought, he was living on borrowed time—he had been, ever since he'd disarmed the bomb. If he couldn't be of any use where he was, what did it matter whether he got back to his body or stayed out of it? What difference did it make whether or not he could control his mind under strange new conditions? He had no future to worry about. He had only these few days to either help the kids, or know they had no tolerable future either.

Such a shift would demand altered consciousness, he knew. He lay back on the bunk and relaxed his body totally, shutting out his senses, and let himself drift. No doubt it would work like all the other mind skills—he must not fight the fear he felt, but instead welcome it . . . that was the only way to stave off panic. He must not try to maintain control by force of will. . . . He recalled what Peter had told him long ago: *Willpower is counterproductive. In order to gain true volitional control, you must be wholly, unreservedly willing to lose control—to let what comes, come, with full consent to the consequences.*

Ivana . . . he focused on her, deliberately visualizing how she must look, head bent, long blonde hair half-covering her face. . . . That was how they did it for rainmaking, they visualized the clouds they wanted to see, and found themselves there, seeing them. . . . There was a loud buzzing in his ears, an overwhelming sound. Feeling himself sinking, he tried to rise, but his muscles were paralyzed. *Don't struggle*, he told himself. *Just let this happen. . . .* In the next moment he lost awareness of the compartment around him, and the walls dissolved. He saw Kel and Ivana as if there were no wall, but only fog, between them.

Ivana sat motionless on a bunk identical to his own. She didn't appear to be sick. Her head was not bowed but raised, with her eyes open wide, gazing into the distance as if she too had shut out awareness of her surroundings— which perhaps she had. Kel sat next to her, pressing close, but it was obvious that she shrank from his touch.

Ivana? Jesse probed. *Ivana, let me help you. . . .*

There was no response from her. But Kel called out, *Dad? You're seeing Ivana, I can sense it! What's wrong with her?*

I think she's just withdrawn, Kel, withdrawn because she's scared and already grieving. It happens to people sometimes.

Suddenly a cup lurched from the shelf next to the bunk, hovered in the air for a moment, then crashed to the floor. A moment later a hairbrush followed it.

Kel whitened. *She did that! She's moving things with her mind without knowing she's doing it. . . .*

With effort, Jesse remained calm. To let dismay overcome him would break the trance, and at all costs he must stay in touch with the kids, stay where he could see what was going on. *It's happened before,* he reminded Kel. *It won't do Ivana any harm.* Privately, he wondered. Ivana was under a different form of stress than when she had given the stone to Peter, and according to what he'd said earlier, unconscious poltergeist activity was especially likely to occur in adolescent girls. What if it kept on happening? The authorities on Earth would surely hospitalize her, either to pretend she didn't exist or to treat her like a lab specimen. . . .

If Uncle Peter were here, could he bring her out of the state she's in?

Yes. He's done it for other people, he knows how. Jesse did not know how. He hadn't had enough previous mind-to-mind contact with Ivana to get through to her. Kel was the only one who could reach her, he realized. They'd had sex, which meant they had experienced the mind-merge that sexual union produced in telepaths. When accompanied by love and commitment, that bond was indissoluble. Yet Kel hadn't yet had much neurofeedback training, and couldn't intentionally get into the state of consciousness needed to break through her barriers.

Could he himself draw Kel into that state? It might be possible. He'd had telepathic contact with his son since babyhood, though the boy had rebelled against that contact when he reached adolescence—they too were psychically bonded. *Kel,* he pleaded silently, *try to see what I'm seeing, a pattern of colors, like with the feedback machine. . . .* He visualized a mind-pattern he'd been taught in the lab, which in itself would mean nothing to Kel, yet might enable him to share the state of consciousness that accompanied it.

I see it, Dad . . . it's as if I'm falling into the lights . . . what does it mean?

I hope it means you can show it to Ivana. If you can, maybe she'll hear what you tell her. Tell her you need her—tell her she might be able to persuade the crew to go back. . . .

The colored lights of the visualization swirled around Jesse and he heard Kel call repeatedly to Ivana—and then, with relief, he heard her answer. *Kel? Kel? I want to go home! Tell me we can go home and have our baby!*

Only if you wake up, Kel insisted. *Only if you can help me talk the crew into taking us back....*

After a long pause, Ivana stirred and said aloud, "What ... happened? Where was I? There were flickering lights and I couldn't see, but you were there, and Uncle Jesse—"

Though she spoke softly, Jesse heard her voice. With some astonishment, he became aware as his vision cleared that he was now, in terms of perception, in their cabin rather than his own. It was as if he were standing next to them, though he felt no physical contact with the floor. They could not see him, of course, nor could they hear if he spoke; and at the moment they were too absorbed in each other to notice in any case. It was good for them to be in each other's arms, but on the other hand, Ivana needed to take action in the real world if she was to shake herself back to normal. *Take her out of here, Kel,* he urged. *Go find Captain Renard.*

65

WHEN THEY LEFT the cabin, Jesse stayed beside them. It was uncanny, as if he were passing without sensation through the ship's bulkheads. To his surprise he felt no fear, but only a new sense of total, unrestricted freedom. With a part of his mind he wondered if death was going to be like this. He would find out soon, he supposed. But for the present what mattered was that he keep on knowing what was happening to the kids, be present to support them when, as was inevitable, Renard refused to change course.

The officers on deck were cordial but preoccupied. "We have to see the Captain," Kel announced. Jesse, knowing that if the reason for this request was revealed it would be dismissed in short order, had warned him not to say why.

"Sure, in a while," one of the women told them. "He's busy—he's on the bridge."

Abruptly Ivana came alive. "The bridge? Oh please, we have to see him now!"

"Sorry, but he's getting ready to jump."

Intensely, Ivana pleaded, *Uncle Jesse, can you hear me? Tell me how to get there! I can't let him jump, I can't. . . .*

He had perhaps raised her hopes too much, Jesse thought; she would be crushed when they came to nothing. But that she was showing initiative was too good a sign to discourage. Though he had never served aboard an explorer, he remembered the layout from his long-ago Fleet training. Silently he directed Kel and Ivana through the ship, following invisibly as they made their way to the bridge, the hatch of which stood open.

Renard looked up, startled, as the woman officer, right behind, said, "Sorry—they just took off, made a beeline for here, I don't know how they knew—"

"It's okay," said Renard. "The programming's done and there's time to wait. I can show the kids around now."

Kel declared boldly, "Sir, we've got to turn back."

"Back? Of course not, we're a long way out and about to jump." At Kel's obvious dismay Renard, who was not an unfeeling man, said more gently, "Homesick already? Or is it just the idea of jumping through hyperspace? That bothers some people, but your dad will tell you there's nothing scary about it."

Sure, thought Jesse sardonically, nothing as scary as what will happen to us after we arrive.

"You don't understand," Kel persisted. "Ivana's sick. She needs to go home."

"If she's sick, there are fine hospitals where we're going, and she'll get better care than she would on the godforsaken planet you've left. But maybe it's just delayed spacesickness. Nadia," he said to the woman, "get the girl something to take, will you?"

Ivana, despite her previous eagerness to reach the Captain, was silent. Kel pleaded desperately, *There's got to be some way to make them go back. . . .*

And all of a sudden Jesse realized that there *was* a way. One way. The only thing they cared about was the bounty. They would not go back for Edris; whatever he said to them, they knew the others would hide her. But Peter—Peter could not be hidden. They could have him in custody before anyone suspected that they could identify him. If he told them about Peter, they would return.

Peter was going to die anyway. He would gladly give up his last few weeks of freedom to save Ivana and her child. It could be explained to him telepathically once he was aboard, and he would not see it as a betrayal. Though there would be no chance to consult him beforehand, it was undoubtedly what he'd want.

Jesse almost spoke aloud before remembering that he was not really on the bridge, that his body was back in the locked cabin from which he could not be heard. It would be more convincing for Kel to tell them in any case, making it seem like a slip. Kel would never intentionally jeopardize Peter, but he'd see that this was the lesser of evils. . . .

Or was it? On the verge of contacting Kel, Jesse stopped himself. Yes, Peter would willingly sacrifice his remaining time for Ivana—but the colony would need him during that time. The others would be crushed if he was betrayed; they would not understand. Only with his support could they get through those agonizing weeks of waiting without losing heart.

And Ivana . . . if she was the cause of Peter's capture, Ivana would be destroyed just as surely as if she would be if taken to Earth. She wouldn't grasp the fact that it had made no real difference to his fate, that he would inevitably have been caught when Fleet took over. She would always believe that but for her, he might have lived.

So it wasn't a means of escape for the kids after all, Jesse decided in despair. They were in the hands of fate, as the Group always had been. The jump was only minutes away now, and after that, they must begin to face what lay ahead.

Kel was looking curiously around the bridge. *Dad,* he asked, *which is the panel that controls the hyperdrive? The one you hoped to damage?*

That one, Jesse told him, turning his attention to it. His sense of freedom abruptly changed to bitter frustration. The panel was so close! He was invisible, he could smash it and Renard wouldn't see—but of course, he could have no physical effect here. Away from his body, he could no more touch anything than he could be seen or heard. He was helpless.

You'd tear the switches off it?

Not the switches. I'd have to take the cover off and get at the wiring they're connected to, and the components at the other end of the connections.

Just wires and stuff? Wouldn't the hyperdrive engine still work?

Yes, but it couldn't be controlled, Jesse explained. *You can't jump into hyperspace without knowing where you're going to come out of it. It certainly wouldn't be anywhere near Earth. It might be in some unknown part of the galaxy, or even in the middle of a star. You might never come out at all.*

But maybe they could fix the wires.

Not if I made enough of a mess of them and the ICs underneath. They don't have spare parts for those. Why was he bothering to go into this? Two officers were at their elbows; even if Kel was crazy enough to make a move, he'd be grabbed—and in any case the cover couldn't be removed from the panel without tools.

I've got to do something, Kel insisted desperately. *They don't suspect me—maybe I could smash the switches with a stool . . . it would buy time, and at least Ivana would know I tried. . . .*

No, Kel! Jesse commanded. *It would make things worse, much worse! You'd be labeled violent and when you get to Earth they'd lock you up in an institution.*

But Dad, she's losing touch with us! I've got to snap her out of it!

Ivana was unresponsive again. She'd turned toward the panel when he pointed it out to Kel and stood frozen, with glazed eyes. God, thought Jesse, she was unstable! She would end up in a hospital, a tragic irony when the idea of settling a new world had begun with the need to escape from the Hospital on Undine. . . .

Fog swirled before him, obscuring his view—he must be falling out of the trance, Jesse thought dizzily. Once he'd feared not being able to return to his body; now he feared the loss of distant perception more. He prayed that its clarity could be maintained.

Dad, Kel inquired, *why is the panel smoking?*

At the same moment Renard burst out, "What the hell—" and made for the control panel from which, Jesse now saw, actual wisps of smoke were oozing. As he touched it he jumped back with a yell, his hand seared by the hot metal surface.

The cry jolted Ivana out of her daze. Sensitive healer that she was, she must literally feel Renard's pain. She rushed to him and seized his hand. Astonishingly—to Renard, at least—the red burn marks began to fade, as, evidently, did the pain's intensity.

"I didn't mean for you to get hurt," Ivana said contritely.

Renard hadn't time to wonder how she'd healed him. He grabbed a fire extinguisher and, wearing gloves, began to dismantle the heated panel. Jesse's preternatural vision gave him a full view as the Captain cast aside its blackened inner board and gazed with horror into the hyperdrive control module's glowing remains.

Oh, my God, Jesse thought. What did this? What could possibly have caused such a fire under that particular panel . . . are miracles real, or am I hallucinating? He was out of his body, after all; he certainly was hallucinating in that sense, and he recalled hearing that people traveling out of their bodies moved on a different plane of reality. . . .

In dismay he jerked himself back, slipping instantly out of trance and back into flesh, almost with regret at the sudden sense of confinement. He was lying on the bunk in the tiny cabin, bewildered and shaking. It had been mere wish-ful-fillment, then. Perhaps the whole episode had been wish-fulfillment; perhaps he had never stood invisibly beside Kel and pointed the panel out to him. It had looked suspiciously like the hyperdrive control panel on *Mayflower XI* and the freighters with which he was familiar. An explorer's controls might not be the same.

Stress could do strange things to a person, he thought ruefully. He wondered if stress would drive him totally out of his mind before he was executed.

There were voices outside the locked door, audible voices. Jesse sat up as Kel's rose over the rest. "Let my dad out," he was saying coldly. "He's the only one who can explain it to you, you know."

Incredibly, the door opened. "What I don't understand," Jiri Doubek said to Jesse, "is why you intended to blow up the ship if you had a weapon capable of what you've just done by remote control."

Jesse said nothing; he was at a loss for words. He accompanied Doubek to the bridge, feeling the deck firm beneath his physical feet. Renard was staring unbelievingly at the fused mass of what once had been a control module, evidently unsure that he was still sane. The other officers stood behind him, mute with astonishment and confusion. There was nothing, *nothing*, that could produce damage like that—not unless fire had enveloped the entire bridge, Jesse thought in awe. The module was not merely charred, but melted.

Kel had gone to Ivana who, unnoticed, was sitting in one of the officers' seats, her slender body looking small and fragile against the black of the padded armchair. "Uncle Jesse," she asked in a trembling voice, "Did it work? Can we go home now?"

"Did what work?" They were indeed going home to Maclairn, he realized with shock. The ship could no longer go anywhere else.

"What I did. I—I couldn't let them take me to a place where they'd kill my baby."

Not until then did he grasp what had happened.

Ivana . . . she had absorbed all he'd told Kel about the control panel. She'd seen what lay beneath it clairvoyantly. They had known she was capable of pyrokinesis; she'd been trained to ignite fires via psi; but this—!

The magnified power had come from emotion: from her terror for Peter and for her unborn child; from remorse over having inadvertently doomed them; and in the last instant, fear for Kel, who had been on the verge of a rash act that would have led to his imprisonment. In desperation, she had called on the gift she'd never wanted to have.

All psi powers can be used either constructively or destructively, Peter had said. *We have to live with the knowledge that we can unleash them, and be prepared to do it wisely.* Had he been afraid that Brian might develop this much power? Had he known that Ivana possessed it? Had *she* known, underneath, as far back as when she'd first seen fire and had been scared that she too might start it with her mind?

Most certainly this unconscious knowledge was what had frightened her when Peter lit the torch during the Ritual. He *had* known, or at least suspected. And he'd known too that she must face the fear of her own potential while he was on hand to support her.

From the very beginning Peter had been aware that such powers existed, and that he bore the responsibility for their awakening. This was why Ian had urged him to endure. If he had died in the flood—if he had not chosen to live without legs—he would not have been there for Ivana. Without his years of guidance she couldn't have used her power in this precise, controlled way, channeling the stress of her anguish into the one possible means of saving them all.

Jesse drew her into his arms. "Ivana darling, you did just fine. We're going home, and nobody will come to take over our world."

66

CARLA GOT THROUGH the day as if in a dream, not accepting that Jesse was gone. Gone ... forever ... never again to lie with her, merge his mind with hers, give her all the strength and joy that for years now she'd relied on. . . . And he would die! She had resigned herself to his death earlier under pressure of acknowledging its necessity. But as the hours passed, she found herself less and less willing to believe it could really happen.

It had not happened already. If he had grasped her message and blown up the starship, the shuttle would have returned within an hour. Kel, at least, would be here with her. Now she had no one but the younger ones, Tarin and Fran—except, for a little while, Peter. . . .

"He gave us his blessing," Peter had said gently. "He knew, Carla. He said that he'd known for a long time."

"Yes." She had never told Peter what Jesse had once suggested; she was not sure she ever would.

"I could never replace him," Peter went on, "and we can't have what other couples have—but he did not want you to be alone."

And Carla had nearly broken down at hearing that, for she loved Peter, loved him more completely than she had ever realized, despite her long-ago admission to herself that she would be capable of it. But he was not Jesse. And though her awareness of Peter's aloneness tore at her, she did not believe that after Ramón and Jesse she could give her whole heart a third time, even to someone for whom she cared fully as much.

Dear Carla, Peter told her, stroking her hair. *I know you can't. I knew when I gave you to him on Undine that it was forever. But if during the time I have left, you need me, I'm here.* She had left his room then, for she'd known that neither of them could bear the other's sorrow.

It would not be long now before he too would die. He

would be extradited to Undine and she would have to live
with the anticipation, and the unending visualization, of
his execution as well as Jesse's. She did not see how she
was going to endure it.

Working with Kira in the weavery where they'd hidden
from clamor of the kids and the well-intentioned sympathy
of friends, Carla was simply numb. Kira was silent, brood-
ing, uncharacteristically overcome by emotion—Ivana meant
even more to her than a daughter would to a younger woman,
and her grief over the kids' departure, unlike Carla's, was
not overshadowed by deeper pain. *They're adults, now*, Carla
reminded her, *though they won't be treated as adults on
Earth. They'll be better off there than sharing what will happen to us after we're taken over.* If their love for each other
was real, she thought, it would outlast the temporary separation that would be forced on them. To be sure, their psi
gifts wouldn't be nourished there, but the future lay ahead
of them, they were alive. . . .

Or were they? In an instant, Carla's heart turned to ice.
She'd convinced herself that they were alive, that the
starship had jumped and that the reason she no longer felt
any trace of Jesse's presence was that he'd vanished into
hyperspace, far beyond the normal confines of space and
time . . . but it was all too possible that he had not known
that the kids were aboard.

She had no real evidence that he hadn't blown up the
ship. She would not know until a Fleet force arrived, perhaps many weeks from now. She would be torn, dreading
the appearance of more ships yet at the same time fearing
that they might never come, that she might never receive
confirmation that Kel and Ivana still lived.

Kira was staring at her, sensitive, of course, to her sudden surge of terror. Quickly Carla clamped her mind shut
against probing. Kira was mercifully unaware of Jesse's full
plan—Peter had told people only that he had attempted to
disable the starship's hyperdrive and had apparently failed.
He didn't plan to say more unless enough time passed for him

to be sure that Fleet hadn't been contacted. Yet how could such a thing be hidden long from Kira, one of the strongest telepaths in the Group as well as their closest friend?

She ran from the weavery, not stopping until she reached the trees by the cistern, and threw herself down on the ground beneath them. So far she had controlled her tears, upheld by her well-practiced mind training. Through all the crises of her life—Ramón's execution, the long years of mourning, Jesse's condemnation to destruction in the Hospital on Undine, her anguish over Peter's injury—she had managed to stay steady. Often enough she had wept, but not hysterically as she was weeping now. She had come to a point where it no longer seemed to matter. . . .

Carla! Carla! Jesse was calling her. They were dead, then. One could not call from hyperspace; it could only be from some realm beyond death, a realm in which she'd never been sure she believed. Had the dead really the power to reach loved ones, to offer comfort? Or was this only illusion? *Carla . . . it's all right! Everything's okay now, I'm coming to you. . . .*

Jesse! If this is real, if you are speaking from somewhere beyond, tell me that Kel and Ivana are with you. That it's a good place and you're together. . . .

Of course we're together! Where else could we be? We're almost home, only minutes now until we land. . . .

Land? Carla raised her head, shading her eyes against the brilliant afternoon sun. She caught the glint of light on metal before she heard the sound of thrusters. Incredibly, miraculously, the shuttle was descending from space into Maclairn's cloudless sky.

67

IN THE HOURS it had taken to get back into orbit, both Ivana and *Picard*'s officers had begun to recover. At first Ivana had been pale and shaking; Jesse could see that the psychic aftereffects were likely to be severe. It would be a terrible irony if she lost her baby through sheer physical reaction. *Kel, take her back to her bunk*, he'd urged. *She'll need to lie down. She'll need you to steady her.*

She would require counseling for a long time to come, he reflected, but Peter would be well able to provide it. She would be upheld by her love for him and for Kel, and for the child—his grandson Sandy—now growing within her. Her psi gifts would continue to mature, and someday, far in the future, she might lead Maclairn into a new era.

Meanwhile, Jesse had to deal with *Picard*'s crew. They believed he had some sort of remote weapon; from their standpoint there could be no other conceivable answer. The destruction was total. The starship was not going to jump—not ever again, since no repair facilities of sufficient sophistication were available. Somehow, they had to be made aware of what that implied.

They would not be easy to convince, he knew. Undoubtedly they would resist acknowledging the reality of psi powers. Yet they had to be told. They were about to be plunged into a world where everyone used psi, and they'd be stuck there for the rest of their lives. The chances of another starship stumbling upon Maclairn were so remote as to be nonexistent. The explorer crew was stranded, and for everyone's sake as well as their own, they must be integrated into its society. So his Ritual pledge to reveal nothing to outsiders didn't apply in this case—he had to make a stab at enlightening them.

"I haven't got a long-range weapon," he told Renard, "and I wasn't expecting this to happen. But we of Maclairn have—abilities, abilities you'd call paranormal. We communicate by mind alone. We can heal by mind alone, as Ivana demonstrated to you. It's why we stole a starship in the first place, you see. We needed a world of our own where these abilities could thrive and be passed on to children—"

They were all staring at him incredulously, as he had known they would. "Well," Jesse went on, "some of the children have greater mind powers than we, their parents, do. And when you brought one of those children aboard, you put an end to your chance of ever escaping from here. Because when she found out what people on Earth would think about her special abilities, and what they'd do about the baby she's expecting, she stopped wanting to leave our world and she understood why it has to remain isolated. And so she found more power within herself than most of us ever dreamed was possible." Watching their faces, he added, "I know. You don't want to believe this. But facts are facts. You have seen the result."

"Are you saying it was the *girl*?" Renard looked down at his burned fingers, which by now showed only a faint reddening instead of the blisters that ought to have appeared. "But Sanders," he protested, "even if she had such a power, how could she have known which module controls the hyperdrive?"

"I told you, we communicate with our minds. I was in touch with her and with my son." He did not mention that he had been with them on the bridge while his body was elsewhere.

The officers were silent, absorbing this; and Jesse knew they'd need a long time to take it in. But it wasn't too soon for them to concede defeat. "You really wouldn't want us to mingle with other settlers," he pointed out. "It's best for our world not to be discovered, don't you think?"

Slowly, one by one, they nodded.

They had treated Ivana respectfully after that, obviously somewhat frightened to be in her presence. Recalling his own difficulty in accepting the existence of psi powers that were far less threatening than pyrokinesis, Jesse couldn't help but sympathize. He hoped they didn't have families that they'd now never see again—loved ones who would grieve when their ship was reported as lost. But it was unlikely. Officers with families rarely chose explorer duty. Quite possibly the men and women aboard were couples.

"I suppose we'll be prisoners," Renard had said resignedly. "We can't orbit your planet forever without supplies, and

I can't say I'm not eager to get the girl off my ship, so there's nothing to be gained by pretending we can resist."

"Maclairn will be your prison if you look at it that way," Jesse said, "but it's actually quite a nice world. You might find that you like it."

"We won't be treated as enemies, then?" asked Mei Luong.

"Of course not. We're not vindictive. You'll have some difficult adjustments to make, but your skills are needed and you'll be respected for them." They could repair the shuttle abandoned at the salt flat, Jesse realized—they were experienced pilots, and at least one of them must be an engineer. Their know-how, and the equipment from their starship, would be invaluable. Both shuttles could be recharged, there'd now be a third, and ... *Oh, my God!* he thought, his heart swelling with excitement as he recalled facts about explorer ships from his Fleet training. Peter's faith in fate was valid after all. . . .

"But if the rest of you possess powers that we lack—" Nadia Farman was saying.

"They are acquired powers for most of us," Jesse said, with difficulty calming himself enough to respond. "You can gain them if you want to badly enough." Delayed aging would be a powerful inducement, certainly, once they found out that it was attainable. "It's harder for adults than for the kids," he went on, "but the methods are well established. Peter is a very good instructor."

"Peter—Peter Kelstrom?" Renard's tone suggested that this was one more piece of bad news than he could tolerate.

Jesse nodded. "Don't believe what the bounty notice says about Peter. We owe everything to him. Ivana is his foster daughter—a large part of her motive and mine was to save his life."

"He was right in front of you all the time," Kel said. "You didn't notice him because—"

"Let's not tell them," Jesse put in hastily. "I want to see the look on their faces when they meet him."

But that would come later when the shuttle returned, bringing all four bounty hunters down to begin a new life. Now, after the rapture of his reunion with Carla, after he'd made his way, with her and the kids and Kira, through the rejoicing crowd to where Peter waited and had explained the awesome outcome of Ivana's psi training, Jesse spoke of the other miracle he had just grasped.

"Peter," he said, "you've been right all along to trust fate. It looked for awhile as if it had turned against us, yet that wasn't true."

"Of course not. The kids' presence, which I'd have prevented if I could, was what saved your life. In the end it saved mine too, and the freedom of our world."

"Yes. But it accomplished more than that. It saved *Picard*—and the chance that brought *Picard* to us, out of all the countless solar systems where we might have been hunted, wasn't the bad luck we thought it was. You see, explorer ships aren't designed like bigger starships. They can land. They can provide power and high-tech facilities on any desolate planet where they may be stranded, if that proves necessary, and they're crewed by experts cross-trained in many fields of technology. That ship and its officers can jump-start industry here, Peter. We can quit fearing that it won't ever be possible to make use of our resources."

They all looked at each other, comprehension dawning. "They can help us build some of the good stuff there is on Earth?" Kel asked.

"Yes, eventually, and you'll be among the builders—they can teach you everything you need to know."

"We'll make progress on both fronts," said Carla happily, "with Kel to lead his generation in regaining technology and Ivana to lead in developing psi skills."

In Peter's mind they sensed an overwhelming surge of thankfulness. "And so at last," he said, awestricken, "we're on our way toward fulfilling Ian's vision."

Epilogue

Dearest love,

At last I can tell you why I left Earth so suddenly without saying where I was going or why, except that it was to fulfill a family obligation I couldn't ignore. I'm sure you didn't guess that it was connected with the Maclairn Foundation, even though you're aware that the Foundation was established by my ancestors—specifically, two centuries ago by an eccentric billionaire who named it in memory of a friend he had admired.

No one has ever been sure just what the Maclairn Foundation does, other than to publish obscure scholarly papers defending the long-abandoned idea that some humans possess paranormal mind powers. That its money has been tied up in an unbreakable trust is common knowledge. As it accepts no donations, makes none, and pays the taxes due annually on capital gains, it has remained beyond the reach of government investigators. I might never have heard of it myself if it hadn't been for family tradition.

Certainly as a young woman I had not expected any personal involvement with its affairs. Then one day, out of the blue, my granddad told me that the Maclairn Foundation had been the anonymous donor of my law school scholarship, which had required me to specialize in Colonial League law—that I had been chosen from among my cousins as one of those most likely to be sympathetic to its founders' goals. Naturally I protested that despite my in-

terest in parapsychology, as a successful attorney handling
League cases I had no time to take on the management of a
trust fund. He then told me that he knew I longed to travel
personally to other worlds, and that the Foundation was
prepared to give me that opportunity, provided that I would
swear to keep its secrets unless and until they were pub-
licly revealed.

Incredibly, I learned, the Foundation had liquidated its
assets and bought a starship—not chartered one from Fleet,
but actually bought it outright. You will say that there are
no privately-owned starships other than those crewed by
pirates and smugglers. That was what I thought, too; there
is simply no reason for anyone traveling between colonies
on legitimate business to incur the enormous expense of
hiring a full-time crew. There are no trained spacers available in any case, except for retirees from Fleet or officers
who've been cashiered. I don't know much about our captain's background, but I suspect it includes some incident
that gives the Foundation a hold over him, for he too was
sworn to secrecy and no amount of money could ensure
that—or even possession of the ship—if a planet rich enough
to tempt a smuggler were to be discovered.

We were told nothing about our destination. The captain, when given its charted location, protested that it was
an unopened planet that had not been visited for centuries
because it was known to contain nothing of value. He was
informed that we might indeed find nothing, but that there
was some chance of an important scientific discovery, in
which case he was to follow sealed orders that he was otherwise forbidden to open. Considering the Foundation's known
interest in the paranormal, I think the crew assumed that
we were like those cults that claim to have communicated
psychically with extraterrestrial aliens.

Was it possible, we wondered, that some indication of
an alien civilization *had* been found? Our ship, rechristened
Promise when registered to the Foundation, was small; it
carried only five passengers besides myself: an archeolo-

gist, a sociologist, a biologist, a linguist, and a parapsycholo-
gist—all of us distant cousins whose college scholarships
turned out to have been backed by Foundation money. This
would certainly be a suitable team for alien contact if there
were any aliens outside of science fiction, though I couldn't
imagine why an attorney had been included.

We came out of hyperspace only a few days away from
the planet, and it was an impressively beautiful one, golden,
dotted here and there with blue seas. By the time we established orbit we could see that it was inhabited. Numb with
awe, we stared at the unmistakable signs not only of widespread agriculture, but of cities—not huge urban sprawls
like Earth's, but clusters of low buildings surrounded by
groves of trees. The unplanted areas were dry, rocky desert.
"It's not an ancient world," said our sociologist. "It looks
more like a colony. But there are no lost human colonies,
and if it's alien—that implies they've got interstellar travel!
It means . . ." He broke off, stunned. We all knew what it
meant. Humankind might be endangered by these aliens, if
not in a physical sense then simply from culture shock.
Earth's civilization is too decadent these days to withstand
much contact with a totally unfamiliar one.

More dumbfounded than any of us, the captain—who
had expected to find only a barren world—opened the sealed
orders with shaking hands. "If you are reading this, you
have seen evidence of past or present habitation," the message said. "The people of the world to which you have been
sent are, or were, the descendants of a group secretly organized by Ian Maclairn. It was his wish that they not be found
for two hundred years. If they have died out, try to determine the cause. If they still live, land and introduce yourselves, saying that you seek the Stewards of the Flame. They
will recognize you by that phrase and will tell you why they
have been isolated. You are to respect their decision as to
whether you should return to Earth and reveal their existence. Your oath to the Foundation binds you to keep their
secret if they so desire."

Our shuttle could not take us all to the surface at once; we drew lots to decide who would go on the first trip, and I was among the fortunate. We were guided in by an automated landing beacon. On a plateau near a long, narrow lake we spotted a small grounded starship. Next to it were a landing pad occupied by two ancient shuttles and a smaller pad that was empty, on which we set down. People approached to greet us. A white-haired woman who appeared to be in her eighties came forward and held out her hand. "Welcome to Maclairn," she said when I spoke the password phrase. "I am Jessica, the great-great-great-granddaughter of Ivana, firstborn of this world, who was our leader before me. We've long awaited your coming."

I noticed at once that there was something strange about the crowd that gathered. The people were uncannily quiet, but it was neither an awed silence nor a hostile one. Rather, I sensed warmth toward us and joy at our appearance. I can express it no better than to say that I felt immediately comfortable with these people, as if I had come home.

"This is the old settlement," Jessica explained as we walked toward the buildings. "The mines near it are exhausted and the wells have run dry; we live elsewhere now, though we still plant crops on the terraces watered by the lake. But the original power plant and computer complex are here, and the long-range comm in the grounded ship *Picard*, which detected your arrival and responded. As many of us as the boat would hold came up the lake to meet you. It's a day of celebration, you see. I remember from my childhood how Peter, our first leader, spoke of his faith that what we did here would not be for nothing."

"I'm confused," I confessed, puzzled. "You *remember* this world's first leader? It was our understanding that the colony was founded two hundred years ago."

Jessica smiled. "I'm older than I look," she said. "I was twelve when Peter died and Ivana became head of the Council. He lived somewhat longer than most—he surpassed even Ian, who died at one hundred and thirty. His friend and deputy, my remote ancestor Jesse—who died the day I was born and for whom I was therefore named—reached only a hundred and twenty-one, which is the age I am now."

We stared at her, openmouthed, as she continued, "Long life with health is not our only gift. You too will gain it, along with most of our others, if you choose to take on the role we hope you will."

She gave us robes and headgear for protection from the searing heat, to which the colonists were evidently adapted. After touring the settlement with its unique historic houses, built of stone and brick with central domed rooms of solid stone, we went by boat and funicular to a larger and more modern village below the lake's dam. There, in Jessica's spacious home—occupied, she said, by several generations younger than she—we sat around a huge stone fireplace and talked far into the night, learning of the colony's early struggles, its present situation, and its hope to influence the future of humankind. And when at last I found myself in a soft comfortable bed, I slept soundly, hearing in my mind a voice that said, *You are welcome here. It is a place where you can become all you were meant to be, where you can be free. . . .*

I'm sure you'll understand that this letter, which the ship will carry back to Earth, cannot be made long enough for me to even begin describing the marvels we have seen on Maclairn. Its people have the psi powers in which a small minority of human beings have always believed—telepathy, psychokinesis, healing, and more—and the shared possession of them has made their society not only prosperous, but serene and peaceable beyond any other world's dreams.

This may sound too bland, as if peace had been achieved at the cost of diversity. Yet that is not so. On the contrary, differing opinions are respected. There is no pressure to conform; individuals are free to think and act as they wish, provided they hurt no one. Most choose a high-tech lifestyle; there has been no sacrifice of technology here, beyond a temporary one during the colony's first century when neither the capability for industry nor much psychokinetic power over physical processes had been developed. Others prefer to live more simply. There is no sickness because people have conscious control of their bodies' reactions. There is no discord because among telepaths, all motives can be perceived and no one's sincerity can be questioned.

But now the untroubled era of Maclairn's history may be coming to an end. These people did not settle a new world solely for their own benefit. They saw themselves as stewards, for the goal was to extend mind powers to humanity at large. The founders of the colony rightly believed that its existence could not safely be revealed until it was well established and had proven viable over many generations. It was their wish to serve as an example of what human civilization may someday become. And to do so, they must allow themselves to be observed by Earth and its other colonies.

This will entail great risk. There's no danger of their being forcibly taken over on grounds of the colony's illegal origin; too much time has passed, and it has grown large enough to claim independence. But without the protection of Fleet, they will be in danger of invasion by looters and profit-seekers and, no doubt, by desperate people seeking the Fountain of Youth. There may even be some danger of an armed attack. Yet if Maclairn joins the League voluntarily, they will be subject to its bureaucratic policies and to taxes, which without exports they have no means of paying, as the price of obtaining that protection.

Furthermore, there will be strong hostility to the revelation of a culture based on psi powers. Antagonists of the so-called paranormal have prevailed on Earth for many centuries. Its existence is a threat to their worldview, which they've fought desperately to defend in the face of all past evidence; but a modern technological society in which everyone has such powers is evidence that cannot be denied. Who can say how far they will go in an attempt to destroy it?

These are the problems that I, as an attorney well-versed in League law, was sent here to resolve. The people of

Maclairn have accepted my offer of assistance. I am to be their liaison with the larger universe.

I mean to say *our* liaison, for I, like most members of our party, have decided to become a citizen. This involves mind training, which we're warned will be difficult and, at the beginning, both frightening and painful; but we will gain control of our health and many of the other powers the native-born possess. They assure us that it is possible for adults, that all their founders went through it before ever leaving their home world, although for generations now such training has been given only to adolescents who've had such powers from birth. The crew of the stranded ship *Picard* completed it successfully, we're told. All of this seems rash and sudden, perhaps, and yet . . . I *trust* Jessica, trust her as if we were already in telepathic rapport; and she is to be my instructor.

My darling, I don't want to end our relationship, but I won't be going back to Earth except briefly, for meetings at League headquarters. I know you share my disillusionment with Earth and have been wishing to get away. The ship *Promise* will return here after taking our report to the Foundation, and I've asked my granddad to save a place for you on that trip. As a musician you will be honored on this world, and I long for you to come. I want children, and I want them to grow up here. We'll do some traveling, of course; *Promise* will remain at Maclairn's disposal for such contacts as we choose to establish with other colonies— colonies that I'm sure will be more receptive to new ways than Earth will. The future of humankind lies in the colonies, and someday, perhaps, there may be many more like this one.

With love always,

Kathryn of Maclairn
Ambassador-elect to the Colonial League